GAELEN FOLEY

Duke of Storm

MOONLIGHT SQUARE, BOOK 3

Also by Gaelen Foley

Ascension Trilogy
The Pirate Prince
Princess
Prince Charming

Knight Miscellany
The Duke
Lord of Fire
Lord of Ice
Lady of Desire
Devil Takes a Bride
One Night of Sin
His Wicked Kiss

The Spice Trilogy
Her Only Desire
Her Secret Fantasy
Her Every Pleasure

The Inferno Club
My Wicked Marquess
My Dangerous Duke
My Irresistible Earl
My Ruthless Prince
My Scandalous Viscount
My Notorious Gentleman
Secrets of a Scoundrel

Age of Heroes
Paladin's Prize

Moonlight Square
One Moonlit Night
Duke of Scandal
Duke of Secrets

Gryphon Chronicles
(Writing as E.G. Foley)
The Lost Heir
Jake & the Giant
The Dark Portal
The Gingerbread Wars
Rise of Allies
Secrets of the Deep
The Black Fortress

50 States of Fear
(Writing as E.G. Foley)
The Haunted Plantation
Leader of the Pack
Bringing Home Bigfoot
Dork and the Deathray

Credits and Copyright

Table of Contents

Prologue – A Son's Duty 1

Chapter 1 – A Lady's Resolve 9

Chapter 2 – A Duke's Honor 20

Chapter 3 – The Warrior 28

Chapter 4 – The Peacemaker 40

Chapter 5 – A Devil's Bargain 49

Chapter 6 – Pistols at Dawn 58

Chapter 7 – The Dragoon 67

Chapter 8 – Pay the Piper 76

Chapter 9 – A Wicked Notion 91

Chapter 10 – Dragon Lady 106

Chapter 11 – A Model Husband... 117

Chapter 12 – The Country Dance 124

Chapter 13 – A Thorough Report 138

Chapter 14 – Hyde Park 160

Chapter 15 – Battle Royale 175

Chapter 16 – Revelations Unfold 185

Chapter 17 – A Shift in the Wind 195

Chapter 18 – A Light in the Dark 207

Chapter 19 – Gazebo 218

Chapter 20 – The Dandy.. 234

Chapter 21 – The Coach House 245

Chapter 22 – Trumbull... 261

Chapter 23 – On the Hunt 281

Chapter 24 – Aunt Lucinda's Soirée 299

Chapter 25 – The Major 317

Chapter 26 – Killer Unmasked 330

Chapter 27 – Leaving Town 346

Chapter 28 – On the Road 364

Chapter 29 – Dartfield Manor 380

Chapter 30 – Vendetta 393

Chapter 31 – Landfall... 400

Chapter 32 – At Last.. 411

Chapter 33 – Two Lanterns 424

Chapter 34 – Conflagration 435

Chapter 35 – All or Nothing 446

Epilogue – The Fourth Duchess 459

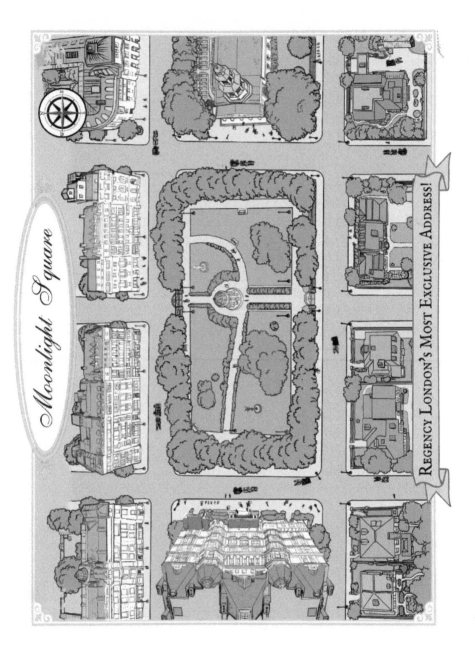

Moonlight Square

Regency London's Most Exclusive Address!

PROLOGUE

A Son's Duty

*H*e did not think of them as victims. In fact, he did not think of them at all.

The Dukes of Amberley were but obstacles to be put down. And how ever many came in the line of succession, he'd just keep killing them, till the title went extinct.

Then surely Father would forgive him.

This one was the last heir in the line, though, he was fairly sure.

He hoped so.

Leaning in the shadows against a net-draped stack of crates, Seth Darrow waited patiently for doomed Duke Number Four to appear.

The ship from Ireland had arrived at the London docks hours late, but the cover of darkness only helped him in his quest. He listened to the Thames' greasy current slap softly against the quay.

A ship's bell clanged somewhere out in the darkness, while an ashy snow flurried down from an indifferent onyx sky to turn the Docklands hoary. It coated the roofs of the dismal warehouses and all the empty vendor stalls, abandoned at this hour. The air had a crisp, cold bite mere days before Christmas, but it still stank of slop buckets and fish brine this close to the river.

Seth shifted his weight, impatient with the need to have his task over with. God, this was as bad as waiting for the moment of a cavalry charge, hearing that bellowed order booming down the line of mounted men.

Wondering all the time if he'd come back alive.

He shoved away the thought of his regimental brothers, for this was not exactly the kind of killing that proud dragoons deemed honorable.

Father, on the other hand, did not trouble himself over such niceties.

So Seth waited, the dutiful son, taming his jitters.

His breath misted through the black kerchief he'd tied around the lower half of his face. He adjusted the makeshift mask restlessly and was irked when the cloth snagged again on his short, narrow beard.

Come on, Amberley, for chrissake. It's cold out here. He fingered the hilt of the knife sheathed at his hip and watched the deck of the Irish frigate, now anchored nearby.

He could hear the voices of a few sailors going about their tasks, securing furled sails, bringing up portage. Meanwhile, farther out across the wide river, the bare masts of moored ships rocked, and creaking hulks of fishing boats shivered under the dark wintry sky.

Down by Parliament, the lanterns along Westminster Bridge gleamed feebly in the gloom. He drummed his fingers on his arm, beginning to wonder if the bleeder had missed the damned boat.

Seth had learned everything he needed to know about the where and when of Duke Number Four's arrival from a fetching maid in Amberley House.

Poor thing actually believed he was courting her—well, in the rough, earthy manner of the lower orders. Which was to say he'd got her onto her back fairly quickly. It helped that she wasn't too bright.

It hadn't taken much to turn the girl to putty in his hands. Little did she know his true intentions.

No matter. Women were made to be lied to.

His thoughts drifted back to something else the scullery maid had said, that half the duke's own staff were disgusted to learn that their new master was three-quarters Irish.

Hell, the man's first name was unashamedly heathen—Connor, she'd told him—like the ancient high kings of that destitute, superstitious backwater.

Seth did not give a damn what the new heir's name was, but he shook his head, bemused. If the duke's own servants found his Irish blood beneath their dignity, then he could not help wondering what sort of reception this Connor expected to receive here in Town.

His bloodlines might fully entitle him to his dead cousin's coronet, but the ton could be deeply obnoxious to anyone who bore the slightest whiff of not being entirely one of *them*.

Seth knew this from personal experience.

There was nothing one could do but brazen it out and try like hell not to make some faux pas in etiquette or speech. Such errors instantly exposed one as an *encroaching toadstool,* as they put it—any lowborn soul attempting to rise up from the shit.

But lucky for Duke Number Four, he'd be spared the ton's mockery. Because he would not be leaving the docks alive tonight.

Finally.

Seth came to attention when, at last, his target emerged from belowdecks, appearing on the snow-dusted deck of the frigate. He could not see him well yet. Just the tall, broad outline of a large man in a long, wind-tossed greatcoat.

He heard him bid the crewmen farewell, then arched a brow. It was a rare nobleman who thanked common sailors.

Seth waited to see how many servants His Grace had brought along that he might have to deal with, but there were none.

Apparently, he'd come alone. Seth cocked a brow as things got even stranger. *What sort of duke carries his own duffel?* But, sure enough, the big man slung it over his shoulder without ceremony, then strode down the gangplank.

Seth heard the deep thud of the man's boot heels striking the planks of the long wooden dock, slippery with snow.

Then Amberley Number Four came closer, marching down the wooden pier toward the concrete quay, where Seth took care to lean out of sight.

He made no move yet, only gauging his target in predatory stillness.

Huh, he thought, bemused.

If the size of that rugged silhouette provided his first inkling that this man might be harder to kill than his predecessors, he ignored it.

Dragoons feared no one, and did not shrink from fights. Maybe this chap would finally give him a challenge. God knew the last three hadn't put up any sort of fight worth mentioning. Two old men and a nancy-boy.

Of course, scullery maid what's-her-name had told him that Number Four was also a military man, but in what capacity he'd served, exactly, not even the butler was quite sure.

Seth wasn't too concerned. Chances were extremely slim that this highborn fool was a real soldier. With his lofty family connections, a rich uncle—either dead Duke Number One or Number Two—had probably purchased his commission for him to give him something to do. Seth had come by his own rank through similar means. Father had bought him his captaincy, pulled a few strings.

Ah, but once Seth had joined his regiment and felt that bold, proud esprit de corps, he'd realized that, for the first time in his life, he had a chance to be a part of something honorable. He'd worked hard to become worthy of the dashing uniform and the brave cavalry horses trained to carry him barreling toward the enemy.

And, to be sure, he'd learned the dragoon's trademark swagger.

Meanwhile, his elegant younger brother had been learning his part, too.

Sadness flickered in Seth when he thought of Francis.

Unlike firstborn Seth, innocent young Francis had never borne the stench of their family fortune's criminal origins. Had never sullied his hands dealing with the real family business. Hell, he'd barely even wondered how Father got so rich.

He'd been shocked the night Seth had finally told him. The night he died…

Ah, but for a time, the handsome lad's rising splendor in the world had made the old man so happy. How Father had laughed and beamed to hear Francis flirt with debutantes in French, or when he'd translate opera lyrics from Italian for him, or the time he'd showed the old cutthroat how to tie a dandy's perfect cravat.

Unfortunately, as the shady Flynn-Darrow family's first real gentleman, Francis had also mastered how to take offense at any slight to his honor, too young and hotheaded to know when to walk away.

And now he was dead.

Seth still felt like he could throw up whenever he thought of that night.

"This is your fault," Father had said when he'd dragged the younger brother's body home in tears. *"You'll avenge him, or you're dead to me, as well."*

And so, Seth had no choice for what he was about to do.

But all his dragoon's swagger was of no help to him in this. Total secrecy was paramount, for in truth there was nothing honorable about his father's private war against the Amberleys.

No matter. Seth was nothing if not a loyal son to his terrifying sire. The old man had taught him everything he knew. Someone had to take over the family business one day, after all. Dark deeds and an iron stomach were simply part of the game.

Besides, Seth knew the guilt he bore for his little brother's death.

"You spoiled little fop, you have no idea how easy you've had it," he'd said that night, losing patience with the boy's fine airs. *"You think you're too good for us? Why don't* you *go collect the money, then — Your Lordship?"* he'd taunted.

Words he'd regret for the rest of his life. For his beautiful little brother, out to prove his mettle, had taken the dare and been destroyed.

Now if Seth had to kill every last damned nobleman in England to redeem himself for sending Francis into that situation, that was exactly what he'd do.

The Amberleys deserved what they got. At least, one of them did. But Father wanted *her* left alive.

To suffer with loss, as he did. Because all of this was her fault. She never should've tried to double-cross him.

Nobody broke a deal with Elias Flynn.

Look sharp, Seth warned himself, snapping to attention as his target finally finished his goodbyes and reached the land. The duke whistled with irritating cheer as he stepped off the wooden dock and turned left.

A fragment of "Good King Wenceslas" trailed out behind him as he marched off, leaving a path of large footprints in the thin coat of snow.

Seth snorted with envious disdain as he watched the blackguard pass. Well, who wouldn't be jolly, having just inherited some six estates and a hundred thousand quid a year, for God's sake?

But his celebration wouldn't last long.

Seth let him gain a little distance, then slipped out of his hiding place and followed stealthily.

It was time.

Is he taller than me? he wondered in surprise as he stole closer, bearing down on him. Most men weren't, for he stood a proud six foot one.

Heart pounding, step by swift, silent step, he narrowed the duke's lead, drawing his knife from its sheath. He gripped it tightly in a leather-gloved hand as he considered just how to spring the attack.

One thing was clear, though. He had to make his move before the bastard reached the street. He couldn't risk any witnesses. God knew if anything went wrong, Father would hate him even more.

Dry-mouthed as the seconds ticked by, Seth shadowed the duke, passing warehouses, rows of fishmongers' stalls, an empty ticket booth for the packet lines. Not a soul around. What little light the moon and a few distant lanterns gave reflected off the snow, casting only vague shadows.

His pulse galloped as Amberley slowed his pace, glancing from side to side as he wandered into a windy four-way intersection of the aisles between various stalls and storage sheds.

Outsider that he was, the Irishman didn't seem to know his way. Then he drifted entirely to a halt, and a thought flickered in Seth's mind that maybe he should just shoot the stupid bastard in the back and be done with it.

The dragoon in him winced at the cowardice of that solution, but, hell, he'd already done worse—look what he'd done to the old men...

Just as quickly, he dismissed the temptation to take the easy way out. The sound of a gunshot would only bring unwanted attention. More importantly, such a move would be too obvious. He had to make this look like a robbery.

Otherwise, Bow Street might start looking into the Amberley deaths, and neither he nor Father could afford that.

So far, Seth had managed not to raise any suspicions with the authorities because he'd been smart about how he'd done it, each time.

His criminal sire had taught him well. There always had to be a logical explanation. Thus, Duke Number Four would perish at the hands of some faceless footpad. Everyone knew it was treacherous down by the docks.

Especially at night.

Now! he thought, but still delayed for a heartbeat, adjusting his mask one last time, his stare fixed on the broad-shouldered form before him as he summoned up his courage for the attack.

Suddenly—before he could move—something startling happened.

Without warning, Amberley dropped the duffel bag and spun around, lifting his arms out to his sides.

"Well?" he challenged Seth. "Come on, then. Are you gonna try it, or you gonna follow me around all night, you stupid bleeder?"

Seth blinked, taken off guard, but it was too late now to back down. He let out a curse and charged.

What happened next was all a blur, violent and disastrous. He seemed to have run, face-first, into a fist or possibly a brick wall.

Somewhere in between the speed at which the man ducked his whooshing blade and smashed his nose with a facer in reply, Seth realized he had...miscalculated.

He was pummeled, grabbed, wrenched slip-sliding on the snow, dragged about, reprimanded and disarmed, knocked about some more, and, lastly, kicked once hard in the gut when he ended up sprawled on the cold, hard ground, seeing stars.

The duke dusted off his hands. "And let that be a lesson to you," he said.

Seth lay there on the snow for a moment, dazed. *What the hell just happened?*

His nose cascading blood, his left wrist either broken or sprained—his knife hurled off to God-knew-where—he clambered to his feet somehow and fled.

"What, leaving so soon?" the man boomed heartily into the night, laughing as Seth scampered away. "That's what I thought! Ye horse's arse."

The last Amberley duke stood there waiting for him to try again, but Seth was focused on staggering away before the towering savage came after him a second time, as he well would've, no doubt, if he'd known his true intent.

Seth flung around the corner of a warehouse to catch his breath and clutch his throbbing wrist. *Son of a bitch!* He'd injured it reaching out to catch himself when he'd fallen on his rear end, after the duke had kicked his feet out from under him.

"You're lucky I let you live—merry Christmas!" the Irishman added. Then he picked up his duffel and slung it over his shoulder once more. Seth could hear him muttering to himself: "Bloody welcome to London."

With that, Amberley marched off, perhaps to hail a hackney to take him to his new home in Moonlight Square, the giant corner mansion he'd inherited.

Shaken, Seth leaned against the warehouse wall and tilted his head back until the gushing from his nose became a trickle. Blood had soaked through the black kerchief on the lower half of his face. It became a bandage now rather than a mask. So much for all his stealth.

And his swagger.

At length, he dragged himself home in humiliation, still completely confounded and clutching his bruised ribs.

When he went into the florid house that Father's ill-gotten gains had procured for the family back when Francis was a baby, he immediately crossed the mahogany-paneled foyer to the red-walled dining room, where he poured himself a much-needed brandy.

Duke of Storm　　7

Dragoon or no, his hand shook as he stoppered the crystal decanter again, then lifted the drink to his lips and tossed it back. *What the hell have I got myself into?* He gratefully let the liquor burn its way down to his belly, then took a steadying breath, and slowly became aware of someone watching him.

He realized Father's study door was open just across the hallway.

Seth cringed at having to face the man.

"Well?" Still seated at his baronial desk, Elias Flynn had looked up from his ledger books and was peering at Seth from across the hallway, his stare blade-like over the tops of his small, wire-rimmed spectacles.

His shorn head gleamed in the candlelight coming from the tapers on his desk. But their soft glow could not conceal the harshness of that craggy, harrowed face, the deep lines carved into the forehead and bracketing the cruel mouth.

Father rose, drifted to the doorway. "Did you get him?" he asked.

Seth hesitated, loath to admit his failure. "Not yet, sir."

Flynn stared at him, rather murderously.

"This one's not like the others, Father. B-but don't worry, I'll see it done. C-can I pour you a drink, sir?"

His father just looked at him in cold disgust bordering on hatred. Then he shook his head, turned his back on his penitent elder son, as usual, and slammed the door of his study in his face.

Seth closed his eyes, flayed alive by his sire's complete rejection. It merely redoubled his resolve.

He took a breath, flicked his eyes open, and swore to God, or perhaps the devil, that if it was the last thing he ever did, the Fourth Duke of Amberley was going to die.

CHAPTER 1
A Lady's Resolve

Four Months Later

Lady Maggie Winthrop nibbled a lemon macaroon, tapped a toe in time with the pianoforte and violin playing between dance sets, and tried not to listen to her sister droning on again about the rigors of choosing a wallpaper for the seventh guest chamber.

While Delia, the Marchioness of Birdwell, prattled on to her audience of mindless followers, debating aloud between stripes and a handsome paisley pattern—and watching herself surreptitiously all the while in a large gilded mirror across from where the group of ladies stood—Maggie washed down her macaroon with a sweet, tart, fizzy sip of champagne punch, then took another discreet look around the ballroom.

Let's get on with it, shall we? Beyond the high arched windows of the Grand Albion's fabled ballroom, a bright half-moon rode aloft in the black April night. But inside, the huge crystal chandeliers filled the lofty space with warm illumination.

The ballroom shimmered, a sea of beautiful gowns on the ladies, their jeweled toques and feathered headdresses breaking like whitecaps as they nodded in the ceaseless roar of conversation.

The men wore black formal coats with snow-white cravats and silk waistcoats, a few smart military dress uniforms shining out among the crowd.

Brilliant red, navy blue. Silver dress swords, gold epaulets.

Very dashing. Maggie took another watchful sip of punch, but still failed to spot her quarry. Lord Bryce, to be exact: the twenty-six-year-old heir of the Marquess of Dover.

Where he'd wandered off to now, she could not say, but so far, she was pleased with their progress this evening. They were getting along well.

Which meant that Delia hadn't found a way to ruin it for her yet.

Indeed, mused Maggie, things were moving along right on schedule, if she dared say so herself.

It was the third Thursday night subscription ball of the new Season, and Maggie felt confident that, this time, she'd soon bring her target up to scratch.

Admittedly, slight misgivings about the fellow in question did nag at the back of her mind. Very well, yes—obviously—Lord Bryce wasn't ideal. But everyone had their flaws, didn't they? And desperate times called for desperate measures.

Besides, her sanity was at stake here.

Why else would she risk her reputation by dancing *three times* in one night with the same gentleman?

Indeed, the urgency of the matter was why Maggie was doing all she could—within the bounds of propriety, of course—to encourage her haughty suitor to pop the blasted question.

Because the sooner those coveted words, *Will you marry me?* left Bryce's sculpted lips, the sooner Maggie could escape out from underneath her sister's thumb to freedom.

Delia was now snorting with laughter at some innocent gaffe one of the maids had committed the other day.

"I mean, honestly, what a fool! I know she's only a maid, but is she blind?"

"You should dismiss her," one of Delia's haughty followers opined. "I would."

"Edward won't let me," said her sister with a smirk. "He feels sorry for the world. The man's ridiculously forgiving."

And you're certainly lucky for that, Maggie thought, gritting her teeth. It was not that she did not love her sister and chaperone. It was simply that Delia had a gift for driving people utterly insane.

No matter, thought Maggie. With any luck at all, she and Bryce would be married by July, and finally, she'd be in a position to establish her own household.

No longer would she have to mouse around in Delia's elegant residence in Moonlight Square, tucked away in an upper dormer like a Poor Relation, at the beck and call of the redheaded empress.

She just hoped that Bryce had not persisted in drinking any more of that scotch he fancied when he came along any minute now to claim her for the promised country dance.

The music should be starting up again shortly, and Lord knew he'd stepped on her toes and tripped over his own feet often enough in their quadrille of an hour ago, though he'd blamed it on everyone around him.

Where is he, anyway? She was growing a little annoyed at her beau's neglect as she scanned the other side of the ballroom, searching the crowd for his curly golden head.

Meanwhile, Delia prattled on, holding forth on the most trivial details of her own existence, as though the fate of nations hung in the balance. "You know, I've heard that *flowered* wallpapers are all the rage just now, but I myself cannot abide them. Of course, Edward likes them, but what do men know? My feeling on the matter is this: why follow the fashions everyone else is chasing? I say, let *them* follow *me!*"

Her devotees tittered in scandalized delight at Delia's brash, devil-may-care attitude. But, then, a woman who'd landed a wealthy marquess who worshiped the ground she walked on could do and say as she pleased.

"Oh, Your Ladyship is well known as an arbiter of taste," one of Delia's hangers-on said with a sigh.

"Well, you know, one *tries*." Delia preened, smoothing her golden dress and glancing at Maggie in smug satisfaction over how admired she was in London's first circles.

Maggie just looked at her. It was possible a white-gloved hand curled into a fist by her side, but lucky for Delia, someone in this family had to be a proper lady.

Why her elder sister, though, had been in competition with her since the day she was born, Maggie had no idea.

The one thing she did know was that the petty tyrant had relished the past year of lording it over her ever since Papa's death had forced Maggie to move in with Delia and dear, unflappable Edward, the Marquess of Birdwell, here in London.

Maggie still ached with homesickness at the thought of Halford Manor and the serene Kent countryside. But, alas, she'd had no choice than to pack up and leave the only home she'd ever known, for when

Papa had died without male issue, his earldom and country house had gone to an unpleasant and repulsively handsy uncle.

Actually, Uncle Wilbur *had* invited Maggie to keep her room and continue living there if she pleased. But she dared not stay.

Everyone knew about Uncle Wilbur.

No, thank you. Maggie shuddered. She had no intention of remaining at the manor just so the nasty fellow could grope her knee beneath the dining table when he thought no one was looking.

Better Delia's tyranny and tantrums than Uncle Wilbur's infamously wandering hands.

Blech.

And so, she'd been nudged out of the nest.

Losing her dearest papa had been awful enough, but with all her heart, Maggie missed having a home where she truly belonged.

She could still visit the manor, of course, but it wasn't the same. The house and gardens she had loved so much—the familiar sculpture of the hills, each of the beloved old trees, the way the morning sun shone through the bay window to burnish the oaken floors—none of it was hers anymore.

It hurt to know she could never truly go home again.

There was only one solution: to make a new home of her own. One that could never be taken away from her.

And if she had to bring down a husband to make that happen, like a hunter after some big game, then *that*, by Jove, was exactly what she'd do.

Even if the one man her sister hadn't managed to scare away on her behalf was completely full of himself, with an unfailingly sarcastic sense of humor.

But beggars couldn't be choosers, so Maggie thrust the disloyal thoughts of Lord Bryce's rude streak right out of her mind.

He'd better not forget about our dance. As she glanced around discreetly, trying to pick the handsome rakehell out of the crowd, frankly, it would not have surprised her overmuch to spy the haughty fellow flirting with some other girl.

It was rather disturbing how little that thought bothered her.

But Society marriages were not love matches. Toleration of one another was sufficient, so long as ranks were suitable, health was sound, family interests were aligned, and other worldly factors made sense. It was all a matter of practicality…

Then her brisk, pragmatic thoughts trailed away when she noticed a man she had never seen at one of these weekly gatherings before.

I say. She blinked, lost all awareness of the other several hundred guests around her. *Who is that?*

Tall, sinewy, and broad-shouldered, he sauntered alone down the colonnade that girded the ballroom, keeping to the shadows behind the white pillars placed at regular intervals.

The man was strikingly handsome, and for a moment, she was confused, wondering how she could've missed such a specimen on the marriage mart.

But no, she decided cautiously, he was new. She certainly would've remembered seeing him here before.

Built on heroic proportions, the black-haired stranger stood a head taller than most of the men he passed, and outweighed them visibly in hard muscle.

Yet he had a guarded air about him—distracted, uneasy.

Whoever he was, it seemed clear that, unlike her, he had far weightier matters on his mind tonight than snaring a spouse.

She did not see him speak to anyone, though sometimes he nodded politely to people he passed. Observing him from this safe distance, Maggie got the feeling the fellow did not know a soul here.

But he must be *someone*, as Delia would put it.

Otherwise, the patronesses would've never granted him a voucher to attend Moonlight Square's exclusive weekly ball. Those fearsome ladies could be high sticklers about such things.

Yet with each passing moment, as the man wandered closer, he seemed all the more alone.

Perhaps that explained his guarded air as he prowled along restlessly, tracking the perimeter of the ballroom, like a sentry keeping watch.

Every now and then, he paused in his slow pacing and scanned the crowd through narrowed eyes.

Which was how he suddenly noticed Maggie standing there, staring at him.

Without warning, the stranger's hooded gaze slammed to a halt right on her.

She gulped, went motionless as their eyes locked.

Even now, caught in the act of ogling him, she could not look away while the crowd buzzed about on all sides, and her sister droned on endlessly.

Pulse thumping, Maggie held the stranger's penetrating gaze for a moment, while a rush of awareness shivered all the way down from her earlobes to her toes. Heat blazed in her cheeks, and she suddenly felt like her stays were too tight.

The stranger studied her, curiously. He reminded her for all the world of some dangerous wild animal who'd just wandered up to the edge of human civilization and was peering in, unsure what to make of it all.

He flicked a wary glance over her, reading her, sizing her up. It was not a lewd gaze, but there was danger in it, nonetheless.

She knew then at once, instinctively, that this was a hard man. A man not to be crossed.

He made her think of rocky coastlines, wild, rugged places, where the fierce wind and the cold, stormy sea crashed against unyielding, jagged boulders, unable to break them down.

His neat, short-cropped hair was glossy black, his eyes bright, astonishing blue. Even from here, she could see their cobalt gleam beneath his jet-black eyebrows. He had strong, even features; a smooth, straight forehead and prominent nose; a square chin and firm, unsmiling mouth.

What struck her most, however, was his weathered, sun-bronzed complexion. His skin was tinged with a vibrantly tanned hue, as though he'd spent years outdoors in sunny climes.

A soldier. The certainty of it whispered through her mind, though he was not in uniform.

Instead, he wore an exquisite tailored coat as black as his hair; it showed off the sweeping breadth of his shoulders, his taut waist. His cravat was simple, unlike the showy concoctions her suitor favored; his silver waistcoat had the sheen of fine silk.

Still, the gentlemanly clothes could not hide the fact that this man was a warrior. She saw it in the stiff set of his shoulders, the proud angle of his chin, the guarded glances, the sharp, wary watchfulness.

The war was over now, she thought, but maybe not for him…

Then she realized she'd been gawping at him like a mooncalf for at least thirty seconds.

Though the sight of him had left her slightly breathless, she cringed as her wits returned. *Oh, how dreadfully awkward.* It was not her habit to gawk at good-looking men, let alone to be caught doing so. But she *had*

Gaelen Foley

just now, and he knew it. They both did.

There was no point in trying to pretend otherwise.

Not knowing what else to do, Maggie offered him an embarrassed smile, inclining her head in a polite nod, while the heat in her cheeks intensified.

A midnight eyebrow shot upward.

Then, to her inexplicably great pleasure, a rueful grin quirked one corner of his mouth, a quick, reckless flash of roguery and charm.

Maggie could now barely breathe.

They shared that fleeting little moment of private humor from across the ballroom, then he winked at her in amusement—and with that, simply dismissed her from his mind, it seemed, for he prowled off on his way.

Heart pounding, Maggie turned away, confused, and, to her chagrin, all aflutter like a henwit. How unlike her! From the corner of her eye, she watched the black-haired stranger amble off into the shadows of the colonnade, continuing his vigilant pass around the outskirts of the crowd.

Whew, she thought, still slightly out of sorts at the mere look they'd shared. But one thing was certain.

For a moment there, she had forgotten all about Lord Bryce.

Welllll, at least there was one friendly face here, Connor mused, and a pretty one it was. Maybe London wouldn't be so bad after all.

As he strolled on down the colonnade, he couldn't resist glancing back for another quick look at the girl.

Aye, a fair English rose—if a man fancied that sort of thing.

Wary of all things English as he was these days, still, Connor wondered who she was. All wide-eyed innocence, ladylike down to the tips of her dainty gloved fingers. *Hmm.* Maybe he should ask her to dance.

But then he remembered that he'd have to figure out some way to get an introduction and sighed at the headache of it all. He did not know a soul here, so whom could he ask to provide one? Never mind the fact that these folk were leery of the Irish interloper. That much was obvious.

She was lovely, though, he thought, slightly wistful.

Slim and demure, with an unassuming air, the girl was a waifish creature with a heart-shaped face, dove-gray eyes, and a luscious, rosy mouth. Her glossy brown tresses were arranged in a fetching topknot with swirling tendrils that hung down to kiss her apple cheeks and brush her milky shoulders.

She wore a diaphanous gown of pale mint-green gauze; below its short puff sleeves, white elbow gloves encased her hands. The square décolleté of her dress was moderately daring, he thought in amusement. Not too low, not too high—just right for a lass plainly born and bred to marry an English lord.

Which he, to his astonishment, had somehow become about four months ago—a fact that Connor still found equal parts annoying and hilarious.

Really, it was the most ridiculous situation.

Me, a duke? he thought for the umpteenth time as he strolled along warily. It all seemed a jest. God knew he had better things to do.

No one had been more surprised than he when that pasty, prune-faced solicitor had shown up in Ireland this past autumn to inform Connor that he had just inherited his granduncle's feckin' title. He barely remembered the old man, Grandfather's eldest brother. Granduncle Charles.

Connor had laughed heartily at first, thinking it was naught but a prank from one of his old Army mates. McFeatheridge, most likely.

Hadn't the fat, jolly sergeant often teased that Connor ought to seize the family title somehow and go fight for Ireland in Parliament once the war was done? It seemed the trusty sarge had got his wish. For the pasty little solicitor had soon explained to Connor how, back in England, the toplofty branch of the clan had been having a dreadful run of bad luck.

Over the past two years, no less than three previous Dukes of Amberley had wound up dead—one by natural causes, two by unfortunate accident.

Supposedly.

Connor's gut—which had seen him and his boys through many a battle—had told him clearly from the start that there was mischief of the first order afoot.

One way or the other, though, Cousin Richard's death left only Connor to take up the title.

Scion of the black-sheep Irish branch of the family.

Grandfather must be laughing his head off in his grave; the soldier of the family, he'd never much cared for his two elder brothers, the duke and the vicar. They'd never approved when the third-born had married an Irish lass.

In any case, as the last man standing, Connor had been apprized by the solicitor that if he, too, should fall to this mysterious run of "bad luck" to strike the Dukes of Amberley, then the title went extinct.

Well, he had no intention of doing any such thing, thank you very much.

Having seen far too much of death, he quite enjoyed living, and intended to continue doing so for as long as possible.

By God, he had not survived fifteen years of highly varied, lethal missions for the Army only to come home and be murdered in his bed, poisoned at his own supper table, or otherwise dispatched by some faceless, cowardly assassin lurking in the shadows.

Rather like the one who'd first greeted him upon his arrival in London, there at the docks. He'd barely stepped off the bloody boat, then came the attack.

For weeks, he had believed it was just what it appeared—some common thief's attempt to steal his purse. He'd shrugged it off.

But the poisoning on Twelfth Night had changed the entire situation, removed all doubt.

In the days before Christmas, he had summoned his longtime band of Army mates to come and celebrate the holidays with him. After all, he'd won a kind of lottery, hadn't he? Becoming a duke, inheriting houses, lands, first-rate stables.

He had to tell them. He knew they'd laugh their heads off right along with him. Besides, the lot of them had nothing else to do, now that the war was well and truly won.

And being home was difficult, made them itchy. Connor knew. He'd felt it, too, back in Ireland in those few months between returning from the Continent and coming here.

So, a dozen of his regimental mates had swarmed into Town to drink and feast with him and buy themselves whatever the hell they wanted for Christmas, on the major. Why not? Connor had just inherited more money than he could ever spend if he had a cat's nine lives. What else was money for? He and the lads had been through hell together.

Upon arriving, they'd each chosen hotel rooms, as it were, inside the ridiculous, giant mansion he'd inherited in Moonlight Square, and there, they had proceeded to feast and drink and live it up like they'd gone to Valhalla.

But then came Twelfth Night.

Thank God that McFeatheridge still had that vulgar habit from the mess tent of delving into everybody's food prematurely.

The portly sergeant's greater (much greater) girth had allowed his rotund body to absorb the poison meant for Connor. It had made poor Rory sick as a dog, but if Connor had consumed it, as intended, he'd be dead.

It was disturbing to ponder how it could have got into his food. That was why Connor had immediately sacked all his servants and hired a few of the boys to stay on, taking their places as best they were able.

For it had become abundantly clear then that someone was indeed trying to kill him, had probably killed his predecessors, too. God only knew why. But until he figured it out, he only wanted people around him that he knew would watch his back.

Of course, you couldn't bring that ragtag lot into a place like this, he thought with a roguish twitch about his lips, scanning the opulent ballroom.

But one thing was certain.

If some unseen foe lurking about held some sort of vendetta against his family line, Connor would suss them out and stomp the bleeders into oblivion before they ever got to *him*.

A man could not be all business, however. Not a three-quarters Irishman, anyway.

Which was why he'd ventured out tonight.

Here in his new home, it seemed sensible to try to meet the neighbors, especially now that the Season had begun.

Throughout the winter, many of the elegant houses on Moonlight Square had stood empty, the families ensconced at their country estates in the snowy English countryside.

Now everyone was back, and the fourth Duke of Amberley could no longer avoid presenting himself to the ton. Oh, he could guess how some of them already felt about him.

Apparently, Cousin Richard, the third duke, had been a popular young man. Not many here looked pleased to meet his replacement.

But…that one smile from the pretty thing back there made Connor hopeful that maybe, just maybe, London wouldn't be entirely awful.

When he glanced back over his shoulder at her again, he caught the sweet creature watching him, as well, but she quickly looked away, her creamy cheeks turning pinker.

Adorable, he thought, stifling a chuckle.

His rascally humor faded, though, when he suddenly spotted trouble ahead.

Up by the doorway of the refreshments room, near the exit of the ballroom, a group of haughty-looking fellows a few years younger than himself had clustered, leaning here and there, watching him, as though lying in wait.

Instantly, Connor went on his guard, and his eyes narrowed. *Well. What have we here?* He sized them up in a glance; what he most assuredly did *not* do was slow his pace or alter his path by one single fraction of a degree.

No.

Instead, he gave the hostile welcoming party a level look—fair warning—and sauntered on, keeping to his course like an iron-hulled frigate sailing straight toward a sleek, lazy pod of sunning seals.

A blond, curly-haired fellow in the center of the group glared at him.

Connor had seen the chap eyeing him earlier. Had not liked the way the man had looked at him from the moment he'd walked in the door.

Like he was planning something. *Guess he was.*

Time to find out what that might be.

The insolent fellow just stood there, arms folded across his chest, as though waiting to confront him. Connor smirked, though he had no idea who the blackguard was.

Didn't matter. If these soft Town chaps wanted a fight, they'd come to the right place.

But if any one of them had something to do with the threat against his family, then God help them.

Because the fact was, he had run out of mercy years ago. Somewhere between Austerlitz and Badajoz.

CHAPTER 2

A Duke's Honor

*M*aggie looked around for Bryce when the intermission music stopped shortly after the handsome stranger had vanished. The caller announced the next set, and the couples who meant to join the country dance hurried toward the center of the ballroom, while she was left gritting her teeth.

Still no sign of her scheduled partner.

She glanced down at her dance card in dismay. Was she mistaken, confused—had she erred somehow? *No.* There was his name, plainly written in—he'd put it there himself—yet her supposed suitor failed to appear. She glanced about, brow furrowed, searching the crowd for him, but when she happened to catch the smile playing about Delia's thin lips, a wave of dread filled her.

Maggie narrowed her eyes at her sister with instant suspicion. *What did you say to him?*

"Weren't you going to dance this set, Mags?" the marchioness asked with a gleam in her eyes as the dancers got into position, forming up two long lines, gents on one side, ladies on the other.

Soon there wouldn't be any room left to join them.

"Yes," Maggie answered, eyeing her sister with a wary frown. "I-I thought I was supposed to."

Delia let out a bray of a laugh. "Maybe he forgot you!"

"Oh, goodness no! I-I'm sure that's quite impossible," Delia's followers protested, looking anxiously at Maggie.

They knew from personal experience, after all, what a bully her sister

Gaelen Foley

could be.

"H-he's probably just...delayed," one offered, giving Maggie a pitying look.

"How embarrassing for you, dear," Delia purred over her glass of punch, clearly enjoying her latest defeat of her younger sibling.

Maggie bunched up her fists by her sides and fought to keep her taut smile pasted in place, determined to appear nonchalant.

"No matter," she said lightly, but, in fact, she wanted to scream.

It seemed inevitable: somehow Delia must have got to Bryce, too. *Blast it!* It really was the greatest mystery.

As much as Delia complained about having to house Maggie under her roof, at the same time, she also undermined her every chance of moving out, as though she could not bear for Maggie to find her own happiness.

Spite seemed the only explanation for why Delia had gone out of her way to quell any interest that different bachelors had taken in Maggie since she'd come to London.

Her sister seemed to think it all a game. To one fellow, Delia had hinted that Maggie suffered from some dreaded, undisclosed disease. She'd left it to his imagination to wonder what that might be.

He hadn't called on her again.

To another, she'd implied Maggie found him repulsive, which wasn't true in the least. He was just a little hairy. But a third, Delia sent away by arrogantly looking down her nose at him, giving the timid young man the impression he would never be found worthy of a daughter of the Earl of Halford.

Delia had always been quite toplofty about Papa's rank.

Now Maggie could only wonder what sort of disinformation she'd fed to Lord Bryce to scare him away, too.

"But, Mags," Delia was fond of saying, *"the right sort of fellow can't be scared away. Don't you see? I'm your big sister. I'm only doing this to protect you!"*

Of course you are, Maggie thought, gritting her teeth.

As for Bryce, she'd wring his neck for this. She couldn't believe he'd snubbed her. How ineffably lowering.

The music began. Delia smirked; Maggie fumed.

At least, upon scanning the line of male dancers now bowing to their partners, she did not see him dancing with anybody else.

Perhaps there was still hope. Although, in truth, she would not have put it past him. She had noticed that her self-important suitor *could* be a wee bit impulsive. If he had become briefly enchanted with some other young lady, she could easily see him forgetting about his promise to dance with her and prancing off to sport a toe with the girl.

They weren't married yet, after all, nor even promised to each other.

Indeed, it was possible Bryce would even do a thing like that just to test her. Merely to see, like Delia would, how much ill-treatment good ol' Mags would take before she snapped.

Little did they know, however, she was made for endurance. Patient as the Rock of Gibraltar. Just like Mama. For her to give voice to temper was very rare indeed.

As an amiable soul who dearly valued peace, she'd long become an expert at keeping her mouth shut and simply doing what needed to be done, in English fashion. Admittedly, it was not always a very pleasant way to go about. But it kept life simple, avoiding fights, avoiding conflict.

Moods passed, after all, and it was so much more reasonable not to make mountains out of molehills.

Admittedly, some molehills did sting a lady's pride.

She let out a disappointed sigh and brushed a stray ringlet back behind her ear, turning to gaze wistfully at the line of dancers now promenading down the center aisle. She loved dancing. The girls skipped and the men paraded along with a bounce in their strides.

Her heart sank to the depths. *Where on earth did he go, then?*

Perhaps he left, she thought with a frisson of worry. Perhaps he'd drunk enough to make himself ill.

She glanced down again at her dance billet, tempted to crumple the useless thing into a ball and throw it out the window.

Why a girl of good family with a pleasant face and a sizable dowry should have so few names on her dance card in the first place was a mystery even to her.

But it was all Delia's doing. The bully had always delighted in tormenting Maggie in small ways, lording it over her.

Just like she was lording it over her followers right now.

"So I told her, 'You must come over for tea tomorrow first thing,'" Delia was saying. "'Tell me everything, and I shall soon have the whole matter sorted for you...'"

Don't you ever shut up? God, only a saintly fellow like Edward could've borne the woman.

Perhaps Maggie should speak to her longsuffering brother-in-law about Delia's meddling in her attempts to snare a husband. The two of them got along well, and he was so kind. Edward hated to fight with Delia, but when it came down to it, as her husband, he really was the only one who could rein her in.

Honestly, thought Maggie, if somebody didn't do *something*, she might be trapped forever as her sister's lady-in-waiting, her captive audience—literally. The pitiable spinster of the family, maiden aunt to Delia's future children.

For all she knew, her sister might force her to serve as governess to her brats, as well, rather than allowing Maggie ever to have a family of her own.

At that moment, as she stood there brooding, a great crash resounded at the far end of the ballroom, breaking into her dire ruminations.

It had come from the refreshments area, and sounded as though a table of dishes had just been knocked over.

A shout followed and then a clamor of voices erupted.

The music jangled to a haphazard halt, the players distracted. Several dancers let out startled exclamations, bumping into each other as everyone turned to see what was going on.

Startled, Maggie did the same. She whirled around and searched the crowd, wondering in alarm if some elderly person present had fallen, like that poor old lady had, fainting in church last week.

But that did not appear to be the case. The whole gathering began turning in a wave toward a location not far from the grand entrance at the top of the stairs.

Then Maggie's eyes widened as she spotted Lord Bryce's curly golden head, there in the thick of the kerfuffle. His hand was up, his finger poking aggressively into the chest of…the large black-haired man she'd seen before.

Who was staring at Bryce rather incredulously.

Oh dear God!

She could see both men in profile, could hear only the muffled, angry tones of Bryce's raised voice. The stranger heard out his apparent rant, then laughed.

It was not the merry sort of laughter.

"You should learn to mind your tongue, whelp," the stranger warned her suitor in a deep, commanding baritone tinged with an Irish brogue.

That voice, unlike Bryce's, carried over the ballroom in the resonating tones of a man used to barking orders over the roar of cannonfire and musket volleys.

The entire room went absolutely quiet.

"I demand an answer!" Bryce yelled, his voice slightly shrill.

The stranger stared at him for a heartbeat. "Tell you what," he replied. "You take back your foolhardy accusations and apologize, and I might just let you live."

"I will *not*, you Irish dog," Bryce answered in withering disdain. "Who's to say that you yourself weren't the one who killed him, eh? You might've killed them all—one by one—just so you could seize the title!"

"Oh my God," Maggie said under her breath, her stomach plunging, nearly falling though the floor.

Bryce and his pack of friends slowly surrounded the black-haired stranger; he glanced around at them from the corner of one eye, then the other.

"So that's the way of it, then?" he asked as Maggie abruptly jolted into motion, fighting her way through the crowd to try to reach Bryce before he did anything even more feckless.

"Very well, coxcomb," said the stranger. "You leave me no choice: I demand satisfaction. Have your second call on me at Amberley House, and state your choice of weapons. I suggest you choose swords."

Bryce scoffed as Maggie elbowed people aside, hurrying closer.

"Nobody duels with swords anymore, Irishman."

"*You* will, if you want to live. Or hadn't you heard I qualified as an expert marksman when I was but a beardless ensign, age sixteen? Had a lot o' practice since then, too," the stranger added with an icy smile. "But do as you please, fella." He shrugged. "It's your funeral."

The stranger started to turn away, then noticed the crowd of gaping onlookers. His handsome lips twisted in a slight, feral sneer, and he bowed politely to the gathering.

Several gasped.

Then he straightened up to his full height, pivoted, and marched out of the ballroom alone.

Instantly, Bryce's friends huddled around him, while Maggie stood there for a moment with her jaw hanging open.

As the entire Grand Albion began to buzz with talk of the impending duel, Maggie snapped out of her horrified daze, and rushed over to her suitor on legs that shook beneath her.

"My lord! Lord Bryce!" Disregarded, she elbowed her way between Bryce's friends, finally laying hold of his lapels to get his attention.

"My lord," she cried in a panic, "what have you done?"

He finally looked down his nose and noticed her. "Ah, Lady Margaret. Don't fret, my dear, it's a small thing." Then he furrowed his brow. "Oh, right—we were supposed to dance, weren't we? Sorry. This was more important."

The stray comment pained her, but she ignored it.

"Never mind that! Did you not hear what he said? An expert marksman in the Army from the age of sixteen?"

Bryce finally looked fully at her, angry turmoil in his eyes. "I must avenge my friend." He tugged at his waistcoat and glanced around at his followers. "We all know there's something not right about that fellow."

She searched his face, at a loss. "What are you *talking* about?"

"I'll explain later. No time now."

"But, my lord, you're not thinking clearly." She could not hold her tongue: "You're *drunk*!"

"Oho!" His friends jeered merrily at her statement of the obvious—one in the back let out a pointed cat's meow—but Bryce laughed.

"Nonsense, my pet, a gentleman doesn't get drunk. Just a trifle foxed."

"Whatever the case may be, you are in no shape to handle a loaded weapon." Setting her hands on her waist, Maggie planted herself in the middle of his path, blocking his exit.

He frowned at her, annoyed.

She did not move, but at least willed a softer tone of voice, still determined to drag him to the altar. Obviously, she couldn't do that if he was dead.

"Lord Bryce, please. This man is dangerous. I am concerned for your wellbeing. You heard what he said; he'll kill you. If you've given offense, you must apologize."

"To that fellow? Hardly." He snorted and tugged at his waistcoat. "He's a bounder. And he's *not* one of us. My only apologies are to you, Lady Margaret, for missing the contra-dance." He executed a beautiful bow to her to show his sincerity.

She managed a sad half-smile. "So you didn't forget, then."

"Of course not. I merely had to take him down a peg. Now, I must beg your pardon, dear lady. I have matters to attend to."

"Bryce. Don't do this."

"Fret not, child. I'll call on you in a day or two. Perhaps take you for a drive, hmm?" He was already strutting away, on a mission now, as though his inborn sense of English superiority had somehow convinced him that breeding alone could help him kill a mere Irishman.

Even a veteran of a long and bloody war.

No doubt, his favorite scotch had helped in the way of liquid courage. Maggie shook her head, halfway between terror and exasperation. *Fool. You're a dead man.*

Her heart was pounding as Bryce shrugged to adjust his coat across his shoulders, like a peacock smoothing out his ruffled feathers. He sent his followers a commanding glance. "Shall we, boys? Now then. Who wants to second for me?"

Without looking back, Lord Bryce strode out with his chin in the air, held at an even higher notch than usual.

Maggie pressed her hand to her brow, her brain reeling, her heart pounding, her stomach in knots.

"Send your second to Amberley House."

At least that answered the question of who the blue-eyed stranger was.

Amberley House was the name of one of the big corner mansions on Moonlight Square, each one occupied by a duke.

Though the latest Duke of Amberley had moved in about four months ago—around Christmastime—he'd kept very much to himself. It was only now that the Season had begun that he seemed to have ventured out into Society.

Slowly, she started putting it all together in her mind.

From what she'd heard, there had been several deaths in that family over the past couple of years, though she did not know the details.

The last duke before this one had been a great friend of Bryce's, but Maggie had never met the infamous Richard. He had died before she'd ever met Bryce.

All she knew was that for her suitor to have publicly accused the new duke of killing his own kin to steal the title was absolutely ludicrous.

Bryce had not even claimed to have any proof. He had just decided who the culprit was, it seemed, based on prejudice and grief for his friend.

But not for all the world could Maggie see that blue-eyed stranger as a murderer. He might be a trained killer, but only for his country. Unsettling but true, she supposed. However, if the new duke had indeed been a soldier from the age of sixteen—and it hadn't looked to her like he'd been lying—then that really meant Bryce was, indeed, about to die. Shed his blue blood all over some stupid dueling field for nothing. Mere false accusations.

Of course Amberley had challenged him for this outrageous insult. What would any man do? What else did Bryce expect?

But one thing was clear. If Bryce went and got himself killed, he wouldn't be marrying *her* any time soon. Blast it, there had to be a way to stop this duel from happening! But how?

Think.

She swallowed hard then, for the only answer that came to mind was for her to go personally, secretly—*now*—and throw herself upon the duke's mercy, for Bryce's sake.

Her pulse raced at the prospect. It was exceedingly reckless even to contemplate, and not proper in the least—Mama would turn over in her grave.

But was it really so dangerous? He seemed friendly enough. The man had smiled at her, hadn't he? Surely she could reason with him. What was there to fear? They were neighbors. He was a duke, for heaven's sake. He dressed, looked, sounded like a gentleman. He'd clearly been an officer in the British Army, and everybody knew that the heroes of Waterloo understood chivalry.

Besides, she thought with a wide-eyed gulp, even an Irish scoundrel wouldn't hurt a lady…

She hoped.

CHAPTER 3

The Warrior

*C*onnor's first reaction as he stalked out of the Grand Albion was fury.

Some gratitude. Aye, that is truly some gratitude, he couldn't stop thinking, over and over again, his jaw clenched. *Bloody useless civilians.*

You risk your life a thousand times—for that lot?

He marched across the landing outside of the ballroom, and then jogged down the long, opulent staircase, ignoring the old knee injury that tended to ache when the weather changed.

All he'd wanted to do was have a look around, try to acclimate himself a bit more to his ridiculous new life as a duke, and even that had turned to bollocks.

God, if only Napoleon hadn't surrendered.

Connor would rather be in battle. But no—that ballroom *was* a battlefield, one he did not understand, one where he did not know the rules, and where every person present was apparently an enemy of some sort. He stood alone against an army of haughty English toffs, stiff as the undead, every one.

His cheeks burned with the humiliation of how it had been made very clear to him just now that he would never be accepted here, never mind his authentic ducal lineage, let alone a decade and a half of loyal service to the Crown.

Fool. Why should he care? These people weren't worth it. So what if they judged him unworthy? He would never apologize for who and what he was.

The lot of them could go to hell.

Connor shook his head to himself as he marched across the entrance hall at the bottom of the marble staircase, then blasted out through the front doors of the expensive hotel and out into the black, windy night, which was threatening rain.

The lanterns on either side of the stately building cast a gleam into the inky shadows. Liveried footmen on both sides of the entrance glanced at him in surprise; he had beaten them to the task of getting the door.

One stepped nearer with a look of chagrin. "Shall I call your carriage for you, sir?"

"No thanks, I'll walk." Connor nodded toward his nearby house, and the footman bowed to him.

Easing a bit now that he was away from that smug crowd, Connor descended the few stairs outside the hotel to the pavement. He turned left and began striding homeward at a fast clip.

Well, bloody what now? he wondered with a curse under his breath as he peeled off his fancy white gloves.

Truly, he was going to enjoy shooting a hole in that young piece of arrogance, if that was what it took to stop this shocking, ugly rumor before it got started. Kill his own relatives?

Ridiculous.

Connor tugged his cravat loose with an irked growl. Every day in this new life of his truly got more absurd. Yet one question loomed: did that fellow have something to do with the plot against his family? Connor knew he could not afford to take anything or anyone at face value. He was surrounded by strangers in this place, and who his true enemy was, he had no idea—yet.

But he would find them in due time, each and every one who might be connected to all this. And as for that haughty chap, well, one way or the other, he would not be a problem for much longer.

Connor strode through the darkness, hoping that maybe, once he dealt with this bastard, others around here might start to get the message. They might *view* him as an Irish mongrel, but to dare speak those sentiments aloud, well, that was insulting his mother, aye, and his Irish granny, too.

So there was that.

Moreover, he would damn well be treated with the same respect due to any man of his rank. If they did not wish to befriend him, well and good; as one of his former commanding officers liked to say, it was better to be feared than loved, anyway.

Yet the whole prospect disgusted and rather depressed him. This was not the peacetime existence he had envisioned for so long.

It all felt like a cynical jest and a damned shame.

The only person back there who had seemed remotely friendly was the gray-eyed girl. Well, she had probably realized by now that he was persona non grata. No doubt, she would keep a safe distance.

Connor sighed. Battle-hardened warriors did not generally admit to being lonely. But deep in his heart, he knew he was, and that annoyed him, too.

Weakness.

Marching along the pavement, he passed feeble gold pools of light where quaint black wrought-iron streetlamps lined the lane. Across the cobbled avenue was a matching swath of pavement, and the wrought-iron fence that girded the garden park in the center of Moonlight Square.

It was a pleasant green refuge in the hubbub of London. He'd taken to strolling its graveled walks, now that spring had come. Each day showed the many flowers planted throughout the park in new stages of development.

This interested him. Perhaps the flowers' progress seemed a silly thing for a trained killer to want to follow and watch with such anticipation. But after all he'd seen, all he'd survived, all the ugliness, horror, and pain, he had learned to take whatever small joys and beauties life offered where he found them.

Tomorrow, after all, was promised to no man.

Particularly one who'd just inherited a dukedom that some hidden foe seemed determined to destroy.

All the more reason to show this fop no mercy when dawn came.

Connor clenched his jaw, itching to feel a weapon in his grip—not that he needed one to send an enemy to his grave.

Ahead, the gigantic house he'd inherited hulked astride the corner.

To be sure, it was beautiful, but Connor still felt a sense of unreality every time he walked in, considering his main residence for years had been a leaky, smelly tent shared with other officers, and that most of his essential items for everyday life could fit on the back of a horse.

This opulence was all just bizarre.

Adorned by a grand, porticoed entrance, Amberley House stood four stories high, with various layers of windows in classical designs, the second being the tallest, what with the drawing room and so forth. The third contained a maze of bedchambers where he still tended to get lost. The fourth was where the servants lived—or had, before he'd sacked the whole treacherous lot.

As he reached the bottom of the few stairs leading up to the front door, which was illuminated by flickering lamps on either side, Connor glanced down warily into the dark exterior stairwell that led to the service entrance, for merchants and deliveries and so forth.

There, a few feet below street level, a plain wooden door was tucked away in the shadows. Behind it lay the working regions of the house: kitchens, pantries, wine cellar, silver vault, butler's quarters, as well as bins for coal storage.

Connor had always thought that that dark, half-underground stairwell looked like a good place for a murderer to hide and lie in wait.

Tonight, once again, however, it was clear.

He harrumphed. Truthfully, he'd have rather fought it out now with his unknown enemy and got the whole thing over with, but no such luck.

He continued up the few front steps to the grand main entrance of Amberley House, unlocked the door, and let himself in without ceremony.

Inside, the mansion was dim and drafty, and though he noticed it was getting a bit messy around here without a proper staff, it was magnificently decorated to suit the taste of one of the previous dukes— or his duchess, more likely.

The floors were marble, the ceilings painted, with touches of gilt. The art adorning the walls was unthinkably expensive, the furnishings so splendid that Connor often still hesitated before sitting down on some of the chairs. Likewise, the canopy bed up in the master chamber seemed vast…and much too empty.

He supposed one of these days he'd have to find himself a mistress. Lord knew, a good daily romp would help dispel the jitters of peacetime and this bizarre change in his station, and all the unanswered questions of who was trying to kill him and why.

Unfortunately, in his current state of well-justified paranoia, Connor doubted he could've found a bedmate who wouldn't have left him wondering if she'd stab him in his sleep, should he doze off after their sport. Bit of a problem there. Thus, he'd become a monk in recent weeks.

But so be it. He had bigger matters to worry about these days than relieving his want.

As he tossed the door shut behind him then locked it, he could already hear Will and Nestor squabbling somewhere in the cavernous depths of the house.

He smirked at the familiar sound. *Those two.*

Of course, as footmen and butlers, his trusty regimentals were generally useless, but they'd have followed him to the gates of hell itself, and had.

Their bickering stopped at the sound of the front door's slam, and a moment later, Will came jogging out onto the landing at the top of the steps, looking more dusty and rumpled than usual from the task Connor had given the men.

Namely, searching each room of the fifty-some rooms of Amberley House for any possible clues about these deaths in the family.

"Major! You're back! Nestor, the major's back!" the skinny lad called over his shoulder.

It comforted Connor immensely to know he would always be the major to his men, rather than the duke.

Little did his humble band of merry men know what a balm their presence here was. This disorienting change in his duties, routine, expectations, command structure—frankly, everything he'd ever known—sometimes made him feel like he was losing himself. But through their eyes, he remembered who he was.

The leader.

Who always knew what to do. Who'd get them out of any scrape alive.

They trusted him, and that reminded him to trust himself.

Then Will looked at him again, furrowing his brow. "Why are you back so soon, sir?" His grin flashed. "Didn't you have fun sportin' a toe with the ton?"

"Not exactly," Connor said dryly. He stalked across the decorative medallion of the foyer's marble floor, practically ripping off his stupid fine coat.

"You need anything, sir?" Will offered, sensing his dark mood.

Connor grunted, and Will frowned, studying him uncertainly.

Private Will Duffy was twenty, but looked younger because of his thin build. His joints seemed oversized on his bony frame. He had a big nose but thoughtful eyes, and wore a gregarious smile on his homely face most of the time.

He couldn't really fight, and indeed, looked like a good breeze could blow him away, but he was entirely goodhearted, and though Connor would never admit it aloud, he credited the lad with preserving whatever was left of his humanity—along with Nestor, who presently joined them in the entrance hall.

The regiment's weathered surgeon took one look at Connor and stopped, resting his hands on his waist. "Ah, bloody hell," the older man muttered. "What's happened now?"

For a man with only one eye, Nestor Godwin always seemed to see everything clearly in a glance.

He was a short, stocky fellow in his fifties, with a wild mass of wiry gray hair and an eye patch.

Nestor had served as the regiment's chief medic until a piece of shrapnel had cost him the use of an eye. Though he could no longer judge distances, he could still set bones and make stitches—more by instinct than sight. He also had wide apothecary knowledge—not to mention nerves of steel.

You'd have to, to amputate limbs, Connor had always thought.

As it happened, Nestor was also—like many old bachelors—a fairly good cook. So he'd become the kitchen staff at Amberley House, while Will was more Connor's valet, butler, footman.

As for everybody's favorite jolly fat man, Sergeant Rory McFeatheridge had gone a-rambling after he'd gobbled down the poison intended for Connor, but he'd be back.

Privately, they'd agreed that once Rory had spent some time recovering from the poison's effects at the home of some cousins near Portsmouth, he'd do some sleuthing hither and yon to see what he might be able to dig up on the Amberley deaths.

That was the thing about McFeatheridge. For all his faults and vulgarities, the bearded sarge was so damned likable, he could get nearly anyone to talk.

He also had a fist like a hammer; Will liked to call him Friar Tuck.

Presently, Will was glancing from Nestor to Connor and back again, alarmed. "Is Nestor right, sir? Did somebody try to kill you again?"

"In a sense, I suppose." Connor let out a huge sigh and scratched his eyebrow. "Seems I've been challenged to a duel."

"*What?*" both men burst out.

"Major!" cried Will. "You can't be serious! A duel? But it's peacetime!"

"I know. I know, believe me." Connor shook his head.

Nestor planted his fists on his waist, his good eye homing in on Connor with knowing disapproval. "What did you do?" he asked sternly.

"What? Me? It wasn't *my* fault!" Connor retorted. "I was minding my own bloody business, I assure you."

"It's a ballroom, not an alehouse, Your Grace," Nestor said wryly. "People are generally on their best behavior in such locations. Which tells me *you* must've provoked the challenge somehow."

"I'm innocent this time, I swear," Connor said with a frown, unbuttoning his cufflinks. These Bond Street clothes were too damned restrictive.

"Ohh," said Will in a tone of understanding. "Was it 'cause you're Irish?" The lad leaned against the newel post, hooking a pointy elbow around the base of the carved marble urn that topped it.

"I'm afraid it's even worse than that," Connor admitted. "If I expected these people to look on me with sympathy over the deaths in my family, or at least to view me with a whit of appreciation on account of the war, it appears I was highly deluded."

"Why? What do you mean?" Nestor demanded.

"Well..." Connor's tone turned grim. "The young jackanapes who challenged me offered a theory that *I'm* the one who killed my predecessors."

"What, the dead dukes?" Will exclaimed.

"To get the title, aye," Connor muttered in disgust. He rubbed the back of his neck while Nestor and Will looked at each other in shock.

Connor began pacing back and forth across the entrance hall. "This challenge might be connected to all that's happened—or not. I really couldn't say for certain whether this chap's involved in it or *what* his true motives might be. Hell, I don't even know his name. Either way, I admit, I did not see this coming."

"Of course not, how could you?" Nestor looked outraged at the sheer absurdity of the accusation. "You? Kill your own relatives? You never even wanted the title!"

"Plus, *how* could you have done it?" Will cried. "I mean, you've been a bit busy!"

"I have no idea!" Connor threw his hands up, bewildered. "The idiot seemed to be suggesting I could've engineered the whole thing from a distance somehow to lay hold of the dukedom, the fortune, the power. This might be the rumor going around now, I hardly know."

"Oh Lord," Nestor grumbled, then huffed. "This is not good."

"It's bloody awful," Connor replied.

"No wonder they've all been so standoffish—well, not all of them," Will amended. "The Duke and Duchess of Rivenwood have been friendly to you, haven't they, sir? I mean, he's an odd one, of course—name like Azrael?—but pleasant enough."

"Right…" Nestor nodded at the reminder of their ducal neighbor on the nearest corner. "You'll have to ask Rivenwood to be your second."

"I shall do nothing of the kind," Connor said, scowling. "*You* can second for me, Nestor."

"Me?" Nestor scoffed and pointed at his eye patch. "There's no way in hell I could ever fight a duel. I'm blind in one eye, remember?"

"Oh, come, you're not going to fight—you'll just do the talking bit, arranging matters. I'm the one who'll do the fighting, obviously. Indeed, nothing would please me more at this point." Glowering at the thought of that golden-haired jackass, Connor pivoted and rubbed his mouth.

Nestor scoffed. "Major, you know full well you need a fellow aristocrat to second you, at least a real gentleman. Not some lowly limb-chopper like me. Why *not* ask the Duke of Rivenwood? Will can go and fetch him for you." The surgeon gestured to the lad. "Go and tell His Grace—"

"No. Stay," Connor commanded. Will froze. "Rivenwood's a newlywed, Nestor. Dragging him into this mess would be poor thanks for the courtesy he's shown me. It's been quite a rarity in these parts, if you haven't noticed."

"Believe me, we have," Will mumbled with a frown.

"That cocky little bastard," Connor said under his breath, thinking of his challenger. Pacing over to the umbrella stand in the corner, he took out his favorite sword, which he had stowed there to have it handy in case of another attack.

Lifting it, he pulled it from its sheath, gazing at the blade. It had seen him through many a scrape. "Aye, I shall make him eat his words. One…bloody bite…at a time."

"Look here, Major—" Nestor began.

"Oh, quit griping," Connor said, and put the sword away again. "Who gives a damn if the ton's scandalized that I chose a commoner for a second? I was one myself until December, wasn't I? Let them choke on their gossip for all I care. Besides, you've got to be there, anyway. I'll need you there to patch me up if I get wounded, so don't forget to bring your doctorin' bag."

Nestor stared at him with his one good eye, hands propped on his waist, fingers drumming. "Perhaps you should just go and talk to this fellow. Try to reason with him."

"What?" Connor retorted. "Hell no. I'm sendin' that one on to meet his maker. Besides, I haven't the foggiest notion who the bastard is."

"*Think*, you Irish hothead," Nestor said without malice. "If some in the ton already suspect that you're a killer, then shooting this chap in the heart in front of witnesses *might not* exactly be the best idea."

"He insulted my honor! He dies."

"Yes, but Major…"

While Connor and the surgeon continued bickering, Will suddenly glanced at the door. "Did you hear that?" the lad asked.

Still arguing with Nestor, Connor ignored the low-toned question. "What, are you suggesting I let the bastard off with a warning shot?"

"A flesh wound, perhaps."

"Nestor, that entire ballroom would've happily lynched me if I'd stayed a moment longer," he said. "If I don't make an example of him, I risk more challenges in the future."

"Oh, you're always blowing things out of proportion," Nestor said, waving this off.

"Well, it's kept me alive, hasn't it? Plan for the worst, hope for the best, like I always say."

"Sirs, I think there's someone at the door!" Will broke in.

"Well, answer it, genius." Nestor smacked the boy on the back of the head, and off he went.

As Will trotted across the entrance hall, Nestor glanced grimly at Connor. "Your challenger's second, already?"

"That was fast." Connor shrugged, planting his hands on his hips. "Told you he was eager for my blood."

Will unlocked the door, but glanced back first to see if they were ready.

Connor gestured at the surgeon. "Talk to him, doc. Negotiate the time and place as you see fit. It's all the same to me. But at least find out the blackguard's name."

Nestor sighed and shook his head. "Very well. I'll speak to him upstairs, Will. Drawing room. And *you*, sir, had best stay out of sight," he said to Connor. "Try to keep out of trouble for once in your life."

"Who, me?" Connor flashed a wicked grin, retreating to the

shadows of the nearby sitting room that adjoined the entrance hall. "Don't forget to ask which weapon!" he reminded the older man in a stage whisper.

"Shh!" Nestor replied, then he nodded at their "butler," and Will opened the door.

"Good evening," he started, then: "Oh—! Er, can I help you, miss?" *Miss?* Connor thought.

"Um, yes, I-I am here to see the Duke o-of Amberley, if I may." The soft voice coming from the doorway had an accent as elegant as cut crystal, but tones as warm as hearthstones where a cat would like to curl up and sleep away a winter's day.

They melted something inside Connor from the moment he first heard the sound.

Even Nestor was startled. Halfway up the staircase, the surgeon turned so he could see through the open doorway with his good eye.

"I-I only ask a moment of His Grace's time, I promise."

"Er, Major?" Will turned to face the sitting room, his eyebrows arched high. "There's a beautiful young lady at your door. Are you at home?"

Always, Connor thought.

Filled with equal parts roguery and suspicion at this extremely unusual news, he sauntered forward from the sitting room and leaned toward the doorway to view their caller.

To his amazement, it was the gray-eyed beauty from the ballroom: the English rose.

What on earth was *she* doing here? Alone, no less.

"Please," she said with an innocent blink, gazing past Will to Connor, "if you don't mind, I should be grateful for a moment of Your Grace's time." She glanced nervously over her shoulder, as though making sure she had not been followed.

Then she looked at him again.

Her heart-shaped face was pale by the dim glow of the lanterns flanking the front door. Her gauzy skirts billowed in the breeze. She wore a lacy white shawl now, draped across her delectable shoulders.

She pulled it closer around herself as she stood in the doorway. He could see her shaking...probably not from the chill, but from the boldness of her visit here. Even he was startled by it.

"May I come in?" she asked with a gulp. "We are...neighbors, after all."

He blinked out of his daze. "By all means."

What she wanted, Connor could not imagine, but he prowled over slowly to brush the lad aside. "I'll take it from here, Will."

"Aye, sir."

Connor held the door for their fair visitor. The girl stared at Will as she tiptoed in warily, looking a little nonplussed at his unconventional butler.

Nestor returned to the bottom of the stairs, watching skeptically.

"I don't suppose there's any chance you're here about the duel?" Connor said, half joking.

He paused to scan the street before shutting the door, then locked it behind her again.

"Actually, I am," she said, wide-eyed.

"*You're* the fellow's second?" Will exclaimed.

"N-no, of course not," she said. She pursed her rosy lips. "I'm his...his..."

Connor cocked a brow, waiting, hands on hips. "His what?"

"His...particular lady friend," she said judiciously.

"I see." His smile soured.

Suspicion promptly won the inner tug of war with roguery. His mood darkened back to normal. "Let me guess. You've come here to plead for the blackguard's life."

She blinked. "Well—actually...now that you mention it..."

He smirked. Her words faltered, and she started turning red, like she had in the ballroom.

"Um, could we possibly discuss this in private, Your Grace?"

Connor considered it. Fraternize with the enemy?

Once again, there was no way of knowing who might be involved with the plot against his family. Indeed, if he were out in the field, running a scouting mission or an intelligence-gathering operation, he would find the most unlikely person to send in to make inquiries for him.

Someone the enemy would never suspect. Someone who could serve as a distraction, diversion, spread false information...or do even worse.

Hmm. Connor's stare homed in on the girl's dainty gloved hands clutching her reticule.

For a moment, he studied her little tasseled handbag, determining after a few seconds that it was too diminutive to contain even a small pistol.

But that didn't mean this lovely little confection wasn't perilous to him in other ways.

Temptation such as this had got Adam and Eve thrown out of the garden, last he'd checked, and *this* was one alluring red apple, ripe and juicy.

He wanted a taste.

She grew flustered at his prolonged silence. "You *are* the duke, aren't you? If there's someone else I should speak to—"

"Oh yes," he said absently, curiosity outweighing his caution. He'd hear her out. *Why not?* "I am Amberley these days, so it would seem. I admit, you've come at rather a bad time, but it's always my pleasure to be of…service to a lady."

His double entendre went over her clearly virginal head, but he folded his arms across his chest and stared at her, far more entertained than he cared to let on.

"How may I be of assistance, mademoiselle?"

CHAPTER 4

The Peacemaker

*E*very quick, reverberating thump of Maggie's heart as she held the duke's stare warned her that she absolutely shouldn't be here. She was not accustomed to doing rash things, and her current venture, she feared, was nothing short of foolhardy.

How she had managed to sneak away from Delia, she barely knew. The entire ballroom had been in an uproar after the outbreak of violence.

But she was here to stop it, if she could.

And so, Maggie swallowed hard and held on tight to her composure.

It was not easy, pinned in the gaze of such a man. Amberley had removed his black tailcoat and tugged loose his cravat. The loose, white, billowy sleeves of his shirt cascaded fascinatingly off the rugged breadth of his shoulders, only hinting at the hard, bulging muscles the crisp fabric draped.

His pale striped waistcoat hugged a powerful chest that tapered toward his lean waist. She gulped silently as her gaze slid lower to the manly regions concealed by his elegant black trousers…

Margaret Hyacinth Winthrop! Mind your manners and get your eyes back in your head. At once, she whipped a blushing glance back up to his disturbingly handsome face.

She found the duke looking not at all inclined to believe a word she said, but waiting patiently for her to speak her piece.

The polite curve of his lips was *almost* a smile.

Flustered by her own wayward noticings, Maggie briefly turned her attention to his companions; if they were servants, they'd have left.

Indeed, she saw no sign of butler, footmen, or maids, and that was very odd—but, clearly, no one was cleaning the place. Her nose twitched in the dust while the homely young beanpole who'd answered the door bathed the entrance hall in the cheery, beaming brightness of his smile.

He wore a shapeless jacket of rough, workaday brown cloth and trousers to match, though his skinny frame swam in them. The boy needed feeding.

The scruffy older chap over near the cluttered staircase did not even have on a coat or cravat, merely an unbuttoned vest over a loose, wrinkled shirt, with suspenders holding up his blue trousers.

His wild gray hair and eye patch made Maggie feel just for a moment as though she had stowed aboard a pirate ship.

A trifle disoriented, she could almost feel the floor at her feet rocking with the waves.

But instead of a ship's deck, the entrance hall had marble floors veined with silver and white, and pale yellow walls.

A curved cantilevered staircase seemed to float up to the chambers above; a wrought-iron banister of slim proportions ran alongside it, curling its way up to the next floor.

There were a few pillars here and there, colorful paintings on the walls, mainly landscapes: Venetian canals, Flemish bridges, mountain cataracts beneath brooding alpine skies, Bedouins on camels in the desert. Overhead, a large crystal chandelier wept amethyst teardrops, but most of its candles were not lit.

To be sure, it looked like a mansion, but the clutter everywhere— and the smell—enhanced the sense that she had fallen in among some all-male band of brigands.

Muddy riding boots had been left to dry beneath the pier table; atop it, an abandoned serving tray brimmed with dirty plates that still bore the petrified scraps of some bygone meal.

Here, a large greatcoat slowly enfolded a Chippendale chair like it would eat it whole. There, a top hat dangled from the lithe raised arm of an indignant alabaster goddess in the wall niche.

What is going on here? she thought, amazed.

A random collection of odds and ends piled in the corners of the stairs, as though some absent-minded soul had set them there weeks ago and kept forgetting to carry them up: books, maps, newspaper, tinderbox, lint brush, some sort of leather knapsack, spyglass, and— egads!—a long gun, broken down into parts for cleaning.

The sight of the weapon reminded her of the grim reason why she was here.

The beanpole, meanwhile, following her gaze, must have suddenly realized how untidy it looked to a visitor. "Oh! Sorry for the mess," he blurted out, then leapt into motion to begin tidying up.

The duke winced. "Er, we've had a bit of a problem with the staff."

"I see," Maggie murmured, nodding as though she comprehended.

"We weren't expecting visitors," the beanpole added apologetically, but the master of the house did not seem too concerned.

The duke hooked a thumb toward the older man. "This is Mr. Godwin and that's Private Will Duffy."

She nodded to the men.

"And you are?" Amberley prompted, arching a brow.

"Oh, yes, um." Maggie brushed off her confusion about his friends. Irrelevant right now. Instead, she focused on the duke, but that proved distracting, too. It was hard to think with his full attention fixed on her.

His presence was potent, elemental, the force of him like standing on a beach at night with a hurricane approaching.

She cast about for her wits. "I am Lady Margaret Winthrop. I live across the square—well, diagonally from here, more or less—with my sister a-and her husband. On Marquess Row." She gestured haphazardly toward the closed door in the direction of their terrace house. "Lord and Lady Birdwell?"

"Ah," the duke said.

She could tell by his blank look that he had never heard of them before.

Delia would be crushed.

It seemed as though he didn't even know which street on the square had been nicknamed Marquess Row.

"I beg your pardon, Lady Margaret," His Grace said with a flicker of impatience, "this is rather a bad time for a neighborly visit, so…?"

"Yes, yes, of course." She nodded briskly. "I saw what happened in the ballroom," she said. "I thought I might be able to help."

"Indeed?" said the duke, lifting his chin.

"In that case, young lady, you are most welcome," said Mr. Godwin, sauntering closer. "What on earth did we miss in that ballroom tonight?"

"Well," she said with a tentative smile by way of apology, "I'm afraid Lord Bryce must've had one too many rounds of scotch."

"So that's his name," the duke drawled. "He never did bother to introduce himself before offering to shoot me."

"Pardon, my lady," Mr. Godwin said. "Did you say that this Lord Bryce is your suitor?"

Maggie nodded.

"Well, well," murmured the duke, and a slightly diabolical half-smile stole across his chiseled face. "Follow me, Lady Margaret. You and I can discuss this in private, as you requested. Won't you step into my…parlor?—or whatever this room is. I still get lost in this place."

He pivoted and breezed toward a sitting room to the right of the entrance hall. By the light of just a couple of candles in there, she noted wood paneling and red velvet furniture.

"Ahem, shall I join you, Your Grace?" Mr. Godwin offered.

"That won't be necessary," the duke replied, beckoning Maggie to follow.

"Not to you, maybe," the surgeon mumbled, and when the duke turned around, the older man nodded toward Maggie with discreet insistence.

It took Amberley a beat longer to catch his meaning—that Mr. Godwin was offering to play chaperone for them.

Gratitude filled her. Pirate or not, he seemed a very civil fellow.

"I think that would be wise," Maggie said primly.

Amberley shook his head. "No, Nestor. Her Ladyship and I must discuss this in private, clearly."

Maggie held up a finger. "I don't mind if they hear this, Your Grace—that is, now that I see that these fellows are your friends."

He flashed a wicked smile. "Perhaps I want you all to myself for a minute or two, my dear Lady Margaret. Don't quit now; you've come this far, haven't you?"

Private Duffy chuckled, but Maggie furrowed her brow in alarm, not as confident as the beanpole that her tall, intimidating host was only teasing.

Mr. Godwin didn't seem convinced, either. "Ahem, two duels, Your Grace?"

Amberley smirked. "As many as it takes, ol' boy. Now run along, you lot. Won't be but a moment," he assured them, then shut the door in the pirate's frowning face.

Thus, Maggie found herself enclosed in a dim room with the Irish stranger.

When they were alone, he turned to her with a decidedly wayward sparkle in his eyes, and—duke or not—Maggie wondered if she ought to worry.

"So. Is the ol' cyclops right?" he inquired. "Should I expect yet another challenge from this brother-in-law you mentioned, on account of your visit here—neighbor?"

The image of Edward's placid smile flitted through her mind. In truth, he was the most even-tempered man alive.

He'd have to be, to marry Delia.

Still, it might be wiser not to tell Amberley that, just in case he had it in his head to try misbehaving with her. He seemed very much a rogue.

Maggie just shrugged, preferring not to lie.

"I see," said the duke, then gestured to a chair. "Do you care to sit, my lady?"

"No, thank you, Your Grace. But do feel free, if you wish to."

"Don't mind if I do." While the duke dropped lazily into an armchair, she walked across the Persian carpet toward the center of the room, putting a safer distance between them.

Then she stood with her feet together, both hands clenching her reticule tight against her waist.

Every drumbeat of her pulse seemed to chide her. This was not the done thing. Not at all. Not proper, not decent, not right.

So, why, then, did she feel such a thrill in this man's presence?

The shadows pressing in on all sides made their secret meeting seem all the more intimate, here in the glow of two candles.

This could get her ruined, she was well aware.

At least, now seated, the warrior duke did not seem quite so large and intimidating. She was grateful for that.

Leaning back in the armchair, Amberley watched her face with guarded amusement. "Now then: Lady Margaret Winthrop. Concerning what happened in the ballroom, if you have information of some sort that could shed light on this whole debacle, that would be most welcome."

"First of all, I'm sorry Lord Bryce was so unpleasant to you—"

"Unpleasant?" He laughed. "The man accused me of murdering my own kin."

She winced. "Yes. He can be rather rude."

"So I'd noticed. What else can you tell me about this suitor of yours? Why don't we start with a name? Who the blazes is he?"

"Oh—Dorian Lacey, the Earl of Bryce. He's the heir of the Marquess of Dover."

"Is he now? Quite a catch there, young lady." His blue eyes sparkled with dangerous mirth in the candle's glow.

Maggie furrowed her brow at his teasing.

"Tell me." He tapped a finger to his square chin thoughtfully. "Has the tot ever been in a duel before?"

"Not that I know of, no."

"Is he a good shot?"

She shook her head. "I've no idea."

"Does he regularly take target practice?"

"I-I don't think so."

"Ah. Then let us rename him Lord Mincemeat, for that is all he is now."

She gasped.

"Calm down, Lady Margaret. 'Twas a jest."

"That's what worries me!" she burst out, staring at him in bafflement. "Shouldn't you be a bit more—oh, I don't know—concerned about this?"

"Sorry, I shall try to look grave. Is he right-handed or left?"

"How should I know?"

"Oh, I should think that a woman would notice such things about her beau's touch. Unless he has not yet dared to explore those lovely—"

"Sir!" she choked out, appalled. Yet her heart skipped a beat. And then began booming.

Amberley grinned at her. "I beg your pardon, my lady. Please forgive a soldier's blunt tongue and rough manners." He paused while she stood there with her face radiating fire like a star. "But after all," he said, "you're on the other side in this matter, clearly. The least you should expect, coming here, is a wee bit o' ribbing."

"But that's just it! I'm not on anybody's side. That's why I'm *here*. I don't want this duel to happen at all!"

"Neither do I. Unfortunately, it's not up to you—or to me, for that matter. It's entirely in the hands of Lord Mincemeat. He's the one who started this. If he wants to live, he can apologize. You're free to tell him I said so. He didn't seem to hear it when I told him myself." He shrugged. "But perhaps he'll listen to you, if you're his sweetheart."

Maggie stared at him, routed. He just looked at her, not budging an inch.

Oh, this was not going at all according to plan. She lowered her head fretfully and rubbed her brow, fighting exasperation.

"Would you like to sit down, Lady Margaret? You look a bit pale. Oh, er—can I offer you some...refreshments?" The great barbarian abruptly stood, blanching with apparent chagrin that he had not remembered hospitality till now.

Some duke he was.

"No, thank you," she said crisply, lifting her head to pin him with a withering stare. "This is not a social call."

He lifted his eyebrows. "Right," he said after a moment. Then his rapid-fire questions resumed. "Do you have any notion why your suitor saw fit to accuse me of murder?"

"He didn't mean that, I'm sure." Maggie shook her head in frustration. "It's just he was quite close friends with your predecessor. Richard? They were of an age and went to school together. From what I understand, Bryce was distraught when he died. I suppose now he probably just wants someone to blame."

"His words were outrageous. Did you hear them?" he demanded.

"I did. And I...I apologize on his behalf."

"Well, that's very civil of you, my lady, but the apology can only come from him."

Maggie sighed. "I'm afraid the chances of that happening are very slim, Your Grace. I don't believe his mouth has ever formed the words *I'm sorry.*"

His lips twisted. "I could accept it in writing."

She offered him a wan smile, and they gazed at each other for a moment.

It puzzled her that Amberley didn't seem to want this duel, even though he'd likely win it.

Capable a fighter as he most likely was, it seemed he only wished for peace.

"Were you really in the Army from the age of sixteen?"

"Aye."

She shook her head to ponder it. "That's little more than a child."

He shrugged with a weary half-smile. "Aristocratic families have to do *something* with their younger sons, don't they? My grandfather, William, was the youngest of three. The first became the duke, the second was for the church, and the third was sent off to the Army. So war-fighting became my line's specialty, I suppose you might say. And now I have a question for *you*, Lady Margaret."

"Yes?" she whispered, entranced by the sound of his voice. His deep purr of a brogue wrapped around her, enchanting her senses.

"Why are you really here, love?" he asked softly. "Beggin' your pardon, but I don't think you came here at all to help *me*. You came wantin' me to help *you*."

"I thought I could at least shed some light on why Bryce..." she began, but her excuses trailed off, and she stared at him. "Will you? Help me, that is."

He studied her. "What exactly do you expect me to do?"

"Spare him!" she pleaded. "I don't want you to kill him. I know you probably could—"

"Oh, aye," he assured her.

"But I've come to ask you not to," she said in a heartfelt, humble tone. "For my sake."

He narrowed his eyes at her, contemplating her request.

She faltered as he sat there, stony. "I know you don't know me, but I-I throw myself on your mercy as a gentleman, Your Grace. That is all."

A low growl escaped him. Maggie saw the chivalry that flickered behind the hard, devil-may-care veneer. But he seemed to fight it. He jumped out of the chair and paced over to the fireplace, where he propped an elbow on the mantel.

"Quite a risk you're taking for that jackanapes, coming here. You know as well as I that if anyone found out, it could destroy your reputation. Are you so in love with this idiot?"

"Well—" The question startled her for some reason. "It...it's my duty."

"How's that?"

She deflated. "I mean to make him my husband before the Season's out, and I think he's almost ready to propose."

"Oho! Is that right?" He began laughing.

Maggie scowled. "You don't know how long I have been working on this! It's...important."

"Well." A wicked grin flashed across his face. "Felicitations, Lady Margaret."

That grin worried her.

"I just want to make sure I understand," he said. "So you set your cap at the future marquess, and now you've almost brought him up to scratch."

Maggie glared at him.

"You're not here for love's sake, then, but ambition, yes?"

"No! Not ambition," she insisted. "Practicality."

"Ah, of course. Righty-ho," said the duke, deviltry dancing a wee Irish jig across his face. He flared his thick eyebrows, then drummed his fingers on the mantel. "Let me see if I have this right: I've got the future wife of my enemy here alone in a room with me. What an interesting state of affairs."

She frowned at him. "We are not engaged yet, but he is nearly poised to propose. Unless you kill him!"

"I see. Still…" His teeth flashed white in the candlelight. "As much as you tug on my heartstrings, my lady, I confess, it does get the wheels in a man's brain turning."

"How now, Your Grace?" she said, and drew back, offended.

Very well, not offended, exactly, but unsettled for certain.

Maggie braced herself for anything, seeing the merry glint in his dancing eyes.

"Tell me this, Lady Margaret." He sauntered closer, leaning down to whisper, "What might you be willin' to do to persuade me to spare your precious boy?"

He reached out and cupped her cheek in one large, warm, capable hand, and Maggie quivered.

"After all, if I spared his life for your sake, as you begged me so prettily, I should need some form of recompense. So tell me, my lady. What's his life worth to you?"

Maggie held perfectly motionless, searching his cobalt eyes. The wicked innuendo in his question stole her breath, but she refused to back down.

Yet it was not the thought of Bryce's survival or her life inside Delia's prison that inspired the next words from her lips, but the scarlet image that unfurled in her mind, of this man raining kisses all over her body. The dark, violent hurricane of him sweeping her off her feet and…

She chased away a whirlwind of wicked thoughts, but her voice came out as a breathy whisper: "What did Your Grace have in mind?"

CHAPTER 5

A Devil's Bargain

Connor jolted at her so-willing answer. *Mother Mary.* Why, he had not been expecting that.

All this time, he had merely been toying with the girl, in truth, pumping her for information, and frankly, he was shocked she had not run screaming from the house.

The little thing had had such a demure, refined look, like sugar wouldn't melt on her tongue. But, much to his roguish astonishment, she had stood her ground. And now, sweet heavens, in answer to his probing, it seemed the lady was game for a bit o' sport.

Perhaps she figured that if she was going to have to make concessions to get what she wanted, anyway, then she might as well enjoy it.

Especially since it was clear that young Lord Mincemeat had never touched her or taught her what that tantalizing young body of hers could do.

Oh, to be sure, having quickly concluded that this naïve damsel had nothing to do with the threat against his family, he could think of a long list of naughty games he'd like to play with her.

But in point of fact, he had a much better use for the elegant beauty than that. *That* he could get anywhere. By contrast, the arrival of an aristocratic young lady on his doorstep offered a rare opportunity.

This one was clearly a very well-behaved young miss under normal circumstances. And she had been brave (if a bit reckless) coming here on her quest to save her beau's life.

Connor could respect that, and had no wish either to harm or to terrify the girl.

Still, he found her unexpected pluck rather hilarious, and couldn't resist pushing her just a little further, bad as he was. He couldn't help it.

After all, he now knew that she was made of sterner stuff than first glance would suggest. She had dared to come here, hadn't she? And if she possessed that sort of grit behind her silk-and-lace demeanor, then, here in the hostile territory of the ton, she could be of use to him indeed — his own native guide to this alien land, as it were, with all its strange rituals and unfriendly tribes.

It was just the sort of alliance he'd have looked for on some reconnaissance mission for the Army deep behind enemy lines. For although he rarely talked about it, Connor had been no ordinary soldier.

Given his three-generation military heritage and all the years he had served from boyhood on, he had tried his hand at many facets of war craft. He'd had a very thorough education. From the geometric calculations of aiming artillery fire, to the care and training of cavalry horses; from the rhetoric of rallying his troops' morale, to the battlefield chess of strategic maneuvers.

He'd become a bit of a jack-of-all-trades, and that had made him valuable to the generals, most of whom had known his father and grandfather. Between his well-known military lineage and his own proven successes in action, the brass knew he could be relied upon in a range of capacities, so they would often pull him away from his usual regiment and send him off wherever he was needed.

Odd jobs, as it were.

Filling in here for a colonel who'd got his head blown off until a capable replacement arrived. Leading a small squadron there to rescue some high-value hostage. Disrupting enemy supply lines, blowing up bridges, and so forth.

He enjoyed the adventure, the unpredictability of his flexible role, and had declined plum promotions to keep it.

But the area where he'd seemed to fit most naturally was in military intelligence. Slipping behind enemy lines to reconnoiter, surveying territory, sketching quick maps, scouting out advantages or obstacles in the landscapes, discovering enemy troop strengths, or, less frequently, charming his way among the locals to connect with any resistance leaders in towns under enemy control, establishing trust and communication with their groups.

From long habit, he *thought* like an intelligence officer.

And he was doing that now, sizing up this young woman.

It disturbed him to admit how taken off guard he had been by her beau's accusation—that he, himself, had murdered his own kin. However outrageous the claim, he chided himself for not realizing in advance that the idea could have occurred to *somebody* here, especially given his outsider status.

The fact that he hadn't thought of it—or had deemed it so daft that he hadn't given it serious consideration—just went to show how out of his element he was in this place.

England. London. Peacetime.

Being a damned duke.

In this situation, he felt like the quintessential fish out of water—but this was Lady Margaret's world. All the more keenly, he felt the need for an ally who knew her way around the ton, had been born to it.

Lady Margaret Winthrop could help him.

God knew his life had been saved often enough by sharp-witted local guides. They could tell you whom to avoid, who held the real power in these parts, where not to go in town unless he wanted trouble, and all manner of local customs and pitfalls, the ignorance of which could lead to disaster.

In short, she'd make an ideal recruit for the job.

But that prim pursing of her mouth warned him that she had remembered her morals, alas.

Chances seemed slim that she would willingly go along with his request.

No matter. He'd simply have to get the fine lady to compromise herself here just a bit, then she'd have no choice but to help him.

Otherwise, if Connor simply agreed to her request and spared her beau's life in exchange for her promise of cooperation, who was to say she would still honor their bargain once she got what she wanted?

The duel would be over by tomorrow morning, and she could easily back out, fluttering her lashes, playing the damsel in distress. Take advantage of his sense of chivalry, which, deep down, Connor knew was both his greatest strength and his Achilles' heel.

No. He could not assume that she'd keep her word to help a stranger—an Irish one, at that, and an enemy of her suitor.

Even so, Connor could tell that the lady liked the look of him.

He had seen that from the first smile they had exchanged in the ballroom. And the attraction was most definitely mutual.

"Hmm…what did I have in mind? An excellent question, my lady."

She watched him with skittish apprehension, one shoulder drawn back, as though she were half poised to flee. It appeared she already regretted her words signaling compliance with his wishes.

"I suppose that depends on how far. How far might you be willing to go to save your suitor?"

She took a tiny step backward, escaping his light touch on her face. "I-I'm sure I have no idea what you mean."

"I'm sure you do," he whispered. "But very well. I shall elucidate."

He lowered his hand to his side again, the heat of her blush still lingering on his fingertips. He backed off a bit, returning to lean against the mantel. He ran a finger through the layer of dust on it and frowned absently. *I really need to hire new servants.*

The inspiration for how to achieve his objective came readily enough. He hid a sly smile, then turned to her. "You see, love, soldier that I am, there was many a night bivouacking under the stars, when, long deprived of a lady's company, I would dream of a finely turned ankle."

Her eyebrows shot up.

He let his gaze slide down her skirts toward her slippered feet. "Would you by chance have a pair of those?" he murmured wickedly.

A blank stare was her answer—at first.

Connor bit the inside of his mouth to keep from laughing as this gave way to a shocked look of missish indignation. The hot female interest of a moment ago was tucked away, snapped closed, and folded out of sight, like a lady's fan.

"Well, of course I have ankles," she said, "but what has that got to do with anythi—"

"Good! Let's see 'em." Connor dropped back down into his armchair and waited for the show.

She stared at him, slack-jawed.

"You cannot be serious!" she spluttered at length.

He shrugged, hiding his mirth. "We all have our weaknesses, love. It's not my fault that yours is Lord Mincemeat. Well?" He rubbed his hands together. "Show us what you've got. Then perhaps we can reach an agreement."

She gaped at him with dubious incredulity; his demand finally seemed to sink in.

"You want to see my ankles," she repeated slowly.

"I do," he declared, then drummed his fingers eagerly on the chair arms.

Is she actually going to do this?

For, really, it was perfect. It was just enough.

It would do her no serious harm, but she'd know she'd gone over the line of propriety beyond just her visit to his house.

Then she'd *have* to do as he asked, or risk him spreading the word about this bit of naughtiness. Not that he'd ever actually carry out the threat. He was no extortionist.

Ah, but lovely Lady Margaret didn't know that.

She stood there, searching his face, as though trying to tell if he was jesting.

"Well?" Connor prompted.

"No."

"Oh, come. Be a patriot." He grinned. "My reward for winning the war?"

"Humph," she said. "Single-handedly, I suppose?"

"Aye." His smile widened as he lounged in the chair. "One arm tied behind my back."

She scoffed at that, and though her gray eyes narrowed as she attempted a withering glare, her lips pressed together like she was fighting a giggle. She cleared her throat, then tilted her head skeptically. "Still. While your victory against the French is very much appreciated, I can think of no good reason why you should need to see my ankles regarding the matter of the duel, Your Grace."

"Well, to be quite honest, I'd like to see much more of you than that, Lady Margaret, especially in the off chance I should die in this blasted thing. But I'll settle for the ankles, I suppose. After all, I am not entirely depraved."

"Oh, aren't you?"

Connor laughed. He liked her spirit. "Time's wasting, my lovely. Come on, girl. Live dangerously, eh? I'll look, I won't touch, promise."

She pursed her rosy lips as she debated with herself, setting one hand on her hip. "So if I...show you my ankles," she said archly, "then that means that you'll spare Lord Bryce?"

"Maybe." He shrugged. "As I said, it depends."

"On what?"

"I haven't got all night, love. If you want me to consider your request, then you'd better start tryin' to persuade me."

A knock on the door interrupted just then. Connor heard her suck in her breath with relief. But if she thought she was saved, she was wrong.

It was only Will.

"Major?" called the lad, his voice muffled through the door. "Your challenger's second just arrived. Nestor took him up to the drawing room to make the arrangements."

"Thank you, William. Dismissed!" Connor added meaningfully.

This was no time for interruptions from those two.

Clearly, Lady Margaret felt differently. She shook her head and lifted her fingertips to her lips. "Oh God," she whispered.

She looked shaken to contemplate the fact that one of her suitor's mates was now under the same roof with her and could feasibly spot her here, where she ought not to be.

Her predicament doubled Connor's amusement about all this.

Then she looked into his eyes, and once more, her anguish preyed upon his chivalry, damn her.

"Must you duel with him?" she asked.

Connor bristled at her plea. "It wasn't *my* doing," he grumbled, even as he acknowledged inwardly that this girl could get to him. *Better not let her figure that out.* "Your little friend shot his mouth off to the wrong man this time, and now he'll have to pay for it. Unless…?"

He flicked a meaningful glance back down toward her lower extremities.

"Oh, very well!" she snapped, her cheeks like strawberries. Slipping her reticule's loop over her wrist, she grasped her pale, frothy skirts with both hands and yanked them up to show her shapely shins.

A triumphant grin spread across Connor's face. It was a very nice view indeed, and the lass still had not caught on that it was all a trap.

Now that she'd done this *shocking* thing, he had what he needed on her. Something he could hold over her head to ensure her cooperation.

It seemed he'd just secured himself a helper. And also learned in the process that she could be pushed.

The hem of her gown dangled about her pretty knees, and in spite of himself, Connor ogled her legs. *Damn…*

White silk stockings hugged her slim, shapely calves, and sure enough, she did possess a pair of finely turned ankles.

Encasing her feet were dainty green dancing slippers with white ribbon lacings that twined round her shins. His mouth watered at an unbidden thought of unlacing those ribbons, peeling those silk stockings down, and feeling her legs wrap around him…

Just as a ticklish flutter tautened his belly and a warm surge of lust stirred in his loins, the curtain dropped on his private show. Her skirts swished back down to the ground again.

"Happy now?" she said.

No. Not at all. Now he was merely frustrated.

Yet strangely proud of her. The girl had a certain toughness to rise to his challenge.

She'd need it, to help him in his goal.

"Bravo, my dear." Connor smiled in approval and drew a deep breath to will down the throbbing in his trousers. "Trust me, you have nothing to be embarrassed of there."

She huffed with exasperation and looked away, beet-red.

He let out a low, congratulatory whistle. "No, I mean it," he insisted as he stood up again, drifting toward her. "Those are some of the finest ankles I've ever beheld, and trust me, I've seen quite a few."

"I'll bet," she muttered.

"Makes me wonder about your thighs," he added in a purr, unable to resist.

She gasped with shock, then suddenly whomped him on the shoulder with her reticule, and Connor exploded with laughter.

"I'm jesting, lass!" he exclaimed, fending her off.

"Ruffian!" she cried as she beat him.

"Calm down! It's a lark! I'm not goin' to hurt you!"

"*What?* A lark, did you say? Jesting?"

He nodded.

Outrage filled her face, and she whacked him again. "You think that makes it better? You cad! A man's life is at stake! Is this all just a joke to you?"

"Aye, more or less," he lied, laughing. It was never a joke when killing was involved, but that was not the sort of thing one said to a lady.

She harrumphed with disapproval, and swung her wee tasseled handbag at him again. But this time he grabbed it—and used the strap to tug her gently closer.

"Enough, you," he chided in a husky tone, smiling. It mystified him, how easily she came into his arms, no longer fighting him.

Instead, she allowed it when he pulled her playfully off balance so she crashed against his chest; at once, he hooked an arm behind the small of her back, capturing her.

She didn't seem at all to mind, laughing along with him reluctantly, shaking her head. "You're mad."

"I'm fun," he corrected.

"I think you're dangerous."

"Yes. But not to you, Lady Margaret. Never to you."

Holding her lightly like that, catching the floral hint of her perfume, feeling the warmth of her flesh, the soft swells of her breasts against his chest, the pounding of her heart against his body, it was all he could do not to kiss her.

But that might prove far more dangerous than even the major dared contemplate.

She intoxicated him more than any fine whiskey.

"Very well, lass," he conceded in a husky murmur, his face mere inches from hers. "You've earned it. I'll spare your suitor. But remember—now you'll owe me."

"Owe you how?" she asked softly.

Her whisper beguiled him.

Yet when he saw the relief on her face to hear that she'd just secured the life of her suitor, Connor experienced a baffling twinge of jealousy.

His glance dipped to her lips. Somehow he fought the temptation to drive any thought of that other fellow right out of her head with his kisses. "Could use your help," he said.

"What sort of help?"

"I'll explain later. Nothing too scary, I promise."

She frowned.

"Don't worry. I won't ruin your life."

"I think you could," she said very softly, and somewhere inside him, a cold, stony chip of his battle-hardened heart melted at her aching vulnerability.

"Tell me something," he murmured.

"Yes?" Her hand rested on his chest, delicate as a bird.

How dainty she was in his arms, almost fragile. The top of her head barely came up to his collarbones. For some reason, she filled him with wonder.

"Why come to me instead of your suitor?" he asked. "Why not just go to Lord Bryce and prevail on him to bow out of this duel?"

She lowered her lashes. "He'd never listen to me."

Connor furrowed his brow. "Well, that isn't right," he said. He lifted her gaze by tipping her chin upward with one finger. "A man ought to listen to his lady in matters of such consequence. He should respect you."

"Like you have?" she challenged him ever so softly. Then she pulled away, sliding free of his hold.

Connor winced, dropping his gaze. Based on what he'd just done, he supposed he had no room to argue that. *Touché, my dear.*

"I must go," she informed him. "My sister will be wondering where I am. So, do we have an agreement, Your Grace?"

Connor nodded.

"Thank you," she said, then slipped past him, flitting off across the parlor at her tiptoeing walk. Instead of leaving straightaway, though, she turned back at the door, hesitating as she studied him.

"What is it?" he asked.

"Do be careful tomorrow."

He snorted. "If that blackguard kills me for your sake, I'll come back and haunt you, I swear."

She smiled at his jest, though her eyes filled with worry.

He waved her off. "Go. Before I change my damned fool mind."

She nodded, then opened the door a crack and peeked out, obviously determined not to be seen by Lord Bryce's second. No doubt it would be difficult to explain why she was here, in the enemy camp.

Connor heard Will greet her from the entrance hall.

Once she saw the way was clear, she cast an uncertain last glance back at Connor, then went whisking away.

Will showed her out, as the click of the front door promptly confirmed.

Connor stood there alone for another long moment, smiling wryly at the floor. *I know I will regret this.*

Then he let out a sigh and sauntered out of the sitting room, the image of lovely legs in white silk stockings still dancing before his eyes.

Thrusting the legs and the rest of Lady Margaret Winthrop out of his mind, he went to learn the time and place of his duel.

CHAPTER 6

Pistols at Dawn

*I*n the gray half-light before sunrise, the dewy air of Hyde Park throbbed with the cacophony of countless birds hunting for their breakfasts. Their squawking and screeching, endless caws, and shrill tweets set Maggie's nerves on edge.

She wished every feathered one of them would be quiet so she could hear herself think. Her heart was in her throat, and she still couldn't believe any of this was happening.

Her efforts to stop the duel had failed.

A ring of fine carriages surrounded a remote grove, far removed from the well-traveled Ring, the Serpentine, and the border of Kew Gardens. Fashionable folk of all sorts had come to watch the duel, some two or three dozen in all.

There was not just Bryce and his friends, Amberley and his two peculiar companions, but coaches full of ton folk come to watch the grim spectacle, including a noisy, probably still-drunk group of dragoons in their showy uniforms, and, of course, Delia, Edward, and Maggie.

A bizarre sort of festival atmosphere hung over the grove, but for her part, Maggie felt freezing-cold with fear.

She pulled the pelisse she'd donned more tightly around her body. It was five thirty in the morning, and she was still dressed in her ball gown.

Delia chattered on beside her, eager to watch the pageantry unfold, as though this were a horse race at Ascot or some silly acrobatic show at Vauxhall—like that indecent, near-naked woman who walked across a tightrope as high as the roof there, with crowds waiting to see if she'd fall to her death.

Maggie felt a little like that woman right now after her secret visit to the duke's.

She frankly couldn't believe she was here *now*. But she had to know the outcome. She had not thought Delia would agree to come, but she should've known better. Her sister adored being close to the action.

As an eyewitness to the scandalous event, Lady Birdwell would relish describing every morbid detail to her followers in the days ahead. It was as good an excuse as any to make herself the center of attention.

Indeed, Delia's only regret seemed to be that it was Maggie who was more directly involved in the drama than herself, as the lady being courted by one of the duelists.

But reflected glory would have to do.

Meanwhile, Delia's husband and Maggie's brother-in-law, the plump, unflappable Edward, Marquess of Birdwell, had insisted on escorting the ladies to the duel, thank God, though he found the whole thing reckless and distasteful.

He did tend to be the voice of reason in their family.

Maggie and Delia had climbed out of the coach to watch the proceedings, but Edward had lain down in his carriage to doze.

"Wake me up if anybody dies," he had said.

Maggie didn't know how she would bear it if anybody did.

She had poured out her pleading in a letter to Bryce and sent it off with a footman in the middle of the night, just to try. Amberley's question, after all, had got her thinking.

It remained to be seen if her efforts would do any good. But at least she'd attempted to get through to him.

So far, the results were not encouraging. The duel had obviously not been called off yet, though it still might. No doubt that would disappoint the gawkers, but at least then both men would be safe.

She looked anxiously from the carriage of one to the other.

Bryce was pacing about, tapping his lucky beaver hat against his leg. It seemed he meant to wear it in the duel.

She knew he never played cards without it. He laughed when he said so, but he swore that hat was responsible for winning him hundreds of pounds at the card tables.

She watched him pacing back and forth, putting on a brave face for his companions, but surely, he must be frightened, she thought.

Her gaze then traveled to the opposite end of the grassy meadow, where Amberley stood perfectly still, feet planted wide, his hands propped on his hips, like a statue of Mars garbed in Bond Street clothing.

The two fellows from his house were there, moving around nervously. They seemed more on edge about this contest than the duke himself.

For a long moment, Maggie stared at him.

Of course, she was scared of anyone learning of her visit to Amberley House. But as for the man himself, she still did not know *how* to feel about him.

Having met him in person, spoken with him, having won the concession from him that she'd sought—though, Lord knew, it had cost her a moment's immodesty—only increased her distress over all of this.

Bad as he was, the man had his charm, to be sure. She could not forget the soft pressure of his warm, muscular arms encircling her, the blue glow in his eyes as he'd held her lightly, the coaxing lilt of his deep, velvety voice.

When she had invaded his residence, her only concern had been saving Bryce. Now she realized she had asked Amberley to stand there across from his foe like some inert human target, declining to defend himself.

How could she do such a thing? How could the man have *agreed*, for heaven's sake? For naught but a look at her ankles?

Surely he must have some trick up his sleeve. She hoped so. Because if anything happened to him, Maggie was not sure she could forgive herself.

She repented of her selfishness, and the fear that had blocked her from seeing it sooner. As the moment drew near, she begged divine intervention.

Maybe the angels could step in somehow and steer Bryce's bullet wide of its target. *Please, God, let there be no bloodshed today.*

What still puzzled her, though, was the duke's cheeky humor before the dawn's battle. Show him her ankles indeed. She shook her head, baffled at what sort of courage it must take to be cracking jokes in the face of death.

She supposed he was used to it, and that, she found sad.

All that merriment must be simply a soldier's defiant graveyard humor, but one thing she knew: there was no way that man was a murderer, as Bryce had accused him.

What he might still expect of her, though, *was* cause for some worry. He'd made it plain that if he spared Bryce for her sake, Maggie would owe him.

She trembled to contemplate what that might mean.

As though he felt her watching him, just like in the ballroom, Amberley looked across the grove and captured her gaze. She went motionless; the rest of the park disappeared for a heartbeat.

He offered her a discreet nod of greeting, then turned away to chat with his skinny young friend.

Exhaling at last, she could not believe how nonchalant the man looked.

Maggie rubbed her hands on her arms, trying to warm up, but when she spotted Bryce coming over to see her, she licked her lips and fixed her face into a guarded smile.

"Lady Birdwell." Bryce gave Delia a debonair nod, then bowed to Maggie. "My lady."

"How are you?" Maggie asked softly.

"I'm quite well," the earl said. "You?"

"Terrified," she whispered.

He chuckled, though it sounded rather forced, and took her hand. "There, there, pet. It'll be all right. I know such things can be difficult for ladies to watch—well, some ladies." He glanced wryly at Delia, who was chatting merrily with her friends; one of the handsome dragoons had joined the banter.

Maggie ignored the lot of them.

"But I'm glad you're here," Bryce continued, gazing into her eyes. "It shows how much you care for me."

She pressed her lips together, guilt pulsing through her. Guilt for the thrill that visiting Amberley had given her. Guilt for going behind Bryce's back to try to save his blasted life.

Guilt for her motives in pursuing him in the first place.

How starkly she saw in that moment that she did not love this man. Not as one's future husband deserved.

The unsightly fact of it stood out in her awareness like the scraggly branches of the huge dead tree emerging from the fog at one end of the grove.

"Of course I care." She cleared her throat. "Y-you got my letter?"

"I did." He nodded.

"Did you read it?" she asked, noting his lack of reaction.

"Yes, of course. It was most affecting."

"But not enough to change your mind."

He looked away with a superior smile. "A man's got to do what a man's got to do, Lady Margaret."

She stepped closer to him. "You *really* think the duke killed your friend?"

Bryce glanced across the grove, eyeing his enemy. "I think he's killed many people. He learned it at war."

"But he wasn't even in London at the time."

"Of course he'd keep his distance to avoid looking guilty. He could've easily hired someone. Why could he not? With so much at stake. Fortune. Power."

"But that's just it! I don't believe he ever wanted the title. Look at him. It doesn't look to me as though he even enjoys being a duke."

"Who wouldn't enjoy being a duke?" Bryce laughed at her like she was a foolish chit of a girl.

"He should respect you…"

"Why are you defending him, anyway? It's irksome," Bryce said.

Maggie tamped down her impatience. "Please, don't go through with this."

"Sorry. It's done."

"Fine! If you won't apologize, at least don't shoot him."

"But that's the whole point of this."

"Fire into the air," she pleaded. "You can still delope without dishonor."

"Why should I? You think the authorities will come after me, is that it? You're worried I might get arrested?"

"I'm worried you might get killed!"

"No. Right is on my side. Such things have been decided by combat since King Arthur's day."

"Bryce, he was a legend, just like your theory. This is ludicrous!"

"If you don't like it, then leave," he said coldly.

She looked away, stung. If he kept this up, she might be tempted to shoot him herself. "Maybe I should go and fetch the constables, hmm?"

He smirked. "They don't dare interfere when the fight's between aristocrats. You know that."

"Very well, then. What of your soul?"

He laughed. "My *soul*? You little silly-head. You should know by now I haven't got one."

She rolled her eyes. "Surely you don't want to live the rest of your life with blood on your hands."

At that, he peered more deeply into her eyes, and she saw that behind his outward bravado, he looked like a frightened boy.

He dropped his gaze, the morning's breeze rippling through his golden curls. "I must avenge my friend's death," he said once more.

"Is this really what Richard would want? For you to kill his kinsman?"

Bryce did not lift his head, but sent her a guarded look. She was encouraged to think that perhaps he was finally listening to her.

Then he took her hands, and she noticed that his palms were clammy; his hands were shaking.

Instantly, Maggie felt a rush of compassion for the haughty fool, though she hid her surprise.

She knew then why Amberley had referred to him so many times in their chat as a lad. He must have seen through Bryce's façade in a glance.

Jarring as this insight was, it doubled her resolve to stop the duel from happening.

"Listen," she soothed, knowing this was her last chance to avert disaster. "Surely His Grace wants to know as badly as you do what really happened to his cousin. Instead of trying to kill each other, why don't you work together *with* him to try to get to the bottom of this? If you truly suspect foul play—"

"I do, and that man has the strongest motive for killing him! Besides, he's Irish, and everybody knows they're just a race of barbarians. Now stop trying to talk me out of it!"

Maggie fell silent, offended enough by his tone and his bigotry to wash her hands of him altogether.

Bryce's glare faded as he saw by her cool demeanor that she had just quit the conversation. He glanced around at the audience that had gathered to watch the duel, then looked at her again.

"Almost time. How about a kiss for good luck?" he said.

She gave him a withering stare. *Are you jesting? After how you just spoke to me?* "I think not," she answered, but he laughed, leaned down anyway, and gave her a peck on the cheek.

Amberley must have been discreetly observing the two of them together the whole time, for when Bryce kissed her, the duke looked over sharply.

His glance reminded her that he was the one in real danger here, having already promised not to pull the trigger.

Bryce, for his part, had made no such pledge.

Then came the dreaded announcement.

A portly viscount whose name escaped her seemed to be in charge of the event, a neutral party.

"Gentlemen," he called from the center of the grove, "if I may have your attention, it is time to begin!"

Bryce looked grimly at her, unaware he was quite safe, thanks to her covert maneuverings. "Farewell, my lady."

Maggie couldn't answer. Her voice had fled, having failed her in her effort to stop this madness. She just shook her head at him.

Bryce's eyes hardened with the task ahead; he pivoted and marched back to his side of the battlefield.

Meanwhile, Amberley slapped his eye-patch friend on the back encouragingly; the one-eyed Mr. Godwin trudged out to the grove to shake hands with Bryce's second.

Maggie's heart took up an ominous drumbeat inside her ribs.

Amberley checked his pistol while Private Duffy stood by. Maggie noticed that the warrior duke held the gun naturally, with such familiar ease that it almost seemed an extension of his hand.

"Birdy, wake up," Delia ordered her husband through the carriage window. "They're about to begin!"

"All such stupidity," Edward grumbled from inside the coach.

A ripple of excitement traveled around the ring of carriages. Wagers were being laid. The few ladies present fetched scarves, fans, and bonnets to hide their eyes with, in case watching the thing proved too ghastly.

The noisy dragoons were still boasting about their own victories as Edward tumbled sleepily out of the coach and yawned.

Maggie clasped her hands together and prayed hard.

Her pulse pounded as both contenders swaggered out to the center of the grove and received their instructions.

"Gentlemen: twenty paces, turn, and fire. Any questions?"

They had none.

"Godspeed to you both."

Maggie winced and bit her lip, hugging her pelisse more tightly around her.

The next thing she knew, Bryce and the Irishman stood back to back.

Their seconds retreated from the field of battle, and Maggie noted that Amberley stood half a head taller than Bryce.

In every way, he was the more formidable man. Surely, Bryce had to see that.

What could have compelled her suitor to challenge such a dangerous foe? She still could not comprehend why Richard's death should have affected him so deeply.

For some reason, it never crossed her mind to wonder whether Amberley would keep his word not to kill Bryce.

His honor she trusted. After all, he could've done much worse to her in that candlelit sitting room than demand a peek at her ankles.

She just hoped that her secret pact with Amberley to spare Bryce did not encourage the peacock to think he had won and that he should do this more often...

Then the portly viscount retreated, calling for quiet.

The spectators fell silent—even Delia, holding her breath.

The dragoons went motionless, leaning forward as a group, as though poised for battle themselves, one of their cavalry charges. Edward shook his head in regret at the foolishness of it all.

Maggie turned to him in distress.

Her kindhearted brother-in-law saw the panic in her eyes and offered his hand. She took it, and he squeezed.

"You don't have to watch, Mags," he reminded her softly.

Indeed, she couldn't, when the crucial moment came.

One hand clasping her brother-in-law's, instinctively, she turned away, shielding her eyes as the viscount numbered their paces aloud: "Seventeen, eighteen..."

As the duelists neared their ends of the grove, Maggie felt ill.

Stomach churning, she squeezed her eyes shut. Held her breath. *God, don't let him die.*

Shots exploded in the grove, a twin crack-crack.

She heard a curse, smelled the acrid scent of gunpowder smoke invading her nostrils. Exclamations ran around the clearing.

She was afraid to look, but when she drummed up the courage to peek through her fingers, the field was a scramble of activity.

Both contenders were concealed by their helpers. The audience was murmuring.

"What happened?" Maggie asked Edward and Delia in alarm.

Edward was squinting at the two clouds of drifting gun smoke. "I'm not sure..."

But Delia was shaking her head in amazement. "Did you see that?"

she cried.

"No!" said Maggie.

Delia pointed. "The duke just shot Bryce's lucky hat clean off his head!"

"*What?* He shot Bryce in the head?" Maggie shouted.

"No, he shot Bryce's lucky *hat*," Delia said in amazement. "What a shot!"

Her sister started laughing, clapping for the duke. "Bravo, Your Grace!"

Even the dragoons applauded, looking impressed by the shot.

Maggie was trembling from head to toe as Bryce swept his black beaver hat up off the dew-covered ground, held it up, and peered through the hole in the crown. The brilliance of sunrise shone right through it.

"Oh no," Delia said suddenly, standing on her toes to see through the hubbub. "I think Amberley's hurt. He's bleeding."

CHAPTER 7

The Dragoon

*N*o. Maggie took a step forward and drew in her breath. The duke was on his feet, but holding his side. Blood flowed through his fingers, and in the rosy light of the rising sun, she saw the snarl of perfect fury on his face.

He might've been making sardonic jokes about all this earlier, but now he looked tempted to give Bryce the thrashing of his life.

Amberley ripped off his jacket and stalked toward his carriage, where his eye-patch friend had taken out a physician's bag with cool, calm efficiency.

Throwing his coat on the ground in disgust, the duke shrugged out of his waistcoat, stepped somewhat behind the open door of his carriage, and lifted his bloodied white shirt off over his head.

A collective gasp went up from around the grove, especially from the ladies.

Maggie's eyes widened with shock at the sight of his towering, herculean physique. In all her twenty-two years, she had never glimpsed so much of the male form before, but for his part, the warrior duke did not seem inclined to give one damn who saw him shirtless.

Not that he had *anything* to be ashamed of.

On the contrary, Maggie thought with a gulp. His shoulders were massive, his chest thick with smooth, sculpted muscles; his arms bulged; and when he turned away, his back was a glorious expanse of rippling strength, his lean waist chiseled as though by a sculptor's tools.

Unfortunately, across the right side of his waist, the bullet had torn through his flesh. He twisted about to peer down at the wound, then muttered a curse, and lifted his arm out of the way so Mr. Godwin could assess the damage.

Time seemed to slow as Maggie stared at the scarlet liquid running down Amberley's side.

His very lifeblood.

Some girls might have fainted at the disturbing sight. But for the well-behaved Lady Maggie Winthrop, it was as though something inside of her snapped.

A lifetime, perhaps, of always trying her best to follow the rules.

This man had been *shot* for her sake.

If not for her plea, Bryce would be dead, true—but he was the one who'd picked the fight. She had never meant for Amberley to be wounded as the price for his restraint.

The next thing she knew, she was in motion, launching herself across the grove without warning, without explanation, without looking back.

She lost all thought of anyone else there and went running to Amberley, her pulse slamming.

All that mattered in that moment was finding out how serious his injury was. If he would die.

She couldn't bear it.

Near him and his companions, she skidded to a halt on the wet grass in her dancing slippers.

Mr. Godwin was already giving him bandages to press to his side, while young Will offered the duke a flask. Amberley swigged from it as Maggie barreled into their midst, breathless with terror.

"Is it serious?" she blurted out.

They all looked at her in surprise, having barely noticed her arrival.

She saw at once that the blue of Amberley's eyes had darkened to that of stormy seas, while the red blood flowed down his side.

"Now you *really* owe me," he said matter-of-factly.

"I'm so sorry!" she cried, gaping at the blood.

"Never fear, milady. 'Tis but a flesh wound," Mr. Godwin reported. "Don't worry, he'll live." The one-eyed surgeon clapped his large friend solidly on the arm. "He's had plenty worse, this one."

"True," Amberley agreed.

Maggie pressed her hand to her chest, where she could feel her heart pounding. "Oh thank God. You gave me such a fright."

"I'm touched by your concern," the duke drawled.

"Lady Margaret!" Bryce called indignantly from across the grove. "Get away from there this instant!"

"Mags!" Delia brayed a loud laugh. "What on earth are you doing?"

Maggie glanced back at her sister, and then, scanning around the grove, discovered the whole audience staring at her in surprise.

Her cheeks flooded with belated embarrassment at her own utter breach of protocol.

"S-sorry," she said faintly to no one in particular, "I-I don't know what came over me."

"Go back to your carriage, if you please!" Lord Bryce said. He stepped away from his companions as though he meant to march over and drag her back physically to her family.

Amberley went very still, narrowing his eyes at Bryce.

Maggie noticed the change in his demeanor; Bryce must have, too, for he said nothing more and stayed on his side of the grove.

She turned back to the duke in misery. "I'm *so* sorry he shot you. This wasn't supposed to happen. I did try to talk him out of this madness, but he simply wouldn't listen."

"It's not your fault, m'lady." He gave her a rueful smile as he pulled a blood-soaked bandage away from his wound and quickly applied a fresh one.

She grimaced at the sight.

"Run along now, before you start a scandal. You can't be of any help to me if you're disgraced."

She stiffened instantly at his pointed reminder of why he had shown mercy.

It was not from the goodness of his heart; he wanted something from her. Exactly what that might be, she had yet to discover.

"Don't worry, miss," said Private Duffy, "we'll take good care of him. We're used to this one bleedin' all over the place."

She winced at the realization that, indeed, they probably were.

"Go," Amberley murmured softly. "I'll call on you soon."

Maggie eyed him in distrust, but accidentally flicked one last wayward gaze over his magnificent body, unable to stop herself.

He grinned, noticing her stray glance. His chin came up a notch. "Just say the word, darlin'."

She sucked in her breath with embarrassment, shot the rogue a self-conscious scowl, then hurried back to her sister.

"What was all that about?" Delia asked in amusement.

"I…I don't know. I just…"

Edward came to her rescue. "The sight of blood can be very disturbing for young ladies, obviously."

So can the sight of a half-naked demigod. Maggie refused to let her gaze wander in that Irish scoundrel's direction again.

"Are you all right, Mags?" Edward asked, laying a hand on her shoulder, searching her face.

She nodded. "Thanks. I'm not sure what came over me. I-I thought I could help."

Delia chuckled. "At least you didn't faint. I'd have lost all respect for you."

You respect me? Maggie thought. *Since when?* Then she shook her head. "I hope I haven't caused a scandal."

"What, you? The girl who never does anything wrong? Mama's perfect little angel? Don't be ridiculous," Delia said in a breezy tone, but Edward frowned at his wife's snide comment.

Dismayed, Maggie lowered her head, while across the grove, the dragoons also seemed to find her unthinking response to the bloodshed quite diverting.

Some of them were chuckling as they studied her and her family, though one of their number, a sinewy, narrow-faced man with dark brown hair, neatly trimmed side-whiskers, moustache, and goatee, leaned against a carriage, staring at her with a motionless intensity that gave her a chill.

She almost preferred the other dragoons' mockery to that man's watchful detachment.

She quickly forgot about him, though, when she noticed Bryce headed her way—and, *ugh,* her suitor did not look amused.

Maggie braced herself when she saw him marching through the wet grass toward their carriage in high dudgeon.

"Lady Margaret! A word, please!"

The spectators paused from getting back into their carriages and turned to look. Hearing his bellow, they realized—no doubt with delight—that the morning's entertainment was not yet over.

"Why were you over there talking to him?" Bryce demanded. "That man has no decency!"

"Because I thought you'd killed him, that's why!" she burst out, much to her own shock, then quickly reined in her temper. "The surgeon said his wound isn't serious, if you were wondering," she coldly informed him.

"Pity," said Bryce.

"My lord!" she said in startled reproach.

"What?"

She shook her head, speechless.

First, her suitor had made a fool of himself, accusing Amberley without proof. Then he'd shot the man and refused to acknowledge— despite the expertly placed hole in his hat—that he had been deliberately spared by a superior marksman.

After all, that bullet could have easily been placed two inches lower and dropped him dead to the ground like a mallard in hunting season.

But did he show the slightest gratitude?

Of course not. On the contrary. Unaware that *she* was the one who had bargained to procure his continued existence, now the little coxcomb dared to come over here and scold her.

"Well?" he demanded.

"You, sir, are quite beyond the pale."

Bryce frowned at her. "Me? What did I do?"

Unable to stomach another minute of his company, Maggie simply held up her hand, shook her head, and climbed back into the coach.

"What's wrong with her?" Bryce asked Delia.

"Who knows," said her sister with a shrug.

Edward was distressed. "I should never have allowed you two to come here. Obviously, such things are too upsetting for a young lady's sensibilities," he said stiffly. "Now, if you don't mind, I daresay my sister-in-law does not wish to speak with you any further at the moment, ol' boy."

"Women," said Bryce.

"La, she's always been temperamental. Moody," said Delia, clearly unfazed by the bloodshed. "That was quite something, though! Lucky you came out of it unscathed. You were very brave."

"Why thank you, Lady Birdwell..."

As Bryce chatted with her sister for another moment or two, Maggie stared out the opposite window, facing away from the grove.

She shook her head, furious in ways she could not even put into words.

The worst part was her grim new understanding of her suitor's nature. Perhaps she had known all along. But after this whole obnoxious display, she could no longer ignore it.

All of a sudden, out of nowhere, she wanted nothing more to do with him, ever. She did not give one fig in that moment if she never even spoke to him again.

Maybe this anger would pass, but she did not see how she could possibly marry such a vain, reckless fool. Her heart sank as she realized there was no point in pretending.

Their courtship was over.

❖

As a garish red sunrise crept across the grove, Seth Darrow leaned watchfully against a friend's carriage, camouflaging himself amongst his fellow dragoons.

His heart still pounded from his fleeting, bloodthirsty hope that the pampered rakehell, Bryce, might get rid of his problem for him, without Seth having to lift a finger this time.

But no such luck.

Word swept around the grove that it was just a flesh wound—that the bullet had only grazed the duke. Once again, Amberley Number Four had proven irritatingly hard to kill.

Seth gritted his teeth. *Damn.*

His mates from the regiment seemed relieved by the news. A few decided to go over and congratulate the major on his fine shooting.

Seth declined to join them. It was enough of a risk just being here.

They had all been out drinking last night at the Officers' Club when news had arrived that some marquess's son called Lord Bryce had just challenged the Duke of Amberley to a duel.

Since some in the club had heard stories of the major and his supposed prowess, many had jumped at the chance to see "the legend" in action.

Everyone was sure he would murder Lord Bryce.

Seth had never heard these tales himself, but he certainly wished he *had* before he'd tried attacking the savage on those docks.

From what they had said at the club, the reason not everyone knew about it was because he had served in intelligence.

Bloody hell, Seth had thought, hearing this.

In any case, he had joined his companions so he might observe his enemy unnoticed.

But while his mates were firmly on the side of their fellow veteran, he, for one, throbbed with unholy hope that Bryce would shoot the Irish son of a bitch in the heart. Drop the bleeder like a stone.

For his part, Seth had failed twice now to expunge the last Duke of Amberley from the face of the earth.

Indeed, the first time, the bastard had nearly killed *him*. It had taken weeks for his broken nose and sprained wrist to heal after that debacle on the docks.

In hindsight, it was abundantly clear that he'd made the near-fatal mistake of underestimating his enemy. But that night, to be sure, he'd learned his lesson.

Namely, that Duke Number Four was nothing like his weakling forebears.

Those three had been easily dispatched. For Number One, a pillow over the face had sufficed. He was old. It was easy. For Seth, a matter of choosing his timing and picking a lock.

Duke Number Two really should have been more careful when out taking his daily constitutional. An older gent really ought to watch his footing, maybe use a walking stick so he wouldn't lose his balance near those high precipices around the West Country...

Most unfortunate, and him so well regarded by his parishioners.

Yes, Duke Number Two had enjoyed wandering out across the moors, and finishing his daily walks with a meditative visit to that soaring promontory on the edge of his estate, overlooking a wild river in a deep, rocky gully.

No doubt the vicar-duke had felt inspired there, thinking his deep thoughts and praying his holy prayers.

Seth had soon sent him on to his eternal glory. He still smiled in amusement to recall the yelp the vicar-duke made when he'd been shoved off the cliff.

Rupert's son, Duke Number Three, called Richard, had taken nothing but a bit of tinkering with the axle of his dainty curricle to bring him low.

Ah, Richard. Bryce's friend. Spoiled young hellion, with his flawless clothes and perfect hair.

He seemed to enjoy being naughty as much as his father, the reverend, had striven to be virtuous. Between a few turns of Seth's stealthy wrench and his own wayward habits, Amberley Number Three had practically killed himself, which had been convenient.

But now came Number Four, and for the life of him, Seth could not figure out how to get to the mean, giant bastard.

He might as well try smashing Gibraltar.

Worse, if he was honest, *this* Amberley had rather shaken Seth's nerve after their first meeting.

He still could not comprehend how the duke had so fully trounced him. The whole experience had been humiliating, not to mention painful.

But the task of killing him remained Seth's duty. After all, his younger brother was still dead, and Father was still disgusted that it was he who lived on, instead of his darling Francis.

Seth still wasn't sure how to do the thing, and after two failures, he was in no hurry to risk a third. The third time simply had to be the charm.

After receiving the thrashing of his life from the duke, unable to use his weapon hand properly, Seth had begrudgingly resorted to the woman's weapon: poison.

Of that, he was not proud. If his regiment ever found out, they'd shun him for certain. But not even *that* had gone as planned. The duke's fat, loud hog of a friend had gobbled down the dish meant for Amberley.

Both failures had only managed to put the blackguard on his guard.

So here he was, and frankly, Seth had no idea what to try next... Until the moment the lovely little debutante had sprinted across the grove to the duke's side, her face stamped with panic.

Well, well, he'd thought as he'd watched her skid to a halt and anxiously ask how serious the wound was. *What have we here?*

Does His Grace have himself a sweetheart?

Seth had stared, observing the whole scene with hawklike intensity, while his friends had chuckled at her reaction.

Neophytes who had never seen violence before could have all kinds of unexpected responses to their first look at bloodshed. Hell, they'd all been there. They'd seen it in countless new recruits.

Some fainted the first time they witnessed a man being shot in front of them. Others threw up; many fled, some froze like frightened rabbits, a few counterattacked, but a fair number rushed to the side of the wounded to see if they could help.

This chit must be one of the latter sort, Seth mused as he watched with all due vigilance.

Then Bryce boomed at "Lady Margaret" to get away from the duke, and Seth realized it was the curly-headed fop who was her suitor, not the major.

His fellow dragoons also figured this out. They began laughing.

"Aha, now I see why he spared him!" they said.

"Hell, *I* wouldn't have the heart to make that angel cry."

"Bryce is courting her?"

"Looks that way. Sweet little thing. Wasted on that ponce, you ask me."

"Maybe the major will steal her away from him," one of his friends jested.

"Maybe I will," another replied.

"Not with that face, mate. You'll need a dukedom first."

"What? Your mother didn't mind my face when she was riding it last night."

"Fuck off, you're disgusting."

Halfhearted punches were traded, and then, amid laughter, questions exchanged about where to eat breakfast, "speaking of eating."

Seth ignored the soldierly banter, watching the girl.

His stare tracked her like a prey as she returned to the couple she'd come with. He'd elbowed one of his mates. "Who are those people?"

"Ah, that's Lady Birdwell and her husband, the marquess. Good chap."

"And the girl?"

His friend shrugged. "I believe that's Her Ladyship's unmarried younger sister."

"I see," Seth replied.

He knew then that he'd keep an eye on her, this Lady Margaret, for he'd seen the soft way that Amberley had smiled at the girl.

And everybody knew that even a legend had an Achilles' heel.

CHAPTER 8

Pay the Piper

*C*onnor awoke hours later in the small, ordinary bedchamber he'd chosen for himself on the third floor of the mansion, at least until he got used to this place.

The master suite was opulent beyond belief. He'd never fall asleep in there. But this simple room reminded him of his chamber back at his seaside cottage in Ireland, though he sorely missed the view and the sound of the ocean.

Lying motionless, his eyes still stubbornly closed, he could admit that at least the four-poster bed was fairly comfortable.

He did his best to continue dozing, ignoring as best he could the clatter of carriages passing on the street below, the barking of a dog somewhere in the neighborhood.

But it was no use. His side hurt. His head ached, too, from the whiskey he'd drunk to chase away the pain of the gunshot wound—and his disgust with his entire situation.

Peacetime.

He couldn't believe he had been shot. He'd truly thought that part of his life was over, that there'd be no more bullet holes in him, that he'd never have to fight again. Swords into ploughshares.

Pipe dream.

Ah well. Food would help his headache. But more than the torn flesh at his side, his pride stung from those little bastards' mockery of him, Bryce's friends. His fists curled at his sides when he thought of their jeering.

He'd like to call out every last damn one of them and teach the surly whelps some respect.

But beneath his ire, the truth was, he was just so damned disappointed.

He was a simple man, really. He didn't need any of this, and with the war's end, all he'd wanted was a chance to be happy.

Inheriting the dukedom had struck him as the most hilarious windfall raining down on him like a leprechaun's gold. Rank, power, wealth beyond imagining. Happy? Hell, he should've been ecstatic.

Except that everybody here seemed to hate him before he ever opened his mouth. Well, perhaps that was a wee exaggeration, for plenty of ladies here seemed eager to give him a go. He'd seen them ogling him.

But twenty paces at dawn against the likes of Lord Bryce had made it quite clear that he would never be accepted here, and since it was all down to his Irish blood, there was not a thing that he could do about it.

Aye, not a thing he *wanted* to do about it, either. If they didn't like it, let them go hang. The Irish were good enough to go and fight for England, eh? The cannon-fodder boys who relished a fight, they and their fellow tribe, the Scots.

God forbid the purebred English should get their own hands dirty when it could be avoided.

But these were dangerous thoughts.

Opening his bleary eyes at last, Connor stared at one of the posts at the foot of the bed. Feeling too lazy to get up and check the clock, he wondered if he could use it as a sundial to guess the time.

The duel had cost him a good night's sleep. Judging by the sunshine trying to get in around the edges of the curtains, he supposed it must be nearly noon.

Was that damn dog ever going to stop barking?

He shut his eyes again, annoyed.

It was hard enough getting used to civilian life again. Now with his radical change in circumstances, he felt like he didn't belong anywhere.

At least a gunshot wound was familiar, though.

With wry pleasure, he imagined the thing going differently at dawn if he had not listened to Lady Margaret Winthrop.

He pondered the far more pleasant subject of the girl for a moment, she of the lovely ankles. A roguish smile tugged at his lips.

The thought of her helped him cast aside his torpor. It was time to go collect on their bargain.

Taking a deep breath, he sat up, still dressed in his linen long drawers, held up by suspenders.

The bandaging around his waist hugged him like a tubby gent's corset.

Whispering a curse at the pang when he sat up, Connor glanced down at it. A copper stain of blood marred its ivory expanse, but it wasn't fresh.

The stuffy room stank of sleep, mingled with the astringent odor of the comfrey salve Nestor had given him to smear over his stitches.

Head pounding, Connor wanted to eat, to bathe—though getting a wound wet was always tricky. He also needed a shave, he noticed, glimpsing his jaw's dark scruff in the mirror.

But first, he went to the window, pushed the curtains aside, and opened the sash, letting the fresh air in.

The cool breeze waving into the room helped bring him fully to awareness.

He began removing his bandage, sauntering over toward the chest of drawers as he unwound it from his waist. He wanted to see how the injury was looking. As he put the length of linen on the chest of drawers and peered down at his side, he found the skin still inflamed around the stitches, but that was to be expected, he knew from long experience.

Just then, Will came racing into his room, barely bothering to knock. "Major, Major!" The skinny lad skidded to a halt over the hardwood floor. "Oh, good, you're up."

"Morning," Connor said serenely, pouring water from the pitcher into the white washbasin.

"Noon's more like it, sir," Will said, striding in.

"Ah. Well, what are you on about, then?"

"This!" Will marched toward him, holding up a small, leather-bound book. "Remember how you told me and Nestor to search your cousin's room again for any clues?"

"Did you find something?"

"His diary! We just discovered it a few minutes ago. It was wedged in a secret compartment built into the underside of that big canopy bed. I didn't mean to read about your cousin's private business, sir, but I wasn't sure what it was, so I looked at a few pages."

"Ah, no matter, Will. He won't mind at this point. Give it here."

"Yes, sir. Take a look at the last entry." Will handed the book to Connor, who quickly dried his hands, having barely had a chance to splash his face. "Duke Richard was scared, sir. Seems he had suspicions, just like you, about the other dukes' deaths. It seems like he started investigating it."

"Hmm." While Connor flipped through the neatly scrawled pages his dead cousin had penned—well, first cousin once removed, actually—Will marched back to the doorway and bellowed: "Nestor, he's up!"

Connor scanned the page in fascination, reading what the Third Duke had written:

> First Grandfather, and now Papa both dying within six months of each other? This cannot be a coincidence. I feel it in my bones that some unseen enemy wishes the destruction of my lineage, and I live in dread that if I cannot stop them soon, I may be next.

Connor snorted softly. "I know the feeling, mate."
Then he read on.

> I have no idea what the substance of this vendetta against us might be, nor does Mama. But I've got to start somewhere. After speaking with my father's secretary, I've managed to assemble the list below.

> These are the last few people Papa met with before his death, according to his appointment book. I believe one of these could be the culprit.

"Good work, Number Three," Connor murmured.

> I shall begin looking into them at once. Unfortunately, the person I really must speak to is Grandaunt Lucinda. To be sure, the Dowager Duchess is a mean old bird, but those eagle eyes of hers don't miss a thing. If anyone might know the source of some ancient grudge against our family, it will be Her Grace.

> The question is, will the old harpy reveal it?

Connor frowned. He had not yet met Grandaunt Lucinda, the First Duchess of Amberley, who'd been married to Granduncle Charles. She'd been giving him the cold shoulder since he'd arrived on account of his Irish blood. Still, Connor couldn't imagine why, if she had information, she'd decline to share it with the family.

Then he scanned down the page to the list of five names Cousin Richard had recorded. None looked familiar to him...

But Lady Margaret might know who these people were.

"Hungry, Your Grace?" Nestor swept in at that moment, carrying a tray with Connor's breakfast.

He snapped the book shut and set it on the chest of drawers. "God bless you, man! I'm starved."

"How's the wound?" asked the surgeon.

"Just a glorified scratch, really." Connor shrugged. "I'm alive."

"Good." Nestor glanced at the diary. "What's this?"

While Will picked it up and handed it to Nestor, explaining what he'd found, Connor guzzled the entire glass of orange juice, then took a large sip of strong, sweet tea.

Sitting down on the edge of his bed, he set the tray on his lap. Under the pewter lid covering his plate, he discovered scrambled eggs and several fried sausages. There was toast and jam as well as cinnamon-topped muffins, and he ate them like some ravenous wild dog.

"You're a good cook, Nestor," he said heartily. "And possibly a saint."

"Pshaw," the surgeon said dryly.

Connor stabbed a sausage with his fork and bit it in half, feeling much better already. He put his hand out for the book, gesturing to them to give it back.

Will brought it to him, then drifted over to the window. "It's a nice day out." He paused. "Don't you ever wonder, sir, where all the servants ended up? If they found new jobs, I mean."

Connor frowned at him. He didn't need more guilt in his life. "Not really. Why?"

Will shrugged. "Some of them were nice."

Nestor, meanwhile, began gathering up the used bandages. Will planted his hands on the windowsill and watched the busy world below.

Eating with one hand and reading with the other, Connor flipped through his cousin's diary at random, when suddenly, his eyebrows shot up.

He read a startling page or two.

"Huh," he said under his breath, then wrinkled his nose.

Nestor turned to him. "Find something?"

Connor nodded. "An explanation as to why that idiot this morning was so keen to kill me."

"Lord Bryce?"

He offered Nestor the diary to read for himself the true nature of the two fops' *friendship.*

"At least now I know why he was so…passionate about my cousin's death," Connor muttered.

Nestor read the passage and then looked at Connor, his eyebrows jumping up high on his lined forehead. "Good Lord. Are you going to break the news to Lady Margaret?"

"Hell no," Connor said. "I couldn't."

"I don't see how you can't," Nestor replied.

"She's an innocent young girl!" Connor said.

"Huh? What's happening?" Will asked, leaving off his daydreaming and turning from the window.

"Never mind," Nestor said.

Speaking of innocent…

Connor snorted, then shrugged off the matter. *Not my business.*

"Oh, come, you can't let that sweet young lady marry that fellow!" Nestor insisted with a frown. "Doesn't she deserve a proper husband?"

Connor looked at his friend as he wolfed down his breakfast.

Will scratched his head. "Did I miss something, sirs?"

"No," they both said.

For they both found it dear and rather amusing that Will was a virgin, despite being twenty years old.

"When will you see her next?" Nestor asked.

"Today," Connor said around a mouthful of toast and eggs.

"Lady Margaret?" Will chimed in, his brow still furrowed in confusion.

Connor nodded. "She owes me, especially now, and I plan to make good use of her."

"Sir!" Will said.

"Not like that," Connor replied with a scowl as he stabbed another sausage. "Although…"

"Major," Nestor said sternly.

"She is pretty, though," Will said with a sigh. "And elegant."

Connor shrugged. "I suppose. I'm merely developing an asset."

"You, sir, are so full of horseshit," said Nestor.

Connor laughed and wiped his mouth with the back of his hand, then held up his cousin's list of names. "Bet she knows who these people are. Lord this, lord that. Toffs, the lot o' them." He tossed the leather-bound book down again.

"I see." Nestor gave him a look of disapproval. "So you mean to use this innocent young lady as your spy in Society."

"*Spy* is such a dirty word, Nestor. I much prefer source, scout, reconnaissance expert."

Will chuckled. "You would know, Major."

"Aye. But I'll tell you one thing," Connor said, his face hardening. "When I find whoever is responsible for harming my family, well… Let's just say I won't be shooting anybody's hat."

Nestor and Will exchanged a grim glance at his ominous vow.

Connor took a polite sip of tea, murder coursing through his veins.

Later that day, Maggie ambled along morosely after her sister through the smart new shopping arcade not far from Bond Street. Green-painted wrought-iron posts held up the fanciful, transparent roof, which was vaulted, like the inside of a fine conservatory.

The afternoon sunlight streamed through the thick glass as the voices of countless well-to-do shoppers rebounded beneath. The quaint, narrow lane the arcade enclosed was lined with fashionable shops frequented by fashionable folk—and few were more fashionable than the inimitable Lady Birdwell.

Maggie trailed after her sister alongside her lady's maid, Penelope, while Delia held forth on the morning's events.

"No one could believe their eyes," the marchioness told her friends with great gusto. "He ripped off his shirt, blood everywhere. I've never seen anything so barbaric!"

Or magnificent, Maggie thought, then let out a dull sigh, remaining outside as Delia and her followers stepped into the linen-draper's shop.

For her part, she did not care to relive the thing again.

"Will you wait with me, Pen? I don't care to go in there," Maggie said.

"Of course, my lady," Penelope said, then the two of them leaned against the wall, waiting idly.

Penelope, a handsome, flaxen-haired woman in her mid-twenties, studied Maggie with a vague look of concern. "Are you all right, my lady?"

"Just a bit glum," Maggie admitted.

Penelope had been her trusted lady's maid for years; she had come with her from home and was thus permitted a certain degree of familiarity.

She could read Maggie well.

Certainly, Penelope knew her better than all the ton folk Maggie had met since she'd moved to London. Truth be told, her maid probably knew her better than her sister did.

"You didn't get much sleep," Penelope said. She knew all of Maggie's comings and goings, since it was her job to help her dress for each social event and to wait up until the wee hours to help her undress, too, since so many of the ball gowns and such were difficult to navigate without assistance.

Then, while Maggie tumbled into bed, Penelope would have to see to the proper care of all those fine gowns. No earl's daughter could live without such an ally, especially in London.

Maggie just counted herself fortunate that *her* lady's maid was not simply a clever and hardworking servant—expert with needle and thread, inventive with millinery, and managed not to pull Maggie's hair too much when she styled it in all the latest modes—but was also a kindhearted person, and sensible.

As Penelope studied her, Maggie let out a sigh, thinking of the duel again.

"Yes. I am rather tired," she said. "And I've learned that I don't like violence."

"I should think not," Penelope said, giving her an arch look.

Maggie watched the people milling about in their finery. The little tea shop across the lane seemed intriguing. Perhaps they'd go there next. Her body felt heavy with fatigue, but a nice cup of sweet China blend might help wake her up.

"Do you wish to go home ahead of Her Ladyship?" Penelope asked. "I could fetch us a hackney coach."

"No, I can wait. But then, a long afternoon nap might be lovely. Oh, look at these muslins..." The fabrics on display in the bow window of the linen-draper's shop caught Maggie's eye, and they both turned to contemplate this far more pleasant subject than that of men trying to kill each other.

"That blue watered silk would look perfect on you, my lady."

"You think so?" Maggie's gaze wandered absently over a luscious greenish-blue watered silk and various swaths of printed muslin in charming patterns. Flowers, checks, little paisleys…

But her thoughts drifted far away again, and her heart was all a-tangle, more than she could have explained even to Penelope. Conflicting sentiments crashed within her like the waves of an uneasy sea.

She hated chaos, in general, so she tried to sort her emotions out neatly, as though she could stack them into organized piles, like the linen-draper's bolts of fabric laid out on a shelf. First: relief that the duel was over and no one had died. Next: guilt that His Grace had been shot, even if it was just a flesh wound.

Beside that: anxiety at her sudden realization this morning that she would have to end her courtship with Bryce.

She simply had to. She knew that.

After the way he had behaved, the true colors he'd shown, she could no longer talk herself into believing that their match would all work out fine. He made her feel small…and stupid.

"He should respect you."

Yes. She must call it off before things proceeded any further.

Otherwise, she'd probably find herself bullied about by him for the rest of her life. And if she was willing to put up with that, then she might as well stay at Delia's.

Ending it was the right thing to do, but he wasn't going to like it. And that made her nervous. Indeed, part of her was tempted to ask Edward to do it for her, but she wasn't *that* much of a coward. She'd simply sit him down and tell him herself.

Last on her tidy shelf of emotions came her feelings toward Amberley.

No—Amberley got a shelf all his own. The size and complexity of her feelings concerning him warranted that. He confused her. He thrilled her. He awed her.

Above all, he worried her.

What might he want from her now? What exactly had she agreed to in all this? She'd shown him her ankles—now what?

He had said that he needed her help, but he'd never explained how or why.

Just last night, she'd been desperate enough to agree to that blindly, to save Bryce's life.

Maybe he'll forget about our agreement, she thought halfheartedly, staring through her own reflection in the glass, her face framed by a mullioned window pane.

It did not help matters that she could not stop envisioning the mighty major with his shirt off.

The blood that had been streaming down his side was of course upsetting to see and must've hurt, but he hadn't even seemed to feel the pain at the time.

She could not make heads or tails of how perfectly at home he seemed to be in his half-nude state in front of so many people.

It almost made her laugh. She could never have conceived of such a thing.

Perhaps it came of his being a soldier, having to live day and night packed into tents with his regiment.

Privacy was probably as rare for the troops as it was for the servants—at least those that ranked beneath lady's maid. Penelope, like the butler and cook, got her own room.

In any case, the question led Maggie to wonder about Amberley's life before he'd become the current Duke of Amberley.

How on earth did anyone become that strong? The force and vibrancy of his character had engulfed her, along with the entire dueling field…

Then, speaking of those with dominating natures, Delia came back out with her coterie, still chattering away at the pace of a racehorse gallop, and the ladies drifted en masse on to the next shop, this one selling shoes.

Maggie followed like a leaf pulled along by a stream.

Penelope glanced at her. "Shall we ask about the tea shop, my lady?"

"I doubt we'll get a word in," Maggie said wryly, and shrugged. "Might as well look at shoes, I suppose."

Penelope chuckled and followed her into the shop.

Inside, a cobbler sat working in one corner, tapping away with a little hammer, spectacles perched on the end of his nose. The shelves all around them brimmed with shoes of all kinds.

Dainty mules, half-boots in velvet or kid, embroidered dancing slippers, smart riding boots, even metal patens.

"Oh, look at these! Aren't they beautiful!" one of Delia's friends said, speeding over to fondle a pair of satin mules with a slender heel.

Maggie smiled absently at the woman's gushing, still in a state of distraction.

If the Duke of Amberley was confused by his change of station, she was even more so with the sudden disruption in what had, until this morning, been her single-minded goal to marry Bryce.

What the deuce was she to do now?

One of Delia's friends ordered a pair of shoes in her size, then they drifted back out into the sunny arcade.

As before, Maggie trailed along behind her sister's cohorts, still contemplating her marital options, or current lack thereof, when suddenly, Penelope gave her a nudge.

"My lady?" she whispered.

Maggie jolted back to awareness. "Yes, what is it?"

"I think that gentleman over there is trying to get your attention." Penelope nodded discreetly across the arcade to a tall, powerful, by now-familiar figure leaning idly on the wall next to a bookshop's display window.

The duke!

Below his smart black top hat, but above the newspaper he was pretending to read, Maggie spotted Amberley's tanned, square face. His cobalt gaze was fixed on her, and his lips curled into a half-smile when she saw him.

At once, her heart lurched; he tipped his hat, then sent her a meaningful nod toward the bookshop.

Maggie gulped. So soon he came to collect on their agreement?

"What is he even doing out of bed?" she mumbled. "Shouldn't he be in hospital?"

"Who is that, my lady?" her maid whispered in amazement.

"That, my dear Penelope, is our new neighbor."

"Handsome," she said.

"Quite. But he's trouble, believe me." *Unfortunately, I could develop a taste for that.* Maggie watched, pulse pounding, as Amberley pushed away from the wall and sent her another insistent stare as he folded his newspaper.

Then he took off his hat and stepped into the bookshop.

"I think we're meant to follow," Maggie said, wide-eyed. *I wonder how he found me.*

Penelope gave her a skeptical look. "Is that wise?"

"Probably not," Maggie said in amusement.

As far as the world knew, she and the duke had never been formally introduced, and there were so many Society folk milling about the arcade.

But Maggie had given her word to cooperate, and he'd already upheld his end of the bargain by sparing Bryce.

At least getting away from Delia and her friends wouldn't be difficult.

He'd been clever to choose the bookshop, for such *fashionable* ladies would never venture into such a place.

Delia read as little as possible to avoid developing, she said, a squint.

For a moment, Maggie lost her train of thought, watching the smooth way Amberley glided into the shadows of the doorway, his broad shoulders straight, nearly as wide as the doorframe, his head held high.

He gave no outward sign of being wounded.

"My lady?" Penelope asked worriedly.

"I suddenly find myself in need of a good novel. You *will* come with me, Pen?"

"You think I'd let you go in there alone?"

Maggie sent her a conspiratorial smile, but Penelope did not smile back, clearly concerned. To make her excuses, Maggie hurried after her sister. The women had gained a lead of some yards on them, but a moment later, she tapped the redhead on the shoulder.

"Delia, I'm going to step into the bookshop over there for a moment." Maggie glanced around innocently at them. "Do you want to come with me?"

"Oh God no," Delia said. "What do you want in there?"

"Don't you remember? Lady Delphine has invited me to be a part of her book club for all the ladies of Moonlight Square. I want to see if that bookseller has the title they'll be reading this month. I've written it down somewhere…" She opened her reticule and pretended to search it in order to avoid her sister's gaze.

For Maggie knew she wasn't good at lying.

"Book club. Right." Delia wrinkled her nose, and some of her friends tittered. "You run along."

"I-I'll take Penelope with me," Maggie said. "I'll be right back."

"Oh, take your time," the marchioness drawled. "We'll be in the milliner's, probably, or the tea shop."

"Good. I'll find you when I'm done. And don't leave without me again!"

Delia stuck her tongue out at her playfully in reply.

Perhaps her sister still remembered the wigging that Edward had given her for abandoning Maggie at Trinny's baby shower in January.

She'd simply got bored and left her at the hostess's house in St. James's. She'd had to beg a ride home from her friend, Felicity, the Duchess of Netherford.

In this case, however, Delia's self-centeredness might prove a boon. Once Maggie walked away, Delia would most likely forget she existed, at least for a while.

Penelope and Maggie hurried across the quaint cobbled arcade, passing the open doorways of several establishments: jeweler's, glover's, tobacconist.

When they arrived under the hanging placard for the bookshop, Penelope hesitated. "Are you quite sure about this?"

"Don't worry, he's a good man—I think. Come," Maggie added, assuming a businesslike air. "Let's see what he wants and get this over with."

Whether her brisk attitude disguised her crazed inward fluttering at the prospect of speaking with Amberley again, she could not say. But she smiled and nodded to a few random customers with her usual outward serenity as she walked into the cluttered bookshop.

She kept her footsteps measured and sedate, but gripped her reticule hard with both hands, heart pounding.

She did not see the duke at once, given all the tall wooden racks that crisscrossed the shop's length. But just knowing he was here made her flesh tingle with awareness. She could feel her petticoat brushing back and forth against her legs. Her skin seemed to grow a few degrees warmer.

She very much feared this emotion was lust, and despised herself for it.

So much for *Mama's perfect little angel*, as Delia had said with a sneer.

Wandering deeper into the quiet bookshop, Maggie nodded back to the ink-smudged clerk who greeted her from behind the counter.

Penelope followed, an obedient step behind.

Then Maggie spotted the top of a man's glossy black hair on the other side of the long wooden rack she was passing.

There he is.

Her pulse raced as she laid hold of her courage and walked around the shelving. Amberley was standing with his hands clasped politely behind his back, perusing the titles on offer. But he glanced over at her with a smile that made her stomach flip-flop.

The vibrant tone of his bronzed face, the clean line of his jaw, and the knowing and strangely intimate twist of his lips as he looked over at her knocked her world slightly off its axis.

He returned his attention to the shelves. "So, what are we reading?" he greeted her with a playful murmur.

For a heartbeat, Maggie feared she had forgotten how to read, even how to speak, standing beside him.

Though she felt fevered with his nearness, she ventured a step closer so they could converse quietly enough not to be overheard.

Turning to the shelves, she stared blankly at the titles for a moment, for he absorbed all her awareness. The cliff-like angle of his shoulder to her right, looming above her, the subtle spice of his cologne, the smooth brown wool of his tailcoat…

She shuddered. *Oh my God. I* want *this man.*

Penelope hung back at the end of the aisle, standing guard, as it were. Maggie would have to give her a nice little gift for that.

"How is your side?" Maggie finally whispered, collecting her wits.

"How are your ankles?" he countered softly.

She shook her head and pressed her lips together to hold back a laugh, as Amberley picked up some thick tome.

He glanced at her, eyes dancing, then he fanned idly through the pages of the book in his hand, stirring up a breeze. Alas, it only fed the blaze that he'd already stoked in her cheeks.

"You're sure you're all right, then?"

He winked at her. "Never better. Thanks for asking. What about you? You all right?"

"No!" she whispered. "That was horrible this morning."

"Could've been worse."

She shook her head. "I didn't expect to see you so soon."

He chuckled very softly. "No doubt."

"I'm so sorry he shot you, Your Grace. I can't begin to tell you how appalled I am —"

"Apologizing for your suitor once again, Lady Margaret?" he said. "I fear you may spend the rest of your life doing that."

"No," she said meaningfully. "Probably not."

"Aha. Rethinking this marriage, then?" He looked askance at her. "That is good news."

"Is it?" She hid her hopeful gulp, trying to glean his meaning.

"Of course. You can do much better than that idiot."

If only he knew how many suitors her sister had scared away.

"Well, thank you for sparing him, anyway."

"My word is my bond, love. However…" He cast her a droll look and snapped the book shut. "You might not want to thank me just yet."

CHAPTER 9

A Wicked Notion

The girl looked at him in alarm, but at that moment, Connor heard her maid sharply clear her throat. They stepped apart a heartbeat before some portly old gent wandered into the aisle and began studying the bookshelves.

It was time to take their conversation outside.

Connor gave his chosen accomplice a discreet nod toward the back door of the establishment, indicating that she follow.

She furrowed her brow, but he did not wait for her to object, slipping out of the aisle. As he walked out the back door of the bookshop, he glanced over his shoulder and saw the look of baffled worry that she and her maid exchanged.

He must have intrigued the lady, though, for a moment later, both women followed him out into another cobbled shopping lane. Unlike the arcade, however, this one had no roof.

It was also considerably less crowded, and for his part, he was glad to get out of the dim, stuffy shop on such a pleasant spring day.

Outside, horses were tethered in front of different establishments here and there, tails swishing, stirrups run up neatly to the saddles, but at the moment, no carriages were passing, so the street was quiet.

Candy smells sweetened the air from the confectionery a few doors down. Hanging baskets of flowers swung in the slight wind.

There were playbills and other advertisements plastered on the wall near the spot where they stood. They flapped in the breeze, and the pub from which the smell of food and the sound of laughter spilled out a short distance down the way seemed interesting.

He wished Lady Margaret and he could have had the luxury of strolling here together merely on promenade, visiting the shops, having a bite to eat at that cheerful pub with its door propped open. He should have liked to buy her some trifling bauble or other, since God knew he had more gold than Midas now.

She deserved spoiling, he thought. But at the moment, she was staring at him dubiously.

"Give us a moment, would you?" he said politely to her maid, and though he said it with a smile, his tone made it clear this was an order.

"Oh…!" Lady Margaret said when he commandeered her hand and tucked it into the crook of his elbow.

"Walk with me a moment." He led her away a few sauntering paces, keeping his voice down. "Though our chat requires privacy, the bookshop was not inappropriate, for, as it happens, I have a story to tell you, my lady."

She had to turn her head all the way to see him past the brim of her bonnet. "I'm listening."

Connor shortened his strides as they strolled so she could keep pace with him more easily.

"Once upon a time," he began, "there was an Englishman who'd been a marquess for decades. But after some obscure personal favor he'd done for King George, this chap was made a duke. Let's call him Granduncle Charles."

"Ah," she said. "The first Duke of Amberley?"

He gave a terse nod. "Yes. He had great wealth, vast power, wide influence and many friends, and, one assumes, some enemies as well. But when he died peacefully in bed about two years ago at the ripe old age of seventy-one, his exit from this earth was deemed of natural causes.

"Since the first duke had no son," he continued, "his younger brother took up the title. Granduncle Rupert was the churchman of the family, as I mentioned to you last night. You do remember that, don't you, amidst all the excitement of showing off your ankles?"

She huffed at his mischievous reminder, but said, "Of course I do. A duke, a churchman, and a soldier, you told me."

"Precisely. You look very pretty today, by the by."

"Oh—thank you," she said with a blush.

It was true. She wore a cornflower-blue pelisse, he believed it was called, over a cream-colored muslin gown with a small pattern of muted blue flowers. The brim of her golden chip bonnet was swathed in an airy scarf, but he noted the nutmeg-brown tendrils that escaped from underneath it, and found himself wondering how long her hair was when it hung loose.

To her shoulders? Down the middle of her back?

But thinking about her back was dangerous. For he imagined it bare, and his mind offered up a ready fantasy of creamy skin, delicate shoulder blades and a supple spine, the curve of a slim waist, the flare of her womanly hips...

When his fingertips started to tingle with the need to glide all over her body, he dropped his gaze to the well-polished toes of his black boots, tapped his hat against his thigh a few times, and continued his story.

"Well," he said as they strolled on, "as it turned out, the poor vicar-duke lasted less than a year in his new role. He went out walking one day, contemplating heaven, I suppose, when he lost his footing on a high promontory overlooking a river on his estate, and fell to his death. It was deemed an accident."

"How awful!" She glanced anxiously at him. "I am sorry for your loss."

He shrugged. "Thanks, but I only met him once, as a boy. My grandfather brought me to London to meet all my English relatives. He didn't really get along with them, you see, which is why he moved to Ireland after leaving the Army.

"In any case, Rupert's son, Richard, became the third duke. Did you know him, if he was such great friends with your suitor?"

"No. He died before Bryce and I were introduced."

"Ah." Connor nodded. "Here is where things start to get interesting. By the time Richard came into the title, it seems he'd begun to suspect that something was, er, rotten in Denmark."

"How so?"

"He found his father's fall from that cliff quite suspicious, and began looking into it. But before he reached any certain conclusions, Richard had an unfortunate carriage accident of his own several months into his tenure as duke."

"Dreadful." She shook her head.

"To be fair, he was known to be fond of driving too fast. Still..."

"Yes." She gave him a troubled glance. "One does start to wonder."

"Indeed. It was at that point that Mr. Rollins, the family solicitor, tracked me down in Ireland to let me know I'd just become the fourth duke."

"Were you shocked?" she asked with a smile.

"Flabbergasted." He smiled back. "I'd barely finished unpacking from the Peninsula. I stayed on for several months after Waterloo to help with the occupation, so I had just got home."

"Why?" she asked abruptly, sounding mystified. "Hadn't you had enough of the war?"

He shrugged. "Fighting's what I do. Well," he added awkwardly, "it's what I used to do, anyway." He shook off the uncomfortable topic and forged on.

"When the solicitor explained this run of 'bad luck' that had befallen my relatives in England over the past two years, it probably should've alerted me that something was wrong. But in my shock at the news, I must've ignored any inner warning. Either that, or I'd got so used to being surrounded by death that it just seemed normal to me—at first, anyway."

She made a soft sound of sympathy.

"But then," he continued, "I arrived in London to claim the title. And in the short four months since I got here, there've been two attempts on my life. Not counting the duel."

She stopped walking and turned to him. *"What?"*

He sighed. "Somebody's trying to kill me."

She stared at him. "Oh my God."

He shrugged, smirked a bit. "Nothing new in that, really. But, I confess, when your suitor called me out, and then you came knocking at my door moments later, I thought you both might be a part of it somehow."

She gasped. "Me?"

"Silly, I know. Sorry. I've become a bit paranoid of late."

"One can hardly blame you!" She looked dazed at his revelation, and indignant on his behalf. "How awful. I'm so sorry you're going through this."

"Thanks." Her show of instant support comforted Connor more than he would've expected. A bit of sympathy was welcome for a change — especially coming from a beautiful woman.

Even if she did have a suitor.

Not that he intended to let that match continue. How could he, now that he knew Bryce's secret?

94   *Gaelen Foley*

Thinking of Bryce brought him back to the matter at hand.

"So, you see, your suitor was not so far off the mark when he made his accusations, claiming that Richard was murdered. I think so, too. But I assure you, I had nothing to do with it, or any of their deaths. You *do* see that, don't you?"

"Yes, yes, of course. But tell me what happened. Who tried to kill you? Where and when did this occur, and do you know why?"

"No! The who and the why of it are utter mysteries to me. One of my predecessors must've wronged someone—badly—it would seem. Someone who now seems bent on revenge and won't be happy till they've altogether ended our line."

An appalled sound escaped her, then they walked on.

"As to the when and where of it, the first attempt happened moments after I'd stepped off the boat from Ireland onto the London docks. This was a few days before Christmas. I was attacked by what I assumed at the time was a footpad. Fought him off, no harm done. I had all but forgotten about it.

"But then, at Twelfth Night, a good friend of mine, a guest, was poisoned under my own roof, at my own table, and that's when I realized...I had a problem."

"Good Lord."

"That's why the house is a shambles," he explained. "I sacked the whole staff, since one of them had to be involved somehow. Called in the lads from my regiment to help watch my back. Loyal, they are, but cooking and cleaning?" He chuckled. "Not exactly what they're trained for."

"You poor man." She shook her head. "What of your friend who got the poison? Did he die?"

"No, thankfully, he recovered. There has not been a third attempt—yet—and I don't intend to sit around and wait for it. I'm trying to piece together information on my predecessors' lives so I can figure out who bears this vendetta against us.

"It hasn't been easy. The family is, er, closed-mouthed about many things. They, like the rest of the ton, see me as an outsider, and, of course, that's what I am. Which is why I was hoping for a little help from you, Lady Margaret."

"What can *I* do?" She stopped and turned to him.

Her dove-gray eyes were wide, their expression grave. Her lips, primrose pink, were drawn into a thoughtful little frown.

He let his gaze roam admiringly over her peaches-and-cream complexion, down her regal neck to the demure lace frill around her alluring throat.

He had a fleeting vision of tearing that delicate lace asunder with his teeth, claiming her pearly neck with his lips. God, what was this effect she had on him? Even his wound stopped hurting in her presence.

Yet her nearness made his body feel hot and constricted, like he was wearing too many damn clothes.

Perhaps her maid sensed his errant thoughts, for she cleared her throat loudly from a few feet behind them, playing chaperone.

They both glanced over and saw the woman's pointed look that clearly said, *That's far enough, you two.*

Lady Margaret looked up at him, her gaze troubled. "We should turn back," she murmured.

"As you wish."

They retraced their steps, and the maid stepped obediently out of the way, waiting till they passed to trail after them again.

"You were saying?" she prompted.

"You can go places and talk to people I can't." Thankfully, by now, Connor had managed to curb his more primal urges. "You fit in here, Lady Margaret. These people trust you. Me, I'm a stranger in a strange land."

She passed an uncertain glance over his face. "I suppose I could help to introduce you around…?"

He snorted. "Frankly, if last night in the ballroom was any indication of my future in Society, I'd rather spend time with my horses."

She winced. "Rest assured, there are good people, too, Your Grace, but never mind that for now. What exactly would you have me do?"

"Advise me on who's who in Society. I could really use an insider's knowledge about various people so I can narrow the list of who is probably *not* the killer. They're all strangers and thus all suspicious to me. I'll need answers about certain people. Basic backgrounds. Where they're from. With whom they associate. On occasion, you may have to act—in a limited way, mind you—as my…well, as my spy in Society."

"Spy?" she burst out, then started laughing. "Me?"

Connor saw nothing funny. "Will you do this? You gave me your word."

"Yes, I know, but…" She hesitated, and her laughter trailed off as she searched his face. "I'm not sure I *can*. That is, I know we made an agreement, but...I wasn't expecting anything involving murder!"

"Shh! Keep your voice down." He glanced around, annoyed at her wavering, exactly as he'd feared.

This was precisely why he'd connived her into baring her ankles. Only, now that it came down to it, Connor did not want to have to use that against her.

He wanted her to help him willingly.

"You'll be perfectly safe. I would never put you anywhere near the danger. As I said, I just want a wee bit o' guidance. You can provide me with the information I need from the comfort of your own home. Nobody even has to know you know me, if you'd rather not acknowledge me as an acquaintance. Well—except for your maid, since she's already seen us together."

"It's not that, it's just..."

"What?" he demanded.

"Well—I'm a lady!" she blurted out, bewilderment filling those pretty eyes beneath her long lashes. "This all sounds quite reckless, and I-I'm not very adventurous, you see. A spy? I don't like deceiving people, and I haven't much experience sneaking around."

"You did fine last night," he drawled, sending a meaningful glance toward her ankles.

She scowled at the reminder of how she had flirted with scandal by coming alone to his house after dark.

"Are you trying to say you're just some helpless female? Because that claim won't work. Not with me."

"Well, I didn't say *that*." She gave a little humph.

An indulgent feeling filled him as he gazed at her in soft amusement, half wanting to let her off the hook, though he really couldn't spare her.

Besides, this would be good for her.

For a moment, he assessed her the same way he did every new fresh-faced recruit they had sent to his regiment. She had more strength than she knew.

He saw a careful young woman, perhaps slightly lacking in confidence, and holding herself a little too tightly in check.

But she had heart. She had shown herself capable of startling bravery last night when she'd come knocking on his door, risking any young lady's most valuable asset—her reputation—to save a man's life.

That he respected.

Clearly, though, his little English rose was buttoned up a wee bit too tightly, lived too often on her best behavior. He could see that. A thoroughly nice girl, but a creature caged.

And, suddenly, the wild side of him wanted to free her.

"Do you trust me, lass?" he asked softly.

"Can I?"

"What does your heart tell you?" Connor watched her closely, ignoring the worried look from her maid.

Lady Margaret consulted the sky, as though the answer floated amid the big, puffy clouds drifting by overhead.

Then she looked at him once more, squaring her shoulders decisively.

"All I know is that you kept your word to me. And so, of course, I shall do the same. Whatever the cost," she added with a gulp.

Connor pondered her with a sudden flood of tenderness inside. Relief unfurled inside his solar plexus, and a smile spread across his face. "I knew you wouldn't fail me."

"Just remember"—she gave him a disapproving poke in the chest—"you promised not to ruin my life."

"Wouldn't dream of it, Lady Maggie. Do you mind if I call you that?"

"Actually, I prefer it."

They smiled warily at each other for a moment, and then walked on. This time, when she took his arm, she held on to his biceps with newfound determination.

"No one out there is going to kill any neighbor of mine, I assure you," she said.

Connor grinned and looked askance at her. The kittenish protectiveness in her grip both touched his heart and amused him.

"So, what does this entail?" she asked. "Where and when do we begin? And how?"

"There are a few members of Society I want to ask you about—general information, whatever you know about them. Whatever gossip you might've heard concerning them. This will save me from wasting loads of time investigating people who are most likely innocent, and time is of the essence. The quicker this is sorted, the sooner I can get on with the whole horrid business of being a duke."

This got a chuckle from her. "Is it so bad?"

"It's bloody miserable," he grumbled.

"Perhaps you're just not used to it yet."

He heaved a sigh. "Perhaps. But if I have to hear one more fool make some snide remark about the Irish, I may put him through a wall."

"Ah, they're just jealous of you."

"Testing me, I think."

"Hmm, probably some of that, too. But you are the rightful Duke of Amberley now, and too bad if they don't like it. You outrank them, and that's that. It's their lot to conform themselves to you, not the other way 'round."

"You think so?" he asked in skeptical amusement.

"I know so," she said. "Act the part and they will fall in line, as they've all been trained. And that, Your Grace, is the great secret of how to go about in Society."

"If you say so." He smiled at her, warmed by her surprisingly cynical advice. She was very dear in her way. "Unfortunately, I've got bigger things to worry about now than my lack of popularity."

"Indeed," she said with a twinkling glance.

The next shop window caught his eye as they strolled past, showing him their reflections together. They looked like a real courting couple, maybe even married. The thought so distracted him that he almost missed her next question.

"So, who are your suspects, Your Grace? Do we have anyone in our sights yet?"

"We do." Thrilled at her turn of demeanor now that she'd put her will into his cause, he snapped back to awareness. "But first things first. We need to establish a convenient method of communication away from prying eyes. Tell me, can you see Amberley House from where you live?"

"Yes, easily. My sister's residence is Number 71 Moonlight Square. It's in the middle of the south terrace, across from your home."

"That's Marquess Row?"

She nodded, smiling. "Several marquesses live side by side there. My brother-in-law being one of them. But yes, I can see your house easily from my bedchamber window."

"Good. Then let us devise a system of lantern signals. Whenever you need to see me, if some urgent matter should arise, or if you uncover information that I need to know quickly, put a lantern in your window, and I will contact you. I'd prefer if you tell me your findings in person. I don't expect you to learn any codes, but I'd really prefer you not write these things down where others might find them. Since I don't know yet who might be involved, and have even had trouble with servants, I want all this treated with the utmost secrecy. Between you and me only."

She nodded, wide-eyed. "I understand."

He nodded back. "Good. Now, to signal that you need to see me, simply put a lighted lantern in your window after dark. To let *you* know, in turn, that I've seen your summons, I'll answer by doing the same, and vice versa.

"However, if a serious emergency should arise, if you feel yourself in danger at any time in all this, put *two* lanterns in your window. This will tell me that something is wrong, and I will come to you at once. If you're not at our meeting place, I'll come and find you and make sure you're safe."

"Meeting place?" she echoed.

"Yes. We must agree upon some mutually convenient location, where we can meet without drawing attention to ourselves. Any ideas?"

"Well, there's the garden folly in the middle of the park. It's a normal place where either of us might be seen, since we live on the square, yet secluded enough among the trees that we should be able to avoid notice, especially after dark. And," she added, "we can both get there quickly, as it sits halfway between our two houses."

He nodded, impressed. "That should suit."

Encouraged to find her warming to her role, he reached into his waistcoat pocket and pulled out the small folded list of names that he had copied down from his cousin's diary. "Put this in your reticule. Wait until you're alone to read it. Study it well. Learn it. Then burn it."

"What is it?" She took the square of paper from between his fingers and obediently tucked it into her reticule.

"It's a list of names my cousin assembled before he was killed. These are the last five people known to have dealings with Granduncle Rupert before he 'fell' off the precipice. Memorize this, then destroy it. Mark me?"

"Absolutely."

"Good. Keep these names in mind, and if you see an opportunity where I might be able to approach any of our suspects in Society, I shall drag myself out to the ballroom again, if you'll point them out to me."

"I'd be glad to," she said. "But, for that, it sounds like you and I are going to need a formal introduction, Your Grace. Otherwise, this all becomes entirely complicated, given Society's rules. Especially after my, er, outburst this morning."

He smiled wryly at the reminder of how she'd come running over to him.

"I couldn't help it!" she said, blushing. "I was horrified. I still don't understand how you could be so calm about it all."

He laughed. "Used to it. But who could we get to introduce us in a manner that would satisfy the ton? I doubt we have one mutual acquaintance. Well—aside from Lord Bryce, but I doubt he'd indulge us."

"Leave this to me," she said proudly.

He arched a brow.

"Edward."

"Who's that?"

"My brother-in-law, Lord Birdwell. I will tell him to befriend you. Oh, you'll love him dearly. He's the most pleasant of men. Which reminds me...I should get back to my sister."

"Was he the chap who brought you to the duel this morning?"

She nodded. "And don't worry. Edward can be trusted. I can vouch for him wholeheartedly."

"Well, that is excellent news. There's one name I can cross off my list of suspects." He sent her a grin. "Only nine hundred, ninety-nine thousand more souls in London to go."

She chuckled, and he was loath to let her go, but her maid was starting to look seriously worried at the length of their conversation.

"My lady?" she called in a stage whisper.

Connor glanced at his fob watch. "She's right. I've kept you long enough. It's been nearly twenty minutes now." He snapped his watch closed. "I daresay we've already tempted scandal enough over the past twenty-four hours."

"I am glad you were not too badly hurt, Your Grace."

"Ah, well, much to my enemies' dismay, I've proven vexingly hard to kill."

"Indeed." She narrowed her eyes, studying him, then started to turn away, but paused. "What kind of soldier were you, exactly?"

The question took him aback, then he feigned an ominous tone. "A very nasty kind indeed. I'll tell you all about it some other day."

"You will find me an attentive audience, I'm sure—but do leave out the gory parts, if you please."

"Then it'll be a brief conversation." He winked at her, and to his delight, the roses crept back into her cheeks. "Au revoir, my lady."

"Good day, Your Grace. And do stay safe until we meet again." She turned away and glided back to her attendant.

Connor tipped his hat to the maid, who'd opened the back door of the bookshop for her mistress.

Before she stepped inside, Lady Maggie sent him one last parting smile, looking intrigued, then disappeared into the establishment. Her maid followed in her footsteps, and the screened door banged shut behind them.

Well, thought Connor, pleased. It seemed he had himself an accomplice.

Maggie's heart was still pounding over what she'd just agreed to as she returned to the close confines of the bookshop with her maid in tow. Her eyes quickly adjusted to the dim, and her nose twitched with the dust of the countless tomes lining the shelves. But as she wove by browsing customers, her feet barely seemed to touch the floor.

Oh, she knew that Amberley's demands were entirely improper, but she could not deny he was a thrilling man.

Sussing out a murderer? She had never been involved in anything so daring in her life.

Nor had she ever met anyone like him. She only wished he weren't so handsome. It would've made concentrating on their shared task far easier.

Frankly, it would've made refusing to help him easier, too. But those blue eyes glimmered with Irish charm, and what could she do?

For heaven's sake, someone was trying to kill the poor man, and was he not one of her neighbors? If she were in a position to help and did nothing, that would be most unchristian. Like noticing that one of the houses of Moonlight Square was on fire in the middle of the night, but rolling over and going back to sleep with a yawn, instead of sounding the alarm.

In short, it would be hideously wrong, as would be giving her word and then abandoning him to this troubling situation.

And she wasn't scared, per se. She believed him absolutely when he said he'd keep her out of danger. The man clearly knew how to fight. So she wasn't worried about her safety. Not yet, anyway, though things might become dicey...

Lord! Maggie thought. This might prove to be the first bona fide adventure of her entire life.

But certainly not his.

In truth, Maggie doubted that this unknown enemy of his would have the slightest success. This villain, whoever he was, probably hadn't realized yet that he had sown the wind, and would soon reap the whirlwind.

With full confidence in Amberley's ability to conquer, she tingled with excitement over her role in lending a helping hand. This pursuit of justice made her feel strangely important.

To think, an ordinary young lady like herself might somehow help preserve the life of a mighty warrior! Besides, His Grace had shown her great honor by seeking her assistance, placing his trust in her under such delicate circumstances.

Maggie burned with curiosity about the slip of paper tucked away in her reticule. She could hardly wait to get started.

Disoriented by all the thoughts spinning in her head, she stopped in the middle of the aisle, needing to collect herself. Penelope bumped into her on account of her sudden halt, then mumbled an apology.

"No, it's my fault," Maggie said absently. She scratched her brow for a moment, out of sorts, then glanced toward the counter of the bookshop. "You know, I dare not go back to my sister empty-handed. I have to buy something."

She scanned the nearest shelves, still too much aflutter to concentrate on any particular reading material. Striding over to the rack of fashionable ladies' magazines, she snatched up the latest issue of *La Belle Assemblee.*

"This will do the trick," she murmured, heading for the counter. "Of course, my sister will steal it from me the moment she sees it."

Penelope grinned.

Delia did love keeping up with the fashions. Her greatest thrill in life was identifying herself as the anonymous "Lady B—" whose latest handsome outfit, observed in the park or at the theater, was described in detail by the fashion writers to their readers so they could copy the look.

Ah, Lady Birdwell was competitive in all things. She'd probably be entirely annoyed if she found out that lowly Mags now had important secret dealings with a duke. But she was never letting Delia find out about this.

She would ruin it for certain.

Finally beginning to settle down, Maggie stepped up to the counter and purchased the magazine.

A moment later, a small bell jangled over the shop door as they stepped back out into the sunshine. Penelope and she drifted into the center of the arcade, glancing around.

"I wonder where they've gone," Penelope said.

Delia and her followers were nowhere in sight.

Maggie shook her head. "We'd better find her before she decides to leave without us."

They began hurrying along the arcade, glancing into the shops and trying to find Delia and her friends, when the group of ladies emerged noisily from the milliner's. They could hear Delia braying with laughter from a few shops away.

Maggie nudged Penelope.

"Oh, good, you're back," Delia said loudly as the two of them returned to the fold.

"We're going to the tea shop next," one of Delia's friends said. "We didn't want you to miss out on taking refreshments with us."

"How kind!" Maggie said. "Thank you for waiting."

"Did you find your book club novel, Lady Margaret?" asked another.

"You know, they were sold out," Maggie lied—easily—to her own astonishment. Maybe she was a better liar than she realized. God knew she had been lying to herself well enough where Bryce was concerned. "I bought this instead."

"Ooh, *La Belle Assemblee!*" Delia snatched it out of her hand, right on cue. "Am I in there?"

Maggie bit her lip as Delia began flipping through the pages while they sauntered along, heading for the teashop. Even Delia's hangers-on looked surprised at this rude display.

Despite her embarrassment at her sister's behavior, Maggie managed another placid smile. But behind her mask of equanimity, she was gritting her teeth.

God, maybe it would be worth it, marrying Bryce, just to escape her sister's house…

But, suddenly, a wicked thought dawned in her mind. It took her so much off guard that she stopped for a moment.

Amberley.

Why not set her cap frankly at him?

Maggie's pulse jolted. She dropped her gaze, amazed by the notion. Her first thought was that it was wrong to think of marriage in such

104   *Gaelen Foley*

mercenary terms. But then, if Amberley was using her for what she could do for him, then why should she not contemplate the practical advantages that she, in turn, could gain from a possible match with him?

Her second thought was how furious Delia would be if she, lowly Mags, the inconsequential younger sister, should go and snare herself a duke, when Delia had only got a marquess—never mind how completely that marquess adored her.

Maggie bit her lip, scandalized by the temptation forming in her mind.

After a lifetime of Delia's belittlement, for once, she would outrank the insufferable firstborn.

Oh, don't be petty, she scolded herself. *You don't marry someone for such absurd reasons.*

And yet, half an hour later, she was still contemplating the wicked notion of getting such sweet revenge on her sister, who had already ruined so many matches for her. It was bad of her, she knew, and she did not normally think this way. But somehow, today, the temptation of a match with this wild Irish duke tasted even more delicious than the glazed apricot scone that Maggie nibbled at the teashop with her lemony cup of Ceylon blend.

What a catch he would be. Rich and powerful, a war hero, handsome as sin?

Maybe it *wasn't* the maddest idea. He was unattached, after all, and they had already forged this unlikely alliance. *The Duchess of Amberley...*

It had rather a nice ring to it.

Of course, the man was a bit of a lunatic. She'd have to take him firmly in hand, try to tame him just a little.

As if that were even remotely possible.

A smile twitched at her lips with the thought.

But then she abruptly remembered that someone was killing off members of his family. And she wished to risk becoming one?

Was she mad, too?

Lud. A cold chill ran down her spine. *Perhaps not my best idea ever.*

In truth, being Amberley's friend seemed dangerous enough. She did not care to attract the attention of a killer, to boot.

Not that she'd be backing down from their bargain, of course. They had a deal. And although her hand might tremble a bit as she lifted her teacup to her lips, whatever her faults, Maggie Winthrop always kept her word.

CHAPTER 10

Dragon Lady

After Lady Margaret had gone, Connor ambled down the lane, pleased at his good fortune in securing her help, and still mulling over their exchange. But near the corner, the wafting smell of food reached his nostrils from the pub he'd noted earlier.

He decided to stop in for a bite to eat and a tankard of ale before returning home. No man could live continuously on Nestor's cooking, after all.

He got to chatting with some of the fellows there, ordinary men who had no inkling of his ducal station. He played a round of darts with some, then the serving girl brought him a highly agreeable roast beef sandwich.

But when his side began to hurt, he remembered it was probably time to change his bandages, wash the wound, and reapply the ointment. So he bade his new mates goodbye, bought them a round of drinks on the way out, then hied himself home.

"Will? Nestor?" he called when he stepped into the entrance hall.

At once, Will came speeding out with a finger to his lips, hushing Connor with a wide-eyed look of consternation.

"What's the matter?" he asked.

"You have a visitor, Major," the boy whispered.

Connor's eyebrows shot upward. "Who?"

"One of your relatives," Will said. "The old duchess, sir. She's upstairs waiting for you in the drawing room. And be warned, she's not happy."

"Which old duchess, lad? There are two."

"I don't know!" Will exclaimed in a hush. "She nearly bit my head off when I asked her. Somehow I was supposed to know this already, who she was. She has a second lady with her, but that one's not as scary."

"Hmm," said Connor. "Sounds like she might be 'the mean old bird' from my cousin's diary. The dowager duchess? Grandaunt Lucinda?"

Will nodded with a blank, rattled look. "That'd be a safe guess, sir."

"Right," Connor said, lifting his head, squaring his shoulders, and feeling altogether intrigued. "I take it she heard about the duel."

"Afraid so, Major."

"Well, this should be interesting." Though he'd never met the matriarch of the Amberley clan before, Connor gathered he should expect a scolding. He pressed his hand to his torn side as he marched up the staircase to the drawing room. Tending to his wound would just have to wait a little longer.

It felt uncomfortable as hell, but he could not have asked for a better opportunity to interrogate the very woman whom Cousin Richard had mentioned in his journal.

Richard had said that Her Grace seemed to know more than she cared to say about the deaths of his predecessors.

But when Connor stepped into the drawing room, he saw with a glance that the formidable First Duchess of Amberley would be the one asking the questions, thank you very much.

Grandaunt Lucinda was a great, scowling mound of a woman dressed all in black, but for a ruby in the shape of a teardrop that hung from her black satin turban. Her hand was braced atop an ivory-handled walking stick.

She had the hanging jowls and pugnacious stare of an aging bulldog.

"Finally!" she said with an impatient huff when Connor stepped into the doorway of the drawing room. "At last you show your face."

He stifled his surprise at the greeting. "I beg your pardon, Your Grace, I was not expecting you."

She humphed in knowing disapproval. "No doubt."

"Ma'am." Connor bowed to the second old lady in the room.

Standing near the dowager duchess, as though ready to leap to attend her—being slightly younger and rather more spry—was a second old lady, a slim, cringing creature, frail as a bird, with white hair in a bun and papery skin.

She, too, was dressed in widow's weeds, but at least this one offered

Connor a slight, anxious smile.

"Since I see you are not in the habit of conducting yourself in a formal fashion, Major, I will do the introductions, and let us get it over with," the grand, seated woman said tersely. "I am Lucinda, the First Duchess of Amberley. This is Florence, Lady Walstead, your kinswoman, though God alone knows how exactly you're related."

"Oh!" said the little bird lady, startled. "I am your aunt twice removed, Your Grace…or is it third cousin? I get so confused about such things."

"Doesn't matter," said Lucinda, rolling her eyes.

"The family simply calls me Aunt Florence," the woman offered. She glanced nervously at Lucinda. "Y-you may do the same, i-if you wish."

"Thank you. Aunt Florence, then." He smiled at her. "I am honored by your visit, ladies. May I offer you refreshments?"

Grandaunt Lucinda was sizing him up. "Your man has already brought us tea which is too strong, so no."

"My humblest apologies it was not to your taste."

"Why do you not have proper servants?" Lucinda demanded. "This house was a proper ducal residence under my domain. But now you've turned it into an army camp. Where are your butler, footmen, maids?"

"Oh, yes, do please tell us nothing unfortunate has happened to dear old Trumbull," Aunt Florence chimed in. "He's been the butler here for ages."

"Do sit down, Florence! You so irritate one with all your nervous hoverings."

"Sorry," Aunt Florence whispered, and obeyed, flitting down into an armchair.

Connor remained standing, still digesting Lucinda's terse bark. Mother Mary, he'd met brigadier generals who were less formidable that this beastly ol' gal. But, as Her Grace was clearly a woman not to be trifled with, he decided to tell her the truth.

"I dismissed them," he said.

Aunt Florence gasped in horror. "Even Trumbull?"

"Whatever for?" the dragon demanded.

"Because someone tried to poison me, dear aunts, and since most of the food that evening came from my own kitchens, I could not be certain the staff was not involved."

"Never!" Aunt Florence whispered, aghast, then glanced anxiously at Lucinda, who sat stone-faced. Lucinda didn't move, staring back

108   *Gaelen Foley*

skeptically at Connor, while Florence perched on the edge of her seat, clutching her chest and looking like she might have an apoplectic fit.

Good thing Nestor was available, just in case.

"Poison?" Aunt Florence squeaked. "B-but Trumbull has always been a model butler! He would never let this happen! He started with the family as a pageboy! O-oh, my nerves, my nerves can't take it."

"Becalm yourself, you ninny," said Lucinda.

Connor arched a brow. "You don't look too surprised to hear of this, Your Grace."

"Why should I be, after all our misfortunes?" she retorted. "This family is cursed."

"Don't say that!" Aunt Florence pleaded. "It was probably just a-a case of spoiled milk or tainted meat, or some passing illness. Yes, that's it!"

Connor shrugged and sat down across from the pair. "I have my doubts."

"Well, then? What happened?" The dowager looked him over from head to toe, her beady eyes guarded. "This *poisoner* of yours obviously failed."

"Thankfully, yes." He decided not to elaborate, for fear of Aunt Florence dropping dead of sheer terror. "All's well that ends well."

"Not for poor old Trumbull, though, I fear," Aunt Florence whispered with a shake of her head. "To end a life of exemplary service in such humiliation! Poor man. Poor, poor man."

"Never mind about the butler!" Lucinda snapped. "I, for one, had to remind that conceited little rooster far too often of his place. Got above himself, you ask me. I cannot abide impertinence." With that, Grandaunt Lucinda's eagle-eyed stare homed in on him.

"Now then," she said, gripping the head of her walking stick, as though she was considering beating him with it if he acted up. "Explain yourself, sir."

Connor blinked. "Pardon?"

"'Tis all very well that you survived this alleged poisoning. But am I to understand you survived one attempt on your life, only to go out this morning and nearly get yourself killed in a duel? I will not stand for it!" Aunt Lucinda bellowed at him. "It's not the done thing. Moreover, 'tis against the *law*."

"Hmm. Well…at least I won," he said serenely.

She glared at his cheeky response. "How did this come about?"

He was silent for a beat, frankly puzzled at how to deal with her. He was used to giving orders and taking no lip.

But apparently, so was she.

"Well? Speak, man! I am getting old, sitting here waiting for you to find your tongue. Unless you are busy concocting some lie in that twisty Celtic brain of yours, eh?" she goaded him with a gleam in her eyes.

Connor's lips twitched. He let the Irish jab pass for once, though, since she was an old lady and his kin.

"The Marquess of Dover's heir challenged me last night at the Grand Albion, quite out of the blue," he told her. "I never saw the man before in my life. But he accused me of involvement in Richard's death, so I had no choice but to defend my honor."

"Did you wound him? Is he dead?"

Connor smiled patiently at her. "I suspect Your Grace knows full well that I did the fool no harm. I merely shot a hole through his hat to teach him a lesson, that is all. He did not do me the same courtesy," he added.

"Yes. I'd heard you were wounded," she grumbled. "If you die before producing issue, I shall be most displeased. That, in fact, is why I am here." She lifted both of her double chins. "What are your plans regarding marriage, Your Grace?"

He blinked. "Marriage? I, er, hadn't really thought about it yet—"

"Men," she muttered. "Of course you didn't."

He frowned. "I am not opposed to the married state, aunt. It merely seems wise to find out who's trying to kill me and eliminate the threat before I take a wife, don't you think? I should not wish to endanger my duchess."

"No, no, you are looking at it backwards," she said. "You must marry and have a son, post-haste, lest the enemy succeed."

It was not lost on him that, with those words, the dragon had all but admitted that, contrary to her prior words, she, too, believed deep down that there was foul play afoot.

But before he could respond, she forged on with a shocking announcement.

"To guide you in making a proper alliance, I have prepared a list of a few acceptable gels from approved families, from whom you may choose the next Duchess of Amberley. Florence, give him the list."

Lucinda handed Florence a small piece of paper, and she started to rise to bring it to him, but Connor quickly left his chair and spared her the trouble.

Aunt Florence offered him a tepid smile for his courtesy, but she still seemed distraught over his dismissal of longtime family domestics.

As Connor took the folded slip of paper from her bony hand, he could not help but notice the unexpected echo of how he, himself, had just handed another list of names to Lady Maggie.

Wouldn't it be something if she was on here? He unfolded the list and read the names, but hers did not appear.

"Now then," Lucinda continued. "In order for you to meet your prospective brides, Florence and I will be hosting a soirée at our house in Mayfair to complete the introductions. Once you've seen these few ladies, I am sure 'twill not take long for you to decide which one will suit you best. Then, 'pon my word, you must get to breeding! The family line must be replenished, and quickly."

"Well, that part sounds fun, anyway."

At his low-toned quip, Lucinda pinned him in a withering glower. "Does something amuse you, Your Grace?"

He cleared his throat and dropped his gaze. "No ma'am."

"Good." She pursed her lips. "For these are serious matters. In the meanwhile, you cannot continue to live in this house without a proper staff. Though it pains me to part with them, I shall send over some of my most trusted servants to work here temporarily for you. They shall soon put everything back in order, and I can certainly guarantee that none of them will try to murder you. Unless, of course, you give them *cause*." She sent him the evil eye.

Did she just make a joke? Connor wondered in astonishment. He hoped so. Indeed, he quite believed she had, though there was no smile to confirm it.

Still, he had no intention of accepting her offer.

"I appreciate your generosity, Your Grace, but you may keep your staff. They're not needed."

"But I insist. You have no choice in the matter," she answered, annoyed.

"Of course I do." Connor gave her his most winning smile. "Come now, ma'am, I won't have you filling my household with your spies."

Her jaw dropped. "Spies? What are you imply—"

"I wasn't born yesterday, Your Grace. Your offer's very kind, I'm sure. Let's just leave it at that. I can staff me own household as I set fit."

"I very much doubt that," she muttered.

Unwilling to argue over trivia, Connor changed direction on her without warning. "What can Your Grace tell me about young Richard's death?"

She blinked, visibly taken off guard. "You read the reports. You spoke to the solicitor. I'm sure Mr. Rollins apprised you of all the unpleasant details."

"Yes, but all the same, I should like to hear what happened to the last three dukes from those who knew them best. People who were there. Their wives, their kinswomen. Starting…with *you*."

Lucinda eyed him warily. "I have nothing further to add to the information you've already seen. My husband died in his bed of natural causes, and Rupert died of clumsiness. Tell the duke, Florence."

"It's true, Your Grace." Aunt Florence nodded, wide-eyed. "Charles died of his heart ailment, his brother of misadventure, and young Richard of that dreadful accident."

"I see," Connor said. "And by the way, never mind the formalities. None of this 'Your Grace' business, dear ladies. Call me Connor. We are family, after all."

Lucinda glared at him, as though irked to be reminded of that fact. Florence offered a wan, uncertain smile.

Connor turned to the duchess. "May I say, Aunt Lucinda, that I am truly sorry for your loss. After fifty years of marriage, it must be dreadful for you." Her eyebrow shot up. "I only met Granduncle Charles once, but he seemed very…dignified."

The dragon let out a sudden huff and looked away. "This conversation grows tedious. Come, Florence. We must go."

"So soon?" Connor rose in chagrin, feeling awful. "I'm sorry. I did not mean to upset you."

"Pfft! Don't be absurd."

Her glower bewildered him. Was this grief?

The woman was so hard to read, cloaking herself in ill-temper.

"We were here waiting for you for half an hour before Your Grace condescended to join us."

"I-I'm sorry, I didn't realize you were coming," he stammered, entirely routed to think he'd upset a grieving old lady.

"Besides, your Aunt Florence has yet another appointment with her physician."

"Oh no." More cause for family concern. "Are you unwell, aunt?"

"Look at her!" Lucinda snapped before Florence could reply. "The little mouse has always been anemic, if you ask me. Thin as a rail, and prone to the vapors."

"It's…my nerves," Aunt Florence said in a small voice, and looked at him apologetically.

Connor suspected he knew the source of her problem; Grandaunt Lucinda now heaved herself up from her seat, one gnarled hand gripping her walking stick.

Aunt Florence scurried around to the other side to help lift the dragon by her other elbow. The duchess brushed her off impatiently once she had gained her feet. Then she stared down her nose at Connor.

He wasn't sure how she accomplished that, since he was over a foot taller than her. But, blueblood that she was, she had probably learned that look from her cradle.

"Now then," she said. "The date for the soirée is in a fortnight. May the ninth. Please do be on time, try to dress like a gentleman, and avoid acting too…Irish," she said with another goading glint in her eyes.

Connor grinned at her tiresome attempt to needle him, playing up his brogue. "I'll do me best, ma'am."

Oh, she did not like his stubborn refusal to let her get under his skin.

"You listen here, young man." She poked him in the chest with her cane. "You may find your change of fortune all very droll, but I am here because, for good or ill, you are this family's last hope.

"Which just goes to show how far our lot has fallen," she continued before he could speak. "But you're all we've got. And if you foolishly permit yourself to die before producing male issue, our line goes extinct. Do you understand? No. More. Duels."

"Yes, ma'am."

"If you die, nearly everything we have reverts to the Crown. Is that what you want?"

"No. Nor do I fancy an early grave, for my part." He dared to lay a reassuring hand on her arm. "Come now, Your Grace. Try not to worry. I have no intention of dying."

She stared at him. "That's what they *all* said."

"Mark my words, ma'am, I'll soon have it sorted. After all, there's a chance that you're right. That it's been a heart problem and mishaps. But if someone has done this, you'll have your revenge. I promise you that."

"Humph." She flicked his hand away and marched on, yet he suspected she felt comforted by his assurance.

Connor stepped out of her way and escorted the ladies back out to the top of the staircase. After gesturing to Aunt Florence to support herself on the banister, he took hold of Aunt Lucinda's elbow to steady her down the stairs.

She scowled at him but did not argue; Florence went ahead, as bidden, and they began their slow descent. Connor pondered their exchange while he braced the dragon's elbow.

Though he was stung by her general rudeness, he was not as offended as he might have been, all things considered.

She was a hard one, probably by nature, but on top of that, she was the ruling matriarch of a great house that had watched its heirs drop like flies for the past two years, starting with her own husband.

Connor had served in the military long enough to have seen a similar effect come over soldiers from regiments who'd suffered heavy casualties. They simply stopped letting themselves care about others, at least openly, refused to learn the names of new recruits, withdrew from their friends.

It was just a way of coping so that one could carry on.

Either that, or the woman was genuinely evil, and, given her sharp tongue, there was always that, he thought with sardonic humor.

When they reached the bottom of the stairs, Will ducked out the door and sent for the ladies' carriage.

Lucinda's walking stick made a slow, steady thump over the marble floor.

"No more duels," she repeated, pausing in the doorway as her carriage glided up in front of the house.

"I'm not going to let some fool insult my honor," he replied, folding his arms across his chest.

"Pigheaded man!" She seemed amazed at his quiet, steady defiance.

But he'd be damned if he was going to be pushed around by an old lady.

He got the feeling the dowager herself was starting to realize that too, as he assisted her down the few front stairs of his house, ignoring her fussy, ill-tempered attempts to brush him off every step of the way.

While the dragon thumped over to her barouche, where a footman cowered, Connor turned to assist her frail, wide-eyed companion.

Aunt Florence looked awed that he had not caved in to Lucinda's fire-breathing. Since she probably bore the brunt of it, he felt truly sorry for the dear little thing.

Taking pains to be solicitous, he helped her into her side of the ladies' carriage, then shut the door gently for her.

"Your Grace?" Aunt Florence said hesitantly through the open window. "I mean Connor."

"Yes, Aunt Florence?"

"I hope you will reconsider hiring Trumbull back someday. He could never... Poison?"

"Perhaps," he conceded, finding himself unable to disappoint her out of hand. "I will think on it."

"Oh, thank you!" She beamed. "Good day."

He bowed to her, then retreated to the pavement outside his house.

On that side of the carriage, Lucinda looked at him through her window. "We will see you in a fortnight. Come ready to choose a wife."

Connor gave no reply.

He had no bloody intention of marrying yet, let alone having his wife picked out for him from a preapproved stable of highborn broodmares.

There was no point in saying so, however. Not yet.

If the dragon sensed he was willing to at least heed her guidance on this matter, he stood a better chance of getting on her good side—provided she had one. That was probably the only way he'd ever get her to share with him whatever information he was already sure she was hiding.

"Good day, Connor!" Aunt Florence called again, leaning forward to be seen.

"Good day to you both. Thank you for calling on me, ladies. It was a pleasure meeting you."

"Humph." Lucinda glared at him out the window, as though she did not believe that for one second.

"Come back again soon," he said gallantly, tongue-in-cheek.

"Hang your Irish charm," she mumbled, then barked at her coachman: "Drive on!"

The carriage trundled off and drove to the corner, where it turned left, leaving Moonlight Square.

Connor stood there for a moment, pondering their exchange, as Will crept out onto the pavement toward him.

"Is she gone?"

"Aye. You can come out now."

"What a terrifying woman," he whispered.

Connor glanced wryly at him. "Cousin Richard was right. She

knows more than she's letting on."

Will frowned. "But, Major, if the duchess has information that could help solve murders in her own family, then…why wouldn't she share it?"

"Indeed," Connor murmured, nodding as he stared down the street. "That is the question."

CHAPTER 11

A Model Husband

When Maggie, her sister and maid returned from their shopping excursion, Delia marched off with her copy of *La Belle Assemblee*. "Lord, I'm exhausted! Think I'll lie down for a spell. Don't mind if I take this with me, do you, Mags?"

It was more a statement than a question, as she was already halfway up the stairs, but Maggie didn't object. "Just don't tear out any of the pages this time, please. I'd like to see them all first!" she called as her sister walked away.

Maggie and Penelope exchanged an arch look in the entrance hall, then Maggie gave her maid leave to go about her duties, and retired to her own room, ostensibly to relax.

Both she and Delia had no further social activities scheduled for the day, which left her afternoon free for getting started on her mission for Amberley.

Once she reached her room, a spacious chamber with pale blue wallpaper inspired by a Wedgwood design, Maggie set her reticule down on her dressing table, then took off her bonnet and set it on the wicker head form atop her chest of drawers. Next, she drew off her gloves, glad to be rid of them. She loosened her simple round gown, unbuttoned the lace collar, and then kicked off her shoes.

Finally, at her leisure, she returned to her dressing table and sat down on the cushioned stool, then picked up her reticule with an ominous feeling.

The time had come to memorize the duke's list of names.

And then burn it.

She shook her head at such peculiar instructions, but so be it.

It was all rather exciting. She opened her reticule with a momentous feeling, then drew out the piece of paper Amberley had given her and unfolded it, trembling a little to find out whose names would be written on there.

It was hard to imagine that anyone in Society could be so diabolical… Was it possible that someone she knew might turn out to be a murderer?

The first thing that struck her as she gazed at the list was Amberley's bold, decisive handwriting. He made his letters small and square, each deeply pressed into the paper, scrawled with force and certainty. She ran her fingertip over his writing, then turned her full attention to the names:

Lord Clayton Bexley
Gideon, Earl of Curnow
Mr. Benedict Dewitt
Bishop David, Baron Humphries
Mr. Barnaby Lynch

Oh, not Mr. Lynch. That's just silly, she thought at once, thinking of the kindly old man known to the ton as the Christmas elf. But the others? *Hmm.*

So these were the last men who'd met with Duke Rupert before someone had pushed him off that cliff. The other four names looked familiar, but she'd have to do some checking to find out who was who.

Of course, Amberley wanted more than what he could've easily learned for himself in any copy of *Debrett's*.

Some might be trickier than others, but as she began sinking her teeth into the task, she certainly felt equal to the challenge. She was just relieved there were no names listed that would give her an instant alarm. She resolved to provide her ally with a simple background sketch of each suspect.

But first she had to get them memorized.

As she worked on drilling the names into her brain in order, she was distracted by the sound of an argument that broke out a few minutes later one floor below her bedchamber.

Maggie rolled her eyes to realize Delia was badgering poor Edward again.

What is the matter this time, Your Majesty? she wondered.

In between her sister's shrill rasping came the lower, muffled tones of Edward's attempts to reason with her. God, why did the woman agitate herself so? Whatever anyone did for her, it was never enough.

Maggie did not understand why her sister was like this, but as usual, all she could do was shake her head and try to mind her own business.

Thankfully, the marital spat was short-lived. As usual, Edward must have surrendered or capitulated in one way or another, for that was the only way anyone could satisfy the redhead.

Delia had to win.

Maggie really did not know how her brother-in-law put up with it. The man was a saint. In any case, quiet was restored.

When Maggie was confident she'd memorized the names, she took the list and held it over a candle until the little flame consumed it. Holding it between her fingers, she set it on the wide brass base of her candleholder.

Then she carried it over to her bedroom window and opened the panes, letting the smoke escape and the ashes blow away.

While she stood there, she scanned Amberley House, wondering which window he would choose for their exchange of signals. There were so many to choose from, large as the house was.

With that thought, Maggie left her window and made sure she had two lanterns of her own on hand that she could use, should the need arise.

Soon she would start her research on each suspect, but with the first part of her assignment completed—the names memorized, the list burned—the next order of business was securing a proper introduction to the Duke of Amberley.

Edward.

The prospect of speaking to her brother-in-law about their handsome new neighbor admittedly made her feel a little embarrassed— and nervous, as well. As much as she adored Edward, she could not tell him the full truth. Amberley had bound her to secrecy.

Maggie gave herself a hard look in the mirror, then went to find Edward.

She followed the sound of his pianoforte all the way to the music room, where she found the marquess immersed in his playing.

Edward always practiced his music when he was annoyed. He was a very skilled player, quite fond of dreamy études.

Pale and pudgy as he was, Maggie sometimes suspected that her unassuming brother-in-law had a bit of a poet's soul.

She drifted in, enjoying the music and the glimmer of the late day sunshine reflecting off the pianoforte's glossy surface. A luxurious bouquet of spring flowers in a vase on a round table nearby perfumed the room.

Maggie leaned her hip against the scrolled arm of the striped satin couch and folded her arms across her chest, listening with pleasure.

Edward stopped practicing abruptly, glancing over at her in surprise.

"How now, sister," he said pleasantly. "Have you been there long? I only just noticed you."

"Only for a moment." She smiled.

"Ah. And how is our dear Mags this afternoon?"

"Very well. You needn't stop on my account. I was quite enjoying listening to that. You really are so talented."

"Nonsense," he said with a shine of pleasure in his eyes at her compliment. "I merely amuse myself."

"Well, I like it," she declared.

"Was there something you required?" he asked as he turned to her on the bench and stretched his fingers, cracking his knuckles.

She opened her mouth, ready to launch into her request, but she remembered the couple's spat and gave a sympathetic wince. "Are you all right?" she asked tactfully.

"Of course," he said. "Why wouldn't I be?"

"Oh, I, er… I don't mean to pry. I heard—a bit of a commotion earlier. I hope Delia wasn't too awful to you."

He laughed. "I don't let these things concern me overmuch."

Still, Maggie couldn't help but wince. "I know. Still, I'm sorry if she was hurtful to you. I love my sister, but I know she can be…difficult at times."

Edward slid her a conspiratorial smile and tinkled the high keys with one hand. "She is fiery," he admitted, but that was all.

Maggie studied him, intrigued.

"What is it, Mags?" he asked. "You look perplexed."

"How in the world are you so patient with her? Doesn't she drive you absolutely mad?"

He laughed. "I'm good at forgiving," he said, unruffled.

Maggie nodded. "Apparently so." She stopped herself from saying

120   *Gaelen Foley*

more, though. She did not wish to overstep her bounds.

"Ah, don't worry, you see, I have a strategy." Edward ran one hand over the keys, serene as ever.

"You do?"

"Mmm." He nodded. "Back when we were courting, and I first realized your sister's...mercurial nature, I decided to forgive her in advance for whatever she might do. With a few specified exceptions, of which she is well aware. Beyond that, I simply let it go."

"That is admirable, I suppose."

"Love doesn't hold a grudge."

"How sweet," she murmured, and meant it. "She's fortunate to have so devoted a mate."

"To be honest, Mags, I think she's harder on you than she is on me." He glanced at her as the tune he was playing shifted keys. "You must be awfully ready to marry Lord Bryce and be on your way from here."

She lowered her gaze, a little chagrined that he'd noticed her unhappiness. "Please don't think me ungrateful. You've given me such a lovely home here. Your house is beautiful, and you and your staff could not be kinder. It's just—"

"Now, now. You should know better than that. You never have to explain yourself to me, my dear. Our home is your home. You are Delia's flesh and blood. I can only imagine the disruption you've experienced since your father died and left you with no choice but to pack up your things and move out of the only home you'd ever known. Trust me, you will always be welcome here."

She smiled tenderly at him. He was such a rock, this man.

"Thank you, Edward, but..." She sighed. "I'm not sure Delia would agree."

He sent her a twinkling glance, then played a few formidable chords in the low keys, as though dramatizing Delia's wrath. "Oh, but you are mistaken. Her Ladyship loves having someone else to boss around besides just me. And I, for my part, appreciate having a fellow prisoner to commiserate with."

He sent her a wink, and Maggie laughed with affection.

"So, what is on your mind, then?" he asked as he played more slowly.

"Actually, it has to do with Lord Bryce."

He looked askance at her, then turned the page of his music book. "I trust you are well recovered from the duel? It was quite upsetting. I was not in favor of going, but of course, the redhead insisted."

"Edward, may I be frank with you?"

"Always."

Maggie went over and propped an elbow on the pianoforte, gazing at him earnestly. "After Lord Bryce's behavior, calling out the duke and making such outrageous accusations against him, I suddenly find myself wanting nothing more to do with him." She shook her head. "I don't want to be courted by him anymore, and I certainly don't want to marry him. It was awful, how he treated Amberley. To make such accusations against a newcomer to town without the slightest proof. I could simply never marry such a lug-head."

He laughed, glancing up at her. "Well, Mags, if I may be frank with *you*, in turn, I always thought that Bryce was a bit of a horse's ass, m'self. Sorry."

She lifted her eyebrows. This was the strongest condemnation of anyone she had ever heard Edward utter.

"If he is a hothead, to boot, starting duels like that, then I fully agree. He is not for you. As a husband, he could really leave you in a lurch if he went out and got himself killed. But, of course, the heart does what it wills, so if you love him—"

"I don't," she interrupted.

He scanned her face. "You sound very sure."

"I am. I'm sorry if I sound like a fickle female, but after the way he acted today, I find myself suddenly and completely indifferent to his existence. I'm not even angry." She shook her head. "I just want to be done with him."

Edward winced. "That is bad."

"I know." Maggie nodded. "Our courtship...is over. I just have to inform *him* of that—which I am not looking forward to—but there's no point in pretending. I only wonder how such a coxcomb will take the rejection."

"Probably not very well," Edward admitted. He paused. "Do you want me to speak to him for you?"

"Thanks, but I couldn't live with myself if I took the cowardly way out." She sighed. "He deserves to hear it from me. Or read it, perhaps... Yes, that's better. I think I'll just write it out in a note."

Edward swallowed any comment he might've made about that.

"In the meanwhile," Maggie continued, "I am troubled by the damage he's done to the Duke of Amberley's reputation, all for no reason. This man is our neighbor. Bryce not only shot him, he also cast aspersions on His Grace's honor before anyone else even had a chance to get to know him. It's really not fair."

"I don't disagree. I daresay that whole debacle at the Grand Albion reflected poorly on all of Moonlight Square. Made all of us look arrogant and inhospitable. Amberley *does* seem to keep to himself. Still."

"I am so glad to hear you feel that way," Maggie said. Her pulse was pounding now that she'd come to the heart of the matter. "Because, as it happens, I was rather wondering…if you don't mind…the next time you see His Grace at your club, perhaps it would be an appropriate gesture of goodwill if you could, um, introduce yourself to him? At least to show him we're not all like Bryce around here."

"That," he replied, "is an excellent idea, my dear."

"You'll do it?"

"Yes, why not?" He eyed her curiously.

Maggie beamed at his answer. "And then…once he's become your acquaintance—if it wouldn't be too much trouble, of course—maybe you could introduce him formally…to me?"

"Aha." Edward's fingers slipped across the keys in a discordant jangle as he turned on the piano bench to stare at her. He started laughing and wagged a finger at her. "Clever girl. Oh, you Winthrop girls are such vixens. So quickly poor Bryce is replaced!"

"Yes, but what an improvement, don't you think?" She laughed along with him. She couldn't stop grinning as she rocked back and forth on her toes, then gave a nonchalant shrug. "A girl could do worse."

"Well, by Jove," he said softly, "if you've got to marry someone, might as well aim high, what?"

"The debutante's creed, dear brother."

"Quite so. How else could the likes of me have snared a beauty like your sister?" He let out a self-deprecating laugh. "Imagine you, a duchess."

"You never know." Maggie left her perch beside the pianoforte and went over to give him an affectionate half-hug while he plinked a few ivory keys. She kissed him atop his balding head. "Thank you, dearest Edward. You are truly a prince among men."

"Ah, those Winthrop girls," he drawled as she twirled around and headed for the door, "always dragging a fellow into mischief."

Maggie laughed, her step light as she went on her way.

CHAPTER 12

The Country Dance

onnor could not deny that Lady Maggie had been right. Her brother-in-law, Edward, Lord Birdwell, was a most amiable fellow.

The portly, balding marquess had ambled over and introduced himself to Connor at the club, where he had been sitting alone, reading the *Times*.

In all, Connor was a little amused to find Maggie's plan progressing along so nicely, since this much of it was her doing.

Tonight, precisely one week after Bryce's challenging him to the duel, at the next Thursday night subscription ball at the Grand Albion, Connor was expecting Birdwell to provide the promised introduction.

For his part, it was not altogether easy for him to walk into the place after last week's explosion. He'd become even more of a curiosity now after the duel.

The music did not stop playing when he walked in, but a significant number of people turned to stare.

Thankfully, he did not have to stand around by himself for very long. Rivenwood and his beautiful bride, Serena, spotted him among the crowd and made their way over at once to greet him.

"Amberley." The pale-haired, silver-eyed, and decidedly mysterious Azrael, Duke of Rivenwood, tore his attention away from his raven-haired duchess to shake Connor's hand.

"Good to see you," Connor replied.

"Your Grace," Serena greeted him with a knowing smile. "We hear you've been *busy*."

"Ah yes," he said with a sigh, grinning at her. Rivenwood had himself a great beauty in his new bride, all bristling velvet lashes, rosy cheeks, and generous curves. Serena offered him a curtsy, and Connor bowed in turn.

"So how have you been getting on?" Azrael asked discreetly, a knowing gleam in his quicksilver eyes.

Serena gave Connor a cheeky poke in the arm. "Fancy that, darling," she said to her husband, "our own neighbor getting into a duel. I never heard of such shocking behavior."

"Well, I didn't start the thing," Connor said.

"I hear you ended it, though," said Azrael.

"And with some style," Serena said, nodding.

Connor frowned at her teasing, unsure how to take it.

The duchess laughed. "Ah, do not be troubled, Your Grace. I'm merely delighted that my husband is not alone in being the oddment around here anymore."

"Welcome to the club, sir," Rivenwood said.

"Don't worry, their morbid curiosity about you will pass," she assured Connor.

"I just hope I don't get shot again," he grumbled.

"Yes, do try to avoid that," Serena agreed.

"I'll drink to that." Azrael lifted his glass, and Connor clanked his own with it gratefully, while the crowd milled around them, sending both men surreptitious glances.

"Ah, Lord Birdwell," Connor said, turning when he spotted his newest acquaintance approaching, his haughty wife on his arm.

Lady Birdwell studied Connor guardedly. Behind her, peeking over her shoulder, Connor could just make out his lovely accomplice.

Though Maggie was still somewhat hidden by her sister and brother-in-law, he could see her peeking over her sister's shoulder at him. The intricate design of her chestnut hair was beautiful, entwined with strings of pearls that caught the light of the chandeliers.

His heart skipped a beat, like a horse's quick stumble beneath him.

Edward gave Azrael a wary smile. "Your Grace."

Greetings were exchanged. Lady Birdwell curtsied to the Rivenwoods, and Serena curtsied back with a hint of irony dancing in her dark hazel eyes. Connor got the feeling she bore no great love for Maggie's elder sister, and, indeed, seemed to take all the pretensions of

Society as a lark.

No wonder Azrael and she were so well suited for each other, Connor thought. The outsider and the blithe, daring beauty. He couldn't help rather envying the couple's effortless harmony with each other.

Then Birdwell pulled his wife aside so that dainty Lady Maggie could come forth into view. Connor hid a dazzled gulp when he saw her.

She looked absolutely ravishing in a pink ball gown with rosettes pinning up the overskirt at about knee level, to reveal a lacy white petticoat beneath. He could just make out the toes of her cream-colored dancing slippers.

The gown had a generous sweep across her milky-white bosom, revealing far more of her tempting flesh tonight than the high-necked lace collar of the day gown she had been wearing at the arcade. It exposed the tops of her shoulders, and he was filled with a longing to kiss them.

"Ahem, Amberley," said Edward, "I'm not sure you've had the pleasure of meeting my womenfolk yet."

"No, I have not, my lord."

"Delia," he said, turning first to his wife, then smiling conspiratorially at his sister-in-law, "Maggie. Allow me to present Connor Forbes, the Duke of Amberley. Your Grace, this is my wife, Delia, Lady Birdwell, and her sister, Lady Margaret Winthrop."

Connor bowed, his pulse surging as he tried to keep from openly gawking at Maggie. "Lady Birdwell. Lady Margaret. The honor is mine."

"Your Grace," the sisters said in unison. They both curtsied to him, the marchioness bowing her head, but still eyeing him skeptically.

Lady Maggie, however, blushed on cue like a rose. He saw with amusement that she had been telling the truth: she really *was* terrible at hiding her emotions. But he was delighted by her obvious excitement to see him again.

The feeling was most definitely mutual.

"It's a pleasure to meet you, Your Grace," she said demurely—as though she'd never whacked him with her reticule, let alone shown him her charming ankles.

As Connor met her sparkling gaze, it was all he could do to temper his smile. He felt oddly relieved to be with her again. At last there was one true ally for him in this place—never mind that he'd roped her into it.

"Are you enjoying the ball this week, Your Grace?" her sister inquired.

"A great deal more than last week, to be sure, Lady Birdwell."

Delia's lips quirked at his refusal to shy away from what everybody knew had happened.

"What a frightful situation," Maggie interjected, glancing worriedly at her sister, then back at him. "Is your side feeling better?"

Connor brought a hand unconsciously to his still-bandaged wound. "Thank you, yes, Lady Margaret. I heal quickly." He paused. "I was fortunate."

"I daresay it was Lord Bryce who was fortunate," Birdwell mumbled.

The others agreed.

Just then, there was a pause in the music; a moment later, the caller announced a country dance.

Serena turned to her lord with a radiant smile. "Shall we, darling?"

Azrael tilted his head, shoulders drooping. "Must we?"

"Oh, come, husband!"

"Can't we at least wait for the waltz? I don't mind that one so much," he protested, but he nevertheless let her lead him away by the hand as the others laughed.

Connor turned to his "new" acquaintance once more and seized his opportunity. "Lady Margaret, would you do me the honor of a dance?"

The slight, bell-shaped flare of her skirts swayed as she took a step toward him at once. "Why, I'd be delighted!"

Her sister glanced warily from one to the other. "Um, that could start another duel."

"Doesn't bother me," he said. "Though, next time, I don't think I'll miss."

"I can dance with whomever I please," Maggie said pertly to her sister.

The marchioness stared at her, as though sizing her up. Then Delia just shrugged, looking miffed.

Connor offered Maggie his arm and she took it. Her touch did things to him. Made his blood leap, his pulse quicken.

The Birdwells did not join them, staying behind as Connor escorted his petite partner toward the lines forming up for the country dance.

Lady Maggie held her chin high, as though acutely aware of everyone staring at them.

He wondered if she knew this was his first foray onto a dance floor as a member of the London ton. He was no more enthusiastic about dancing than Azrael was, but he'd had the usual training for a lad with aristocratic bloodlines. It wasn't as though he'd embarrass himself.

Ah, but fair Lady Margaret, *she* carried herself like a swan. Her grace was impeccable. Even his mother would be impressed, Connor thought.

He was proud to be seen with such an elegant beauty on his arm.

As an added reward, her choice of him as her partner this evening was a bold and obvious rebuke to Lord Bryce for his behavior at last week's event.

It took courage, he thought, to stand with him against this roomful of strangers.

"Well?" Connor murmured discreetly as they joined the queue of dancers lining up with their partners for the opening promenade. "Was your sister correct? Do you think Bryce will call me out again for asking you to dance?"

"If he does, you have my permission to shoot him this time," she said wryly.

"Huzzah," he replied.

Her smile widened. "I very much doubt it, though, considering I broke off our courtship several days ago."

Connor froze. "Did you, now?"

She nodded sweetly.

He could not hide his satisfaction on hearing this news. "Bravo, my lady. Sounds as though we have much to discuss."

"Yes." She gave him a meaningful nod. "I have obtained the information you wanted, as well."

"Not here," he murmured, then glanced around and gave her a look that said, *Too many people.*

Perhaps later this evening, they could manage to steal a few minutes apart from this throng to speak privately.

She nodded, but could not resist one cloaked comment. "I will tell you this, though: it's all good news."

He glanced at her in surprise; she smiled with a coy shrug.

Then the music began, and the promenade line began streaming forward.

They had to follow the row of couples striding up the center of the dance floor, hand in hand. Maggie's gloved fingers rested atop Connor's as he led the way, paying watchful attention for the next moves expected of him.

"Is your wound really healing well, or were you just saying that in front of the others?" she asked with a fretful glance.

"I wasn't lying," he answered. "I am still keeping it bandaged, though, so I won't be dancing too vigorously."

She looked at him in alarm. "Are you sure you want to do this? Perhaps we should sit down—"

Her words broke off when he scowled at her for being a mother hen.

"Or not." She arched a brow, then looked away and licked her pretty lips. "Well," she said after a moment, "at least now we are officially acquainted, Your Grace."

"Yes," he agreed as they took a playful backward hop with the rest of the line. "That will make things easier."

"God bless Edward," she said.

"He is a good man. But I must ask you—" Alas, his question had to wait, for the two lines duly separated then, leaving them facing each other with five feet of dance floor between them.

Lady Maggie stood across from him now, twitching her skirts a little with a saucy glow in her eyes, and Lord, he enjoyed the view.

"Why have you not signaled for me, dear lady?" he murmured when they stepped together again briefly. "You left me bereft all week."

"I knew that I would see you soon enough. Besides, the news is not all that exciting, as I said. And…" She hesitated. "To tell the truth…I was afraid."

They backed apart again on the beat, while Connor pondered this.

"Not of me, surely?" he asked in a soft tone when he'd captured her again, one hand around her waist for a slow, stately, and almost intimate spin.

"No, not of you, of course," she said warmly, gazing up at him with that open sincerity that he'd already grown used to somehow.

It was an enchanting quality, this artless vulnerability of hers, and as for her sweet body, she felt so delicate in his arms. She barely came up to his heart, and everything in him wanted to shelter her from a world that held more darkness than the innocent creature knew.

"I told you, Your Grace, I am not very daring. I'm glad to help you figure out who's been trying to—you know. But it did not seem like *such* an emergency, since I knew I would be seeing you here tonight. Why risk the scandal? Besides," she added as they changed directions, "there's not much to tell. I'm glad you didn't waste *your* time on this list, because it would've merely sent you chasing down a rabbit trail. I'm afraid there's nothing *there*."

"Hmm." They parted again, but as the dance picked up in tempo, it was impossible to discuss much of anything, especially since Connor had to concentrate on the half-forgotten motions.

God knew, he had not had much occasion for dancing over the past decade. But he took his cue as discreetly as he could from the other gents in the line.

At one point, while they waited for alternating couples to sashay past, weaving back and forth, Connor noticed a pretty auburn-haired lady waving eagerly to Maggie, trying to get her attention.

Connor pointed her out, and Maggie gasped when she saw her, waving back. "Trinny!"

"Who's that?" he asked when it was their turn to join hands and sashay along.

"That's my friend, Lady Roland. Oh, I'm so happy to see her out in Society again! She had a baby—her first—at the end of February, so she's been in confinement for ages. 'Twas a boy," she added.

"Well done," he replied.

"Ah, she's very dear. I'll have to introduce you to her and her husband, Gable, Lord Roland. You'll like him. He's very, hmm, easygoing."

"Like Edward?"

"No, Gable's much more of a cynic."

Connor smiled. When Maggie flashed another fond grin in the new mother's direction, he noted the glow in her eyes. Her affection for her friend made her even lovelier.

"What?" she murmured when she noticed him gazing at her as they stood still again.

"You look very beautiful tonight."

The compliment appeared to startle her. "Why thank you, charming sir. You're looking rather dashing yourself."

He arched a brow, enjoying this young lady's company more than anything he'd experienced yet in his new life as a duke.

Far too soon, the figures of the dance pulled them away from each other, and, much to his surprise, Connor felt a twinge of jealousy when he had to surrender her to a smiley, yellow-haired chap.

"Lord Sidney!" she greeted him.

"Why, Lady Maggie, my dear! Heard you gave ol' Bryce the sack, you little vixen," the man teased her. "You must tell me everything."

She laughed. "What, didn't you already hear the details at your club?"

"There were wagers on it, actually."

"I say!"

"Couldn't take him anymore, eh?" the smiley chap jested, while Connor grew increasingly annoyed at his familiarity with her.

It did not help that this Sidney fellow was unreasonably good-looking. The man-about-town sort of rake that made ladies swoon.

"Still," Lord Sidney continued, "glad as I'm sure you must be to get rid of him, isn't it a bit soon to be fraternizing with the enemy?" The chap sent a mischievous glance in Connor's direction—and promptly caught him eavesdropping.

Never mind that Connor was a trained intelligence officer.

Sidney flashed a knowing grin, and Connor quickly looked away—but not before he noted that there was nothing but harmless mirth in the man's eyes. He realized then that Sidney's roguish attitude toward Maggie was that of a friend, not an interested suitor.

Connor harrumphed anyway, and thankfully managed to look elsewhere before Maggie also realized he'd been listening. He smiled at the woman he'd been paired with for the moment.

She regarded him with uncertainty, while he continued eavesdropping on his erstwhile partner's conversation.

"Well, he's not *my* enemy," Lady Maggie declared, much to Connor's satisfaction. "It was ridiculous of Bryce to call him out. Amberley is a lovely man, and our neighbor."

A lovely man? McFeatheridge would've laughed his head off at that one.

"A crack shot, too, from what I hear," said Sidney.

"To be sure," Maggie said. "I'd be pleased to introduce you. Then you could help me introduce Amberley around."

"I'd be honored," Sidney said, while Connor bristled with self-consciousness.

No, thank you. Still chagrined over being caught in his odd moment of jealousy, Connor did his best once more to try paying at least *some* attention to his current partner.

He forced a smile despite the fact that the lady took his hand for the next figure with a pursed-mouth look of distaste. Connor rolled his eyes at her obvious prejudice against him as an Irishman and gave her a matter-of-fact stare.

Her judgmental expression turned to a blanch as she caught on that her rude thoughts were written all over her haughty face.

Connor had never been gladder to return to his original partner than when Maggie came skipping back to him, sprightly and charming.

Thank God.

"You dance well, my lady," he said, holding on to her hand firmly this time, like he'd never let go. The thought of keeping her was tempting indeed.

She beamed. "Why, thank you, Your Grace. So do you."

"No, I don't. And everybody hates me."

She laughed. "No, they don't! *I* don't. The Rivenwoods don't. Nor does Edward."

"Well, your sister does."

"Oh, Delia hates everyone, including me."

"Impossible," he said. "Listen—" he started, but she was snatched away from him again by the old, familiar grapevine move, the lines of the dancers whisking along, hand over hand.

Dammit, couldn't he just sit her down and have a simple conversation?

But of course not. He was a bachelor, she was a deb, and they'd have to have a chaperone present, at the least.

He tried to stay agreeable, but he was losing patience with this.

Hang Society's rules.

"Psst, Amberley," she whispered when they were briefly reunited. "There's the fourth person from your list. Over there." As her dainty hand alighted on his, she flicked one finger just for a heartbeat toward the doorway.

Connor looked over, intrigued. Since he, too, had memorized the list of names culled from Richard's diary, he recalled that the fourth man was Bishop Lord Humphries. "Red waistcoat?"

She nodded, and he inspected the fellow: a portly, middle-aged man, bald on top, shaggy fringe of hair around the sides of his head.

The unassuming clergyman stood peering through his spectacles at the gathering, thumbs hooked into his vest pockets.

Admittedly, he did not look like any sort of vicious murderer that Connor could've imagined. There was absolutely nothing threatening about the man.

"See what I mean?" Maggie said. "They're all like that: harmless as houseplants. I'll give you details when we talk."

Connor was looking forward to that with increasing fervor.

In fact, his hunt for his would-be murderer aside, a second goal had begun taking shape in his mind. And it had everything to do with his pretty accomplice.

"So, who is your friend, Lady Margaret?" he asked with a nod toward Monsieur Smiley, who was now working his charm on some ravishing blonde.

"Oh, that's just Sidney." She chuckled. "If Moonlight Square had its own mayor, I daresay, it would be him. He knows *everyone*. I shall introduce you!" she said brightly.

"That's all right," he said.

"What? You don't want to meet him, grumpy face?"

Connor just looked at her.

"He's very friendly. Though a bit of a prankster."

He looked like a well-heeled dandy to Connor. The sort of idle rake for which a military man had no use.

"Trust me, you'll like him. It's impossible not to."

"Want to bet?" Connor said, playing the curmudgeon.

"Pshaw," Maggie said, a knowing twinkle in her eyes. "I thought you said you needed allies. Well? I mean to give them to you. People I know. People I trust."

He supposed he couldn't argue with that. He nodded his thanks.

The dance set ended on that note, and they exchanged the obligatory curtsy and bow.

Connor was loath to let her go, but he'd barely released her hand when her auburn-haired friend was already by her side, greeting her with a quick hug.

"Maggie, my dear!"

"Trinny! You are radiant. How is the baby?"

The woman released her to clutch at her heart with a sigh. "Wonderful!"

"Except for all the screaming, of course," drawled an urbane-looking man with black hair, who now joined them. "The boy's got lungs fit for the opera house."

Maggie laughed; Connor couldn't take his eyes off her.

"Congratulations, Lord Roland. Listen, you two," she said, "I don't know if you've met our new neighbor yet. Your Grace, these are my friends, Lord and Lady Roland. Trinny, Gable—the Duke of Amberley."

"Oh, it's so nice to meet you!" Lady Roland gushed as Connor sketched a taut bow. "I've been locked up in my house for months—well, not literally—but, I tell you, I have been *so* intensely curious to find out all I've been missing, which I see includes you! How do you like living in Moonlight Square, Your Grace?"

They had a friendly chat and more people accrued around them. Azrael and Serena drifted over along with another couple, the brawny, dark-eyed Duke of Netherford, whom Connor had noted at the club, and the gorgeous blonde whom Sidney had been chatting up. *She* turned out to be Netherford's wife, Felicity.

True to her word, Maggie introduced him to them all.

Connor took a guarded interest in all his new acquaintances, but, still feeling like a fish out of water among all these English aristocrats, he was glad that Maggie stayed nearby. Watching the group, he soon concluded that, while Trinny and Felicity were the best of friends, both women clearly loved Maggie.

Serena got on well with her and the rest of them, too, though the raven-haired beauty was a bit more reserved, just like her mysterious husband.

Connor tensed anew when Lord Sidney strolled over to them, all elegant nonchalance. Maggie introduced the two of them, as threatened. Connor greeted the chap skeptically, but Sidney merely seemed amused at this wariness.

Apparently, the territorial glint in Connor's glance earlier had not been lost on the happy-go-lucky viscount. But Sidney seemed to have shrugged it off, and it dawned on Connor that the ridiculously handsome man was probably used to that reaction from other males. Begrudgingly, he supposed it wasn't Sidney's fault that women likely adored him wherever he went.

Yet all the ladies present seemed to have sensibly figured out for themselves that Lord Sidney was a natural flirt, whose attentions, though pleasant, meant absolutely nothing.

"So you were in the Army, then, yes?" Sidney did not wait for Connor's reply, beckoning to someone through the crowd. "You'll have to meet Felicity's brother—also a major, as it happens. Major Peter Carvel. I'm sure he'll be happy to meet a fellow soldier in this place, instead of all us lie-abouts."

"It's Danger-man!" Trinny whispered to Maggie with a giggle as Major Peter Carvel came sauntering over to them, answering the summons from Sidney.

Unlike Connor, this major was in full dress uniform for the formal occasion. He had the weathered complexion, rugged air, and haunted eyes of so many of their breed. But he smiled as he joined his sister.

"Yes, what is it, Sid?"

"Peter, we've got a new neighbor," Felicity informed him, slipping one arm around her brother's waist.

Connor noticed the siblings had the same blue-green eyes, though Peter's hair was light brown, while Felicity's was golden.

"Ah," said Carvel. The fellow veteran looked questioningly at Connor, and Sidney made short work of the introductions.

"Your Grace, this is Major Peter Carvel. Pete, this is the Duke of Amberley. I hear he was at Waterloo."

"Were you?" Carvel asked, sounding impressed, though he gave Connor the brief once-over, assessing him in a glance, as was the way of their kind.

Connor nodded, sizing him up in turn. "You?"

"Missed it," Carvel said, shaking his head. "I was in India. Thought the damned thing was over after Boney's first abdication, sold my commission, and wouldn't you know it, missed the best part."

"Oh, I don't know about that," Connor said ruefully as they exchanged a handshake of mutual respect.

It turned out Sidney was right. After taking each other's measure, both Connor and Carvel seemed to take a certain relief in finding a fellow veteran among the civilian crowd.

"So, what did you do in India?" Connor asked, genuinely curious.

"Bit of surveying for the East India Company. Then, with Netherford's funding, undertook a private expedition to explore the northern provinces."

"Fascinating," Connor said.

"It was. Like entering some fantastical realm. Jungles. Cloud forests, tigers, wild elephants. Went as far as the Himalayas..."

Felicity beamed with pride in her adventurer brother and Maggie smiled as the two majors embarked on a conversation about their various experiences.

Bit by bit, Connor could feel his tension dissolving. When he noticed Maggie listening, he sent her a discreet glance of appreciation. It was no small gift she had given him tonight.

Perhaps he would yet find a welcome in his new home.

❖

It was later in the evening, while Connor was nursing a brandy alongside Gable, Lord Roland, when the first-time father offered him unexpected condolences. "You know, I was very sorry to hear about your cousin Richard dying in that accident, Your Grace. It must've been horrible for your family."

"Thank you. That is very kind of you to say. To be honest, though, I hardly knew any of my London relatives before I inherited the title. I only met my uncles once as a lad—the first and second dukes. And Richard was just an infant at the time."

"What a spate of bad luck to hit your family," Gable remarked.

"Indeed," Connor said darkly.

"Well," Gable said with a nonchalant shrug, "as it happens, my father, Lord Sefton, knew all three of your predecessors rather well through his efforts in the House of Lords. If you'd ever like to ask him about them, I'd be happy to introduce you."

Connor cocked his head. "Really? I'll take you up on that, if it's not too much trouble. There's so much that I'd like to know."

"Of course," Gable said, then quirked a half-smile. "Although it might cost you a vote or two in the Lords, knowing him. Father lives and breathes politics. If you're a Whig, he may try and convert you."

"A Whig." Connor scoffed. He had yet to find one in the Army.

Gable grinned. "Tory, then? In that case, I'm sure you will find him at your service, Your Grace. Shall I set up the meeting?"

"I'd be much obliged. I have quite a few questions regarding my predecessors."

"Consider it done," Gable replied. "Father usually takes appointments on Mondays, if you're free."

"Certainly, just let me know what time. And thanks."

Standing on the other side of Gable all the while, his wife had been talking to the other women, but must have been half listening to their exchange, as she now jumped into the conversation.

"I'm sure my father-in-law can enlighten you about your deceased relatives, Your Grace, but what about the *living* relatives?" Trinny asked pertly. "Have you been getting to know any of them yet?"

Connor smiled at the question. "Well, actually, my Grandaunt Lucinda came by to scold me after the duel—as if I'd called myself out."

Silence dropped, and every one of his new acquaintances blanched at the mention of the dragon. A few even gasped at the name. The ladies went wide-eyed, the men pulled back with diverse looks of dread, and though no one dared utter an impolite word, Connor laughed.

"I take it you know her."

"Er, yes, Your Grace. The dowager duchess is…quite a grand lady," Sidney offered with admirable tact.

Connor grinned. "That's one way to put it, I reckon."

They all started laughing self-consciously to realize that he, too, had experienced Aunt Lucinda's fearsome ways.

"Bless her," he said, "Her Grace is hosting a soirée in my honor, officially welcoming me to London. You all should come—if you dare."

They laughed at his quip.

"When is it?" asked Maggie.

"Friday next. Do come, all of you, if you're free. I know it's late notice, but I'll make sure you receive invitations. I'd be quite pleased to see you all there. Especially you, Lady Margaret," he teased, glancing over.

He caught her gazing dreamily at him, and she bit her lip. But watching him chatting with her friends clearly made the girl happy.

Connor held her gaze just a little longer than he probably ought in front of so many people. But in that moment, he made a decision.

Now that she was no longer attached, he was placing Lady Margaret Winthrop's name at the very top of his aunt's silly bride list.

Whether the ol' dragon liked it or not.

CHAPTER 13

A Thorough Report

*M*aggie couldn't believe how fast two hours had sped by in Amberley's presence. Perhaps he possessed some mysterious Irish magic that he'd brought with him from the Emerald Isle. But certainly, he'd brought his Irish charm, and he'd used it to work an effortless enchantment on everyone around them that night.

Especially her.

In her fascination, she noted several new things of interest about him. One: his brogue deepened after his third draught of whiskey, though his brilliant blue eyes never turned red or glazed. *Good.*

Two: he was polite to the ladies, but the formidable major was clearly a man's man. He got on well with the lords of Moonlight Square, easily earning their respect with his authoritative bearing.

It had pleased Maggie deeply to look around at her circle of acquaintances and know they had taken him in—in part because of her. She'd certainly never needed to take such bother for Bryce, who was as nonchalantly independent as a cat. But the threat to Amberley's life, and the gunshot wound he'd received from her former suitor—these things had jolted her out of her anxious preoccupation with her own marital fate, and back to her more customary mode of concern for others.

She regretted having let the discomfort of her current living situation turn her so self-centered for a while there. It really wasn't like her. She did find, however, that it was easier to ignore Delia's petty insults and so forth by focusing on Amberley's far more serious situation. What did courtship really matter when someone out there was trying to kill you? Her problems seemed so small by comparison. No, courtship could wait.

Although, she mused, taking another long sip from her second glass of strong fruit punch, *it might be possible to think of both at the same time…*

To be sure, it filled her with a spinning sense of excitement to look over and catch Amberley's eye amid the crowd; the way he looked at her reminded her afresh—viscerally—of their secrets together and their shared task.

He remained discreet, though, true to his word. She was quite sure her reputation was safe with this man.

As he carried on his conversation with Netherford and Major Carvel, Maggie savored the sight of him in their midst, his raven-black hair and cliff-like shoulders towering over the ladies gathered in their group.

She refused to stare, half listening to Trinny detailing her new baby's habits, but inside, Maggie was still counting things she'd noticed about her new neighbor.

Three: someone must've told the Irishman at some point in his life that blue was his color, for the sky-blue waistcoat he'd chosen beneath his impeccably fitted black tailcoat turned his eyes the dark cobalt of the sea just below the horizon, like she'd seen once on a trip to Brighton.

Finally, the fourth thing she noticed was that he did not dance with any other girls that night, and this pleased her immensely. She should not have liked to share him. But then she remembered abruptly that, in fact, he was not *hers* to share or withhold.

Not yet. But maybe, one day, when no one was trying to kill him anymore…

And so passed two hours in this fashion, much to her surprise. When Amberley meandered his way over to her side and leaned down to murmur in her ear, her heart pounded faster.

As he headed toward her, she wasn't sure if he was going to ask her to dance again or what, but he suggested, with his warm breath a beguiling tickle at her ear, that now might be a good time for them to steal away for a brief, private talk.

Oh God yes. Talk? Her body had other ideas, but she ignored them.

She knew he only meant so she could give him the information she'd collected on his list of suspects. Hiding her eagerness, she glanced up at him with a subtle nod. He straightened up to his full height and gave her a *follow me* sort of glance, like at the bookshop.

Of course, she had the sense to let him get a good lead on her before drifting away from her friends. Tall as he was, it was easy to note his winding course through the thronged ballroom; it was past eleven, and the Grand Albion was now bursting at the seams with the crème de la crème of London Society.

The music played on, the couples danced, the wine and spirits flowed, and the hum of conversation had now risen to a dull roar.

Clever boy, she thought as she watched him saunter out of the wide doorway at the back corner of the ballroom.

Beyond it, Maggie knew, lay a landing, where a red-carpeted staircase both descended to an outdoor terrace, where the gentlemen were welcome to smoke, and ascended to the next floor, where the hotel had provided an opulent ladies' lounge with all the conveniences.

These two options were clearly meant to provide the two of them with their ruse.

His Grace had planned this rendezvous with care, she thought with slightly giddy amusement. But it was well that she'd already drunk most of that second glass of punch—the remainder of which had gone warm in her hand—otherwise, she might not have had the nerve to follow her co-conspirator into the recesses of the hotel with hundreds of people present.

A tipsy giggle escaped her for some reason—what, she now laughed at the prospect of ruin? But she shushed these thoughts away like wooly sheep blocking a country lane. Everything would be fine.

Amberley's self-assurance was contagious.

So far, so good. With the ballroom at full capacity, it was easy to weave her way among the crowd until she was far away from her usual circle of friends.

When she finally stepped through the back corner doorway, the staircase was thankfully empty—except for His Grace, who was already racing up the stairs at top speed, passing by the floor with the ladies' lounge.

She pressed her lips together to hold back another nervous laugh as he bent down to beckon her with an insistent look before springing up the last stair, out of view.

It was only after he'd vanished that she noted he had somehow kept his footsteps silent. *One might almost deduce he has done this sort of thing before,* she thought, holding back another giggle.

Anyway, since *he* was the one venturing into forbidden territory around the ladies' lounge—not her—Maggie took the stairs at a more dignified pace, moving sedately. All the while, she was still fighting tipsy laughter. Sneaking away to meet a man in the middle of a ball?

She had never done anything so daring in her life. Well, except for last Thursday night, when she'd gone knocking on his door close to midnight. Lord, if anybody ever found out...

She smiled politely as two ladies emerged from the women's private lounge and came bustling down the steps. Maggie nodded to them, waited a beat, and then, with her glass dangling from her gloved fingertips, she climbed the rest of the stairs oh so casually, one hand sliding along the banister.

But the moment she reached the landing, instead of heading for the nearby lounge, she glanced up at the next story, where, suddenly, a handsome head poked out over the staircase, peering down at her.

He beckoned to her again, and Maggie grinned. With a glance this way and that, she whirled to set her glass on a tray table by the wall, then hitched up her skirts and bolted up the next flight of stairs in a flurry of petticoats.

Heart pounding, she found her friend already gone when she reached the next landing, but the staircase continued upward, and so did she.

The continuous deep drone of voices from the ballroom gradually faded away as she ran up three more flights of stairs, zigzagging back and forth until her chest heaved like her bosoms might burst out of her gown.

He'd probably enjoy that.

At last, reaching the top floor of the luxurious hotel, a faint layer of perspiration dampening her brow in the several layers of her hot, formal clothing, Maggie spotted the duke waiting for her some distance down the corridor.

When he saw she had arrived, he strode on.

She continued to follow, still at a safe distance—and fortunately so. For just then, a door opened ahead and a pair of guests stepped out of one of the hotel suites. Maggie moved politely to one side of the hallway as the pair walked toward her, heading for the staircase.

Hiding her gulp, she lowered her gaze with a demure smile as the couple passed, engrossed in conversation.

Beyond them, Maggie saw that in that second she'd looked away, Amberley had disappeared around the corner ahead.

Given that more guests could pop out of any random door here at any moment, Maggie pressed on with a newfound surge of desperation not to be caught at her mischief. She all but tiptoed along the patterned carpet runner lining the elegant hallway.

Upon reaching the corner, she glanced around but did not see Amberley at all. The start of dread gripped her.

Oh no. I've lost him.

She'd be stranded up here and not even achieve what she'd taken this daft risk for. The hallway was silent.

He would not have slipped into one of these rooms, would he? Since this seemed unlikely, she ventured over to the one door she was rather sure wasn't a guest chamber, as it was much narrower.

Ever so discreetly, she opened it and peered inside.

"*Psst!* Dukes do not hide in broom closets, darling," came a roguish whisper. "Even I know that. Over here!"

She spun around in shaky delight, grinning again in spite of herself.

Amberley motioned to her from behind a swoop of velvet curtain framing an alcove niche at the end of the corridor. Then he ducked out of sight behind it.

Maggie closed the broom closet silently and stole over to the alcove, her heart skipping a beat as he pulled her into the shadows with him, whisking her out of view.

"You made it," he murmured, steadying her gently when she stumbled and crashed against his chest.

"Barely!" she whispered breathlessly, not minding their contact a bit. She pushed a stray wisp of hair out of her face, and he grinned at her like a rascal.

Maggie smiled back, then realized she was blushing again.

"Oh, look at that view!" she whispered suddenly, averting her gaze in a wave of self-consciousness.

Their cozy little alcove turned out to be a recessed window nook, from which hotel guests could enjoy a marvelous view of London, presently lit up in all its nighttime glory—especially with the Season in full swing.

Maggie turned her attention to the view, refusing to gawp at her handsome neighbor again like the smitten virgin that she increasingly feared she was.

He drifted to her side and gazed at it with her. "Yes… Lovely."

The sky was black above them, but below, the endless streets of London unfurled. Rows of streetlamps illumining the cobbled lanes, through which miniature carriages rolled back and forth.

Glowing mansion windows sparkled throughout this part of Town as Society played, and in the distance, bridges were strung with lanterns, while the onyx river flowed on, glittering with silver moonlight.

Yet with all the beauty of the capital laid out before him, she could feel her companion eyeing *her*.

She didn't dare look over to confirm this sensation, however.

Not when the rich, caressing timbre of his baritone made her insides quiver with strange, fitful yearnings as he murmured, "Very lovely indeed."

She bit her lip, acutely aware of his tall, muscular body beside her, his arm brushing against hers. All of a sudden, it dawned on her that this was *want* she was feeling. Raw, urgent desire, like nothing she'd ever experienced before.

The newness of it shook her. As did the realization that he probably knew exactly what to do with it. How to relieve the breathless agony that quivered through her for a moment, heating her blood.

"Did you have any trouble getting here?" he asked softly.

Somehow, she hid her thoughts and found her voice. "Um, no. Not really." Calling back sanity somehow, she managed to look reasonably natured as she turned back to him. "It was actually rather fun."

He took this in with a curious smile.

Maggie cleared her throat and sternly reminded herself that they were supposed to be here for practical reasons. *Right.*

She had to give him—as promised—the details she had learned about the suspects on his list of names.

This was part of their bargain.

Still, it was hard to clear her head and focus when he stood so near. A proper girl should've worried that, alone like this, he might try something inappropriate. She rather wished that he would.

Stop it, she ordered herself. This was not like her at all.

She looked up again to find the duke studying her intently, as though sensing the war going on inside of her. Those shrewd blue eyes glittered in the starlight coming in through the window, while the darkness of their alcove wrapped around them...like a black satin bedsheet.

God. She shuddered with another subtle pang of desire, then fought the impulse away, staying her mind on the task at hand as best she could. A lady was not a creature filled with lust, ever.

Mama would be so ashamed of her. *Maybe I'm drunk. I don't think I am, but…ugh.*

With that, Maggie remembered her morals. *Right.* She ignored his magnetic appeal and turned her full attention to the business at hand.

She had already told him she had serious doubts that any of the men on his list might be the killer, but the major was the expert on such things; he could decide for himself if any of these fellows warranted further inquiry.

For her part, Maggie was eager to show him what a useful ally she could be.

Just in case there ever came a time when he did not have to worry about being murdered anymore, and could start looking for a wife.

After all, with her Bryce match terminated, she still had to marry *someone*, and getting out of Delia's house sounded all the more appealing if it meant joining Amberley in his. Especially when she thought about a husband's marital rights…

Ack! Stop it, now.

Her smile was ever so polite as he touched her elbow gently, bending down a little to speak more intimately with her. "My lady, I wanted to thank you for introducing me around to your friends. That was…so kind of you."

"Nonsense." She blinked away the spell with a bright smile. "I said I would. Besides, they're your neighbors, too. You'd have met them eventually."

"Ah, but your introduction, I think, disposed them to look more favorably upon me than they might have otherwise done."

"Well, they all seemed to take to you at once. Not that I'm at all surprised. You're a decidedly likable fellow."

His eyes twinkled. "Don't tell my troops that."

"War's over, Your Grace."

"So they tell me. And your friends aren't bad, either, for Englishmen."

She snorted at his teasing. "How now! Enough of your cheek, sir. Wait till you hear all I've found out for you. I have been a *very* busy bee this past week, so now I shall dazzle you with my full report."

Dazzle me? Connor thought. Didn't the lass know she'd done that from the first moment he had laid eyes on her?

It was strange, actually, to think he'd only known her for a se'nnight. She felt so much more familiar to him than that by now.

They worked together well, he decided as he listened to her begin filling in the details on the last five men ever to see Granduncle Rupert alive. She was proud of herself for all the facts she'd sniffed out, it was plain, and he found her pleasure in the telling rather adorable.

But he forced himself to focus on the information.

"Lord Clayton Bexley is an undersecretary at the Treasury," she said, keeping her voice down. "He's a younger son of the Marquess of Liddicoat, and he was seeing your uncle on business, according to my sources. His father, Lord Liddicoat, wanted your uncle's vote on a budget proposal he was circulating. Harmless, in my view."

"Sounds it," Connor said cautiously, trying to be subtle about his enjoyment at inhaling her perfume.

"Second," she continued with a businesslike air of importance that made his heart clench, "we have Gideon, Baron Curnow. You may have noticed Lord Curnow out and about. Bit of an eccentric. Tweed hat, walking stick, beard, country clothes in Town, always travels around with at least one dog."

"Does he?" It was difficult not to touch her, let alone pay attention.

She nodded briskly. "He writes in lots of periodicals about agricultural improvements. That's his expertise. Enclosures, livestock, irrigation, the proper care of the woodlands on one's estate. All matters pertaining to country life."

"Interesting."

"Your uncle must've thought so. From what I was able to learn, Duke Rupert sought a meeting with Lord Curnow to get his advice on land usage at Dartfield Manor, his favorite of the estates you apparently inherited."

"That's where he died," Connor said.

"Is it? Well, that's why they met. Most likely, to talk about land."

"Hmm. That one sounds harmless, too," Connor said.

"Third, we have Mr. Benedict Dewitt, a gentleman in his sixties. Spectacles, soulful stare, pipe. He lives in Hanover Square. Mr. Dewitt is a wealthy widower whom your uncle counseled, probably falling back into his former role as vicar out of habit, after Dewitt lost his wife. Mrs. Dewitt died unexpectedly of typhus, and several ladies told me the poor man took it quite hard."

"Aha. Ladies' gossip? That's where you gained your information?" he asked in a mild tone, raising his eyebrows.

"Ladies know more about what goes on than you may imagine, Your Grace. Those scandal-broth sessions we love so much can yield more than just idle gossip, you know. But all this comes from a variety of sources. Don't worry, I was entirely discreet."

"I'm not worried," he said, surprising himself to discover it. "Do go on." He was enjoying this immensely. *What a clever girl. Resourceful. Reliable, too.*

A man could do worse.

"Fourth," she continued, "Bishop Viscount Humphries, whom you saw downstairs in the ballroom. Your uncle and he were acquainted since divinity school."

"Oh? Were they friends?"

"Except for a few pointed disagreements on matters of theological doctrine, they were."

"Hmm." Connor furrowed his brow. "Hard to think of a bishop as a killer, anyway."

She chuckled. "To be sure. Last on the list, we have Sir Barnaby Lynch, who I can personally vouch for—a dear old man, nearly eighty. Smiling, buoyant, happy. Around Town, we call him the Christmas elf. I would wager he was in touch with your uncle for his usual Christmas charity drive, benefiting war widows and orphans."

"I see. Harmless again," Connor murmured.

She nodded. "Especially the Christmas elf."

Connor sighed. "Then I'm no farther in all this now than I was a week ago."

"I tried," she said with a shrug.

He squeezed her arm in reassurance. "No, no, I'm not blaming you, my dear." Then he froze, wondering belatedly if touching her like that was far too familiar.

He withdrew his hand awkwardly, lowered it to his side, and cleared his throat a bit with chagrin. Last week, it hadn't bothered him to make her bare her ankles, but now, he cared very much what this girl thought of him.

Which was highly unusual in itself.

He cast about for a quick change of subject. "Actually, it's astonishing that you managed to do all this in a week. Wellington should've hired you for a spy."

She laughed, not looking at all offended by his brief touch. "Well, Your Grace, a lady has *vast* swathes of free time, and I'm dreadful at needlepoint."

He snorted at her jest. He liked her sense of humor.

"Besides, I've become rather a dab hand at research through studying possible future husbands." With a wry chuckle, she glanced back toward the picture window and folded her arms across her chest. "A practice I frequently had to repeat, after all the men Delia chased away."

"What? What do you mean?" he asked at once, crossing the alcove in a step or two to stand beside her.

But it was not the view of London that enchanted him.

She waved his question off idly. "Delia did her best to make me look like a fool to any man who showed an interest."

Connor jolted to attention. "Did she indeed? Why would she do that?"

"To amuse herself, probably. She claimed she was protecting me. It was 'for my own good.'"

"I don't like hearing this." He stared at her. "Your own sister got you jilted?"

"Well. At least they weren't *rude* about it, usually."

"I don't understand."

"Neither do I, really."

"Huh," he said after a moment, setting his hands on his waist. "So...that explains your former match with Bryce?"

"He wasn't my first choice," she admitted. "At least he wasn't frightened away by Delia's games, though. I'll give him that." A low, awkward laugh escaped her. "Yet I got rid of him all the same, didn't I?"

"You're better off," he said automatically, then realized perhaps it was too blunt of him—as usual.

She didn't seem to mind. "Oh, believe me, I know."

Connor was relieved he had not offended her. Still, he could not suppress his indignation on her behalf. "I can't believe your own sister would do that to you."

"She's been picking on me since we were little girls. I'm used to it." Then she elbowed him, clearly wanting a change of subject. "What of your own progress? Did you find out anything useful this week about all this?"

"Alas, no." He checked his roiling anger at her sister to answer the question. "Though I tried. I spent the past week retracing my steps."

"What do you mean?"

"In hopes there might've been something I missed back in January after the poisoning—because, believe me, I was nigh blinded by rage for a few days—"

"I'll bet."

"They nearly killed my best mate."

"Oh...I'm so sorry. Who's that?"

"Sergeant Rory McFeatheridge." He grinned. "Don't think ill of me when you meet him. He's not the most refined chap. But there's more to Rory than meets the eye."

"I'll look forward to it. Is he in London?"

"No, he went to some family in Portsmouth to recover from his ordeal. He'll be back at some point."

"And this week you said you retraced your steps?" She folded her arms and leaned against the window frame, watching him, listening.

"Yes, I went back and spoke again to the family solicitor to see if he had any opinion on the dukes' deaths, any possible leads. He didn't." Connor shook his head. "He's a fact man. He believes it all happened exactly as stated in the coroner's reports.

"After coming up empty-handed there, I wrote to Uncle Rupert's secretary to see if he had learned anything of interest in the meanwhile. Zed there, as well.

"Last, I summoned the two Bow Street officers who interviewed my servants before I sacked them all. Ugh, these two dunces were as useless this week as they were back in January." He shook his head in frustration. "Turns out Bow Street decided weeks ago—without bothering to tell me—that the case was closed."

"What was their conclusion?"

"That Rory was never poisoned. That it was either bad food, too much drink, or simply a stomach flu of some sort. Obviously, they don't know the sergeant's iron constitution," he muttered. "I swear, that man could eat hardtack full of maggots and never even notice the wriggling— Oh, er, sorry," he mumbled when she wrinkled her nose.

His heart sank at his blunder. *You don't say that sort of thing to a lady. Dunderhead.* Dammit, it was all down to too much time spent in the rough, rowdy company of men. "Sorry," he muttered again, embarrassed. "It's just, well, unfortunately, spoiled rations are a soldier's frequent lot in life."

"Lud." Her grimace had faded, thankfully, but when he noticed that the sparkle of amusement had never left her eyes, he smiled in rueful relief.

Maybe she was getting used to his rough-and-tumble ways, learning to see past them. He hoped so. He didn't want her to think him, as so many English folk did, a typical "Irish savage."

"What about your relatives?" she asked. "Have you been able to question them?"

"No." He lowered his head and scratched an eyebrow with his thumb. "Those who aren't in mourning still see me as an outsider. Aunt Lucinda doesn't *want* to tell me what she knows; Aunt Florence doesn't dare; and as to Aunt Caroline, I've been giving her and her daughters a wide berth, considering Uncle Rupert was her husband and Richard was her son. To lose them both in so short a time?" He shook his head. "I'm sure the sight of me, as the new titleholder, would pain the poor woman, and I've no desire to make this any worse for her than it already is."

"That is considerate of you." She paused. "Do you think *she* suspects her menfolk were murdered?"

"I really couldn't say." He growled under his breath and moved up restlessly to the window, staring out. "You know, I almost *wish* this blackguard would try again to kill me. That way, I could confront him, catch him, and be done with it. But he hides now. He knows I'm onto him, I think."

Connor glanced over his shoulder, saw her apprehensive frown, and realized the lady found this a chilling subject.

"It's all right, don't be frightened," he reassured her softly. "He failed twice now. He'll fail again."

"But I worry for you." She laid a hand on his forearm.

"No need," he told her with a gentle smile, sliding his arm up to capture her hand in his. "I'm ready for him now." He lifted her gloved hand to his lips and gave her knuckles a confident kiss. "He attacked with poison, for God's sake. The man's obviously a coward, whoever he is. But never fear, Lady Maggie. The major eats cowards for breakfast. Just ask Will," he said with a wink.

Her smile returned.

That's better, he thought. She was studying him, and he grew mesmerized by the starlight sparkle of her eyes. *Such beauty.*

Then she moved closer to him of her own accord, and Connor held his breath, wanting so much to take her in his arms. But rare hesitation held him back, for hadn't he forced her into this?

The risk to her reputation shook him, in hindsight. He hadn't even thought about that much until now. He was ashamed of his own selfishness...but such was the power of a warrior's well-honed survival instincts.

The morals of a high stickler were a luxury that only civilians could afford.

Then he glanced down in wonder as she laid her hand gently on his chest.

"Well, Major," she said, her voice beguiling him with its slight, breathy note. She peered up at him from beneath her lashes. "In the interests of ending this threat to your life as quickly as possible, I stand ready and waiting for my next assignment—especially since this one got us nowhere. What can I do to help next?"

He willed his mind away from a hundred naughty answers.

She deserved better than that from him, his delicate English rose. Something tenderer than his usual roguery when it came to women.

Connor shook his head and ran his hands gently down her arms. "You've done enough, my lady. I fear it was wrong of me to involve you in all of this in the first place."

"What? No," Maggie protested, but he barely heard, realizing how incredibly glad he was at that moment that her batch of suspects had turned out to be harmless.

God, what if he had sent this innocent girl chasing after the real killer?

How could he have been so cavalier about her safety, simply brushing any the notion of danger reaching her? It had seemed remote enough, but his heart sank with disappointment in himself.

He could only conclude that, in the same way that Maggie had grown accustomed to putting up with her sister's abuses over time, he, likewise, had come to take danger for granted as a normal part of his daily life, not worth bothering about. But just because life-or-death situations no longer impressed him, that didn't mean others around him were equally equipped to shrug it off.

God, he thought with a shudder. If anything had happened to her...

It just went to show how hardened he had become after all those years of war. *Maybe I'm less ready for peacetime than I thought.*

Clearly, this new life before him would take more adjusting to.

Meanwhile, he barely registered her continued protests until her light touch on his chest became a small, cajoling caress.

"Please, Amberley, I want to help. It's meaningful for me…"

At that, his senses homed in on her with his full, fiery attention.

"I'm sure I can be useful somehow," she said.

Oh indeed. His mouth watered as he failed this time to rein his roguish thoughts back into line. *You could help me, all right, love. Sit on my lap and let me show you exactly how…*

"Well?" she prompted, sweetly oblivious to his wayward thoughts.

Connor jolted back to his own haphazard version of propriety. "You astonish me, my lady." Alas, his voice had gone husky, and then his blood burned when Lady Maggie licked her lips.

"I do?"

"Aye," he forced out, throbbing. Then he turned his gaze with determination toward the window, and decided to open it a crack.

God knew he needed air, suddenly finding it much too warm in this dark, tiny alcove. He clicked the lock open and slid the casement up, striving for a businesslike tone as he continued.

"I thought I would have to compel you to help me in my search for information. Thus my demand to see your…you know." He glanced down wryly toward her skirts' hem as he turned around again, dusting off his gloved hands. "Thought I'd have to blackmail you into cooperating. Sorry," he added with a rueful grin, "I was desperate."

"Oho, is that what that was?" She started laughing, then poked him in the arm. "Oh come, you wouldn't have blackmailed me! I'll never believe that."

"Shh!" he scolded, laughing along quietly with her as he glanced past the curtain to make sure no one was coming.

The chilly thread of air whispering in felt wonderful. It stirred the tendrils of her hair—and helped to cool his lust enough so he could think again.

"Very well—you're right. The threat of it was about as far I as I could have taken that, to be honest. But I must admit, I don't regret makin' the demand. 'Twas a very nice view." He sent a hearty glance toward her shins, and she smacked him lightly in the chest for it this time.

"Ow! Careful of the gunshot wound, little hellcat."

"Oh my goodness—I forgot!" Her hands flew up to her mouth.

"I was only teasing," he told her.

"Humph! Ruffian," she said, narrowing her eyes at him.

God, he wanted to kiss her.

"Well?" She propped her fists on her waist. "I want my next assignment, duke. Tell me what to do."

"I don't think I will," he murmured, holding her gaze.

"But why? Didn't I do a good job?"

"You did an excellent job, my darling girl. But this could get dangerous, and I couldn't bear for any ill to befall you for my sake."

"Well, that is very gallant, I'm sure, but I am your friend, and I am not afraid," she declared, stealing his breath.

He could not resist reaching out to cup her cheek. "I know you're not, sweeting. I can see you're at your bravest when you're defendin' someone whose part you've taken up. You and I have that in common."

She pondered his words, but a crestfallen look crept onto her sweet face. "There must be something I can do to assist. Safely, as it were, behind the scenes?"

He lowered his hand to his side. "If I think of anything, I'll let you know."

"Very well," she said. But she looked so disappointed that Connor felt as though he had taken something important away from her.

As much as this puzzled him, he didn't want to be the cause of that dejected slump about her shoulders, that forced smile on her lips.

"You really want to assist?" he asked, trying to think of something for her.

She nodded eagerly, brightening at once. "I didn't at first, but now I really do. Did something occur to you?"

Something had. But it wasn't a task, it was a question. One he couldn't help asking, given the slight twinge of doubt nagging at him.

How reliable *was* her information, if she claimed to do thorough research on her prospective husbands, and yet had never found out that Bryce preferred men?

Connor looked toward the window, puzzling over any tactful way to probe the subject with a sheltered, virginal miss. There wasn't one, he was rather sure.

"How did Bryce take the jilt, anyway?" he asked abruptly, opting for a flanking maneuver on the subject.

"About as well as you might guess. Why do you ask?"

"Er, my lady, are you...*sure* you knew everything about him that a woman would want to know before marrying a chap?"

"Well, not everything, of course. But as much as I needed to. Why? You don't still think *he's* involved in trying to kill you, I hope?"

"No, no. I just wondered how clear your picture of him was."

She shrugged. "Fairly accurate, I think."

Connor hesitated, then decided that, above all, he owed her his honesty. "So I assume you heard the rumors," he said as delicately as possible, eyeing her.

She froze, stiffened, then lifted her chin. "Yes. I heard them," she said tightly. "And ignored them, of course. Disgusting lies. Who could believe such a thing?"

"Ah. So, it wasn't true, then?"

"People talk about everyone behind their backs in Society," she said, which he noticed was not a direct answer to his question. "I'm sure they say plenty of things about *me*."

"Like what?"

"Who knows? Who cares?" she said firmly. "The gossips of the ton twist the truth and delight in hyperbole. Take you, for example."

"Me?" he said, startled. "They're already talking about me?"

"Of course."

"What are they saying? Wait—maybe I don't want to know. As long as it's not that I killed my own relatives."

"No, no, no. Don't worry. I don't think anyone else took hold of that theory other than Bryce himself. However…if you really want to know, there is actually a tale going 'round that the fearsome major once discovered and then blew up a secret tunnel through which some French-held town under siege was receiving supplies."

He winced.

"Unfortunately," she continued, "they say that when the explosives were laid to bring the tunnel down, there were a dozen Spanish civilians inside, making their way through it, trying to reach freedom."

He looked away, his face taut with the memory. "They weren't supposed to be there."

She gasped. "You mean, it's true?"

"Aye." He gave her a hard glance. "It was pitch-black in that tunnel, and those families did not make a sound in their fear of being discovered by the French soldiers while making their escape. If I had seen them, heard them… Dammit, I'd watched for the pattern of how that tunnel was used. Their presence was a fluke. Do you think I'd have killed them on purpose?"

"Oh God," she whispered, staring at him. "I-I didn't think it was true."

"It doesn't matter." He turned away and shut the window again, sufficiently cooled by the night's chill. "It happened. I cannot change the past."

When he turned around, she was gazing somberly at him. "Forgive me, Your Grace. I should not have spoken out of turn. What does a lady know of war?"

"It's all right." He shrugged, stoic. "That's war for you."

She gazed at him in tender silence.

Connor shook his head and leaned against the windowsill, folding his arms across his chest. He lowered his gaze to the floor. "These idiots who think it's all glorious cavalry charges and sunlight flashing on sabers make me sick, to be honest. It's horror and pain and it ought to be outlawed."

She was silent for a moment, then he glanced at her to gauge her reaction.

"Yet you went in so young, and stayed there so long."

"Aye. My father signed me up. Family tradition."

"I'm sorry," she whispered.

"I'm not," he said in a steely tone. "If a war must be fought, then it must be won. So of course I was there, and stayed to see the thing through."

She appeared to have been rendered speechless. She turned away a little, lowering her gaze, touching her brow. "I feel like a fool for bringing it up."

His lips curved in the darkness, the tension easing from him again when he saw her dismay. "It's all right, Lady Maggie. I only bring it up as a means of suggesting that, um, perhaps you might consider that the rumors about your former beau might be true, as well. Actually"—he hesitated—"I'm certain they are."

Her chin jerked upward, and she looked at him, amazed. "No..."

He gave a noncommittal shrug. "It would seem that that was why he was so upset about Richard."

She grew increasingly appalled. "You mean...?"

Connor lifted his eyebrows and looked away discreetly, tapping his fingers on his arm. "Yes."

"Good heavens." Her voice had dwindled to a whisper. "Are you sure?"

"I found my cousin's diary."

"I...I see," she whispered, then furrowed her brow. "But if that's the case, then why did he court me? Only for appearances?" A soft, pained laugh escaped her as she turned away, apparently in shame.

Connor scowled at the floor, wishing he had never brought it up.

"It was all a lie," she said. "I was just…"

"There, now," he said softly, going over to her. He laid a hand on her shoulder. "You gave him the benefit of the doubt."

"I'm blind."

"No. You are just one of those rare souls who chooses to see the best in people. It's a beautiful quality. Do not berate yourself for this."

She looked up at him mournfully. "No wonder you don't want my help anymore. I am a dreadful judge of character. Yet…I am quite sure that the men whose names you gave me mean you no harm. They are not capable of murder."

"I believe you. I trust in your word. And you do have good judgment with people. Your choice of friends downstairs proves that."

He saw her swallow hard as she hung on his words.

"That's not the reason I said I did not want you involved anymore. I just want to keep you safe, my lady."

She searched his eyes, but then nodded, her lips pressed together. She took a breath and chased back the shimmer of tears that had threatened in her eyes.

Her gentleness moved him so deeply. He wanted with all his heart to take her into his arms and shield her from the world. But, as the target of so many threats, Connor knew that he mustn't do that.

Not yet.

"Well," she said, gathering herself, "speaking of my friends, I should probably return to the ballroom before they all start to wonder where we two have gone."

Connor gazed at her in dismay. He did not want her to go, did not want to leave this alcove yet. "Tell you what. If I think of any way for you to help that doesn't seem too dangerous, I'll summon you to our meeting place."

"Really?"

He nodded, determined to come up with something for her. He had no idea why exactly it meant so much to her, but clearly, it did. "Watch for my signal."

She finally smiled again at his reminder of the lantern signals. "I will. At least you and I officially know each other now," she added.

"Believe me, the pleasure is mine. Be careful going back downstairs.

I don't want to give the Town gossips any more fodder for their — what did you call it? Scandal-broth sessions?"

She nodded, chuckling. "Good night, Your Grace."

As she started to turn away, Connor stopped her. "One more thing."

"Yes?" She looked at him hopefully.

"Do come to that party I mentioned. My grandaunt's soirée."

She grinned. "Send me an invitation and I'll be there."

"Done. You promise?"

"I do. You'll need moral support that night?"

"I just like seeing your face," he said softly. "And…" He glanced down meaningfully at her ankles.

She giggled. "*That* never happened, Your Grace."

"You catch on quickly," he said with a smile, then he found himself holding her stare, and it seemed neither of them could look away.

She suddenly clapped both hands to her cheeks. "Why can't I stop smiling when you are near?"

"Perhaps the same reason my wound feels better when I see you." He touched his bandaged side vaguely.

"Your Grace—"

"Connor," he whispered.

Suddenly, Maggie moved toward him, and his own resistance crumbled entirely. As she lifted her arms to embrace him, he pulled her to him, sliding his hands around her waist. She tilted her head back in eager abandon, offering her lips as he leaned down and claimed them.

He devoured her, his blood thrumming with triumph, with awe. Her lips were warm and silken beneath his, far sweeter than he could have imagined. She returned his kisses with neophyte wonder, letting him lead her, parting her lips at the stroke of his tongue.

He moaned as he tasted her, tightening his hold around her waist. Fantasies of taking her here against the wall in this darkened alcove flooded his mind.

But, somehow, he held himself back. He checked his wild impulses, slowed his fierce kisses, and gradually loosened his clutching grip around her waist.

Both panting a little, they ended the kiss.

"Oh my," she breathed. As her dreamy eyes swept open, he scanned her face, praying he had not completely overstepped his bounds.

He did not want to botch this.

"Um, I hope…that was all right," he ventured.

"Pardon…I've forgotten what planet I'm on."

He laughed softly. That seemed a good sign. "Shall I apologize?"

"Please don't. I would have kissed you if you hadn't kissed me." She bit her lip after this admission, while, beneath her velvet lashes, her gray eyes smoldered with silver desire.

Connor shook his head, amazed, and hard as a rock. She was playing with fire, but when she slid her arms around his neck and tilted her head back for another kiss, his restraint splintered into shards.

He clamped his arms around her once again, yanking her slim body flush against his. All that existed was this woman's softness, her pliant, yielding warmth as she parted her lips again, luring him into her mouth. He reveled in the way that she clung to him, but when a feminine groan full of yearning escaped her, it ignited his instincts.

With two steps like a dance move, he drove her back against the narrow wall beside the window and consumed her as she consumed him. He could feel her carnal delight. Here, they were cloaked by the darkest of the shadows. Here, with the solid wall behind her, he could explore the beauty of her sleek, firm curves. He touched her waist, her neck, and she did not protest. So he let his palm glide cautiously down the bare, alluring expanse of her alabaster chest; it heaved beneath his touch, rising and falling in time with the wild rhythm of his kisses.

Her hand hovered over his on her chest, but she made no move to stop him, even when he inched his touch down the swell of her bosom, lightly rounding its hardened crest. He groaned at the distended nipple swelling under his thumb, longing with all his heart to take it into his mouth. He could have torn her gown asunder with the need to know every inch of this woman.

Her writhing willingness there against the wall had him blinded with lust in seconds, panting.

If only he'd have thought to take one of these blasted hotel rooms for the night. For his delicate English rose wanted him, in all his rough, rowdy, seething storm, like she yearned for the rain. He almost couldn't believe it. For one fleeting moment, Connor envisioned having her beneath him in bed. Making her come. He could almost feel her legs around him, her nails raking down his bare back. He could ravish her for hours…

"Oh God," she finally whispered, gripping his shoulders in a halfhearted attempt to bring him to heel. "We…we shouldn't be doing this, Your Grace."

Your Grace.

Her use of his lofty new title jarred him. It sounded so elegant, when he could barely hold back the barbaric frenzy of lust seething inside him.

He wanted so badly to let it all go with her. Give in to the hunger that had raged in him for so long.

He was astonished that she seemed to want this as badly as he did.

Determined, however, to show her that "His Grace" was not the savage Irishman, nor the rough, ruthless soldier she probably thought he might be—very well, the one that he *could* be when the occasion called—Connor forced himself to yield to her wishes. Somehow dragged himself back from her body. He hoped that she was too innocent to know what the pulsating rod that she'd surely felt against her belly signified.

Maggie's chest heaved as she sought to catch her breath. As for Connor, likewise, it took him a long moment to find his voice and bring his flesh back under control.

He did not regret kissing her, though. Not for one, lusty moment of that glorious madness. It had been as rash as hell. But tomorrow was promised to no man. Soldiers' creed.

"You're right," he finally managed with a haphazard laugh, "probably best that you go now. I'll, er, keep my distance downstairs for a while. Wouldn't want to cause a scandal."

She gazed at him, still panting from their brief but passionate contact, her lips bee-stung. "That was wonderful."

"Yes, it was."

"We should do that again sometime," she murmured, torturing him.

A small groan of thwarted want escaped him, and Connor looked away. God, this girl could have him eating out of her hand if he didn't watch his step. "You'd better get out of here before…"

"Before what?" she whispered, a sparkle in her eyes.

He shook his head, marveling.

"You're trouble."

"I bid you a fond good evening, Your Grace," she said coyly.

Connor gave her a playful salute, and she went on her way, leaving him still dazzled and dazed. What a fine town London was, after all, he thought in amusement. This was much better than wartime.

At length, he, too, left the alcove. They returned to the ballroom several minutes apart, entering through different doors.

As far as he knew, no one was the wiser regarding their absence.

But his head was still spinning when he caught sight of her again amid the throng. It was about then that Connor sensed, deep down, that something profound had changed in his world tonight.

He had not yet managed to uncover the murderer. But he was fairly sure he'd found his duchess. If she'd have him. Once the timing was right.

And more than just his duchess, truth be told.

It was altogether possible that he'd found his soul mate.

CHAPTER 14

Hyde Park

Put out, petulant and pouty, Maggie decided. That was the best way to describe her sister's mood the next afternoon as they trundled along through Hyde Park at the fashionable hour.

"You really needn't have danced with him *twice*," Delia reproached her. "Why do you always have to make yourself the center of attention?"

Maggie's eyes flared open wide at that. *Me?*

She glanced in amazement at her sister, but there was no point arguing, she knew from long experience. She merely let Delia have her say, giving the sort of noncommittal nods and halfhearted shrugs and evasive monosyllabic responses that she had learned from Edward.

Instead, as they rumbled along sitting side by side, both facing forward, Delia closer to the oncoming traffic, all the better to display herself, Maggie focused her attention on the dramatic sky that stretched out across London.

Much of the firmament overhead was bright, sunny and springlike, pale blue, with complex layers of clouds. But England's weather was never to be trusted entirely. The strong though pleasant breeze rustling in from the north prodded before it several dark, ominous thunderheads.

The wind riffling through the trees throughout Hyde Park made the waters of the Serpentine choppy and tried to blow away her hat.

The slight threat of rain merely added an air of excitement to the daily ritual of the promenade. People zoomed back and forth in their carriages, the ladies showing off their fancy equipage gowns, eyeing up each other's pelisses and spring wraps and hats and bonnets.

Gentlemen went cantering by on fine, leggy mounts, while the usual collection of waterfowl drifted on the lake.

It was a perfectly ordinary day, at least for now. As the dark clouds crept closer overhead, inch by inch, their deep blue tone reminded Maggie of the Duke of Amberley's eyes.

He was the cause of Delia's current pique. God forbid her little sister should have a duke paying attention to her.

If only she knew, Maggie thought. Savoring the memory of what had happened in that alcove last night, she hid her wicked mirth from her opinionated sister.

What did this man bring out in her? Wild urges, the most unladylike yearnings…

To her amazement, a match with him was beginning to seem genuinely possible, but she barely dared entertain the thought. If she let herself hope, the disappointment could be crushing. Because, frankly, he was *wonderful.*

Suppressing a shiver of remembered delight, she stared into space for a moment as the carriage rolled along. Delia went on complaining. Maggie didn't listen, didn't care. Nothing could burst her bubble of happiness today.

Not when she could still feel the pleasant, scratchy roughness of his jaw against her chin, the brandy-flavored warmth of his mouth consuming hers, and the satin glide of his fingertips skimming her face, her neck, her bosom…

She had never known such kisses were possible. Even now, perched on the seat of her sister's luxurious open coach, the memory of it made her toes curl.

Oh! The thought came in spite of her efforts to stay measured about it all. *I may die if I can't marry this one.* If Delia ruined it for her somehow, this time, Maggie swore she'd do a violence to her sister.

Connor. She savored his first name on her tongue, now that she'd been given permission to use it.

There was just something so dear about the man… Those glimpses of melancholy behind his humor. The restless, uneasy churning within him, of chivalrous ideals at odds with ruthless killer instincts.

At the duel and last night in the alcove, she had seen how he trusted those instincts—and his passions. This was not the English way, in the main. He seemed amused by the decorum, the restraint customary to the English as a breed, and Maggie found his attitude oddly liberating.

The sense of freedom it gave her felt like an invigorating gust of fresh air.

Unfortunately, the *actual* breezes blowing back on them from ahead smelled like sweaty carriage horses.

Maggie wrinkled her nose as Delia's driver, Hubert, in brown Birdwell livery, urged the clip-clopping team along the graveled Ring.

For a moment, she wondered what the coachman must think of the way Delia continued nagging and needling her.

"I don't see why you went out of your way to try and throw yourself at him."

"I did nothing of the kind," Maggie said serenely.

Delia huffed. "He is unsuitable, in any case. He may be a duke, but he's Irish—"

"Only three-quarters."

"—and besides, it is completely inappropriate for you to set your cap at him after he dueled with your beau."

"Haven't you heard, Delia? I am no longer receiving Lord Bryce."

"What? Why?" Delia turned to her indignantly, feigning ignorance. "Why am I only learning of this now? Since when?"

"Since he behaved in such a repulsive manner last week at the ball and the duel. Bryce is of no consequence to me anymore—as you know full well."

Delia shook her head. "God, you are so spoiled."

"Spoiled?" Maggie echoed in shock. "Why would you say that? I am *not*."

Delia's eyes gleamed. Then she glanced toward the stream of oncoming carriages. "Oh look, there's the Duchess of Rivenwood."

Thank God, Maggie thought, clenching her jaw. Delia usually behaved a bit better in front of Serena or anyone higher-ranking than herself, the phony.

"Ugh, but she's with that insufferable Portia Tennesley again," Delia added under her breath.

"What's wrong with Lady Portia? I thought you liked her."

"She never shuts up about her stupid wedding."

Maggie held her tongue, though there was some truth in that. Still, it was far preferable to hear the latest minute details of Portia's wedding plans than continue listening to Delia's browbeating.

Poor Portia. Everybody knew that the only reason she was obsessed with planning her wedding was because the man her parents were forcing her to marry was said to be such a crashing bore.

Maggie could not confirm this, since she had never met the groom. The Duke of Fountainhurst rarely came to Town—never mind that Fountainhurst House was one of the giant ducal mansions that graced the four corners of Moonlight Square. Rumor had it the man was rich as Croesus, but, alas, he had remained single on account of his keen scientific interest in studying—of all things—insects.

Lord Gable enjoyed astronomy, and that was nice enough a hobby, Maggie thought. Netherford supported the arts, while Serena's Azrael housed wild animals at the menagerie he had inherited from his father.

But insects? Creepy-crawly, wriggling little vermin?

No. This was really just a bridge too far for any fashionable young lady. Even if the amateur entomologist in question *was* a millionaire duke.

Poor girl, Maggie thought with a sigh. There were rumors of some other young fellow whom Lady Portia had adored a Season or two ago, but he had disappeared and nobody knew what happened to him.

Dead, probably.

To prevent her becoming a spinster, and for the many advantages of any family alliance with a ducal house, her parents had pledged their daughter to the renowned eccentric. For her part, having lost the suitor she'd preferred with no explanation given of his fate or his whereabouts, Portia cared little what happened to her anymore, and, wishing to benefit her family, had not given serious protest to the match. But in her heart, Maggie knew, her friend was already set against her future husband.

In the meantime, the unlucky bride had decided that if she could not have the *man* she had wanted, then at least she'd have the wedding of her dreams.

"God, I don't envy her," Delia said out of the corner of her mouth, but when their friends' carriage rolled into earshot, she turned all sweetness, waving eagerly. "Hullo, ladies! Halloo, Your Grace! Lady Portia! So nice to see you both again! Stop the coach, Hubert," she ordered her driver. "I wish to speak to the duchess."

As Serena's carriage glided toward them, Delia wrinkled her nose adorably and waggled her fingers, looking faker, Maggie thought, than those costumed wax likenesses of famous historical figures designed by that French émigré artist, Madame Tussaud. For a few pennies, the curious could wander through her studio inspecting everyone from King Henry VIII to Napoleon himself. But with Delia, such entertainment came free of charge.

Maggie prayed for patience as their carriage glided to a halt by the edge of the Ring.

Her Grace of Rivenwood, likewise, bade her coachman pull up alongside, though the other two women were heading in the opposite direction.

"How are you both today?" Serena asked pleasantly. The raven-haired beauty looked striking in a light beige carriage gown with ribbon trim the color of red wine, and a jaunty hat to match. "Quite recovered from the ball, I trust?"

"Oh yes. You?"

They exchanged pleasantries for a moment, then Delia beamed artificially at Serena's companion. "And how goes the wedding planning, Lady Portia?"

Maggie nearly choked at her sister's hypocrisy. It was so transparently insincere that she saw fit to chime in quickly, showing a more genuine interest. "Yes, have you decided on your flowers?"

Flaxen-haired, with guarded blue eyes and a thoughtful face, Lady Portia Tennesley sighed and shook her head. "Sadly, no. Fountainhurst informs me through his clerk that he is concerned we should not choose flowers that disturb the *bees*."

"Oh God," Delia whispered.

"There, there, don't worry, darling," Serena said, patting her hand while Portia looked forlorn. "You have plenty of time to sort it out. The wedding is still far off."

Lady Portia shrugged. "At least he hasn't given me any trouble over the music. Who can disagree over Mozart? Better than a band of crickets chirping, at least."

Maggie laughed while Serena shook her head. "She's making a joke of all of this," Serena said.

"What else can I do? It *is* a joke," Portia replied with a weary half-smile.

"And at least now you've got the invitations settled," Serena insisted.

"Thanks to you," Portia said, smiling at her friend and then looking ruefully at Delia and Maggie. "Serena is so much more resolute than I. I couldn't decide between silver embossing on white linen cards or gilt engraving on cream."

"They both sound beautiful," Maggie offered.

"They were," Portia said. "I could've taken another month to make up my mind, but...ah well. Delay will not prevent the inevitable."

"Darling, he may be...different, but different can be lovely," Serena said, turning to Portia. "Take it from me. The Duke of Fountainhurst probably has fine hidden qualities."

"What," Portia said with a bit of smirk, "like a caterpillar?"

They couldn't help laughing, and Portia tipped her head back to look wryly at the sky, as though imploring heaven.

"At least he's handsome. Well, when he takes off his spectacles," Serena pointed out. "And, er, combs his hair."

"I'd hardly know," Portia said. "I've only seen him twice."

"Exactly. You have to give him a chance," Serena said.

"I just hope I don't have to share the marriage bed with a colony of ants," Portia drawled.

"I'm sure that won't be the case!" Serena chided as they laughed sympathetically. "But, you know..." The duchess looked askance at Portia with a twinkle in her eyes. "Tall and strapping as he is, I'll bet he's got a *big worm*."

Delia hooted with laughter. Portia pressed her lips together and looked at Serena matter-of-factly while Maggie giggled.

Portia finally shrugged. "Guess I'll find out. Whether I like it or not."

"Don't worry—you can always have an affair if he's horrible," Delia assured her with a wave of her hand, horrifying Maggie, her first thought of Edward. "We'll never tell," Delia said blithely. "And look on the bright side. At least you're not in Maggie's shoes. She'll probably never get married, the rate she's going."

The casual cruelty of Delia's remark took all three others off guard. Maggie drew in her breath, hurt, while Portia blinked in astonishment, and Serena's eyebrows shot upward.

Serena looked at Maggie and pressed her lips shut, as though holding back a cutting rejoinder to Delia. A spark of indignation flared in her dark hazel eyes.

Portia cleared her throat. "Oh, I don't know," she spoke up, sending Maggie a conspiratorial smile. "Any girl who's got peers of the Realm dueling over her is sure to have her choice of husbands, I should think."

"Indeed," Serena said sternly, pinning Delia with a hard look. "I daresay even Sidney's thinking of sweeping her off of her feet, as well, and he's always been the most committed of bachelors."

Maggie doubted it, but gave no reply. They all knew beautiful Lord

Sidney was nothing but a flirt. For her part, she was too busy trying to school her face into a semblance of nonchalance while her very soul quivered with shame.

"Well!" Delia said crisply, recovering from her momentary falter at the ladies' polite reproach. "We really should be moving on. This weather, don't you know."

"Yes," Serena said blandly, "it looks like it might rain."

"Good day, ladies. Hubert, drive on!" Delia barked.

Maggie forced a smile and waved goodbye, still badly stung by her sister's rude remark, but touched by her friends' defense. Portia sent her a wink as the two carriages rolled off in opposite directions.

Delia sat stiffly and did not make a sound for a good minute or two. "Don't look so smug," she finally grumbled. "They didn't fight the duel over *you*, obviously."

"I'm well aware of that." Maggie paused, but found she could not hold her tongue. "Why do you always do this to me? Single me out like that just to mock me?"

Before Delia could answer, the sound of cantering hoofbeats approached from behind them, and they heard a deep familiar voice with a hint of an Irish brogue. "Good day, neighbors!"

Oh, thank God. Like the answer to a wish, Amberley appeared, clad in gentlemanly riding attire; slowing his magnificent dapple-gray thoroughbred to a rangy walk on Maggie's side of the carriage, he greeted her with a bright smile.

Relief coursed through her at the sight of him after Delia's unkindness. He had no idea how glad she was to see him.

"Well met, Your Grace!" she greeted him.

"Ladies." He tipped his hat, and Delia grumbled at him with a sour look.

Maggie beamed, however, not caring who noticed her pleasure in seeing him. His gaze caressed her with affection in return as he made his tall horse keep pace with Delia's open coach.

But his blue-eyed stare homed in on her; he instantly seemed to notice that something was wrong.

Maggie was already feeling much better with his arrival. His effect on her was magical, scouring away the hurt of a moment ago like a blast of clean water from a strong fountain's jet. She did her best to dismiss Delia's petty cruelty from her mind and gave him her full attention, instead—a far more congenial subject.

"What brings you out this afternoon, Your Grace?" she asked pertly.

Why, you do, my dear, his twinkling gaze seemed to say, but his smile broadened. "Oh, just tryin' to get meself some Town bronze, if I'm to be a duke and all." He glanced roguishly at Delia's haughty face, and Maggie suspected he was playing up the Irish accent just to annoy her. "I hear ridin' up and down this stretch o' turf around five o'clock is one o' the rules of good ton."

"So they tell me," Maggie replied.

"Did you have fun at the ball last night, Lady Margaret?" he inquired then, as though he couldn't resist.

Maggie knew full well he was not talking about the dancing. "Oh yes." A blush crept into her cheeks at the memory of the alcove. "The company was...particularly scintillating, I thought."

Connor grinned.

"La, but you are a glutton for punishment, aren't you, Your Grace?" Delia interjected, jolting Maggie back down to earth.

"Whatever do you mean, Lady Birdwell?" he asked.

"I should've thought you'd had enough of my sister for a while after the way she clung to you like a nettle all evening."

"Never," he said with a charming smile. His glance at Maggie assured her it was all right; what she'd told him last night in the alcove about Delia's habit of undermining her must have prepared him to expect this sort of thing from her sister. "I'd throw her dance card away and keep her to myself all evening if it wouldn't shock the world. But I fear she'd be the one getting sick o' me."

Maggie's smile widened while Delia absorbed this, looking startled and rather more annoyed. Even if he was only being gallant, Maggie appreciated his ready defense of her. Delia, alas, began to fume. Her milky complexion started turning red.

"Lady Margaret," said the duke, "I hope you'll save me another dance at next week's ball. You were such a patient partner for so clumsy a dancer as myself."

The man did not have a clumsy bone in his body, Maggie was sure. If he did, she had yet to find it, but his innocent look told her he was only rubbing it in for Delia's sake.

He was so delightfully naughty.

Maggie mumbled an assurance that of course she'd dance with him again, but couldn't help smiling, even though she already knew from experience that every compliment he paid her would only make the queen bee's sting sharper.

"Actually, we won't be attending next week," Delia announced, much to Maggie's surprise. "All these gowns of yours are getting very expensive, sister."

Maggie raised her eyebrows. Papa had left her money of her own.

"She's very lucky to live with us, you know," Delia informed Connor before Maggie could remind her of this. "When Father died, she had nowhere else to go. Not that she's at all grateful to me and Edward for that."

"I'm so sorry for your loss," the duke said, ignoring the barb and trying to change the subject, bless him. "When did your father die?"

"Last year," Maggie said, giving her sister a warning look.

"She's been with us ever since. And believe me," Delia said, "without my influence, she'd have even less Town bronze than you, if that were possible."

"Ah, then that must explain why the two of us get on so well together. Just a couple of diamonds in the rough, aren't we?" He winked cheerfully at her, and Maggie quite fell in love with the man.

Though he maintained his easy smile, the stubborn set of his jaw hinted at immovability on this point.

He sent her sister a hard but polite glance, clearly informing the marchioness that he would not hear Maggie abused in his presence.

Delia turned to Maggie with a stare full of skeptical astonishment.

For her part, Maggie could've kissed him for his willingness to stand up for her, though, admittedly, she had long since noticed that the Irishman did not shy from confrontation.

It seemed to come to him as naturally as breathing. Unfortunately, so it was with her sister. And Delia did not like being contradicted.

The hostility brewing between the two hung in the air with a roiling tension, like the distant storm clouds starting to take shape in the north.

Though she'd laughed at first, Maggie began to feel intensely uncomfortable about this, considering *she* was the one caught in the middle.

At the same time, her conscience sent her a pang of distress. *Don't drag him into this*, it whispered. *He's got enough problems of his own. He doesn't need more enemies, what with somebody out there already trying to kill him.*

"Well," Delia finally said with a needling smile, "it's so *sweet* how you've befriended each other. But, I'm sorry to say, Your Grace would do well not to grow too attached to the poor creature. She's not in very good health. She'll probably end up an invalid."

"Absurd," he replied.

"No, it's true—"

"No, it's not!" Maggie exclaimed.

"We do what we can for her, but she's so weak and sickly."

"Is she, now?" He slid Maggie a sparkling glance. "Looks the picture of health to me. Radiant as a rose."

"A rose, eh? One that reached its peak two Seasons ago, and is now nearly withered."

"You're older than me!" Maggie reminded her with a glare, but Connor played along.

"Hmm. Let's have a closer look." Leaning down from his horse, he gave Maggie a good, long inspection. "No. With all due respect, Lady Birdwell, ye need your eyes checked. Take it from me." He sat up tall in the saddle again. "I've a great deal of experience assessing female beauty, and I say Lady Margaret Winthrop is one of the loveliest girls I've ever beheld."

"Why, thank you, Your Grace," Maggie said, beginning to feel rather desperate for this whole conversation to end.

Oddly enough, Delia eyed the duke with an air of newfound appreciation, almost respect. It was rare indeed for anyone to give the redheaded tyrant a run for her money, and he did not give an inch.

He smiled back at her, unflappable.

Very well, Delia seemed to say to herself. *That game failed. Next tactic.* "Perhaps Your Grace is right," she conceded. "The physician may be wrong about her health. But, really, it's her wits that are the problem."

"Delia, please!"

"She's quite thick in the head," she continued. "Always has been. You should've seen her as a child. It took the little simpleton the longest time to learn how to read."

Connor shrugged. "Maybe she had better things to do. Like playing with her dollies. I'll bet they were better companions than other children nearby," he said pointedly, meaning Delia, of course.

And was he ever right about that.

Delia tossed her head. "All I know is that it was quite distressing to our parents. For years, they weren't even sure if the little widgeon could speak."

"Because *you* never let me get a word in!" Red-faced and bristling now to think of her childhood and all the years of torment she'd endured as Delia's little sister, Maggie pushed away the anger churning inside her, and instead changed the subject. "What a beautiful horse that is, Your Grace," she said with determination.

"Isn't he, though?" Connor leaned down and patted the powerful animal's sleek neck. "This is Hurricane. Thoroughbred racer. He can be a right handful, but he's behaving himself in front of you ladies. Fine Irish stallion, he is."

"Like you, Your Grace?" Delia drawled.

"Delia! That's enough," Maggie said, mortified by her sister's comment.

Delia whipped around and narrowed her eyes. "What are *you* going to do about it?"

Maggie stared at her, but with Amberley right there on his horse, witnessing all, bolstering her courage, a strange thing happened.

She felt infused with a fight she usually nullified within her, and decided on the spot that she would not be humiliated for one moment longer by her sister.

Not this time. Not in front of *him*.

"Your Grace?" She glanced up to find Connor studying her with a stalwart expression of readiness.

"Yes, my lady?" That battle-ready look, that loyal stare—why, it quite stole her breath. For a moment, Maggie was in awe, having it directed at her.

The warrior needed no words to make her understand he was prepared to lay his strength at her feet, if she but gave the order.

No one, Maggie trusted, had ever yelled at Delia like the major seemed quite prepared to do if she but gave him the nod and stepped out of the way.

But no. This was her fight. One she had avoided for far too long in the interests of keeping the peace.

There came a point, however, where even the most well-bred lady had to stand up for herself.

And that moment was now.

If she refused, the man she desired would lose all respect for her, she feared. More importantly, she would lose all respect for herself.

"Would you kindly excuse us?" she asked him, trembling with wrath. "I wish to speak to my sister—privately."

He furrowed his brow as if to ask, *Are you sure?*

Maggie nodded while Delia scoffed. "Oh no! I'm in trouble now," she said sarcastically.

Connor narrowed his eyes at Delia. "Well then. I shall bid you two ladies adieu." As he gathered the reins, his hands low over the stallion's withers, he sent Maggie a bolstering glance. Then he chirruped to his horse and guided Hurricane away, cantering off toward the Serpentine in perfect form.

❖

Have at it, girl, Connor thought as he rode away, glad in that particular moment that he didn't have any siblings. *You shouldn't take that from anyone.*

God, he never would've believed Maggie's sister could be so obnoxious unless he'd seen it with his own two eyes. *Poor Maggie...*

Poor Edward!

He hoped he hadn't goaded the lass into anything she was not ready for, but he hadn't been able to resist antagonizing her sister a bit when he'd heard her saying such nasty things about gentle little Maggie.

All the same, as he glanced back uneasily over his shoulder, he knew deep down that, as difficult as this might be for the girl, putting Delia in her place would be the best thing for her.

In his experience, people treated you about as well as you let them.

It angered him, though, that her sister would take advantage of Maggie's easygoing nature and, even worse, exploit her lower status as a dependent in her household, rather like he'd seen Aunt Lucinda do to Aunt Florence.

Well, it was time for his little English rose to put a stop to that nonsense.

She could handle this, he knew. Connor had seen the kind of backbone the girl could show. She had certainly had no trouble standing up to *him*.

As he neared the Serpentine, where the rising breeze drove ripples across the surface of the water, riffling them almost to the point of causing whitecaps, he could hear the water sloshing up around the graveled edges of the man-made lake over the cadence of Hurricane's hoofbeats.

He checked the stallion's rocking canter, murmuring reassurances as they approached a chaotic cluster of riders ahead. Hurricane's ears twitched obediently at the sound of his voice, but he seemed to sense Connor's authority.

It was always a dicey proposition, taking a stallion out in the world as an ordinary riding horse. The temperamental beast needed exercise, however, and it felt oddly important to Connor to prove to Hurricane that he could be more than just a racehorse.

That he could go about in the world, be among ordinary folk.

At any rate, even if Hurricane got a little lively, Connor was a highly seasoned rider.

His grandfather had raised horses back in Ireland after retiring from the military, and Connor had pitched in around the stables from the time that he could walk. Then, at age twelve—being lighter than the trainer—he had started helping with the sometimes perilous task of breaking green horses.

He had been away at war when Grandfather had given Hurricane to Granduncle Rupert as a gift for his sixtieth birthday. Hard to believe that was just three years ago, Connor mused, and now both men were gone.

Hurricane had been but a weanling then, and now here he was, a splendid three-year-old racing colt, whickering amorously to every mare they passed.

With the knot of riders approaching ahead, Connor urged the stallion onto the grass, then he saw a wide, empty stretch of green alongside the road and felt the pull of temptation.

"That looks like fun, doesn't it?" he murmured to the horse.

The gray tossed his head, his dark mane flying.

"Let's give it a go, shall we, boy?" Loosening his firm hold on the reins, Connor squeezed Hurricane's sides with his heels.

The response was instantaneous, explosive. The gray leapt into a gallop like he was born for it—which, of course, he was.

They flew. Connor reveled in the wild burst of speed the thoroughbred unleashed, leaning slightly over the horse's withers.

In the blink of an eye, Hurricane had crossed the greensward. As they hurtled toward the next grove of trees, Connor gently reined him in, pulling the racehorse back to a restless trot.

"Good boy, good boy," he said heartily, while Hurricane tossed his handsome head with pride, wanting more. "By Jove, I think you're ready for the derby."

"Amberley!" someone called just then from the Ring.

Connor looked over as a rider waved, then guided a tall, slender chestnut away from the busy park lane and swept toward him at a canter.

"Easy," Connor told the stallion, slowing to a walk, and watching the gray's black-rimmed ears for any signs of rebellion.

Hurricane danced sideways a bit as the chestnut approached, but it must have been a gelding, for the other horse held little interest for the stallion.

As the rider approached, Connor recognized Gable, Lord Roland.

"Damn, but that's a fine bit of horseflesh you've got there," his new friend said, running an admiring gaze over the gray.

"Thank you." Connor grinned. "He's fast."

"I'll say! Did you run him at Ascot?"

"Missed it. Next year."

"Ah. Listen, I'm glad I spotted you. I'm headed over to see my father and I thought you might like to come along, if you're available."

Connor shrugged. "I've got nothing else to do. But are you sure now's a good time for him? I don't wish to impose."

"It's a fine time. In fact, it may be your only chance for a week or so. Last night, when I offered to arrange a meeting for you, I had forgotten that my parents are leaving on Sunday to visit my aunt in the country." Gable suddenly yawned. "Oh, pardon me."

Connor quirked a brow. "Late night?"

"The baby was up around two o'clock and then again at four. Therefore, so were we." Gable smiled. "Lack of sleep has shot holes through my memory of late."

Connor chuckled. "Well, if you can stay awake for it, I'm game to meet your father now. In fact, I'd be grateful."

Gable nodded. "Follow me."

"Oh, but first—do you think he'll have an extra box-stall in his stable where I can leave this fellow while we talk? Stallion," Connor said, patting his horse's neck. "I don't want him causing any trouble."

Like I just did, he thought, stealing another glance in the direction Maggie and her sister had gone. He hoped he had not started a war between the two sisters, or, if he had, that Maggie was holding her own.

He was intensely curious—and, in truth, a bit worried—about how the lass was faring. But the ladies' carriage was no longer in sight.

A haunting thought trailed through his mind. *Maybe I shouldn't have left her.* He frowned to himself.

But it was too late now to second-guess his actions.

"Plenty of room in Father's stable," his friend said. "That won't be a problem."

"Then lead on," Connor said, resolving to trust Maggie to take care of herself in this. He'd ask her later how it had gone at the first opportunity.

"Where are we off to?" he added as Gable turned his quiet-tempered gelding around. Its long tail swished gracefully over the turf as the viscount answered, "St. James's. Follow me."

They rode.

CHAPTER 15

Battle Royale

$\mathcal{M}$oments after Connor had ridden away on his silver stallion, Maggie was still gathering her thoughts, trying to figure out how to begin. Unfortunately, her sister beat her to the punch.

"Why, look at that, Mags," Delia drawled, gazing off in the direction Amberley had gone. "You managed to scare away another one. That didn't take long."

Maggie scowled, drawing herself up. "Delia," she said, "I have had it with you."

"Beg pardon?" Her sister's green eyes glittered as she turned.

"I am sick and tired of your attitude. What on earth is wrong with you?"

"Me?" The marchioness let out an indignant huff of laughter. "There's nothing wrong with *me*, I assure you."

"Then why would you say such awful things to Amberley about me? And to Serena and Portia earlier? Why are you always trying to make a fool of me wherever I go?"

Delia rolled her eyes. "Oh, can't you take a joke?" Then she waggled her fingers politely at a carriage full of people she knew going by in the opposite direction. "Halloo! Good afternoon."

"This goes far beyond humor, Delia," Maggie said, ignoring them. "I'm not stupid."

"Hmm," Delia teased, then waved again to someone else—Trinny's mother and a horde of red-haired younger sisters went trundling by, enjoying the sunshine. "Lady Beresford, so nice to see you. Hullo, girls!"

The youngsters all waved back cheerfully.

Maggie managed a nod to their neighbors, noting with a pang that the Beresford girls all seemed to get along well together.

Delia's coach rolled along inevitably as Fate, wheels crackling over the gravel. The empress seemed to bask in the view of the flat, pleasant green and all the liveliness of a busy Hyde Park afternoon, but Maggie knew Delia was watching her from the corner of her eye.

Perfect. Now she's ignoring me. Maggie fumed at her sister's obtuseness.

Very well, perhaps this wasn't the best place for the confrontation she finally felt ready to have.

Maggie glanced at the coachman, who was sitting up on the box, ramrod straight, and, no doubt, trying desperately not to overhear anything he shouldn't.

"Hubert!" Maggie called. "Would you kindly take us home now?"

"What? Never mind that, Hubert! Don't tell my driver what to do," Delia snapped. "He's my coachman, not yours. Hubert, continue 'round the Ring!"

"Er, yes, milady."

"I'd head home if I were you," Maggie warned her sister.

"Why?" Delia demanded, the jaunty feather on her hat whipping in the wind, which had begun blowing harder. "If it rains, we'll simply put the top up."

"This has nothing to do with the weather." Maggie braced herself. "I have something to say to you."

"Oh really?"

"Yes. And I don't think you want me to say it here."

"Speak your mind, by all means, sister!" Delia folded her arms across her chest and sat back as though she welcomed the challenge.

Maggie swallowed hard, going a bit dry-mouthed. She could not deny she had always found Delia intimidating when she went all cool and superior like that.

For a moment, she was tempted to back down, simply out of habit. But no. Not this time. "You really want to have this out right here, in the middle of Hyde Park, with half the ton present?"

"Have what out, Mags?"

"Oh, I think you know." Maggie started trembling, but not from fear, exactly. Nervousness, perhaps. It seemed to be some sort of automatic response to the prospect of a row. But still, she didn't falter, holding her sister's gaze. "We are going to end this now. For once and for all."

Delia studied her for a moment, then shook her head. "You don't have the nerve. Look at you, already shaking like a leaf. Drive on, Hubert!" she ordered, sending Maggie a smirk of defiance.

Of casual domination.

Maggie's nostrils flared as she inhaled sharply, glaring at her sister.

The coachman sent an apprehensive glance over his shoulder, looking torn between the two conflicting orders he'd received.

Maggie knew full well that all of Delia's servants preferred her to their mistress. But she didn't want to get the poor man sacked.

Noticing Hubert's distress, Maggie waved it off. "Do as she says," she muttered, shaking her head and looking away as a trio of male riders went galloping by in a cloud of dust.

Pleased with her petty victory, Delia folded her arms across her chest and eyed Maggie. "That's what I thought." Delia shook her head after a moment. "You have some cheek, complaining to me about anything, after all I've done for you."

"I'd have fared much better by now if you'd done far less, believe me."

"What's that supposed to mean?"

"If you're so keen to be rid of me, you should've tried to help me find a husband instead of driving them all away just to humiliate me. But no. You do the exact opposite! When I meet a man I like, you start meddling, planting your little seeds of destruction, and end up ruining it for me every time. I only wish I understood why."

"What rubbish! You ungrateful little monster, I do nothing of the kind."

"Yes, you do!" Maggie said. "If you had not been hellbent on ruining my life at every turn, I'd have already finished *imposing* on you for the dreadful burden I've placed on you, having to share your roof! Never mind that I'm your own flesh and blood."

"I promised Papa that I would look after you, and I've kept my word," Delia said. "It's not *my* fault if you can't conduct your own affairs. Do you know how many times I have kept you out of trouble?"

"All you ever do is tear me down!" Maggie cried.

"It's for your own good," Delia said oh so reasonably.

"How's that?"

"I am keeping you from becoming any more conceited than you

already are, Margaret Hyacinth."

"I beg your pardon?" Maggie stared at her in disbelief.

Delia preened and looked forward as the coach rolled on. "I suppose there'll be no living with you now that you think you've got a duke sniffing around your skirts. You know he only wants one thing from you, anyway."

Delia's crudeness revolted Maggie almost as much as the outlandish accusation. "No, he doesn't, and I am *not* conceited! You're the one who's completely incapable of honesty."

Delia arched a brow.

"Why do you hate me so much?" Maggie asked softly. "What did I ever do to you?"

"Oh, don't be so dramatic. I don't hate you."

"You act like it. You clearly have some sort of grudge against me and always have. So, why don't you just come out and tell me what it is?"

Delia looked forward down the road and said nothing.

"Well? Tell me! If you make me understand, perhaps there's something I can do to try and change it."

"You can't change it," Delia said.

"Why not?"

"Because it's in the past!"

"Apparently, it's not, if it still comes between us every day. So?" Maggie waited.

"Fine. You really want to know?" Delia said tightly after a moment.

"I'm asking!"

"It's not fair," Delia said crisply.

"What's not fair?" Maggie said, mystified.

"Mother always thought you hung the moon, while I might as well have not even existed. It's not fair; it's not right!" Delia burst out. "They both spoiled you, taught you how to be all puffed up about yourself and put on airs. You think you're better than everyone else—"

"That is utterly ridiculous! Delia!" Maggie said. "You cannot honestly believe that."

"You can't even see it in yourself!" Delia cried, turning fully to Maggie. "Take *him*, for example." She flung a gesture in the direction Amberley had gone. "How arrogant do you have to be to think that *you*, the mere daughter of an earl—and a younger daughter at that—have any business setting your cap at a duke? Especially one like him, rich and handsome. He'd be better off with Portia. At least her father is a marquess."

Maggie stared at Delia, floundering. "I-I am not setting my cap at Amberley."

"Oh, spare me the sickening protestations of innocence, Miss Perfect. I see you drooling over him. Big stud with a coronet and a huge fortune? How fine you must think yourself to have snared his attention!"

Maggie felt herself color, certainly not about to tell her sister anything. "He is a nice man! That is all."

"As if that has anything to do with marriage among our class. No. You just want to outshine me, as ever." Delia stared at her as though waiting for a response, but Maggie just sat there. "Well? Have you nothing to say for yourself?"

"I-I… Y-you've flabbergasted me," Maggie finally said. "I have *never* outshined you in anything, Delia! How could I? People don't even notice that I exist when you are there. You're the eldest. I've lived in your shadow all my life.

"As for my friendship with His Grace… Well, I feel sorry for you if all you can see of other people is their fortune and rank. But that's how it is with you, isn't it? As long as I've known you, you've always been jockeying for position, trying to put yourself above everyone else in the pecking order. Especially me. And you know what that means?"

Delia sneered at her. "Enlighten me."

"It means I'm not the arrogant one—*you* are. And if you don't realize that, then you are beyond anyone's help. Mine. Even Edward. How the man puts up with you, I have no idea."

"Don't you dare talk about my husband!"

"Why? Because I'm the only one besides the servants who knows how badly you treat him? That man is far too good for you, you know."

"How dare you?" Delia gasped, but Maggie warmed further to the fight.

It was so much easier defending her dear brother-in-law than standing up for herself. "It's true! Edward is a saint. You may only care about his rank and fortune, but that man adores you. Mark my words, Delia. If you hurt him one day badly enough to lose him, no one will ever love you like that again."

Delia's face had paled into a frozen mask of rage.

"Get out," she suddenly spat. "Get out of my coach right now! Hubert, stop the carriage!" Glaring at Maggie, she pointed to the carriage door as the coach slowed.

"Delia—"

"You heard me. Get. Out! You can *walk* the rest of the way home, or don't come back at all, for all I care!"

"Delia!" Maggie felt a surge of panic at this unexpected turn of events. "Don't do this—"

"Remove yourself, please. I can't stand the sight of you a moment longer, you ungrateful little witch." Delia turned away, blocking Maggie from view behind the brim of her hat, muttering furiously to herself. "Telling me about my own husband. *Go!*" she barked.

Maggie's first impulse was to apologize, as ever, and plead with Delia not to throw her out of the carriage in the middle of Hyde Park, to be humiliated in front of all Society.

Granted, it wasn't very far to Moonlight Square. But there were so many people present.

Even Hubert looked appalled. "A-are you sure, Lady Birdwell?"

"Of course I'm sure!" Delia said, red-faced. "I'm always sure!"

Maggie waved off her sister's order, excusing Hubert from culpability. She mumbled to him not to bother when he set the brake and hastily started to descend from the driver's box to come and hand her down.

As if such courtesies made the slightest difference right now.

"Just keep your distance, Hubert," Maggie said stiffly.

He looked relieved, though uncertain. The man had a family to feed, after all.

"Look forward! Do you mind?" Delia said.

Hubert turned around, facing the horses.

"Well? Go!" Delia ordered.

"I'm going." Maggie stifled a growl and rose to her feet.

A glance around revealed that their very public argument had already drawn more than a few stares from all around the green.

Thank God, Amberley was nowhere in sight to witness her total defeat.

She could just imagine how the mighty warrior would cringe at her failure to win a simple argument—even one where she was in the right!

But as the image of the fearsome major blossomed in her mind, in all his Irish fight and rebellion, Maggie suddenly decided, *So be it.* And all in an instant, she mentally washed her hands of her sister.

This was pointless.

"You know what?" she finally said, opening the carriage door. "You win, Delia. I'll get out, gladly. And I'll enjoy the walk home. But in the meanwhile, you had better figure out what you're going to say to Edward when I tell him about this."

"He's *my* husband, not yours. Whose side do you think he's going to take? You're just miffed that you haven't been able to land one of your own, poor, ugly spinster!"

Stung by this lowest of blows, Maggie narrowed her eyes to angry slashes, but pressed her lips shut. She did not trust herself not to scream.

"You think I care if you run and tattle on me to Edward? I'm used to it, Maggie," Delia added bitterly. "You did the same thing to me throughout our childhood, running to Mother and Father to tell them everything I ever did wrong. *You're* the reason they never loved me."

"Yes, they did—despite the fact that you were a horrible child! Oh, yes, you were!" Maggie shouted before Delia could deny it. "You wreaked havoc whenever you got the chance! Half the time you were a danger to yourself—and others. Was I to keep them in the dark about your antics?"

"I was never bad, merely high-spirited—except compared to you, Mama's perfect little angel!"

"High-spirited?" Astonished, Maggie paused. "Maybe you've forgotten, Delia, but I certainly haven't—how you browbeat our nursery maids until they burst into tears and quit. How you picked on all the other children, kicked the pets, tore the limbs off my favorite dolly! And when you were twelve—remember how you stole Papa's cheroots and a flask of his brandy? You were a spoiled little horror, Delia! Half the villagers walked on eggshells for fear of your little tantrums, and frankly, you haven't changed a bit. I just hope that one of these days, you will *finally* grow up!"

"Will you *please* get away from me?" Delia yelled, rising to her feet, as if she had half a mind to throw Maggie bodily out of the carriage.

"I'm going!" Maggie bellowed, jumping out of the coach. "Good *day!*"

"Good riddance!" Delia roared back, red-faced.

Maggie slammed the carriage door, shaking with rage.

"Hubert, put the damned top up!" Delia ordered. "All these bloody people gawking at me. Why don't you mind your own business?" the marchioness hollered at some wide-eyed passersby.

Maggie shook her head in disgust. "What elegance, my lady."

"Step aside or I'll bloody run you over, Margaret!"

Glaring at Delia and gripping her reticule tight, Maggie stepped off the graveled roadway and somehow managed not to bite her thumb at her sister.

It was the only rude gesture she knew, from a Shakespeare play. She was too angry right now to remember which, but at least she knew that famous line: *"I bite my thumb at you, sir!"*

Hubert had scrambled to comply with Delia's order, raising the folded-down leather top over the open coach. He sent Maggie a frantic look as she pivoted and began marching off alone across the grass.

"I'll send Miss Penelope to find you, ma'am," he ventured.

Maggie waved off his offer, already stalking away. "Don't bother."

It was Penelope's day off. She was probably wandering through various mantua-makers' shops right now with her two friends who also worked as ladies' maids, styling aristocratic women. They went out now and then to peruse the shops and get ideas, for a good lady's maid made it her business to keep her mistress abreast of all the latest fashions.

Sometimes Maggie thought Penelope was more like a sister to her than Delia was.

Humiliated by her ejection from the carriage, she felt sick to her stomach as she headed for the nearest copse of trees, desperate to take cover from all the prying eyes.

She could feel countless stares upon her, while her pulse pounded and her legs trembled. *What a disaster.*

With her wrath starting to recede once she'd escaped Delia's infuriating presence, she regretted ever having tried to stand up to her in the first place. *Why didn't I keep my mouth shut? All I've done is make everything worse.*

When, at last, the shadows of the grove she had entered screened her from view, Maggie blew out a shaky breath, fighting back tears.

She glanced toward the road and saw Delia's coach rumbling off around the bend. Her chin trembled, eyes prickling with moisture. Her sister's words were hurtful, to be sure. Hurtful and false. But that was not what made Maggie give way to a sob. It was the sheer, intolerable powerlessness of her situation.

That and the specter of a deep, aching loneliness.

Spinster, Delia had called her. What if she really did end up alone...forever?

It was too terrifying to contemplate.

God, it was intolerable sometimes, being a lady, forbidden from making a living of one's own, forced into being a dependent. If she were a commoner like Penelope, she would've at least had more options.

Ah, and if she were a man, she could've forged her own way in the world and lived exactly as she pleased.

But, of course, that would never be. She was who she was. The daughter of an earl, trained to be a wife and mother and run an upper-class household. Which meant she had to marry someone.

Quickly.

For she really couldn't take this anymore. No doubt Delia would treat her even worse after that debacle. Fear gripped her as she wondered if her sister would even let her back into the house. If not...then what?

Blast it all, Delia had no right to do this to her! Surely Edward would not stand for it. Frankly, Maggie did not even want to go back to their house, but where else could she go?

For a while longer, Maggie remained hidden among the trees, leaning against the smooth, whitish trunk of a slender elm until she had managed to calm down and gather her composure.

When someone drove slowly past the place where she'd gone into hiding, she decided to get out of here before this ordeal became any more embarrassing.

For now, she had no choice but to return to Birdwell House.

Blotting away her last couple of tears with the fingertips of her ivory kid gloves, she took a deep breath, pushed away from the tree, and lifted her chin.

If anyone stopped her, she would simply tell them that she had decided to walk the rest of the way on her own. Yes, she and her sister had bickered. But what sisters in the world didn't now and then? If anyone knew the true depths of Delia's cutting comments, it would only bring dishonor on their entire family.

Delia must be shocked that Maggie had stood up to her for once, though.

That at least gave Maggie *some* satisfaction as she squared her shoulders and finally strode out of the other end of the pretty grove of trees.

Time to start walking. One could always do with a brisk constitutional.

Unfortunately, she had not gone far when the wind picked up and a few rumbles of thunder rolled across the firmament, coming ever closer.

Then, before she had even reached Hyde Park Corner, lightning streaked through the air, piercing the dark, heavy clouds.

Which promptly disgorged a miserable torrent of rain on her head.

Maggie let out a huge sigh and dropped her chin nearly to her chest. *Worst…day…ever.*

CHAPTER 16

Revelations Unfold

"So, military man, eh?" Gable's father said, shaking Connor's hand. A trim fellow in his sixties, the Earl of Sefton had salt-and-pepper hair and a shrewd, searching gaze behind his spectacles. "I was pleased to hear your inclinations lean Tory. Though perhaps not on the Irish question, eh?"

"Father," said Gable, "I did not bring Amberley here today to speak about politics. Not yet." He shut the door to the earl's wood-paneled office.

"Oh?" Lord Sefton gestured to a seat in front of his huge oak desk.

Connor nodded in thanks and flipped the tails of his riding coat out of the way as he took the leather chair on the right. Gable drifted over and dropped into the chair beside him.

The two of them had made it to the earl's fine house in St. James's without incident, though the skies had gone gunmetal gray on the way over. Having secured Hurricane in an extra box-stall, they had no sooner stepped out of the stable into the cobbled mews when the brewing storm broke.

Then they'd run for the house, pelted by raindrops.

Gable had laughed, said it helped to wake him up.

Now the deluge pounded against the wide window behind the earl's huge oak desk. As Gable glanced over his shoulder in expectation of the tea the butler had offered, Connor supposed it would have been all rather cozy if he were not worried about Maggie.

Perhaps he was becoming a proper mother hen, but he hoped the ladies had made it back to Moonlight Square safe and sound.

"No," Gable said, "I'm afraid the reason Amberley needs to talk to you is a bit more serious than the vote of the day."

"Well, that sounds mysterious." Sefton glanced from his son to Connor. "What can I do for you boys?"

"Someone's trying to kill him," Gable informed his sire, gesturing at Connor.

"Really?" the earl asked. His eyebrows lifted. "Whatever for?"

"That's what I'm trying to find out, sir," Connor answered in a hard tone.

"This needs to remain confidential, Father," Gable added.

"Of course," said Sefton.

Gable began to explain. Having taken the man's measure and decided that he trusted the suave, quiet viscount, Connor had explained his situation in full on the way here.

Gable had been startled, but vowed to assist however he could, and had honored Connor's injunction against telling anyone else except his father, at least for now.

"You needn't worry about *him* saying anything, either," Gable had assured him. "Ol' Sefton's known to be a very vault. You wouldn't believe what my father knows about people in this town, actually. You'll definitely be speaking to the right man. I'm so glad you told me."

"Me too," Connor had said. "I am in your debt."

"Nonsense," Gable had answered. "We're neighbors."

Presently, between the two of them, Gable doing most of the talking, they finished telling the earl about the two attempts on Connor's life. Sefton asked a few sensible questions, then sat in silence for a moment.

"Well, I'm sorry to say that positions of power do invite the hatred of the jealous now and then. I've had threats made against me, God knows, but thankfully, no one ever tried carrying them out." He furrowed his brow. "Forgive the obvious question, Your Grace, but do you have any particular enemies?"

"Not poisoners, to be sure," Connor said with a snort. "Nor the sort to attack in the dark from behind." He shook his head. "But looking at the three deaths in my line in the space of a mere eighteen months, I don't think this is about me. I think someone's got a grudge against *all* the men in my family. But I have no earthly idea who or why, or what the cause of it might be, because I barely knew my English relatives."

"That is where I told him you might be able to help, Father," Gable said. "Anything you could tell him about the past three Dukes of Amberley might offer some hint at what's at the root of this problem."

"Any dodgy characters that one of my predecessors might've been involved with?" Connor asked.

"Dodgy characters?" A half-smile tugged at Sefton's lips. "Well, of course, the First Duchess springs immediately to mind—begging your pardon. But I'm sure you must know about that."

Connor looked at him blankly. "Grandaunt Lucinda?"

Sefton stared at him. "Don't you know?"

"Know what?" Connor asked.

"Oh dear." Sefton frowned and sat back, briefly tapping his desk with the tip of a pencil. "This is awkward."

"It's quite all right, my lord. Please, enlighten me."

"Father?" Gable said.

"Well…" Sefton cleared his throat and gave them both a rather sheepish look. "I was referring to the lady's past."

"Meaning?" Gable prompted.

The earl glanced from one to the other, hesitating. "I don't wish to be rude, Your Grace."

"Please," Connor said with a wave of his hand, "you won't offend me. Speak freely, by all means."

Sefton shifted uncomfortably in his seat. "Well, I suppose it's not so strange that you weren't aware of it. All families have their secrets, and after all this time—it's been, what, more than fifty years now—the scandal has faded with time. But, you see, ahem, well, many years ago, Lucinda Bly was the toast of the demimonde."

"What?" Gable cried.

"Lucky Lucy Bly, they used to call her. Drove the men mad, until your Granduncle Charles snared her. She was the First Duke's mistress before they wed."

Connor's jaw was nearly on the floor.

Gable likewise wore a look of incredulity. "The dragon lady?" he finally exclaimed. "The highest of sticklers?"

"Oh yes. Compensating for her scarlet past, I should think. Ah, she was magnificent in her day. I was but a boy of nineteen when I first saw her on display in her theater box with the other courtesans. I remember it well…how she leaned over the railing to blow a kiss to her admirers with her gown cut clean down to here." He gestured at his midriff with a grin.

"Good God!" Connor whispered, astonished, and feeling a tingle of hilarity.

Gable was gaping at his father as though he'd never seen him before. Then he and Connor looked at each other in amazement, and—both familiar with the fearsome old dragon that the dowager duchess had become—both burst out laughing.

Maggie was still running through the streets of London in a torrent of rain.

It came down in sheets at her, this way and that, tossed by the wind. The loud drumming of it everywhere striking the road and the pavement filled her ears. Growls of thunder rolled overhead, but it was the few impressive lightning streaks that urged her on with a slight shriek any time her pace slowed.

Instinctive fear of nature's wrath lent an odd touch of exhilaration to her mad dash. But, at least, running kept her warm, for the cold downpour coursed down her back.

By now, her fine carriage gown of blue striped muslin was ruined beyond all repair. The rain spilled off the brim of her chip bonnet, soaking her hair.

In the midst of her panicked, bedraggled state, lost and alone, with neither umbrella nor maid, for the final humiliation, who should come driving up Park Lane toward her than Bryce?

Faint hope of rescue stirred when she saw him approaching.

Snug and dry beneath the raised hood of his curricle, her jilted suitor was—thank God—alone. The fewer people who saw her like this, the better, Maggie thought, her teeth chattering.

Considering that she had ended their courtship, she did not expect cordiality, per se—although this would've been a perfect opportunity for him to try to change her mind about their match. Show his true worth by playing the role of her rescuer.

Alas, this was Bryce they were talking about.

He'd heard of chivalry, of course, but as it turned out, it didn't much interest him. Maggie could already see the smirk forming on his lips as he slowed his curricle to a halt beside her and took a good, long look at her in all her sopping misery.

Pausing her sprint, Maggie turned on the pavement, looking up at him with a shiver running through her frame, the rain dripping off her bonnet, and squishing through her shoes.

"L-Lord Bryce," she said hopefully over the noisy patter, teeth chattering, as the water trickling down her neck gave her a chill.

"Tsk, tsk, my dear Lady Margaret." He shook his head, clearly enjoying this. "A word of advice? Always take an umbrella."

"Bryce!"

"Au revoir, cherie." Laughing, Bryce cracked the whip over his horses' backs and splashed off through a huge puddle in the cobbled street, sending a large plume of muddy water fountaining right up into her face.

Doused all over again, Maggie sputtered with indignation as he drove away.

"Cad!" she shouted after him.

But after the row with her sister, feeling the rain dripping down her nose, and splashing through puddles up to her ankles, it was hard to say which was worse: marrying Bryce or living with Delia.

Putting the whole maddening question out of her mind, she pushed on, running across the next street, and half hoping at that point that she caught the ague. *That'll teach her—Bryce, too! If I catch my death*, then *they'll be sorry…*

Amid such woeful thoughts, she clambered on through the rain-scoured streets, the cobblestones slippery under her feet, her cold, sodden skirts clinging to her limbs.

When she flung around the corner into Moonlight Square, passing the Grand Albion, the rain blew at her from the right now, rather than pelting her in the back.

Cringing at the prospect of her neighbors seeing her like this, she put her head down, hiding behind the brim of her bonnet. She wished she could've cut through the garden park's acreage to avoid being spotted, but the nearest gate was not in a suitable location. It was easier just to go around till she reached Marquess Row.

Just get this over with!

The large, elegant square seemed to have grown even wider, while the wind rocked the plane trees and went riffling through their lush, leafy branches.

As Maggie hurried toward the corner of the south terrace, she heard another carriage clattering up behind her.

Her first thought was that Bryce must've had a change of heart and decided to come after her. But if that was the case, he was too late now. She was almost home—such as it was.

Besides, that bounder was dead to her.

Maggie marched on, her angry stare fixed straight ahead, but it was not Bryce's haughty tones that reached her just then.

"Excuse me! Excuse me, miss?" came a gravelly voice over the constant hiss of the rain striking the pavement.

Maggie turned, startled, shivering in the spring chill, and soaked through to the skin.

A small black coach built on the narrow lines of an expensive vis-à-vis rolled up beside her. The team of liver bays pulling it had turned nearly black with the rain drenching their coats.

Then a lean, sinewy young gentleman with a neat, narrow beard jumped down from the shelter of the roofed driver's box.

"I say!" he called, holding on to the brim of his top hat to keep it from blowing away. "May I be of assistance, my lady?" He gestured gallantly to his coach, his black greatcoat billowing in the wind. "This is no weather for anyone to be out walking!" He spoke loudly to be heard over the thunder that made Maggie jump once again.

The stranger offered her a reassuring smile. "It's all right." He stepped closer. "Let me assist you. I see you were caught unawares by the weather. Allow me to offer my conveyance to wherever your destination might be."

"Oh! How very kind," she said, managing a startled laugh despite the slight chattering of her teeth. "If only you'd found me a mile ago! Thank you, but that won't be necessary—"

"No, I insist," he interrupted, taking another step toward her. "You're freezing. You'll catch your death in this tempest. Climb in." He held the carriage door open for her. "I'll take you wherever you need to go. It would be my honor."

Maggie studied him for a heartbeat, unsure what to think.

He had a gentlemanly bearing, and even looked strangely familiar.

But everyone knew it was unthinkable for an unchaperoned young lady to get into a man's closed carriage. Not even a thunderstorm was any sort of excuse. Any real gentleman knew that.

And his smile unsettled her. It did not reach his eyes.

No doubt, he was only being kind.

Yet a tickle at the back of her awareness whispered that something here…wasn't quite right.

Fortunately, she was too close to her so-called home now to require the stranger's assistance. So she blinked off the unsettling thought and smiled anyway, because she was Maggie Winthrop. Well-bred. Polite.

Unsuspecting.

"Thank you so much. I'm thrilled to see chivalry is not dead in Town after all. But I live just here, you see. I'm already home." She gestured vaguely toward Marquess Row.

The stranger squinted in the direction she indicated, then looked at her again with an almost predatory stillness.

With his stare fixed on her, he did not even seem to feel the rain coursing down his face. "Still a bit of a walk yet," he pointed out. "I don't mind."

His cold tone did not match his courteous words, and the distinct ripple of uneasiness running down her spine intensified as he took yet another step toward her.

"N-no, thank you." She shook her head and began backing away, her smile turning brittle. "I'll be there in a moment. But I-I appreciate your concern. Good day!"

A flinty hardness flickered in his eyes as she sketched a curtsy, then turned around and ran.

She did not stop till she reached Edward and Delia's front door after some fifty yards.

As she grasped the door handle, she stole another wary glance over her shoulder and found him still standing there.

Watching her.

When he saw her look back, he sketched a gentlemanly bow, as though to confirm he had merely waited to make sure she had got in all right. He waved a friendly farewell, then jumped back up into his coach and picked up the reins.

Maggie made no move to enter the house until she was sure he was gone.

Not quite tipping his hat, he sent her a little salute as he rolled on by, driving past their house to exit Moonlight Square by the other end.

It was that slight, unthinking gesture—the salute—that jogged her memory all in a flash after he'd gone.

Of course! Relief flooded her as she remembered where she had seen him before. *Oh, you silly thing,* she told herself.

A shaky laugh escaped her at her own paranoid imaginings. For a moment there, she had thought… Oh, never mind what she'd thought.

She shook her head ruefully. *I knew he looked familiar.* He had not been in uniform just now—and perhaps the fellow *was* a little intense overall—but in hindsight, she understood that his offer of help was naught but the typical gallantry of a military man seeking to aid an obvious damsel in distress.

Maggie rarely forgot a face. It was a knack of hers. After the terrible day she was having, she'd been slow to remember, but now it came to her.

He had been at Connor's duel—one of those dashing dragoons.

He probably knew Connor. And so, greatly relieved, she put the man out of her mind, bracing herself to go into the house. For, after that row with Delia, heaven only knew what waited for her behind that door.

Lady Margaret Winthrop, Seth mused as he drove around the corner and circled back one more time to observe, gain the lay of the land.

Watching her scamper away, he'd been disgusted but not surprised that she'd slipped through his grasp.

Ah well. It had been a whim, anyway. He was never one to overlook an easy opportunity that presented itself. But he hadn't pressed the matter, unwilling to stir her suspicions—or the duke's.

She was the girl from the duel, of course. The one who'd run to Amberley's side looking more stricken over his gunshot wound than he was.

It had been easy to learn her identity, since the ton had been abuzz about the whole event, from the hole in Lord Bryce's hat to the young lady's outburst.

Hmm. Well, now he knew where she lived. A fruitful day, in all.

Seth had discreetly followed Amberley Number Four from his house today—from a safe distance, of course—and tracked him to Hyde Park. When he'd seen the duke ride over to the two ladies in the open coach, he had recognized the brown-haired beauty as the girl from the duel, and now that he could put a face to the name, Seth had watched their exchange carefully, lurking amid the crowd.

When Amberley and the ladies had parted ways in Hyde Park, Seth hadn't been sure at first whom to follow. The duke had simply begun exercising his impressive dapple gray, taking the beast for one hell of a gallop across the park's sprawling acreage.

Seth had nearly lost him then, thanks to his mount's speed, but he'd caught up just in time to see Amberley go riding off with some other chap.

Seth had followed the pair to some aristocratic mansion in St. James's, but they'd gone inside. Shut out, he'd decided to return to the Ring to try and find the females again.

By sheer luck, he had spied Lady Margaret walking off by herself, looking very upset. Then the weather had turned foul, and he'd been caught in the crush of traffic fleeing Hyde Park. He'd followed and finally managed to catch up with her in Moonlight Square.

Debating with himself about how to proceed once he had her in his sights, he had watched her progress through the screen of plane trees and lush greenery shrouding the park.

Then he'd been arrested by the way her wet gown clung to her body; you could almost see through it. An arrow of lust had pierced him, and he'd started thinking that thought again.

The one that would probably get him in trouble someday.

The wicked desire in the back of his mind for a lady.

A real one.

He'd never had one. Not once. Of all the hundreds of females he'd sampled for fun or broken in for Father's establishments, they'd all been whores of one sort or another.

Never *that*, with class seeping out of her pores.

Her kind fascinated and rather scared him, almost, in a sense. Bona fide ladies. Mother had been one, though he barely remembered her, small as he'd been when she'd died birthing Francis.

All he really knew about his dam was that she had been the last vestige of a once-great Darrow family, which had bankrupted itself generations ago.

That was the only way, obviously, that the rough-and-tumble likes of self-made millionaire Elias Flynn could have captured such a bride. One who'd brought to the marriage that precious whiff of respectability that Father had yearned to bequeath to his sons, the one possession he himself could never have.

The reminder of Father's displeasure brought Seth back to the grim reason he was here. He glanced over to the mansion on the corner: Amberley House.

His face hardened, a surge of jealousy in his veins.

Oh, to be sure, the likes of His Grace could have all the Lady

Margaret Winthrops that he could consume.

How they must cast themselves at his feet. But this one, Lady Margaret, well, Seth had seen how Amberley had gazed at her at the duel, and no wonder.

She was a jewel, a wet, dewy flower, so innocent. She even moved with refinement, he'd noticed, the way she went hurrying through the rain so lightly and delicately, like she was in danger of melting, made of marzipan.

And now, having gone in the house, she'd be peeling those fine clothes off, piece by piece, with the help of her maid...

Seth swallowed hard and clapped the reins over his horses' backs, driving on. Best not press his luck here.

It wouldn't do to be noted lingering about.

He'd continue watching both Duke Number Four and the girl. But, for now, he had gained enough information.

Indeed, he knew now what he could do about Amberley, if all else failed.

The idea was riskier than he liked. Very much so. It would not be his first choice of how to complete his assignment.

It could ruin everything for him — and for Father — if even one thing went wrong. But it would work, to be sure. And if he committed to it fully, it would be easy to carry out.

Realist that he was, Seth could acknowledge that he might *never* manage to beat the major in a fair fight, as much as it stung his pride to admit it.

Ah, but with that damp, dewy goddess in his grasp, it would be a simple matter to lure Amberley to *him*.

Then he could blow the bastard's brains out the minute he came to collect her.

And with Amberley out of the way, why then, thought Seth with a lusty smirk, he could finally satisfy his curiosity about how it felt to bed a lady.

He doubted, in truth, it was any different from taking his rough pleasure of a whore. But there was only one way to find out.

Pleased at the prospect of that sweet little miss as his reward for finally completing his task for Father, Seth drove on with a smile on his face.

CHAPTER 17

A Shift in the Wind

"He's a good man, your father. I like him well," Connor said as he walked back out to the mews with Gable, having finished his meeting with Lord Sefton.

"He seems impressed with you, likewise, and believe me, that's no easy feat."

The rain had stopped, and the fresh, damp aroma of it rose from the cobblestones, mingling comfortingly with the smell of horses and hay from the stables.

"You two certainly seem to get on well together," Connor continued. "It's nice to see."

"We didn't always, God knows." Gable smiled wryly while the sound of hungry horses neighing for their supper floated out on the evening air. "He used to think me an utter wastrel. And frankly, before Trinny came along, he was not altogether wrong in his estimation. She straightened me out."

"She seems a fine woman."

"Why don't you join us for supper tonight?" Gable asked as they strolled across the mews, heading for the stable. "I have to stay here a little while longer with Father to go over some things he wants me to see to in his absence, but you could take your horse home and make sure he's settled, then join us at our house in Moonlight Square. We're quite informal, and we'd love to have you. After all, you are our new neighbor."

"That's very kind of you. But won't your lady mind?"

"Not at all. She spent so many weeks closeted in her confinement with the babe that she's eager for company. Besides, I have an ulterior motive."

Connor looked askance at him. "You want to show off that baby of yours, don't you?"

"Oh God, am I that obvious?" the viscount exclaimed, laughing.

Connor chuckled knowingly.

Gable's face flushed. "I try not to be too obnoxious about it, but I am ridiculously smitten with the tot."

"As you should be," Connor said.

"So, are you free?"

"I'd be delighted," he said.

As they went back into the stables, a groom reported that Hurricane had behaved himself, to Connor's relief. The groom led the way to the stallion's temporary stall, but Connor had no sooner reached for the stall door than he furrowed his brow and turned back, his heart sinking.

"You know, on second thought, I should wait until all this trouble is laid to rest before I set foot in your home. God only knows what these enemies of mine are capable of. I could never forgive myself if I were to draw danger to your wife and child."

Gable's expression turned grim. "Damn. I hadn't thought of that... That's a hell of a thing," he murmured, then folded his arms across his chest. "Do you really think...?"

Connor shrugged. "Not worth taking the chance. Let us just postpone it. Better safe than sorry. But thank you. It means a great deal to me."

Gable frowned. "If it were just me, I would say it doesn't matter, but—"

"No, no, not at all." Connor hauled open the stall door and collected his horse.

Gable leaned against the wood frame, admiring the animal, though his eyes showed his concern. "So, do you think you'll confront your aunt and see if your family's troubles now have anything to do with her past?"

"Confront the dragon?" Connor ran down a stirrup and gave Gable a sardonic glance. "Who do you think I am, Saint George?"

His friend chortled.

Connor shook his head. "It's a delicate matter, to be sure. I think she's still grieving and I don't want to make anything worse. I may ask a few cautious questions—*after* this soirée she's holding for me, of course.

Such questions are sure to offend her, and God only knows what she might do to me in revenge at the party if she sets her mind against me."

"My father certainly had fond memories of her beauty back then." Gable shook his head. "I don't think I've ever seen him like that before."

They both laughed at the earl's rhapsody over "Lucky Lucy Bly."

"Well, I'll say this for her," Connor remarked as he went around to the other side of Hurricane, resting his hand on the animal's flank on the way so the temperamental stallion knew where he was. "Difficult as she is, she must be one hell of a survivor to have clawed her way up from that life to being a duchess. There's something in that I can't help but respect."

Gable nodded. "At least it explains how she became so formidable."

"Aye." Connor shrugged and then tightened the saddle girth.

A couple of grooms gathered around to admire Hurricane as Connor led the stallion out. They kept a respectful distance but ogled the tall thoroughbred and ventured to ask a few intelligent questions about the animal. Connor happily indulged them by answering their queries about the horse's lineage and speed.

"He's a fine animal, Your Grace," the head groom finally said with a bow as they let Connor and his horse go on their way.

"Thanks for looking after him," Connor said, and gave the man several coins to pass around to the stable boys.

Gable sauntered after him, hands in pockets, as Connor led Hurricane back out into the cobbled yard.

"You know," the viscount said as Connor threw the reins over Hurricane's withers, preparing to mount up, "supper might have to wait, but surely you could come and play cards with me and the boys tomorrow night."

His ears perking up at the sound of fun, Connor turned to him. "Oh?"

Gable nodded. "We're playing long whist at the club starting at eight, if you want to join us. It's deep play, but we'd be glad to deal you in."

"Sounds a fine way to get rid of some of this ridiculous fortune I've inherited."

"Could be," Gable said with amusement. "More importantly, there'll be a whole crew of us at the table, so you would not appear to be singling anyone out, even if your enemy was watching. But it's doubtful that he would be, since only residents of Moonlight Square can be members at the Grand Albion. Of course, they can bring guests," he admitted. "Netherford always brings Peter Carvel, for example. But Rivenwood will be there. Sidney, me. What do you think?"

"Aye," Connor said, nodding, "that I could do. Thank you, Gable. I'll be there. Sounds a proper way to spend a Saturday night."

"Into morning, usually."

"Aha. And you mean to stay awake for it?" Connor jested, recalling the new father's frequent yawns.

Gable grinned. "Coffee, man. Nectar of the New World. So, are you any good at gambling?"

Connor gave him a cheery wink. "Luck o' the Irish."

"Ha! Well, you'll need it. Watch out for Netherford; he's a shark. And Sidney is a master of the bluff."

With a hearty laugh, Connor swung up onto his horse. "Thanks, mate. I'm lookin' forward to it."

Gable nodded, and they parted ways.

"I cannot *believe* she did that to you!" Penelope cried, pacing back and forth across Maggie's chamber. She had returned from her day off and been appalled at the news. "I simply...cannot...believe it! What is wrong with that woman? Begging your pardon, my lady, but—I'm sorry—your sister's a witch!"

"I don't disagree," Maggie replied wearily, propped up against the headboard of her bed, with several pillows around her and three blankets tucked in about her shivering body. She sneezed again, covering it with her handkerchief just in time.

Penelope rushed to Maggie's bedside as though she were dying. "Oh, I'm so sorry! I feel responsible for this! If I had been there, at least—"

"You'd have caught a cold, too. Don't worry, I'll be fine by tomorrow. I'm hardier than I look." With a half-smile, Maggie reached gratefully for the cup of hot tea that Penelope had brought her.

It was Mama's old remedy for colds, passed down for generations, simply to add a stiff shot of whiskey to a cup of tea and go to bed early.

Worked every time.

Confident she'd feel better by tomorrow, she was not above making her next sneeze extra loud so that Delia might feel her reproach.

Of course, Delia had problems of her own right now, for Edward had never been so enraged.

Penelope and she had tried not to listen to the shouting coming up through the floor.

It was the fiercest fight between husband and wife that she'd ever heard, and if her presence here was now adding this kind of strain to her sister's marriage, then it merely drove home the point that Maggie needed to go.

She did not want to be responsible for destroying their marriage.

"Good God, woman, who are you?" Edward had thundered from below, and though the floorboards and carpet somewhat muffled their argument, it could not hide the fury in his voice. "I've tried to overlook your immaturity, God knows, but there comes a point—I mean, what sort of monster have I married?"

"Monster?" Delia hollered. "I'll tell you what sort of woman I am, Birdwell—one who's too good for you!"

"Oh, really?"

Penelope shuddered while Maggie sank down a bit beneath the covers.

"She's going to ruin her own life," Penelope murmured grimly.

"She might as well," Maggie said. "She's already ruined Edward's. Poor man."

"He should take a mistress," Penelope whispered. "He's too good a man to put up with such treatment."

"I don't disagree," Maggie said.

She did not approve of adultery, of course, but at the moment, she was not convinced that her sister was even capable of love, and Edward deserved it.

Penelope shook her head, pacing. "It could put you off marriage entirely."

Maggie nodded and sipped her fortified tea once again.

Upon her bedraggled return, it had given her some satisfaction to see how angry Edward had been on her behalf. His calm face had flushed with fury, and he had immediately sought out his wife.

Even Delia knew she had gone too far this time, as much as she'd tried to pretend nonchalance. Maggie did not see fit to tell either of them about Bryce's beastly behavior. How he'd enjoyed adding insult to injury. But he'd only brought dishonor on himself, and so had Delia.

The Marchioness of Birdwell now found herself an outcast within the walls of her own home.

Having heard the shocking story from Hubert the coachman, the entire staff had joined the insurrection, each of them, from butler to scullery maid, going out of their way to show their displeasure with their mistress by being very slow to obey any orders Her Ladyship gave them.

Maggie appreciated their silent show of support, but was too fed up to care anymore. She felt miserable in both body and mind and did not know what would become of her.

It was clearer than ever now that she could not stay here much longer. This living arrangement was simply not suitable. It might even be preferable to take her chances at Halford Manor, near handsy Uncle Wilbur.

Only Penelope dared give voice to what she'd told Maggie all the servants were feeling. "Of all the petty, callous, insensitive—"

"It's all right, Pen. I survived it."

"That remains to be seen!" Penelope set her hands on her waist. "Are you sure you don't want me to fetch the physician?"

"It's just a case of the sniffles. I'll finish this good stuff, then get some sleep."

Penelope frowned, scanning Maggie's face. "Very well. But if you start feeling worse, I think he should come and see you."

"As you wish."

In truth, all Maggie wanted to do was pull the covers up over her head and block out the world.

She was already cringing to think of how the mighty major would react when he heard about her defeat. He'd inspired her to fight, and she had—and she'd been soundly trounced.

Having to face him again and admit it merely doubled her shame. He was going to think she was the world's worst weakling. And who would want to marry that?

Certainly not a man who practically personified strength.

He was going to feel sorry for her, and that thought utterly depressed her. She knew how it felt to pity a suitor, after all. She shook her head, then took another deep drink of the tea. She might've been trounced by her sister, but she refused to be laid low by a stupid cold, too.

Her eyes watered at the fiery scotch in the tea, but she finished it all, coughing a little as it burned its way down to her belly. Then she set the cup aside on the tray Penelope had rested on her night table.

"If you'd excuse me, Pen, I really think I ought to get some sleep."

"Oh yes, of course, my lady. Do ring me at once if you need anything at all."

"Thank you. I will."

Penelope gave Maggie a fretful look as she collected the tea tray, and then bustled off to the door and closed it silently behind her.

When she had gone, Maggie stared at the ceiling, then heaved a great sigh. Meanwhile, the fight between Edward and Delia raged on below.

She hoped with all her heart that her sweet-tempered brother-in-law fared better against the redheaded dragon than she had, but deep down, she rather doubted it.

Delia always won.

The next night, a cloud of cigar smoke hung over the green baize table. The card game at the Grand Albion gentlemen's club was well underway.

The smell of tobacco, the taste of good whiskey, the raucous sound of male laughter, and the sight of the colorful playing cards spread out before him...it all brought Connor back to his Army days. Of course, the luxurious club tucked away at the back of the hotel's ground floor was a far cry from the cramped and moldy officers' tent where he used to play. But he could not deny that it felt good to be a part of things once more.

He was not, by nature, a solitary soul—a thought which, inevitably, carried his mind back to Maggie.

Though he watched his male neighbors taking their turns around the table, by now—around eleven o'clock on Saturday night—his curiosity about how she'd fared at Hyde Park yesterday was killing him.

He told himself he was probably being overeager and nosy, to boot.

But, prodded by impatience, he had decided to send her a one-line note: *How are you, my dear?*

He'd had Will run it over and hand it off to her lady's maid. When Will had returned, he had brought back her reply: *Forsooth, Your Grace, I've been better. Fondly, ~M.*

He'd arched a brow at the humorous tone of her answer, but what her words meant, exactly, he still wasn't sure. It perplexed him.

It worried him.

"Your turn, Amberley," said Netherford.

"Right." Stirred from his thoughts, Connor considered his cards.

Netherford frowned across the table. "Rivenwood, what the hell's wrong?"

Connor glanced over curiously as Azrael frowned.

"Yes, do tell," Sidney chimed in. "Why the long face? You're brooding even more than usual."

Major Peter Carvel chuckled at that and took a swig of his ale while they all looked at the blond duke in question.

Azrael let out a huge sigh. "Alas, boys, I am out of my lady's good graces," he announced.

From all around the table, jovial protests erupted.

"What? No!"

"Say it isn't so!"

"But you two never fight."

"Really," Sidney drawled, "it's disgusting."

"What did you do?" Netherford said, amusement dancing in his dark eyes.

Azrael shook his head. "My fair duchess asked for a favor I couldn't grant. Serena," he said, "is not used to anyone telling her no. Especially me."

"What on earth did she want from you?" Netherford asked with a grin.

"Yes, what labor of Hercules did she ask?" Gable chimed in. "Although, for what it's worth, I feel your pain. Trinny has the same unholy power over me."

Azrael laughed softly and sat back in his chair. "Well..." He paused, glancing briefly at Connor, then kept his voice down. "She told me I needed to have a word with Lord Birdwell."

At the mention of Maggie's brother-in-law, Connor looked over his hand of cards, his stare homing in on his fellow duke's angular face. "Why is that?"

"You've probably all heard by now how Lady Birdwell threw her poor sister out of their coach yesterday?"

"What?" a few fellows asked.

Connor went motionless.

"Yes." Azrael winced and nodded. "My wife did not witness the row, but she told me she and her friend, Portia Tennesley, happened across the two sisters while they were taking their drive in Hyde Park yesterday. Serena said Lady Birdwell was extremely unpleasant to her sister, making barbed jests at poor Lady Margaret's expense."

Connor felt a growl gathering in his throat.

"Serena gave the marchioness a bit of a sting to warn her to behave, but they parted ways then, so she did not witness the row itself. But by the time my wife had circuited the Ring, she happened across another friend who'd seen it unfold. Quite a heated exchange." Azrael shook his head. "Apparently, the two sisters ended up in a shouting match, and then Lady Birdwell ejected Lady Margaret from the carriage. Made the poor girl walk home."

Deaf now to the exclamations of shock that rose from around the table, Connor set his cards down slowly, ignoring the worried glances that several of the men cast his way.

Obviously, they knew that he and Maggie were on quite friendly terms; she was the one who had introduced him to most of the men present.

Indeed, half of Society had seen them dancing together.

Though his heart pounded and his hands itched to punch something, Connor held himself back from going on the warpath. He said not a word.

"And so, Serena wanted me to say something to Birdwell, tell the chap to get his wife in line. But, as much as I adore her, I told my darling duchess that a man does not tell another man how to manage his lady."

"To be sure," Netherford agreed, nodding and still looking shocked at Her Ladyship's rudeness. "If anyone ever criticized Felicity in my hearing, let alone suggest to my face how *my* wife ought to behave, whew! Even if she'd been a wild hellion, it would not go well for him."

"Exactly," said Azrael. "If any man said a word to me against Serena..." He did not finish the sentence. He did not need to. But he sighed. "And so she is cross at me now. It pains me to deny her, but this, as I told her, I simply cannot do."

"This is different," Gable agreed, nodding. Then he glanced at Sidney, brightening. "Maybe you can drop a hint to Birdwell, Sid. You're very tactful—when you mean to be."

They all looked at the golden-haired viscount, who had an odd look on his face. A rather taut, rueful expression, as though he knew more about this Hyde Park matter than he had yet revealed.

Connor studied him with a sharp eye, listening to Azrael, who continued.

"Well, someone should warn Birdwell, because my wife is

threatening to speak to the patronesses of the subscription ball about revoking Her Ladyship's voucher."

Netherford's eyebrows shot up. "Well, that would take the woman down a peg, to be sure."

Except that she'd probably just take it out on Maggie, Connor thought.

"What say you, Sidney?" Gable asked. "Will you be our diplomat once more?"

"Yes, you've been unusually quiet," Netherford remarked.

"Um…" Sidney hesitated. He drummed the table with his fingers.

"What?" Connor said.

Sidney sent him a guarded glance. "I, er, wasn't sure if I should say anything. But…I'm afraid there's a further twist to this story that, ah, makes Delia's role pale by comparison."

Connor leaned forward, his elbows on the table. "What are you talking about?"

All his male neighbors seemed to have realized by now that this was *his* problem.

And, oh, to be sure, he would deal with it.

Sidney lifted his eyebrows, as though he feared violence was the inevitable outcome of his words.

Gable glanced uneasily at Connor, then looked over once more at his boyhood friend. "Sidney?"

Connor narrowed his eyes, waiting. "What did you hear?"

Sidney downed his last swig of rum. "Promise not to kill anyone, ol' boy?"

Connor nodded.

"Right. Ah well." Sidney set his glass down with a thud. "Bryce and a few of his set were here last night drinking till late. I'm afraid Lady Margaret's ex-suitor was laughing his head off over having spotted her traipsing home through the streets in the middle of the downpour." Sidney winced. "Bryce seemed to find it amusing that poor Maggie 'had the nerve,' as he put it, to hope that he might let her into his curricle and drive her the rest of the way home. He deigned not to, on account of her jilt." Sidney paused. "In fact, he spoke of steering through a puddle to splash her on purpose with his carriage as he drove away."

"What a cad," Gable murmured in amazement.

Azrael looked appalled, Netherford incredulous. The others were silent, then Carvel looked at Connor expectantly.

Connor was seething. He could picture the whole thing in his mind.

No wonder the poor girl had gone into hiding.

She must be mortified. If she hadn't caught her death.

"Thank you, Lord Sidney," he said through gritted teeth, then slapped his cards down. "Gentlemen, you must excuse me. I have business to attend to."

The room had gone absolutely quiet.

He swept to his feet. "Deal me out. Thanks for inviting me."

"Amberley, what are you planning to do?" Gable called after him as he headed for the door.

Connor did not answer, but gusted away, banging out through the club's double doors in a fury.

I'll kill him, he thought as he marched back out across the marble-floored lobby. *Aye, and I might just wring Delia's neck, too.*

The uniformed doorman saw him coming this time, and must've noticed the wrath on his face, for he quickly pulled the door open and held it. "Good night, sir."

Connor jogged down the front steps of the hotel and paused for a moment, unsure which direction to go.

Part of him burned to go at once to Maggie's and pound on the door, demand to see her, make sure for himself that she was all right.

The other half of him considered marching back inside to get Bryce's address so he might go and kill the man.

Or at least send his second there now to finish what they'd started a week ago.

But no. He had to think.

Clenching and unclenching his fists, he pivoted and began stalking home. Though he was livid, his anger did not dull his awareness of his surroundings.

Casting a wary glance over his shoulder, he scanned the square for any sign of threat, detecting none.

I have to see her. I've got to do something! He could not believe that his goading could have led her into such circumstances. The poor girl. He felt *awful* for putting her up to this.

He'd encouraged her to stand up to her sister and then he'd ridden off to let her face it alone. True, she had told him to go. Still.

I knew I shouldn't have left her.

His heart pounded in time with his footsteps as he marched the rest of the way to Amberley House, his dodgy knee aching from the change in the weather.

When he arrived, he slammed the door behind him with such savagery that they probably heard it in Dublin.

Enraged, he let out a futile war cry. Pacing across his own entrance hall, he unleashed a tirade of obscenities.

Seconds after his bellow shook the house, Will and Nestor came running.

"Major?" the lad cried with a blanch as he flew down the staircase. "What on earth is the matter?"

"And what did you do to that painting?" Nestor frowned at the landscape of *Desert with Bedouins*, through which Connor had just put his fist.

A growl was Connor's only response. He stomped across the entrance hall and began bounding up the steps.

Will and Nestor got out of his way—but then Connor suddenly paused, turning to them. "Any word from Lady Margaret while I was out? Did she send a note?"

"No, sir," Will said.

"What happened, man?" Nestor insisted, but Connor was in motion once more, pounding up the staircase.

"Did somebody try to murder you again?" Will called after him.

"Not this time!" he answered. Churning with fury, Connor ran up to the third-floor bedroom on the corner of his house.

Crossing the dark, little-used chamber, he paused only to plant his hands on the windowsill, briefly peering out across the square at the Birdwell residence.

Most of the windows were dark; a few glowed from within.

With everything in him, Connor longed to see her. He had to know if she was all right. He stared at the window that she'd said was her chamber...

In a heartbeat, his mind was made up. With that, he reached for the lantern and lit it. He set it on the sill and then, for urgency's sake, lit the second one, praying Maggie looked out her window to notice his summons: *Come to me. Now.*

CHAPTER 18

A Light in the Dark

*M*aggie's hands trembled with excitement as she lit a lantern to acknowledge that she had seen Connor's signal and was on her way. Her heart pounded as she hurried to get dressed.

After spending most of the day locked up in her bedchamber, not so much from illness—for she was feeling pretty much herself again, thanks to Mama's ancient cure—but from her own mule-like recalcitrance, awaiting her sister's still-absent apology, she had grown altogether bored and restless by nighttime.

Still refusing to come out of her room until Delia apologized, she had finally, from mere habit, drifted over to the window to see if, by chance, Amberley might have thought of a new assignment for her yet.

To her astonishment, she'd found the signal beaming.

She'd gasped to see not one light but *two* shining in the duke's upper window. Two lanterns meant it was an emergency!

She had leapt into action to go to his aid, rushing about to dress, and wondering how long those lamps had been burning.

I wonder what he wants! Oh God, I hope everything's all right. What if somebody's tried again to kill him?

Or maybe it's good news. Maybe there's been a break in the case and he can't wait to tell me...

If so, she couldn't wait to hear it. She could really use some good news right now.

Wasting no time, she had sent Penelope scurrying downstairs to fetch the key to the tall wrought-iron gates that bound Moonlight Square's garden park, for these were kept locked at night.

Residents of the square could enter the park whenever they pleased, of course, but it was closed to the public after nightfall.

While Penelope discreetly retrieved the Birdwells' key, Maggie slipped on one of her favorite walking dresses, trembling with excitement.

It had been such a pretty yellow before; she'd been disappointed when she'd had to dye it black during her mourning period for Papa. Tonight, however, its ebony hue would serve her well, helping to conceal her in the darkness when she went to meet her Irishman at the gazebo.

Besides, the gown was made of soft merino wool. It would keep her warm after her brush with illness. As reliable as Mama's old cure was, Maggie did not wish to risk another tussle with the weather, for yesterday's rain had returned to sprinkle London again on and off all day, although it hadn't stormed.

Just as she flung a hooded woolen cloak around her shoulders to ward off the night's chill, Penelope slipped back into the room, bringing the key.

Maggie murmured her thanks and put it in her pocket, a bit nervous to go out there and brave the night. The clock read quarter to midnight, after all.

Her maid scanned her face. "Are you sure about this, my lady? It seems awfully risky."

"You will cover for me, won't you?"

"Yes, of course, but is it wise?"

Maggie couldn't help smiling, unable to hide her joy at the prospect of seeing Amberley again after the misery of the past thirty-six hours. "All will be well."

If he had a new assignment for her, she was ready for duty—though she still had not come up with a lighthearted jest to make light of her Hyde Park ordeal. Lord willing, perhaps he had not heard about it. If he had, *ugh*, she barely knew how she'd face him.

Trying not to think about it overmuch, she fastened her cloak around her neck, then Penelope handed her gloves from her dressing table. "Are you sure you'll be warm enough?"

"I'll be fine." Maggie sent her a conspiratorial smile. "Come, you know I'm only playing it up to make Delia feel guilty."

Penelope grinned.

"To tell you the truth, after the misery of yesterday, seeing him will be just the thing for me. I confess, no one quite cheers me up like that rogue."

Especially when he takes me in his arms…

"He is handsome," Penelope admitted with a smile. "Oh, I know! Shall I make a great fuss in fifteen minutes or so, right when you're out there alone in the dark with him? I could arrange for you two to be caught together, and then he'd *have* to marry you. You'd be free of this place at last. Problem solved."

"Clever girl!" Maggie said with a laugh. "Tempting, but no." She paused, lowering her gaze. "I should not want to win him by trickery."

Penelope arched a brow. "Milady is starting to sound like a woman in love."

Maggie shrugged as her heart bubbled with joy. "Perhaps I am." Then she signaled for secrecy, laying a finger over her lips, and they were off.

Penelope whisked over to the door, opened it, and peered out into the hallway, glancing this way and that. Stealthily, she beckoned to Maggie, then guided her out of the house, distracting the butler so she could sneak over to the front door unnoticed.

"Return by the side door," Penelope whispered as Maggie crept out. "I'll leave it open. And do *please* be careful!"

Maggie nodded and pulled the door shut behind her with a quiet click.

Hurrying down the few front steps of the terrace house, she drew the hood of her cloak up over her head, her whole body tingling with anticipation to see that blue-eyed scoundrel again. *Be careful?* she thought. Didn't Penelope know that the safest place for her was right beside the major?

With that, she raced out into the mild spring night to go to him. The darkness glistened; here and there were still puddles, but the streets and the houses had been washed clean by the rain.

Tightly clutching the key, Maggie sped across the street, then glided through the shadows next to the wrought-iron fence. She hurried alongside it, taking pains to keep her footsteps quiet until she reached the elegantly formidable, locked gate.

As she fiddled with the key, squinting in the inky darkness, her trembling hands and the lack of light made it nigh impossible to fit the thing properly into the keyhole.

"Oh, come on!" she whispered.

Just then, a flicker of motion in the shadows near the street corner to her right caught her eye. Already jumpy with the mad risk she was taking simply by being here, Maggie stopped cold and looked over.

She held her breath, and could have sworn she saw a dark figure lurking in the shadows. A man-shaped silhouette, blacker than midnight.

Was it Connor? Her heart skipped a beat. But it couldn't be.

He knew full well that their agreed meeting place was the white garden folly in the middle of the park. So why would he be over there?

Maggie narrowed her eyes, staring into the blackness, but the figure had already vanished—if it had been there at all.

She swallowed hard, slightly unnerved. Perhaps it had been no more than a wisp of fog forming from the rain, or some man's shadow from inside one of the houses over there.

Or just a phantom of her skittish imagination.

Either way, it was gone now. But even so, she fumbled all the more speedily with the lock, glancing again in the direction that she'd seen the spooky shape.

It did not reappear.

To her relief, the lock finally gave way. She twisted the key and pushed the gate open. Its creak in the peaceful quiet of the street made her wince.

She did not need any of her neighbors peering out to see what was going on. No doubt there was already enough talk about her. First, with the way she had run over to Amberley in a panic at the duel, and now, the far more ludicrous spectacle she had made of herself in Hyde Park with the help of her sister.

It was all so unspeakably lowering.

She felt like such a fool. If only she could think of some glib remark with which to make light of it to Connor.

After stepping through the garden gate, Maggie turned back to close it behind her. The squeak that it made sounded so loud in the tranquil night that she decided not to risk banging it shut all the way.

Instead, she left it closed but unlocked, letting the latch-arm rest against the iron strike. That would make leaving quicker and easier, not to mention far less noisy.

Once inside the garden park, she could see how the rain had swollen the flowers—every fragrant petal seemed lush and engorged. The sweetness of lilacs filled the night air, and the blossoms on the fruit trees glowed pale in the moonlight.

With a glance back at Edward and Delia's house, Maggie saw no sign that her escape had been detected. Bless Penelope, always reliable.

Confident that she'd gained her freedom, at least for a while, Maggie whirled around and raced down the graveled path toward the gazebo, her steps light, her heart pounding with eagerness to see Amberley again.

Seth stepped out of the shadows by the corner, shocked at what he'd just seen.

Little Lady Margaret Winthrop, sneaking out of her house and into the garden park close to midnight!

What the devil?

He looked up at the terrace house from which she had just emerged. He had been watching both Amberley House and the Birdwell residence tonight, keeping an eye on both of his persons of interest.

After Duke Number Four had gone into his club, of which Seth was not a member, he had waited a while, growing restless and bored. Then he had wandered around the square and had a good, long look at the block of large, elegant terrace houses where the girl lived.

The last thing he'd expected to witness was an aristocratic virgin sneaking out alone in the deep of night.

What is going on here?

Glancing up at her house, he noticed the lantern that now shone in the upper window. *Well, that's odd.* Why was it sitting there right on the sill?

If people inside the room required light, that was a useless place to set the lantern. His brow furrowed, Seth turned and squinted toward Amberley House.

What he saw made him stare. *Well, now… What have we here?*

In Amberley's window, *two* lanterns now glowed, right there, side by side. None had shone there a short while ago.

Staring at the twin lamps for a long moment, Seth spun slowly on his heel and looked again at the light in Lady Margaret's window.

Realization began sinking in, and his jaw dropped. *It's a signal.*

He laughed softly in the darkness.

Why, you naughty girl. The suspicion brewing in his mind told him to follow her at once. So he did. Stealthily crossing the street, he was quite prepared to climb over the iron fence. But, just in case, he tried the gate.

Open.

Why, thank you, Lady Margaret.

She'd made it easy for him to follow. Seth liked easy. But the thought of her made him hard. Maybe she wasn't as virginal as he had assumed if she was sneaking out at night to meet a man.

After easing the gate back into the same position she'd left it, he avoided the graveled path and the noise it would make, striding through the soft, wet grass instead, surrounded by the heady perfume of spring.

What would he do if he came upon Amberley out here with his guard down, distracted by the girl?

This might be the night.

Of course he had come armed. Knowing Amberley, he'd probably need a cannon, but if Seth got a clear shot, his service pistol would have to suffice. Unfortunately, that did require going rather closer than he liked. Still, he touched the gun hidden under his jacket to reassure himself of his readiness.

The metal was smooth, solid, and cool under his fingertips. As he glided through the darkness on a parallel to the path he'd seen Lady Margaret take, he considered the prospect before him.

As a dragoon with all the usual swagger and at least a few pretensions to chivalry, he found he really did not care to kill the man in front of Lady Margaret, if it could be avoided.

If not, oh well. But there was a practical reason for this, too. She had not reacted well to the sight of blood at the duel, as he recalled. There'd be noise from her.

Screaming.

And that drastically increased his risk of being caught. *Don't get ahead of yourself.* He had made the mistake of underestimating the major once before.

He had not *planned* to kill tonight. These were not ideal circumstances, and Seth had no intention of getting cornered, sentenced, and hanged.

He must be shrewd, like Father. It was probably best for now just to observe and collect information.

Oh, but it was tempting to have this burden over with. Either way, as he prowled through the darkness, his pulse throbbed with the thrill of the hunt.

❖

Connor leaned against the gazebo railing as he waited, arms loosely folded across his chest.

Far overhead, a waxing gibbous moon shone now and then between the shifting clouds. The garden park in the center of Moonlight Square was wrapped in a deep, dripping darkness, puddles gathered here and there from the rain.

He took another draft from his cheroot in brooding stillness, savoring the smoke, then slowly blowing out.

It was a dreadful habit, he knew. He had picked it up in Spain during the war, like so many others had.

But the long breaths in and out helped him manage his fury.

Indeed, Connor was still hot, but he'd calmed himself down a bit ahead of seeing her, because he knew he could come across as menacing indeed, when he was angry. Prided himself on it, actually. He'd built a fine military career on it—but he didn't want to scare *her*.

Especially not after all that she'd been through, thanks to both Delia and Bryce.

Still seething over what he'd learned at the club, Connor only cared about protecting the girl, and perhaps it was rash, but tonight he would follow his instincts.

The frogs sang in the night, unseen, and a puff of breeze sent a scattering of raindrops flying off the trees overhead, dripping off the eaves of the gazebo. He took another pull on his cheroot, and the taste of tobacco smoke mingled with the luxuriant scent of the rain-soaked turf. He watched a moth go fluttering by and wondered if Maggie had seen the signal yet.

Maybe she hadn't, or if she had, maybe she wouldn't come. Maybe the impropriety of meeting a man alone at night would prove too much for his little English rose.

Either way, he, for his part, did not intend to budge. He'd be here as long as the Great Pyramids stood on the desert sands, waiting for her.

She'd see the damned light eventually.

He flicked his ashes over the railing and glanced around, watching for her.

Provided she indeed came, he mused, the garden square was a lovely setting for what he had in mind. Odd to think that, in fact, this spot had once been a hanging ground, long ago, so he'd been told.

Quite the transformation. It gave one hope. After all, if a former site of public executions could become one of the most fashionable neighborhoods in London, then perhaps a three-quarters Irish trained killer could eventually become a proper duke.

Especially with the help and guidance of a proper duchess.

It was about then that he noticed motion in the darkness. His stare homed in on the path to his left. He heard delicate footsteps crunching over the gravel, then a slim, dark-clad figure approached, speeding toward the garden folly.

Connor pushed away from the railing with a smile slowly spreading across his face. *Atta girl,* he thought. She was so much stronger than she gave herself credit for. Like the graceful willow that could bend and not break in a gale that toppled mightier trees or snapped them like matchsticks.

As she neared, he noted with amusement that Lady Maggie had concealed her fair self with a long, hooded cloak to help her blend into the shadows. She wasn't taking any more chances with her reputation, he gathered.

Well, after tonight, thankfully, she wouldn't have to worry about such things for much longer.

If she said yes.

His pulse hammered at the prospect of what he meant to do.

"You're smoking?" she exclaimed as she skipped up the three steps from the path to join him inside the gazebo.

Why, she already sounded like his wife. "You disapprove?"

"I do," she said archly, drawing back her hood.

He flicked the rest of his cheroot away with a smile.

She smiled back with a twinkle in those lovely gray eyes, and set her hands on her waist. "Well?" she asked with a businesslike air. "What's afoot, Your Grace? I see you're alive. You look unscathed. I was worried there might've been another attempt on your life."

He shook his head.

"Oh thank God," she whispered, pressing a hand to her chest. "I was beside myself with worry."

He smiled. "How sweet."

"Well?" She waved a curl of smoke away. "Have you learned something more? Found another clue?"

She seemed cheerful enough, a fact that he noted with relief, for he had been worried about her, too.

"Actually, yes," he said. "But that is not why I called you here tonight."

"Oh."

"Will you sit?" He gestured toward the built-in bench that ran the perimeter of the garden folly. His pulse lurched from a trot to a canter.

She nodded, then lowered herself to perch on the edge of the bench nearby, watching him, wide-eyed. "What is it?"

He sat down beside her, unsure how to begin. For a moment, he stared into her eyes. "I heard what happened yesterday."

She stiffened at once, and her gaze fell to the floorboards. "Oh. That."

He could not hold back. "Did she really make you walk home?" he demanded.

She gave a slight nod but did not look up, as though she were ashamed.

"And then Bryce chose not to help you?"

She looked up. "You heard about that, too?"

He struggled to keep his wrath from showing on his face, determined not to frighten the girl the way he'd sometimes frightened Will back at the war. "Yes."

"Wh-what are you going to do?"

Connor just looked at her.

Her eyes turned as round as an owl's, and she gulped. "Don't. Not another duel—please!"

He growled, but the hard truth was, as much as he wanted to punish that coxcomb for showing her such outrageous disrespect, Connor needed Bryce alive for information on Richard. That was his next line of question regarding the plot against his family. Richard's secrets, Richard's past.

"Don't worry, I'm not going to shoot anyone," he grumbled.

She exhaled with relief.

He couldn't stop staring at her, scanning for damage. "I feel responsible for this."

"No! Why?"

"I provoked her," he said. "I'm the one who picked the fight, and that goaded *you* into joining the fray."

"Nonsense." Her dainty shoulders slumped as she sat back against the railing. "I had to stand up to her sometime. Didn't I?"

"I cannot believe the woman is such a bully to you." He shot to his feet and began to pace across the gazebo.

"Is that the only reason you summoned me?" she asked. "I didn't come here to talk about this. I thought you might have information or something for me to do. You said we'd only risk meeting here in case of emergency."

"Dammit, Maggie, this *is* an emergency!" he retorted. He ran his hand through his hair and rubbed the back of his neck with agitation. "I will not allow you to be treated this way!"

She cocked a brow and folded her arms. "Well, what do you propose? Should I challenge my sister to a duel, hmm?"

He sent her a mild scowl. "Hardly."

Bloody hell, this was not going at all the way he had envisioned. Her hurt pride over the shameful way she'd been used had raised her hackles just when he wanted to rescue her from all of it.

"Well?" She shrugged. "What is it you expect me to do?"

His heart thumped, and for the swiftest instant, the words stuck at his Adam's apple. Then he forced them out: "Marry me."

Her eyes flicked open wide; he did not know how to read her blank look.

In that brief moment, Connor felt a rare bolt of dread arrow through him. It startled him immensely.

Slipping behind enemy lines in uniform, risking execution every time if he were caught: no problem. Leading men into battle, all in a day's work.

But gazing at the girl he suspected had already stolen his heart, the legendary major tasted a moment of pure fear. *What if she says no? Because I'm Irish? Because I've killed men?*

Because I'm…well, me?

Because of a hundred reasons for all the ways in which he wasn't perfect.

Suddenly, the thought of this fine English beauty's rejection sent him running for cover. "It seems a practical idea, and I know you're a practical girl," he said coolly.

"I like practical," she said automatically, staring at him.

Still unsure what to think of her stunned look, he retreated oh so casually to a safer distance, leaning against one of the white posts across from her. "Another bargain between us, as it were."

Her expression was guarded, too, as she scanned his face warily in the silver moonlight. "I'm listening."

"Well…" *Gulp.* Connor folded his arms and tried to look nonchalant. "The situation's very plain, inn't it? You need a husband. I need a wife." He shrugged and gave her a hard, meaningful look.

She seemed speechless for a heartbeat. "Are you…serious?"

"Aye," he said, going perfectly motionless, for that could be taken either way.

"Really?" she murmured in astonishment.

"Yes." His cool, level stare probably would have been better suited for the card table earlier tonight, but here he was.

"Criminy," she whispered, glancing away as if to collect her thoughts.

"Well, it just makes sense, doesn't it? You need a new living situation, and I've got to marry *someone* to carry on our poor, decimated family line. My aunt's already shoving women at me, but I much prefer you because…well, we've already seen we get on well together, yes?" He paused, his heart thumping. "You understand me. And I trust you."

He waited for as long as he could bear; the few seconds of her silence felt like hours, fraying his normally steely nerves.

"Well, lass?" he prompted, losing patience. "What say you?"

CHAPTER 19

Gazebo

*M*aggie sat staring into space, unsure if she was dreaming. Had the Duke of Amberley really just proposed to her? She might as well have won the parish lottery.

Her heart soared somewhere up above the slumbering expanse of Town. Giddy with a swirling sense of outlandish possibility, she stared at her large, intimidating friend like she'd never seen him before, taking in the strapping size of him, with his dark jacket unbuttoned, his cravat hanging untied.

The hard, angular face and thick black hair. The intense eyes, blue as the deep Atlantic. It was too dark now to see their color, but she knew it well; she'd memorized it at the ball.

And now she sat here marveling at the chance to become his wife.

Was she asleep right now, or was this really happening?

She could barely speak as a future more wonderful than she'd ever dared hope for blossomed into possibility right before her eyes, like magic. Not just marriage, not just escape from Delia's. But *him*. A husband who gave her such joy.

Love.

Except…

Connor waited for her answer, palpably on edge, looming in the shadows with a frown, while the moon looked on. Restlessly, he folded one arm across his lean middle and rested the other on top of it, his loosely curled hand obscuring his mouth.

His piercing stare never left her.

And for her part, Maggie was acutely aware of him. A part of her wanted to trap this moment and save it forever. *The night that he proposed…*

Yet she hesitated, sitting there with the hard bench at her back and a scattering of leftover raindrops blowing off the trees around them.

He arched his eyebrows, tapping his finger against his mouth as though he were mentally timing her answer.

Little did he know the reason for her prolonged silence, however.

The truth was, the well-behaved, the generous, the unselfish Maggie Winthrop was privately fighting a savage moral battle with herself.

Take this man, this duke, this war hero for her husband? Share in all his wealth and power? Unleash the fullness of her blazing desire for him—*and* get to leave Delia's?

He was offering her everything she wanted on a shiny silver tray.

But…a marriage of convenience? Because he felt *sorry* for her? Because he felt guilty, and obligated to make it up to her, as if the whole Hyde Park debacle were his fault?

She couldn't possibly take advantage of his chivalrous nature like that.

Could she?

He was so dear, with his concern for her. But Connor didn't owe her anything.

So she grappled with temptation. Wanting, for once in her life, just to give in to her own selfish desires. Admittedly, there was also a certain measure of dismay that her dream man had only offered marriage out of "practicality."

Trying to read him, she noticed that his frown had deepened into an impatient scowl as he waited for her to say something.

"Well?" he said, sounding a trifle exasperated with her. "Tonight, if you please?"

Maggie struggled for words. "Your Grace—"

"Connor."

"Connor," she echoed faintly. *Don't be selfish, Maggie. Don't be like Delia.*

"Connor," she started again, clutching tightly to all her hard-won Christian virtue. *The meek shall inherit the earth.* She forced a patient smile. *Blessed are the peacemakers.* "You mustn't blame yourself for what happened between Delia and me." She took a deep breath. "This is my problem, not yours. Trust me, it's been going on for a very long time. I don't want you to feel as though it's your job to fix it."

He stared at her, his coal-black eyebrows knitting together, as though he had no idea how to take that reply. "Yes…but…" He seemed to weigh every word. "Such an agreement would hold advantages for us both," he pointed out. "We've…already become rather comfortable together. For the most part."

Maggie gulped silently, remembering those lush kisses they had shared in the alcove. Comfortable indeed. "True."

Yet she could not help noticing that *this* Connor, here in the garden folly, was a very different fellow from the self-assured warrior she had met that first night at Amberley House.

When he had proposed their *first* bargain, hiding innumerable secrets up his sleeve, he had seemed aloof, amused, and coolly in control.

Tonight he was volatile, edgy. Maggie sensed that she had better handle him with care.

She did not want to offend the man when he was doing this to try to help her. "You do realize we only met ten days ago?" she asked.

"So?" He shifted away from the post where he was leaning, and the floorboards creaked beneath his muscled weight.

He stood with his feet planted wide and clasped his hands behind his back, as though he were giving his report to the generals. "Matches have been made on far less."

"Yes, but—" Maggie's patience began to fray at the edges. Why was he making this so difficult on her? She held on to her smile, though it thinned. "You aren't listening. What happened between Delia and me wasn't your fault in any way. You are not obligated to me."

"I never said I was." The set of his square jaw was implacable.

Maggie pressed her lips shut and lowered her head, her pulse pounding with the nearness of temptation. *Just give in.*

Oh, it would be so easy to whisper a yes. Selfishly lay claim to all that he was offering, for her own benefit. But she knew that he was passionate, impulsive, hot-tempered, and deeply loyal.

And, right now, he was angry over her misadventures of yesterday. But marriage was too big a decision for anyone to make from a passing mood.

What if he regretted it once his righteous anger passed? She couldn't live with herself if she exploited the moment for her own benefit.

She sought another tack. "What about the plot to assassinate you? I thought you said you want to find the killer first."

"Yes. The marriage itself would have to wait until after the threat is laid to rest. But I'll be better able to concentrate on that task once I can rest assured that your situation will be sorted, as well." His tone was businesslike, grim. "I cannot watch you go through this anymore, Maggie. I won't stand for it. You deserve better in life, and I can give you that."

She quaked a little at his ferocity, then strove for clarity while the frogs sang their springtime serenade. "I appreciate your desire to protect me. I do. You are most gallant. But...it's not your job to rescue me."

"Damn it, Maggie, what if I want to rescue you?" he retorted, nigh glaring at her. "What if that's the reason men like me exist?"

She did not know what to say to that.

Well, actually, the next words that came were ones she did not want to share, because they were so pitiful.

A soft sigh escaped her and she lowered her head, cringing at the prospect of uttering them. But he deserved the truth.

He waited. *"What?"*

She fidgeted with her hands in her lap, unable to meet his gaze, nor to keep the tremor of emotion from her voice. "You can't marry someone because you feel sorry for them, Connor. Believe me, I know what that's like. I had suitors I pitied, too, and I'd rather die than be that to you."

"Pity?" he exclaimed. "Are you daft, girl?"

She looked up abruptly and found him studying her like she'd sprouted two heads.

"This isn't pity! What do you take me for, a saint?"

Startled, she watched him as he began to pace. "What is it, then?"

He did not answer at once, but eyed her warily as he marched the four paces it took him to reach the other side of the gazebo. "Practicality is all, like I told you."

Pivoting, he paced back the other way, toward the stairs, restless as a lion in a cage. "You're easy to be with. You make a person feel...comfortable around you. And you seem to tolerate me more than I would've expected from any Englishwoman. We're well situated to help each other. Besides, you've lent me your assistance, and I never forget those who help me. I always reward me friends and allies. That's how you keep 'em."

"I see." She pondered this for a beat, rather more confused. "So...you want to marry me from gratitude?"

"In part, aye." His Grace seemed to be growing rather nervous.

"And, come," he added with a roguish half-smile, "think of the laugh we'll have. Can you imagine the look on your sister's face when she hears the news?"

Maggie smiled ruefully at him. Thank God that at least it wasn't pity.

"So, practicality and gratitude...and revenge on Delia and Bryce. This is very generous of you, but I'm still not entirely sure such things form the best foundation for a marriage."

"God, you are stubborn," he muttered, but her hesitation only seemed to make him more determined. "There's also the fact that both of our former modes of life have ended now. A man needs a purpose!" he declared. "Mine ended when we trounced Boney. You, meanwhile, got tossed out of your home when your father died—Delia told me so, remember?—with all her bragging about how generous she is to let you live there." He shook his head. "What a piece of work."

"Well, be that as it may," Maggie said uncertainly, "it's bad enough being a burden to my sister. I should never want to become one to you."

"Nonsense." He stopped pacing and frowned at her, resting his hands on his hips. "I've got to take *someone* for a duchess, don't I? Aunt Lucinda's already got some girls she wants me to meet at her soirée on Friday night—"

"What?" Maggie cried, sitting up straight.

"Aye. I told her I can choose my own wife—and why shouldn't it be you? You've got the right sort of bloodlines, don't you? Your father was an earl. You've been trained all your life, born and bred to run a large aristocratic household, have you not? You're perfectly well qualified for the post."

Ouch. Qualified for the post? So, what, he was hiring her to be his duchess? Maggie nodded vaguely in answer to his questions about her bloodlines and education, but failed to hide her wince at what he'd apparently meant as a compliment. Good Lord, he sounded like he was selecting which of his troops to promote to sergeant. Somehow, this was almost as lowering to her as Bryce's rudeness yesterday.

But that had been cruel and deliberate. Connor was being innocently sincere.

Which somehow only made it worse.

For he never even came close to uttering the one word she longed with all her soul to hear.

"Ahem." She finally found her voice and a path to take if she had any hope of smoothing over the excruciating awkwardness that had descended upon them. "Right. So, then. You are proposing a marriage of convenience."

Apparently, he heard the disappointment in her voice, for he bristled and stepped back. "If you don't like the idea, then say so." He lifted his hands out to his sides. "You don't have to come up with any excuses, all right? I can take it. I'm a big boy. Actually," he cut her off before she could speak, "I think I understand you just fine—so never mind, as you wish, no matter. It was just an idea," he muttered, then turned away and went to the railing, putting his back to her.

Utterly confused, Maggie blinked, trying to comprehend the man.

"Jaysus," he grumbled under his breath, "I've heard women are fickle, but 'twas only two nights ago that you were in my arms. Up in the alcove—in case you've forgotten." He glanced over his shoulder at her.

Maggie gulped at the reminder.

"I should've thought then my interest in you was clear," he muttered, turning away again.

Hold on…

Maggie's pulse slammed in her veins as it started dawning on her— or rather, as she slowly let herself dare to believe—that maybe, just maybe, there was more real feeling behind this offer than the rough-and-tumble warrior cared to admit aloud.

"Reckon I read too much into those kisses, then," he said, studying the sky from his spot at the railing. "I merely thought to offer myself as a solution to your problem. But if you don't like the idea, then never mind."

He paused.

"Just tell me one thing." He kept his back to her, his hands planted on the railing. "Is it because I'm Irish?"

Her eyes widened. *"What?"*

Belated understanding flooded in.

"I mean, it would barely come as a surprise—I've been dealing with the prejudice all my life. I just really hadn't expected it from you."

"Connor, no! Never!" Maggie leapt to her feet and rushed across the folly to him, laying a hand on his shoulder. "That's not it at all. I promise you!" Taking his arm to force him to turn to her, she searched his face, which wore a wounded glower. "It's got nothing to do with your Irish blood, my…dear friend." She did not have the courage to call him anything more intimate than that.

"What is it, then?"

"It's because you're so much more to me than some mere solution to a problem, Connor. And I so want to be more than that to you," she finished in a heartfelt whisper.

He scanned her face with a guarded look, as though weighing the sincerity in her eyes.

"It was different with all my other suitors," Maggie confessed. "I just wanted out of Delia's house, and I still do. But with you... Connor, I care for you so much. I know it's fast; I know it's reckless. And I am not trying to be difficult, o-or hurt your feelings. It's just...I would want you to want me for more than just a marriage of convenience."

"But, Maggie, I do." His glower vanished, replaced by a soulful stare as he cupped her face. "God, what a coward I am. Forgive me," he whispered, "I feared what you'd say. I didn't want to look a fool. But I am one. God knows I am." He swallowed hard. "A fool in love with you."

Maggie touched his chest in an awestruck caress. "I feel the same."

"You do?"

She nodded, full of wonder.

He caressed her arm. "Well, then...?"

"Yes," she said, trembling. "I *will* marry you."

His eyes glowed as he savored her answer. Maggie slid her hands up his chest, curled one behind his nape, and pulled him down to kiss her. Connor wrapped his arms around her waist and drew her close against his warm, powerful body.

Ignoring the taste of the cheroot on his lips, the stubble roughening his chin, she wound her arms behind his neck and pressed her lips to his in excitement. He slid his hands around her waist and she clutched him tighter, coaxing his lips apart, but he pulled back as though she'd be offended after he'd been smoking.

"I don't care," she whispered. Then she captured his rugged face between her hands and kissed him more insistently, licking his lips apart with the tip of her tongue.

He groaned and gathered her into a tighter embrace. Thrilled to the core, Maggie stroked his stubbled jaw, devouring the smoky, liquor-tinged flavor of him. His raw maleness intoxicated her.

Reject him because of his Irish blood? Was he daft? She'd had no idea that this small Achilles' heel of insecurity had existed behind his tough, formidable exterior; it showed that he had been wounded in some secret place deep in his heart, and it called to the nurturer in her.

It made her love him even more and vow that, as his wife, she'd take good care of him.

Perhaps if the mighty major possessed this hidden weak spot of a type so familiar to her own, for she doubted herself in so many things, then maybe likewise she could find a little of the strength deep inside herself that was so obvious in him. But as she kissed him, their tongues swirling, lips wet, all she wanted to do was make him understand that he had no such thing to fear from her.

"Oh Connor," she whispered between kisses, "ever since I met you, all I want is to be with you."

As if by magic, her words unlocked a whirlwind of desire from within him.

His hands ran down her sides, then he lifted her off her feet; Maggie gasped in breathless delight and wrapped her legs around his waist, her skirts rustling.

"You are a marvel, girl," he said gruffly, and moved toward the nearby post, holding her with her back against it as he stood between her legs.

"God, what you do to me," he panted between kisses. "I'm sorry I wasn't more direct. I usually am." He laughed at himself, husky and low. "I didn't want it to change anything between us if you said no."

"Say no? To you?" She, too, laughed breathlessly as her body heated with the feel of him against her, his lean hips firm between her thighs. "Have you taken leave of your senses, man? How could I possibly? How could any woman?"

"You're not just any woman, my darlin' Maggie." As he kissed her over and over again between his ragged phrases, she was quite prepared to forgive the scoundrel anything. "You want the truth? Hang the marriage of convenience. Marry me because I'm mad about you. Because we belong together. I feel it in my bones."

"Yes," she gasped out. "Yes, yes." She dug her fingers into his broad shoulders and kissed him fiercely. "I was yours from the first moment I saw you."

"God, I want you," he said with a thrilling note of savagery in his groan. He pressed in tighter between her legs, subtly caressing her with his entire body, while he held her at waist level by the cheeks of her backside.

Maggie undulated against him. It was so deliciously scandalous, but she couldn't stop. As Connor kissed his way down her neck, she unbuttoned her cloak with trembling fingers, baring more of her chest.

All the while, she thrilled to the silk and warmth of his lips and the scratchy delight of his chin chafing the crook of her neck.

Her chest heaving, she ran her hands through his hair, giddy with pleasure; as he lifted his head, she turned her face and flicked her tongue playfully against his ear.

A violent quiver ran the length of him. "Sweet Christ, girl, you drive me mad."

"I want you, Connor. I've waited my whole life for you."

"Angel."

"Take me," she whispered in his ear.

He laughed softly, breathlessly. "Not here. You little madwoman. You're killin' me."

"Uhn, please."

Drawing his face back from hers an inch or so, he gazed at her. Temptation glittered in his eyes. Feeling downright feverish, Maggie licked her lips, waiting.

He moved away from the post where he had pinned her so delightfully, and sat down, putting her on his lap. "No, my lady. I know you, and I wouldn't want you to be doing somethin' you might regret before the wedding. But I can give you this…"

He ran his hand down her chest and over her stomach, resting his fiery palm over her mound through her walking dress. With a shudder of desire, Maggie closed her eyes, her heart pounding.

The next thing she knew, that warm, clever hand of his was gliding up her thigh beneath the fabric of her skirts, unseen. Higher and higher it climbed. He gazed at her with seductive reassurance, then kissed her.

Her pulse slammed, her skin tingled, and her core pulsated, drenched with eager readiness for him. Beneath her skirts, he caressed her thigh and then explored higher…much higher. Maggie shuddered on his lap, panting. Her senses felt electrified with want. Then her legs parted as though with a will of their own as his fingers pressed into her body, his thumb circling her hard, dampened pleasure center.

He kissed her as he touched her, rousing her body to arch and writhe. She draped an arm loosely around his broad shoulders, panting and moaning, flabbergasted at the pleasure that he gave her. She could not believe what was happening to her. The rest of the world ceased to exist.

Virginal as she was, he brought her to climax within mere moments,

226   *Gaelen Foley*

capturing her blissful cries of release on his tongue.

Chest heaving, Maggie lay against his chest and shoulder, dazzled for a long moment, but the major wasn't done with her yet, merely giving her a moment to catch her breath. In that brief respite, she remembered some scandalous remark he'd made to her the first night they'd met. The night of the ankles. Something about how she should've known by then whether Bryce was right- or left-handed.

She now realized exactly what the rogue had meant. But she could never have imagined doing this with any other man.

Connor murmured love words to her, nuzzling his face against hers, his breath ragged by her ear, the rhythm like galloping horses. But before long, his kisses and caresses teased her desire back to a state of torturous yearning. Ever the soldier, he was deliciously ruthless, causing yet another crescendo of pleasure to explode through her body, again and again, twice, three times, until she could take no more.

"Stop!" she finally gasped out, exhausted and shaking.

He gave her a naughty little lick on her cheek, let out a husky laugh. "Are you *sure*?"

"Ohh, you are wicked." She found the strength to wrap her arms around him, and began laughing with astonishment at the glorious mayhem he had just wreaked on her senses.

"That's only the beginning of what we'll do together," he whispered.

She shook her head, dazed. "Oh, Your Grace, I am going to enjoy being married to you."

Seth finally withdrew into the ebony night and crept away from the gazebo in disgust. His heart was still pounding with all that he had witnessed. And though he was throbbing with arousal, he was furious.

Life was so bloody unfair. He shook his head to himself as he stalked through the dark damp of the park, his body on fire.

Why should that bastard have a girl like her panting over him?

Seth wanted her so much after seeing that, he was nearly blind with lust.

Obviously, he dared not make his big move against Duke Number Four in such a state. His head was muddled with want, his blood too hot for him even to think, let alone shoot, clearly.

But his desire for Lady Margaret was now tinged with anger and envy and hate. She'd pay the price for her behavior tonight once all of this was over.

She was *supposed* to be a lady.

Apparently not.

Very well, then—he would treat her accordingly once he had her in his control. He'd enjoy punishing her for letting Amberley paw her like that.

For now, though, he had to release the fire in him, and he knew just where to go. Straight to Father's dockside establishment, to make use of his own personal plaything there.

She was no fine, delicate Lady Margaret, what with her vacant stare, and that pretty mouth of hers always hanging slightly open, like she was in the middle of an astonishing thought.

Which, of course, she wasn't. The little blond nitwit was as thick as a stone.

And yet he had grown oddly attached to Saffie, in a way.

By all rights, he should've drowned her in the river after she had served her purpose, but she was harmless enough. Besides, the girl did literally anything he said, believed whatever he told her.

Her stupidity amused him, and fucking her, he always felt like he was getting away with some horrible sin, and that pleased him, too.

In some ways, she was the perfect woman for him, Saffie was. A warm, always-willing body without much of a mind to naysay him or ask questions.

Simple as she was, the duke's ex-scullery maid worshiped the ground that Seth walked on, and he'd found that a man could get used to that. He couldn't wait to bend her over tonight with her pale, round ass in the air for him.

Oh, she would enjoy the fiery thrashing he would give her, just as soon as he lifted her frilly skirts.

Of course, thoughts of the physical bliss awaiting him between her thighs were not helping him contain his pulsating hardness.

He paused, took a deep breath and got hold of his discipline, then adjusted himself inside his riding breeches. His arousal slackened just a bit with a few deep breaths after he had put some distance between himself and the writhing aristocratic virgin.

Enjoy it, Lady Margaret, he thought cynically as he reached the wrought-iron gate at the edge of the garden square. *You might have a duke's fingers up your quim at the moment, but someday soon, you're going to have me.*

Whether you like it or not.

As he slipped silently out of the gate, the cool metal was a welcome sensation under his burning touch, and finally, Seth managed to focus his mind on the two useful bits of information that this night had yielded.

First, he'd learned the lantern signal that Amberley and the girl were using to arrange their rendezvous. Second, he'd overheard the duke mention a soirée at his Aunt Lucinda's on Friday night.

Which meant that Seth now knew exactly where his target was going to be, and when.

A perfect opportunity.

Better still, he was familiar with the old dragon's house, having been there before. He knew the layout; he had studied it in the past, when it had come time to kill her husband.

But, of course, even before that, the old bitch had been his patroness. Father had forced her into it.

If not for the duchess putting a word in for Seth, he'd never have been allowed to buy his commission in the first place. Not just anyone was chosen for the dragoons.

Since he was familiar with the dragon's Mayfair residence, it would be a simple matter to set up the assassination there.

Oh Amberley, he thought as he crooked a smile, *you're a dead man. Just like all the rest.*

Then he swung up onto his horse, which he'd left hitched to a post around the corner, and rode off to the Docklands.

He'd tucked Saffie away at the lowliest of Father's establishments catering to the Navy and merchant sailors coming and going. No one would take any notice of her there.

In the brothel, the duke's former scullery maid, his unwitting accomplice in the poisoning, was just another whore.

The ride through the dark streets of London kept his libido sufficiently distracted until Seth rode up to the tawdry entrance of the low but lucrative Aphrodite's Cove.

The women here were the workaday harlots, the ordinary cattle with ordinary looks, not those lucky few with dazzling faces, perfect bodies, and enough brains to learn how to carry themselves with elegance—the sort Father picked out to become his high-priced courtesans.

Their kind got fashionable gowns, fine carriages, a box at the theater so that men with *real* money, including lords, could get a good look at their wares.

Sometimes these investments even yielded rich husbands.

But whenever Father managed to marry off one of his top-drawer girls, it did not mark the end of the income he made off them, but only the beginning, for he charged a steep monthly fee that these courtesans-turned-rich-wives had to pay faithfully, on time.

Or else.

That was the deal the lucky few signed with Elias Flynn, and no woman, no former whore, was allowed to break it. Even if fifty years had gone by.

Even if she'd long since become a duchess.

Seth smirked at the thought of the dragon lady.

There wasn't much to smile about, though, considering she was the one who'd got his brother killed. Of course, darling Francis had barely been able to stomach the family trade, but Seth, for his part, admired Father's sharklike business acumen.

The ruthlessness of his sire was a wonder to behold.

As soon as he walked through the door to one of the family brothels, the familiar sights and sounds and smells of it, and his overwhelming awareness of what this place was all about let him discard the burden of what he was sworn to do: kill Amberley.

He let the onerous task dissolve in the cloud of tobacco smoke that hovered beneath the rafter beams and between the red-painted walls. The place was busy tonight. Should be making good money. He took a few steps in, looking for Saffie.

The cheap carpet was sticky underfoot from countless ales spilled on it, and everywhere were the women, Father's human cattle, leaning against the walls, fanning themselves, their faces painted, bosoms on display, all ready and available. Fully under control, too, the way a woman should be.

Seth could feel his blood pumping, and his stare homed in on the waifish little blonde sprawled in the chair by the fireplace, waving her gaudy fan with an air of boredom, clad in a crimson dress.

It had been his idea to rename her Scarlet and dress her up in red so that she'd fit in here. But she was off-limits to the customers.

Saffie was studying the ends of her hair when he walked in, as though it were deeply engrossing.

He shook his head, perplexed. What on earth was she about now? But he shrugged it off. It didn't matter. He wasn't here for conversation.

She looked up just then and saw him sauntering in. The girl lit up, and Seth smiled vaguely, nodding toward the hallway. She jumped to her feet, suddenly animated, but he had warned her not to be too open about their connection.

Instinctively, his little nitwit accomplice started toward him, but then she must've remembered his instructions, for she smiled almost slyly and twirled around to strut off toward the hallway he had indicated and get on her back.

Seth's mouth watered with anticipation. He had corrupted her utterly, he knew, but he didn't give a damn.

"Sir," said the house manager. Who knew exactly who he was.

Most there didn't, for Seth's work for Father regarding the family business was carried out behind the scenes. This degree of anonymity allowed him to maintain his double life.

He gave the cold-eyed man a discreet nod and then headed up to his usual room. The primal drumbeat of raw, mindless sex slammed inside his chest as he surrendered to his want, letting it take him.

He was already hard when he reached for the doorknob to Room 22.

When he went in, Saffie was already waiting for him, sitting prettily on the edge of the cot, leaning back with her hands propped behind her.

Her shapely legs were crossed, those frilly skirts hitched up over her crossed knees. The bobbing of her foot betrayed her excitement to see him.

Seth eyed the bare stretch of thigh exposed above her garter as he shut the door behind him. And locked it.

"Oh Johnny, you missin' me tonight?"

She called him that because one did not tell such a creature one's real name. "Badly," Seth said.

He tore off his jacket and crossed the room, unbuttoning his breeches.

"I've missed you, too," she said with a squirm and a little hungry whimper, like a bitch in heat.

His pulse leapt.

There was a stale smell in the room but he ignored it, pulling off his shirt, throwing it aside.

"When can I get out of here, Johnny?" she asked restlessly as he walked over to her and slid his hand right down inside the top of her gown.

"What?" he mumbled as he grasped her breast and quivered.

"It's so boring here! Why can't I ever go outside?"

The little nitwit didn't seem to realize she was lucky to be alive. By all rights, he should have strangled her and dumped the body in the river to cover his tracks after the poisoning had failed.

But she had been of use to him, and Seth had found he didn't have the heart. No, he had a better use for her for the time being.

So he'd left her alive for now.

"Don't fret, Saffie," he said, laughing at her pout as he pulled the gown off her left shoulder. "I've only given you a few simple rules to follow."

"I know," she whined. "I don't mind the house chores, but—"

"Good. Because you've got to earn your keep here in some fashion. And, after all, you've got nowhere else to go."

She sighed. "I suppose." Then she arched her back, pushing a nubile breast deeper into the curve of his hand. "At least you're here now. I'm getting really good at this for you, aren't I?"

"Practice makes perfect." He squeezed her other breast, nigh bursting from his trousers at her wanton response. "Your hand, dear."

Saffie's hands were strong from scrubbing pots and pans in Amberley's scullery. Her true talents had been wasted there.

Seth groaned at her touch.

Saffie licked her lips, warming to her new work as she grasped his burgeoning erection.

She giggled when she felt him throb. "Oh, Johnny, so randy you are!"

"Because I knew I'd be seeing you, poppet."

She leaned forward as she stroked him and kissed his bare stomach a few times with a sigh of adoration. He petted her head while she sucked him for a while. "Johnny, I love you so much. Have you finished that errand for your father yet?"

"Almost."

"Oh, good! I'm so keen for us to marry."

"Me too," he said, panting. *Idiot.* "Now turn over."

"So impatient," she chided, but obeyed, moving onto all fours at the edge of the bed. "You really needed this tonight."

"You have no idea," he said gruffly. Unceremoniously tossing her skirts up over that round, ready ass, he stood at the edge of the bed, grasped her bare hips, and took her roughly from behind, thrusting in deep.

With Saffie facing away from him and his eyes drifting closed, Seth could ignore the reality of where he was and who he was, and even whose body it was gratifying him. In his mind, it was easy to imagine she was someone else, under his power and taking whatever he gave her.

Someone with class, like Mother.

Someone worthy of him.

Someone he would take, just like this, once Amberley was dead.

CHAPTER 20

The Dandy

A man could not get properly engaged without a ring for his lady. And so, first thing Monday morning, Connor jumped lightly out of his coach after Will had parked it on Bond Street. Nestor and the lad waited with the horses while Connor strode across the pavement to the jeweler's elegant front door.

When he went into the sumptuous shop with its Persian carpet and crystal chandeliers, surrounded by the reverent hush of beautiful, expensive objects, he still marveled to think that he could now afford whatever he wished to buy in this top-lofty place.

Good. An ostentatious diamond on the finger of his duchess would be something Maggie could flaunt in Delia's face.

It would also help remind the ton of his rank as the fourth Duke of Amberley, and how they owed him their respect, Irish blood or not.

He meandered around the shop with a sense of unreality about all of this, until a glittering mass of white diamond flanked by twinkling emeralds caught his eye. Slowly, a smile crept across his lips.

As he went toward the shining glass case where the ring was on display, he could not help mentally poking fun of himself. Who in the world ever would've thought he was such a bloody romantic? If his troops could see him now, wrapped around the finger of a little gray-eyed miss with pretty ankles.

Relishing the knowledge that, soon, everything *above* those ankles would belong to him, he was downright eager to pay the princely sum the jeweler quoted him for the bauble. He ordered the little man to hold the ring for him—he'd buy it, but he needed to find out his fair lady's ring size.

Then he walked back outside, debating with himself whether it was better to surprise his bride or bring her to the shop and make sure she liked the ring first. He still shuddered to think of how close he had come to botching his proposal.

Thank God she was so patient with him. And then she had said such lovely things to him…

With memories of her caring whispers trailing through his mind, he drifted back toward his carriage. Annoyed at the necessary delay in his purchase of the ring, the notion occurred to him that surely he ought to buy her *something* to celebrate their engagement.

He glanced around at the nearby shops lining the famous street. He was already here, after all, and Bond Street was London's premiere place to find treasures for sale. But what should he get her? He was no expert in female fripperies…

At that moment, whom should he spot dancing out of the fine haberdashery on the corner than Maggie's former suitor, Bryce?

Connor's eyes narrowed. He had not forgotten that he owed that blackguard a thrashing for what he'd done to her when he'd seen her walking in the rain.

Connor gestured to Will and Nestor to wait for him with the carriage, and strode after the dandy, eager for a word.

Bryce was engrossed in admiring the new hat he had just purchased, apparently, to replace the one that Connor had destroyed.

Taken off guard when Connor seized him by the shoulder, the marquess's heir flew across the pavement like a rag doll, then found himself slammed flat against the brick wall next to the haberdashery's bow window.

"Amberley!" he sputtered, paling. "Wh-what the hell do you want, you insane Paddy?"

People in the fashionable street turned to stare, noticing the row.

Connor ignored them, irked at the slur.

"A word, my lord." He hauled Bryce into the nearby alley flanking the corner shop.

It was narrow and dim in the shadows compared with the broad, sunlit avenue where the shoppers strolled.

"What is the meaning of—"

"Shut up. I'll ask the questions." Connor flattened Bryce against the wall again by his lapels.

Bryce grew incensed. "Take your hands off me, sir!" he snarled, baring his teeth like a cornered animal. "Unless you want another bullet?"

Connor laughed and glanced at the fop's new hat. "You call me out again, and I guarantee, your hat there might survive it, but you won't. I'll put the bullet right...there." He shaped his fingers into the form of a pistol and pointed it at Bryce's left eyeball.

"Boom," he added softly, pulling an imaginary trigger.

The threat inspired the vain fool to check his anger. "What do you want with me?"

"Oh, we've much to talk about, my lord. First comes the matter of your complete lack of chivalry. You see, I don't like men who are unpleasant to young ladies."

When Bryce started to scoff, Connor shoved him harder against the bricks, itching to punch him. But if he broke his jaw, then the son of a bitch wouldn't be able to tell Connor what he knew about Richard's secret life.

That didn't mean Connor could not still put the fear of God in him, however.

"Did you think it amusing, eh, to splash Lady Margaret with your carriage when you saw her in distress? Make it worse for her? Punish her for jilting you to soothe your ego, you witless little boy?"

Bryce looked startled that Connor knew about it, but he didn't deny it. "What, she came running to you about that?"

"If only that were the case. But no, I heard about it at the club. Allow me to assure you that no one but you and your idiot friends found it amusing."

Bryce scoffed, but looked away, avoiding eye contact, which suggested he at least had the sense to be embarrassed by his behavior. "So she's moved on to you now, has she? Well, don't flatter yourself. She's a tuft-chaser, Amberley, just like her sister. She dropped me, a mere marquess's heir, to set her cap at you, a duke, I'm certain of it." He tugged indignantly at his waistcoat and lifted his chin. "I think I deserved at least a little revenge for that."

"Oh, drop the charade, Bryce. You never had any real interest in the girl. And we both know why."

Bryce flicked a wary glance over Connor, suddenly worried.

Connor let out a brief, cynical snort and shook his head, releasing the man in disgust and stepping back.

Bryce eyed him uneasily. "What do you want from me?"

"Stay the hell away from Maggie in future. Don't speak to her; don't even look at her again. She is under my protection henceforward. Do you understand?"

"Fine." Bryce rolled his eyes and looked away, haughty as ever.

Connor felt sure he'd got the message.

"Well!" said Bryce. "This has all been very enjoyable, Your Grace, but if there's nothing more, then I'll be on my way—"

"Not so fast." Connor thrust Bryce once more against the wall. "I have a few questions for you. About Richard."

Bryce's stare homed in on Connor, a flicker of dread in his eyes. "What about him?" he asked with careful nonchalance.

Finally confident that the little viper wouldn't try to slither away, Connor stepped back and blocked the escape route with a wide stance, his feet planted wide, his fists planted on his hips. "I want to know exactly why you thought my cousin was murdered in the first place, let alone why you blamed it on me. Official reports state his death was an accident."

Bryce stared, weighing the question. "It wasn't."

"How do you know?"

"He knew how to drive his own damned curricle. He was a dab hand! He drove it everywhere. He knew exactly what that vehicle could do—and what it couldn't."

Connor had never driven a curricle, but he had seen plenty of them in Town. They were extremely popular with the dandyish set, those who could afford them. Light, fast, rather spindly vehicles built on elegant, flowing lines, with a leather top that could be folded down, and perched up high on two wheels—the only two-wheeled vehicle drawn by a pair of horses for double the power.

Bryce shook his head. "It's obvious to me that the only way that accident could've happened is if someone tampered with his carriage somehow, or did something to the horses." He fell silent abruptly, as though he felt he'd said enough already, and glared at Connor in mutinous silence.

Connor studied him with a probing gaze. "You must know by now that I am not the killer. At least you can admit that, if I were, I would not have done it in so cowardly a fashion. Tampering with someone's carriage? Shoving an old man off a cliff? Not my style, as you may have noticed. I prefer the direct approach."

Bryce arched a brow and looked away. "I suppose."

"Well? What else do you know? It's plain as day you're hiding something. Were you with him that night? Was he drunk? Was he angry about something before he drove off and got into that wreck?"

"How should I know!"

"Do you want me to find his killer or not? If so, you've got to tell me what you know, Bryce."

Bryce stared at him, clearly feeling cornered.

"Can you think of any other motives about why someone would do this to him? Jealousy? Vendetta? Hatred for your kind, maybe?" Connor suggested with a knowing look when Bryce remained silent.

"My kind? What are you talking about?" he answered, though his face flushed.

"Lovers' quarrel?" Connor asked meaningfully.

Nothing.

"Look, I know you two were more than friends—"

"What?" Bryce's eyes flared and he looked at Connor with dread.

"If anyone has information about what was going on in his life the night he died, I know it would be you. That's why you called me out, isn't it? To avenge him? And I am sorry for your loss—I am. But I need to know more if I'm to figure out what really happened to him. Did he have any particular enemies?"

Bryce shrugged. "No."

"Were any of his other, er, companions especially possessive?"

Bryce made a show of looking utterly offended. "I'm not going to stand here and listen to such filthy, perverted accusations—"

"Bryce, I don't give a damn about your secret, other than it being wrong of you to deceive Maggie. I just want to know who the hell is murdering my relatives. Preferably before they get to me."

Bryce began trembling, but gave up trying to deny it. Ashen, he glanced up and down the alley. "How did you find out?" he whispered with a terrified gulp.

Seeing him like this, Connor did not have the heart to tell Bryce that many in the ton were well aware of his proclivities, according to Maggie. There was no good reason, either, to admit that the information had virtually dropped into Connor's lap, courtesy of Richard's diary.

"Military intelligence officer, remember?" he said instead. "I have my ways." And just like in the field, he attempted to establish trust by being respectful of foreign customs. After all, a man who had blown up twelve innocent people in a tunnel did not have much room to judge. "I, er, understand you cared a great deal about each other."

"Don't be disgusting," Bryce said.

"I told you, I don't give a damn about it, Bryce. But I'm sure Society would. So do, please, cooperate."

"Don't threaten me, you Irish mongrel."

"You really want to push me right now? After how you treated Maggie? I really don't advise it."

"What about how she treated me? Jilting me for no reason?"

"No reason?" Connor exclaimed, then shook his head. "Stop trying to change the subject. Just tell me what you know about my cousin's death and I'll go away. I did not kill Richard or his father or any of them; I had no designs on this godforsaken title. I would've been quite content to live out the rest of my life on my grandfather's horse farm in Ireland. So quit wasting my time." Bryce winced as Connor shoved him back once more against the rough brick. "Start talking. When did you last see him?"

Bryce heaved a sigh. "Richard was obsessed with finding out the truth about his father's accident. He was torn apart with guilt for how he'd treated the old man while he was alive." Bryce scratched his brow and looked away. "His father was a priest. Caught Richard with another boy once when he was younger. And from then on, was fond of telling him he was going to hell."

Connor scrutinized him. "Did Richard kill him? To get the title sooner?"

"No! He merely loved to scandalize him when he got the chance. But that game ended when his father suddenly died. Especially under such strange circumstances.

"Richard didn't believe the story that his father had just accidentally slipped while he was out walking near those cliffs at their estate in Dorset. He suspected foul play, only his father had so few enemies. Bloody virtuous," Bryce said with a sneer. "About nine months into his tenure as duke, Rich left Town again to continue his search for clues out in Dorsetshire. He felt certain one of the locals must've seen *something*."

"Did he speak about finding any leads?"

"Nothing in particular. But he was spooked by it all." Bryce shook his head. "He wanted me to come to the country with him, but I refused. Told him he was being paranoid, and that people have accidents all the time," he added bitterly. "So he left."

"Was he gone long to the country?"

"No. He said he'd be away for a fortnight. But then, well, you see, he came back unexpectedly after just a few days. To tell me that I was right. That he'd realized he was being foolish, acting obsessed. Except…" Bryce lowered his head as he slumped back against the wall. "He came over to my house unannounced and…we had a row."

"Why?" Connor waited. "Well?"

Bryce looked at him in frustration. "I was not alone when he arrived."

"Oh…I see," Connor murmured. "So he found you with somebody else."

Bryce blushed but nodded grimly.

"Who?"

"It doesn't matter now—"

"It might. Who was it?"

"It's insignificant! Believe me," he said, red-faced.

"Damn it, Bryce—"

"Fine!" Bryce scowled and dropped his gaze. "It was Lady Haywood."

"*Lady* Haywood? Oh… I see." Connor had been warned at the club about the so-called man-eater of Moonlight Square. One dallied with her at one's peril, Netherford had laughingly warned him.

Connor cleared his throat awkwardly as the murky picture became just a shade clearer. "Did, er, my cousin also like women?"

"No! Now I've answered your questions. Can I go?"

"First tell me what happened when he found you with her."

Bryce shrugged. "Not much. He gave me this cold, scornful laugh and walked right out. I followed him, but that only made it worse. We got into a shouting match. Before I could stop him, he stormed out and drove away in his curricle in a rage. It wasn't my fault," Bryce insisted, though the tortured look on his face suggested that he had not managed to convince himself of this.

Connor pondered the order of events for a moment. "Richard wouldn't have taken his curricle all the way to Dorset and back, would he?"

"Of course not. A curricle would never survive on rough country roads."

Connor traced the line of his cousin's final hours in his mind. "So, he must've returned to London in one of his heavier-duty coaches.

Probably stopped at home to refresh himself after his journey, then left in the curricle to visit you."

Bryce nodded. "Sounds about right."

"And where did he normally keep this vehicle?"

"It stayed in London year-round, so I should think it would've been kept in the carriage house with his other vehicles right there at Amberley House."

"Did he mention having any problems with the curricle or the horses?"

"God, Amberley. Considering how he found me, we didn't exactly discuss such trivialities. Especially when he told me he never wanted to see my face again. He stormed out, and that was the last time I saw him alive."

"Where did he mean to go?"

Bryce heaved a sigh. "There's an inn on the outskirts of Town, almost as far as Islington, where men go looking for…"

"What's it called?" Connor asked.

"The Ram's Head Inn. That's why he was out there on the turnpike road at such an hour." Bryce swallowed hard. "Not a streetlamp for miles. Nothing but fields and cows. Then he hit that sharp turn. The curricle was smashed. And he was thrown clear of the vehicle. They say he hit some farmer's stone fence headfirst…"

Connor dropped his gaze.

"At least he didn't suffer," Bryce said in a strangled tone. "They say he died instantly."

Connor gave Bryce a moment to collect himself, then asked, "What of the horses? Did anyone examine them afterward for signs of tampering?"

"One was killed in the wreck, the other badly injured and had to be destroyed. Poor Richie. He loved those horses."

"Who was it that found him out there?"

"The mail coach driver came passing through on his route. God, why are you asking me all this? I'm sure it was covered in the coroner's report."

Connor just looked at him meaningfully, and Bryce's eyebrows shot upward.

"You think *I* had something to do with this?" he exclaimed. "You're mad. Absolutely not. I didn't even know he was dead until the next day!" He shuddered. "I've barely slept a wink since."

"You feel responsible?"

"Obviously! He was scared of some wild plot against his family and confided in me, but I didn't listen! How's that for a friend? How would you feel?"

"So it helped allay your own guilt to blame his death on me, instead?" Connor said dryly.

"Well, you had the most to gain! And plenty of experience in killing. I'm sure you could've killed all three dukes easily enough. Just like you could've killed me in the duel. Why didn't you, anyway?"

"Because Maggie asked me not to," Connor said matter-of-factly. He gave Bryce a look of reproach, then turned away. "If you think of anything else that might be helpful, let me know."

With that, he ended his interrogation and left Bryce alone in the alley to compose himself.

No doubt the guilt-ridden soul was glad to see him go.

At last, Connor returned to where he had left Nestor and Will waiting with the carriage.

"There you are!" said Will. "I was starting to worry."

"Any luck?" Nestor asked, getting the door for Connor while Will climbed up onto the driver's box.

"Possibly," Connor said.

Upon their return home, he decided to have a look around inside the carriage house. If Richard's vehicle had indeed been tampered with, then any alteration to it most likely would have been made while it sat in its usual spot, inside the coach house.

Chilled to find the trail leading back once more to his own property, Connor stared out the coach window, deep in thought, as Will drove them back to Moonlight Square.

Upon arriving, the lad slowed the horses, carefully turning in at the narrow passage between Amberley House and the row of large terrace homes beside it.

The passage led back to the mews behind the mansion, where both the stable and carriage house were situated.

The stable for Amberley House accommodated a dozen horses, with the grooms and coachmen housed upstairs in the loft. As for the coach house, it had five pairs of wide, arched wooden doors, behind which lay five carriage bays.

The first usually housed the ducal town coach, in which Connor presently sat, with the Amberley coat of arms emblazoned on the door.

The second contained an opulent barouche, while the third had been empty since Connor's arrival. He presumed that was where Richard's curricle had been kept.

The last two bays housed the sleek, but rugged, longer-bodied traveling chariot, built for comfortable conveyance over long distances, and finally, an old, plain brown carriage for the servants' use.

When Will pulled the team to a halt in the mews to be unharnessed, Connor got out to take a closer look around inside the coach house.

For some reason, he had not given it much thought before.

He also made a mental note to have all the carriages checked for signs of tampering. He'd order full maintenance procedures performed to make sure all vehicles were safe.

After stepping through the man-door on the side of the coach house, since all five of the wide bay doors were still closed, Connor went in to explore the quiet space. His boot heels struck softly over the dark flagstone floors beneath him, while above, the vaulted ceiling with its mellow oak trusses and exposed rafter beams arched over him.

Sunlight angling in from the high windows lit up the fine particles of sawdust that hung in the air. The scent of it mingled with the smell of hay from the nearby stables, and the sharper but pleasing aromas of the oil and polish used in maintaining the carriages.

The bay for his town coach still stood empty, but Connor sauntered through it into the curricle's empty slip and examined the space, his brow furrowed. Unfortunately, he wasn't even sure what he was looking for at this late date. Probably wasting his time.

Any evidence of an intruder would have long since vanished, considering that Richard had died months ago...

Just then, someone spoke up from behind him, breaking into his thoughts: "Good afternoon, Your Grace."

He turned around, a grin breaking across his face at the sight of his favorite face peeking in through the man-door. "Why, Lady Margaret Winthrop! What are you doing here?"

"Just a neighborly call. I was walking in the park when I saw you return. Couldn't resist coming 'round for a quick hullo. Good thing I came, too; you look lost."

Her smile dimpling, her gray eyes beaming at him from beneath the brim of her fetching, lace-trimmed hat, she ambled in, coyly swinging the skirts of her light blue walking dress, clutching her dainty reticule.

She looked so beautiful—and so happy—that Connor lost the ability to speak for a moment. His chest clenched, and his heart beat faster.

His future duchess.

He had not seen her since the wee hours of Saturday night, when they had pledged themselves to each other. Now he couldn't take his eyes off her. All he could think about was that gorgeous ring with the diamond and emeralds, and how it would look on her finger.

She studied him with a playful smile. "Well, my dear duke? I assume there is a reason you are standing in the middle of your coach house staring into space?"

CHAPTER 21

The Coach House

s Maggie ventured into the cool, quiet, expansive space of the carriage house, she gazed with pleasure at her future husband.

It was risky of her to sneak in like this unchaperoned, but she could not deny that her heart welled up with champagne bubbles of delight at the mere sight of him: tall and powerful, elegantly dressed for the day in a smoke-gray tailcoat with a steel-blue paisley waistcoat. Exquisitely well-fitted ivory breeches hugged his legs, disappearing into shiny black boots.

He was indeed a specimen to behold, and Maggie couldn't help thinking as she drifted toward him that such a husband could make even the most mild-mannered woman viciously possessive.

"You, sir," she said, "are a sight for sore eyes."

"Pshaw," he teased, taking her hands and drawing her into his embrace.

She went without the slightest thought of protest, and as his strong arms encircled her, she smiled up at him, thinking how wonderful it was that she could say to him whatever popped into her mind.

It was how they had begun their strange acquaintance, and how they would always continue, she vowed.

Then he bent his head and brushed her lips softly with his own. "Good afternoon, my lady."

"Good afternoon to you." She smiled, gazing into his eyes, then she pulled him down by his nape to kiss her once more.

Closing her eyes, she reveled in his eager response. Connor deepened the kiss, tightening his embrace. They both ignored the sound of the man-door clicking closed several feet away, as some discreet soul outside—probably Will—gave the two of them their privacy.

Maggie wondered if the major had told his trusty followers yet that they were now engaged. But her musings dissolved as his mouth slanted over hers and his hands molded the curve of her waist, soundly claiming her anew.

As his firm hold inched down to her hips, his delicious tongue swirling against hers, Maggie could not stop herself from pressing her entire body flush against his. She could feel the stirring in his trousers against her belly.

He left her breathless several moments later, when he ended the kiss. He stood in silence for a moment, still holding her, as though he needed to collect his thoughts.

"Now that," Maggie panted, "is what I'd call a proper greeting."

He nodded with a low, charming laugh, then met her gaze with a roguish smile. "Aye."

He took a deep breath and stepped back from her. He looked away, running a hand through his thick black hair. "Right. What was I doing, then?"

She laughed, feeling the glow of a blush in her cheeks. "That's what I was wondering."

"Well, it's gone, whatever it was. You've stolen my wits again, dash you."

"And I'm not giving them back." She smiled like a troublemaker and wandered off to admire his luxurious coach house and all its fine vehicles, giving her wondrous fiancé a moment to compose himself.

Mellow wood-polish smells infused the coach house. As Maggie ambled by an opulent mahogany barouche with the top folded down, she could not resist a peek inside the gorgeous vehicle. It was even finer than Delia's, with exquisite light green damask upholstery.

"That must be hard to keep clean," she said, impressed, then strolled on. "You are living *very* well, aren't you, Your Grace?"

Connor snorted. "Nowadays, perhaps. This building alone is bigger than some of the barracks where I've lived."

She smiled at him over her shoulder, and then opened the glistening door of the massive traveling chariot and had a snoop inside. "Goodness. You could sleep lying flat in here. Well, maybe not *you*, you great bruiser."

He grinned and leaned against one of the wooden posts. She could feel his appreciative gaze traveling over her body as she sauntered around the long-distance vehicle.

It was an enjoyable sensation, feeling herself the object of his desire as she meandered around. "So have you told your men about us yet? Nestor and Will?"

"Aye."

"What did they say? Were they happy for you?"

"Happy and shocked," he said in amusement.

Maggie beamed. "I'm bursting to tell the whole world. Don't worry, I won't," she quickly added. "I know—we will, together, as soon as it's safe. Major's orders." She peered around the side of the tall coach and gave him a little salute.

"I am sorry about the delay," he offered. "I just want to keep you safe until this whole bother is laid to rest."

"I don't mind. Just stay alive for me, eh?"

"Yes, ma'am." He saluted her in return. "Say, has your sister apologized to you yet?"

Maggie scoffed. "No, and I won't hold my breath. This is only the fourth day, you see. Delia can hold a grudge for ages." She inspected the plainer brown coach in the end bay. "I have a feeling she is waiting for *me* to apologize for daring contradict her in the first place."

"Ha!" Connor said.

"Ha indeed. But don't worry. That part of my life, trying to please everybody, is over."

"Good."

She shrugged, swinging her reticule thoughtfully. "I have you to thank for that, you know."

"Me? How?"

"*You* don't especially try to please anyone, do you? You just simply *are* who you are, and I admire that. It inspires me. It's quite freeing, actually. I don't care anymore what people think about me. Except for you."

"Well, you never need to worry about that, my darling. I am your greatest admirer."

Hearing the squeak of carriage springs behind her, Maggie turned around in surprise and found Connor sitting back in the luxuriously upholstered open barouche.

He rested one arm along the back of the carriage seat, and, with a devilish glimmer in his eyes, crooked a finger at her, beckoning her to join him. "Fancy a ride, love?"

Maggie gulped at his wicked entendre. At once, a blush bloomed in her cheeks, and her heart leapt at the seductive glow in his eyes.

She sauntered toward him, her pulse suddenly pounding. "Where to?"

"Come and find out." He began unbuttoning his waistcoat. "Have a seat in your future carriage, my lady. I think it would make a fine lady's coach for my future duchess."

Maggie halted in her tracks, for not until that moment had it crossed her mind that everything she was seeing on his property would soon belong to her, as well.

He patted the empty seat beside him. "You'll have to tell me what color horses you'd like to pull this thing." A half-smile curved his lips as he read the astonishment on her face. "Did you just realize that now?"

She shrugged. "I was never the mercenary type." She could see by the look on his face that he was enormously pleased by her words.

"All the more reason for me to spoil you." He leaned forward and offered his hand as she approached, helping her to step up into the barouche.

She sat down next to him, facing the wide, closed door of the bay. Still dazed by the thought that she was about to become a very wealthy and powerful woman, she let her stare travel over the carriage interior. "Oh, Delia's *really* going to hate me now."

He chuckled and studied her, his arm resting on the back of their seat. "I'm glad you like it. Too fancy for my tastes, but I like seeing you in it."

She turned to him. "Do I really get to marry you?"

"I wouldn't have it…any other way," he whispered, then he lifted her hat off her head, cast it aside, and pulled her onto his lap.

Maggie went to him eagerly, peeling off her gloves as fast as her trembling fingers would allow her. She couldn't help herself. She had thought far too often of all they had shared in the gazebo. And, heaven help her, she was hungry for more of this man.

Apparently His Grace felt the same. He took off his tailcoat, kissing her all the while. Maggie used the fleeting respite when he tossed his coat aside to start removing her tight velvet spencer.

He kissed her throat, his hot, silken mouth intoxicating her as he helped strip the snug little jacket off her shoulders. Her hands bared now and tingling with a heightened sense of touch, Maggie caressed her lover's face as he devoured her neck in an open-mouthed kiss. She began untying his cravat, and he joined the effort, yanking the knot free and sliding the length of starched fabric off his neck.

With his cravat removed, the V of his loose linen shirt fell open, revealing his sculpted chest. Maggie caressed it in delight, fascinated by the heat of his skin and the light furring of hair that she discovered there.

His sheer masculinity overwhelmed her senses. It was then that Connor managed to tug the low-cut short sleeve of her white muslin gown off her shoulder. Then his warm, clever fingers slipped inside her décolletage and went exploring.

Her heart raced, and a frisson of delight ran through her when his questing fingertip reached her nipple. He began deftly teasing and playing with it until she was on fire. Moving to the other breast, he ordered her hoarsely to stand.

When she did, he worked her breast free from the gown, and his mouth replaced his fingers.

Maggie tipped her head back, wild with thrill, running her fingers through his hair. He was freshly shaved, so the pleasing roughness of his jaw that she remembered from Saturday night was gone now. It was all just warmth and wetness and urgency. Languorous kisses savoring her flesh…

Straddling his bent knees with her skirts hitched up a bit, her hands propped against his broad shoulders, she grew weak-kneed with desire.

"Oh, I missed you," he whispered as he put that side of her dress back up and pulled the other down. Then he paid homage to her other breast with loving care.

His hands traveled over her all the while, coaxing her body into reckless compliance with anything the man might ask.

She assumed he knew what he was about when he moved her back from him a little and made her sit on the opposite carriage bench. Maggie bit her lip and waited, enthralled, yearning for more of the pleasure he had shown her before, but he had something else in mind for her today.

Waiting in a state of throbbing breathlessness to find out what it was, she watched in fascination as he knelt on the spotless carriage floor between her knees and slowly slid her skirts up, higher and higher.

"What are you doing, you wicked man?" she whispered.

"Trust me. You're going to enjoy this."

Duke of Storm   249

Oh, but he had a gift for understatement, she soon realized. Because when he lowered his mouth to her mound and began to kiss it, playing with the swollen crest, swirling his tongue over and around her center, she began to whimper with pleasure and went positively limp. She could do naught but lie back in the carriage and receive.

He clearly enjoyed the giving as she arched helplessly against his mouth. He gripped her hips, bared to him beneath her skirts, and then slipped a finger inside her passage while his tongue played.

Maggie had no idea such things were possible…

Then all thought dissolved as he swept her on toward a needy climax, his face buried between her legs. Her hips pumped against his face as he licked her faster and faster, and ravished her all the more deeply with his hand. Her wanton cries of pleasure resounded beneath the soaring rafters of the coach house, and she had become deaf to the creaking of the carriage springs.

"Oh, God, Connor." It happened then, the same as at the garden folly, only so much more intense, a wrenching release that seemed to rise and explode from the depths of her very soul.

It lasted several seconds longer, but he kept going until he was very sure he had wrung every ounce of pleasure from her body.

She lay back against the carriage seat, panting, then winced as he withdrew his fingers delicately from her body. He drew his damp chin along the inside of her thigh, smearing her skin with her own dewy wetness, then rose from between her thighs.

When she looked at him, breathlessly incredulous, his lips glistened, but his eyes were full of fire. He wiped his mouth off roughly with his loose white shirt sleeve, piratelike, and gave her the most rakish little smile she'd ever seen.

He then pulled a silver flask out of his castoff tailcoat and washed down her wetness with a swig of whiskey.

He licked his lips and winked at her. "You're welcome."

"Holy God," Maggie finally uttered, and began laughing dazedly. "You…!"

He took a slight bow like an actor on stage and then collapsed heavily onto the opposite bench, laughing. Maggie shook her head and returned gradually to earth, tucking her legs shyly back together again and brushing her skirts down to their proper station.

"You," she said again, shaking her head in amazement.

He flicked his eyebrows upward, playfully smug, then took a second swig of drink. While Maggie strove to reassemble her wits, he replaced the cap on the flask, watching her.

Bliss flowed like a river through her bloodstream.

"Told you," he said, his fond gaze at odds with his cheeky jest.

She laughed and went to him, planting herself unceremoniously on his lap again. She wrapped her arms around him and gave him a shy kiss after that madness.

When he parted her lips with a stroke of his tongue, she noted the taste of her own nectar on his tongue, mingled with whiskey.

More than anything, though, the fevered urgency in his kiss made her realize that, although he was too polite to say so, the man was beside himself with frustration.

Rallying her spent strength and gathering her nerve—emboldened, no doubt, by all they had shared so far—she reached down and laid her hand on his most forbidden region. His manhood stood erect, flush against his body; she could feel it throbbing against her palm and fingers behind the buttoned placket of his breeches.

He went very still, closing his eyes as she ran her hand lovingly up and down the solid length.

"Connor?" She leaned closer, and he shivered with desire when her lips brushed his ear. She smiled, still intoxicated from the magnificent experience he'd given her. She inhaled the clean scent of his cologne. "Can one do that to you, as well?"

He did not open his eyes. "*One* can't, but *you* can, darlin'. Anytime."

She bit her lip. He held perfectly still, as though he dared not scare her away. But Maggie wasn't going anywhere. She could feel his rapt attention, absorbing her every move.

"Would you like that?" she whispered.

He nodded rapidly.

"Only, I'm not sure how."

"It's not complicated," he said hoarsely, and, at once, began unbuttoning his trousers. She drew back, filled with a daring spirit of adventure as he gave her the most seductive look imaginable. Need glittered in his heavy-lidded eyes.

Before guiding her hand to his body, he cradled her face in his palm and kissed her, as if to make it clear that he was not insisting on this. Whatever she wanted to do…

His refusal to pressure her made her adore him all the more. But, eager to learn the ways that she could give him pleasure, she slipped her hand down into his unbuttoned clothes.

He drew in his breath when her fingers grazed the satin tip of his member. "Show me what to do," she whispered.

He seemed to have lost the power of speech as her fingertips traveled down the towering length of his shaft until she came to the furred base of it.

"Oh my," she breathed.

He dragged his eyes open and stared at her like he'd devour her. She wrapped her fingers around the silken steel of his shaft. "Like this?"

He nodded.

She tightened her grip and began to stroke him. He groaned, swallowed hard, and swelled further in her hand.

"Heavens…"

"Oh, Maggie," he moaned as she redoubled her efforts. "Yes, hard is good," he encouraged her. "Fast is even better."

She complied, and indeed, his advice proved most sincere. His massive cock lunged again and again through the tight tunnel of her fingers.

His hand wrapped around her shoulder almost roughly as he clung to her. "All the way up to the tip, sweeting. God, yes—please—don't stop."

She obeyed, mesmerized. She kissed his cheek, and he stole a quick kiss from her lips, but then turned his mouth slightly away, as though he needed air. His breaths came deep and fast, in time with the wild tugging of her fingers.

Maggie clenched her jaw, astounded and thrilled beyond measure at his response to her as a lover. Something in her had taken over, a deep, primal beat in her blood. If she could do *this* to him with a touch…

"But what of kisses, darling?" she whispered in his ear, pausing in her rough caresses. "Down there, I mean."

He drew in his breath sharply at the question, then dragged his eyes open and looked at her.

"Are you sure?" he said, looking slightly astonished.

Maggie nodded so that her forehead brushed his cheek. "May I?"

She heard him gulp. "Aye." Wasting no time, he lifted his hips to push his breeches down several inches more, and then Maggie mimicked his position of a while ago, kneeling daintily on the carriage floor.

Connor bent forward to claim her lips in a passionate kiss. He did not have to say a word to communicate how badly he wanted this. She could feel it in his fevered touch, could practically hear his slamming heartbeat in the quiet of the sleepy afternoon.

After a moment, he ended the kiss and sat back slowly, watching Maggie between his sprawled thighs. She took his towering cock in hand again, lowering her head. A strangled moan of pleasure escaped him as she parted her lips and licked uncertainly at the tip. She was nervous but willing, and quickly caught on to the notion that she was meant to open her mouth wider and take him in.

And so she did, her fingers wrapped around him all the while. She grasped his upright shaft from this angle and realized that open-mouthed kisses all up and down his kingly cock were what he truly desired. And when she took his throbbing member deep into her mouth, so that he nigh bumped the back of her throat, her diligence paid off.

Before long, they found their rhythm together, and she gloried in the fierce pleasure she was giving him. She wasn't sure exactly when his caresses on her head dislodged the combs from her hair, but her long tresses tumbled down around her shoulders as she kissed and sucked his raging erection. His deep groans enwrapped her senses, and she could feel the power of his body, the strength surging through him, though he was holding it back even now.

Maggie wanted all of it—the raw male force of him. He thrust into her mouth, bruising her lips, but she didn't care—she liked his rough, needy savagery; she liked it very much. This man was exactly what she needed, and all she wanted was to give him pleasure endlessly.

She did not stop until she brought him to climax, but by now, she, too, was frenzied, so when she felt the shock of his hot, salty seed fill her mouth, she drank him down with crazed, greedy thirst.

After a long moment, he collapsed back against the carriage bench, his chest heaving. "Oh my *God*. I can't...believe...we just did that."

"Me neither." Still trembling, Maggie laid her head on his thigh, and he petted her hair. His touch was tender, but she could feel his hand shaking with the aftermath of lust.

"Oh, I'm *really* going to like being married to you, my little wanton," he purred, and Maggie laughed a little, the curious taste of him still tingling on her tongue.

Then he helped her to her feet; she sat down heavily beside him and stared into space, dazed. Beside her, he put his breeches back into order.

When he nudged her a moment later, she looked over to find him offering her his flask.

Wryly, she indulged, though it was the middle of the day. They sat in silence for a moment, him in obvious satisfaction, her dazed with virginal awe at what they'd done. What she had the power to make him feel.

She wondered if she ought to feel just a bit guilty over such splendid wickedness. But when embarrassment threatened to rise, she refused to let it steal the triumph of their intimacy, however scandalous.

Instead, she warded it off the same way he would: with a jest.

"So." She looked askance at him, then nodded toward his groin. "You're going to deflower me with that thing, are you?"

He flashed a broad smile. "Oh, I most certainly am."

"When?"

For that, he pulled her onto his lap once more with playful roughness. "What, you need more already, you adorable little fiend?"

She wrapped her arms around him and sighed. "I'll never get enough of you, my dearest Amberley."

"Nor I you," he murmured as he wrapped his arms around her and held her in dreamy silence.

Several minutes passed in fond, doting quiet as they lazed in the carriage in each other's arms, silently rejoicing in the happiness they'd found.

Unwilling to risk any chance of losing it, Maggie sat up and turned to him, wagging a finger. "Now, you'd better not let me catch you flirting with those other girls your aunt is trying to shove off on you on Friday night."

He gave her a chiding look. "There's only you, my lovely."

She gazed at him adoringly. "I hope Her Grace won't be too cross about us."

"Cross is her nature, my love. Might as well resign ourselves to it." He dropped his feet back down to the carriage floor after having rested his crossed ankles on the opposite bench, then he heaved himself up from leaning against the squabs. "Don't worry about her. She has no power over me."

"Well," Maggie said, "let's just hope a lifetime with Delia has prepared me to face the dragon."

He chuckled. "I have every confidence in you." He gave her a light kiss, and she brushed her nose against his, knowing she must go, but treasuring every moment in his presence.

She could not recall one moment in her life in which she had been more ridiculously content than she was right now.

A happy sigh escaped her. "Ah well. I should probably be getting back before anyone notices I'm gone."

He nuzzled his face against hers. "I wish I could keep you here always."

"Soon," she said softly. After giving him one final soft kiss, she rose from his lap and they both went about the business of straightening out their clothes.

"Now then," Maggie said to herself, "I know I had tortoiseshell combs in my hair when I arrived."

Connor was tucking his shirt into his breeches. "I think I ate them."

"Figures." She grinned at him then bent down to the carriage floor and peered under the seat. She spotted her comb, but as she reached for it, something else caught her eye.

A small, round, golden object.

She retrieved it after rescuing her comb, then looked at it: a brass button stamped with some regimental insignia.

"Darling, did you lose a button off your uniform?" She held it up and presented it to him.

"No, I've never used this carriage. I suppose it could belong to one of my men," he added, accepting the button from her.

But when he held it up and looked at it in a shaft of sunlight streaming into the high windows of the coach house, he furrowed his brow.

"That's odd."

"What is?"

"We're infantry. The insignia on this button belongs to a cavalry regiment. Fairly sure it's one of the dragoons, but I've no idea which—" Pausing abruptly, he looked away and muttered, "Oh Lord."

"What is it?"

"Nothing."

"What?" she asked as she twisted her hair back into a tidy formation and tucked it into place with the combs.

Connor frowned. "It's not the sort of thing one tells a lady."

"Am I still considered one after that?" she asked with a rascally smile.

He laughed heartily. "After that, my love, you've risen to *goddess* in my eyes."

She elbowed him as she worked on adjusting the other comb. "What were you going to say?"

Connor shrugged and looked away. "I just wondered if perhaps one of Richard's, er, particular friends might've been a dragoon and took, shall we say, a ride in this carriage with my scandalous late cousin."

Maggie lifted her eyebrows, then dropped her gaze as she realized what he meant. *Awkward.* "I see."

"By the way, expect an apology from Bryce for how he treated you the other day."

She jerked her chin up and looked at him with alarm. "What did you do?"

He lifted both hands. "Don't worry. I merely showed him the error of his ways. There was no blood, I promise."

"Connor." She set her hands on her waist and tilted her head at him, trying to look reproachful, though she couldn't help but smirk. "Well…if it's already done, at least tell me this: did he cower?"

He tapped her on the nose. "What do you think?"

"Ha." She could not deny that she was pleased. "Did he tell you anything useful?"

"Not really. Then again, if Richard had had some sort of liaison with whoever lost this button, I'm not sure he'd have wanted his darling Bryce to find out about it."

Maggie harrumphed at her former suitor's unimaginable two-timing.

"Hmm," Connor said, "I suppose I could ask around at the Officers' Club about it… But to admit to that vice is risking court-martial."

"Oh, Connor, it's plain what you must do," she said, sitting on the bench and hitching her skirts up to make sure her garters were well fastened.

He stared at her legs—and much more than her ankles—like he'd forgotten what they were talking about. "Huh?"

His desire for her was extremely flattering, but she snapped her fingers to regain his attention. "Simply track down your former butler and ask *him* if any of Richard's companions were dragoons. Butlers know *everything* that happens in a household. Trust me." She nodded with great certainty. "If anyone would know Richard's secrets, it's the butler. Always."

"But, Maggie, the butler might've been the one that poisoned me. That's why I sacked him." He shrugged. "Besides, by now, I have no idea where he is."

"His whereabouts would be easy enough to learn, my love," she said. "You'll have all your staff records somewhere in the house—home addresses, references, and so forth."

"Oh..."

"By the way, did you notice there were dragoons at your duel?"

"Yes. They came over and spoke to me after I shot Bryce in the hat."

"Maybe one of them had designs on you," she teased, poking him in his flat stomach.

He snorted. "And maybe one day hell might freeze over."

Maggie couldn't help but laugh as she brushed her skirts back down and rose again. "So cruel, Your Grace!"

He arched a brow. "What can I say—I'm a heartbreaker."

"You'd better not break mine."

"Never." He leaned down and kissed her, and Maggie went all dreamy for a moment.

"By the way," she continued after he ended the kiss and reality gradually faded back in, "I saw one of those dragoons during my jog through the rain the other day. I don't know who he was, but I recognized him from that day. He gave me a bit of a fright, actually, at first."

"What do you mean?" The major instantly came to attention.

She waved off his look of concern. "When he approached me, I thought he had some sort of improper intentions. But he was only offering me a ride home to escape the inclement weather—which is more than my former suitor did."

"You didn't accept, I hope?"

"No, of course not." She shrugged and hopped down from the barouche. "I was practically at my doorstep, anyway. He did rather startle me, though, addressing me by name. For a moment, I took it amiss, but then I realized he must've known who I was because of the spectacle I made of myself at the duel, running over to you like that."

"Ah, I found it very touching." With his cravat draped around his neck, Connor flashed her a jovial smile, then grabbed his tailcoat and jumped down from the carriage after her.

"Well, anyway, he was one of those dragoons. But, as I said, I'd already reached Delia's doorstep, so there was no point accepting his offer. Even if I had a long way to walk, a lady does not get into a closed coach with a strange man."

"But an open coach is all right?" Connor teased, hooking his thumb over his shoulder to gesture at the barouche.

She tilted her head and tried to give him a chiding look, though she could all but feel her eyes twinkling when she looked at him. "An open coach is entirely acceptable," she answered in a prim tone.

"Good. We wouldn't want to do anything scandalous, you and I." Dangling his tailcoat over his shoulder, he rested his other arm around her shoulders as he walked her toward the door.

Maggie looked up at him with affection. "Yes…whatever would the neighbors say?"

He tugged her off balance so that she stumbled into him with a breathless laugh, then gave her a kiss to send her on her way.

When the kiss ended, they exchanged a smoldering gaze and intimate smiles, then she slowly backed away from him, and only gradually let go of his hand.

"So, we'll speak to your butler tomorrow, yes?"

He heaved a sigh. "I suppose. If we can find him."

"Check the kitchen office. Staff records are usually kept somewhere in there, along with the household ledger books. I assume you don't have a steward here in town?"

"No, it was just the old butler, Trumbull." He paused. "For what it's worth, Aunt Florence felt very sure there was no way he could've been involved in the plot against me."

Halfway to the door, Maggie stopped and turned to him. "Who's Aunt Florence?"

"An aged kinswoman… I think she was my granduncle's cousin or something. She lives with Aunt Lucinda, though I don't know how she can bear it. She's a dear old thing, as sweet as the other one is sour."

Maggie was glad to hear that at least one of his relatives was friendly. "Will she be at the soirée on Friday evening?"

He nodded. "Should be. She told me she trusted old Trumbull entirely. That I should consider hiring him back because he had been with the family forever."

She winced. "And you sacked him?"

"Of course! Even if he wasn't the poisoner himself, it happened on his watch."

"Now you really sound like a soldier."

"Shouldn't a household be run a bit like a regiment?"

She arched a brow. "Is the family home a theater of war?"

He digested this for a moment. "Very well. You may have a point."

She chuckled with affection. "Darling, a servant capable of rising to the rank of head butler in a ducal household is nearly guaranteed to be as loyal as the family dog. In all likelihood, you needn't have dismissed him at all. In fact, he probably could've helped you more than I could."

He scowled at this, and Maggie got the feeling he was berating himself for not understanding better how a great aristocratic home functioned.

"Well, it's too late now, isn't it?" he finally said. "Even if I tried to hire him back at this late date, I doubt he'd take the job. He didn't think much of my Irish blood to begin with, and after I sent him packing, he probably despises me now. He's not going to tell me anything."

"Except for one small detail," she said. "You now have a secret weapon."

"I do? What's that, pray tell?"

"Me," she replied. "I'm to be the lady of the house, and I'm not the mean one who sacked the poor fellow." Maggie gave him a smile and then turned slowly, sauntering toward the door. "Don't worry, I'll get him to talk."

"I don't know…"

She paused, resting a hand on her hip. "You think I can't do it?"

He laughed, his eyes sparkling. "I'm sure you can do whatever you put your mind to, Lady Margaret Winthrop."

"Just watch me."

"Didn't I say I don't want you involved in this business anymore? For your own safety."

"You need me in this, duke. Besides, Aunt Florence said the old fellow's trustworthy, and I'm sure that must be true. If he's been with the family for decades, then he must be—"

"Ancient as Stonehenge?"

"Perhaps a bit decrepit," she conceded, "but I was going to say that if anyone will know whether your cousin was having his way with a dragoon, it'll be our Mr. Trumbull. Don't worry, Your Grace, I'll win him back for you."

"As long as he's not a murderer!" he called after her, still trying to sound grumpy, but she detected the underlying note of playfulness in his voice.

Maggie just waved a hand in the air as she strolled on toward the door. "War's over, Major. Not *everyone's* trying to kill you. Bring the household records tomorrow. They'll have his address and those of any other servants we might need to speak to so you can hire them back."

"Maggie!"

"You don't expect me to run your household without servants, do you? If so, you'll go hungry, because my cooking is even worse than my needlepoint. But I do have a way with the household staff. Trust me on this. Hiring back your old butler will be much easier than finding and training a new one. Especially when His Grace is paranoid."

"I have cause!" he said indignantly, but Maggie could feel him smiling behind her.

"Yes, dear."

"What time do you want to go?"

"Let's make it eleven. I have to be back in time for morning calls; they start at one."

"Morning calls…?" he echoed. "Last I checked, one o'clock was deemed the afternoon."

"You don't expect the rules of the ton to be logical, do you? Get that silly notion right out of your Irish head." She blew him a kiss, then went on her way, a giggle of pure happiness trailing out behind her.

As she walked back out into the golden, sunny afternoon, Maggie felt like she was walking atop light breezes.

She couldn't believe it. As much as Connor himself exceeded her dreams, in truth, she'd found more than just her future husband.

At last, she'd found a place to belong.

A home… One that needed her just as much as she needed it.

CHAPTER 22

Trumbull

*A*lgernon Trumbull was not, in fact, as old as Stonehenge, it turned out, but, according to his records, a mere eighty-two, and surprisingly spry, as they found the next day. He lived north of London in a quaint little cottage with a garden, a thatched roof, and blue shutters. He was baldheaded and slight of build, but the old man had a spine of steel, and Lord, thought Connor, Trumbull was a butler down to his fingertips.

Within the confines of the cozy residence Mr. Trumbull had procured for his forced retirement, nary a speck of dust could be found.

Admiral Nelson himself could not have run a tighter ship.

Connor, feeling too large and rough-mannered in the low-ceilinged space, was, admittedly, a little afraid of the tiny old man's polite glare.

Maggie was not.

Upon answering his own door for a change, the former butler gave Connor an icy stare, though he bowed, seemingly in spite of himself. Ah, but when His Grace introduced his future duchess, Trumbull drew in his breath and gazed at her in wonder.

His thoughts were all but written on his wrinkled old face: *Now here is a proper lady!* Then it was "Oh, do come in, come in, please… Tea, Lady Margaret? Cucumber sandwiches? Scones, Lady Margaret?"

"Please," she had said with a grateful smile, though Connor would've thought this was imposing.

He was wrong.

Trumbull drew himself up at this request, becoming a good inch taller, and marched off on his lofty mission to fetch tea for the future Duchess of Amberley.

When he'd gone, Maggie sent Connor a quick, knowing wink; he hid his grin in answer. Penelope stood at attention nearby until Trumbull returned, then Her Ladyship dismissed her. The elegant maid curtsied and withdrew, and this, too, seemed to please the old man.

This was the world he knew, a blessed return to the world that made sense to him, Connor supposed. Here was a lady who knew how to go about, and that, Trumbull could appreciate.

He stood at attention before her while Connor leaned against the softly timeworn mantel.

"The tea is delicious," Maggie told him.

He bowed. But then, seeing her warm, winning smile, he admitted, "I could make it with my eyes closed, ma'am."

She chuckled. "I am sure you could. Oh, please, Mr. Trumbull, do sit. This is your home, after all. And may I say, it is charming."

As are you, Connor thought, watching her in action.

Trumbull considered this, then remembered he was host this time, not employee, and sat, looking rather pleased with himself for the distinction he'd been shown. "How may I be of assistance, Lady Margaret?"

No doubt he was wondering what the devil they were doing there.

She took a dainty sip of tea, nodding at the question, and then began, in her diplomatic way. "First of all, I understand things went somewhat awry leading up to your departure from Amberley House."

Connor managed not to snort. That was putting it mildly.

"And I want you to know," she continued, "there is no suspicion upon you of any kind. In fact, we would be most honored if you would consider returning to your post at some point in the future."

Trumbull looked so astonished that he set the teapot down abruptly, having just begun to pour himself a cup, since Her Ladyship had made it clear that, at the moment, they were dispensing with the formalities. Perhaps he feared that his bony, wrinkled hand might shake at such an offer.

"You needn't answer just now if you don't wish to," she said, "but will you kindly consider it?"

"I-I will. Thank you, my lady." He glanced dazedly at Connor. "I thank you both."

Connor gave him a nod of acknowledgment.

"It is the least that you deserve," Maggie said. "But there is another reason for our visit."

Trumbull cocked his bald head. "Yes, ma'am?"

"Well." Maggie glanced down at her lap, fretting into her teacup. "The authorities *still* have reached no satisfactory conclusion to that whole troubling business at Twelfth Night."

Trumbull frowned.

"His Grace worries that if someone means him harm, then I may be at risk, too."

Connor had not seen her this adorably demure since that first night when she'd come knocking on his door, begging him to spare her stupid beau.

She was irresistible in this mode, in his experience.

She shook her head, topped with a rose-pink bonnet to match her gown.

"And so, you see, we cannot marry until the threat is resolved. We are obviously eager to start our new lives together," she said with a darling blush as she glanced over at Connor by the fireplace.

He nodded in agreement, but kept his mouth shut. He had already botched things enough with the old high stickler.

"Any details you remember from around Twelfth Night might at least help us glean a sense of what we are truly dealing with. So if there is anything at all that you might be able to tell us...?"

Trumbull frowned. "I am sorry, my lady. I have no further information beyond what I've thrice now told the Bow Street officers."

"Hmm." Maggie nodded. "It must have been distressing for you when suspicion slanted toward someone on the staff."

"I never believed that," he said emphatically, still looking routed by the mystery.

"So, you noticed no irregularities amongst the servants?"

"No, nor even the delivery personnel. The coalman, the milkman, the fishmonger's boy. Everything was in order from all that I could see."

"Well, who do *you* think poisoned His Grace?"

"Lady Margaret, if I may be frank, I am not convinced there was poison involved." He shook his head, staring at her. "It...seems impossible."

"So, what do you believe happened?"

"I personally believe that, er, Sergeant McFeatheridge either took ill with a stomach flu, as is common in wintertime or—more likely—

sickened himself with too. Much. Drink." Trumbull very determinedly ignored Connor at this moment. "The gentlemen were very merry, my lady." Disapproval sharpened his clipped, terse voice to fine-edged precision. "*Very* merry indeed."

Maggie pressed her lips together and dropped her gaze, somehow stifling the humor that Connor could feel bubbling beneath her polite surface.

He cleared his throat. "We did become rather rowdy now and then."

Not that he was sorry. *Eat, drink, and be merry, for tomorrow we may die.* The soldier's creed.

"But suppose for argument's sake that someone did put poison in the food," Maggie continued. "Perhaps not to kill the duke, but merely intending to drug him for some reason. Whom would you suspect?"

"None of *our* people, my lady." Trumbull fell silent for a moment, clearly wanting to please her by giving *some* sort of answer. "I suppose, in hindsight, it might have been possible for some *intruder* to have stolen in secretly and done it. With so many of His Grace's regimentals coming and going, the doors were scarcely ever locked."

"Was anyone hanging about who didn't belong at Amberley House?"

"Other than His Grace's twenty-three guests?" he asked pointedly.

Connor was well aware that Trumbull approved neither of him nor his Army mates.

Maggie nodded encouragingly. "Yes. Someone who might've known the staff's comings and goings, and perhaps had access to the kitchens?"

"Well," Trumbull said in an offhand way, shrugging, "there was one person allegedly hanging about, though I myself never saw him. If I had, believe you me…"

Connor suddenly came to attention, though he remained motionless.

"Who was that?" Maggie asked.

Trumbull sighed. "Ah, one day, I overheard three of our chambermaids gossiping about the scullery girl, Saphronia Diggs. Begging your pardon, ma'am, it is a bit improper, what I overheard."

"It's all right."

"They claimed that Simple Saffie, as they called her, was holding trysts in the coach house with a soldier—*not* one of His Grace's guests."

"Certainly not," Connor murmured. Even the rowdiest of his mates would have known that he would never tolerate them harassing his servant girls. Such behavior would have resulted in immediate ejection from the party.

"Naturally," Trumbull continued, "upon overhearing their maids' gossip, I revealed my presence and demanded explanations, but the gels were much abashed, confessed it was just idle talk, and quickly apologized for their impertinence. Even so, I called Saffie into my office and questioned her, for this would be an offense that warrants a maid's instant dismissal, as I'm sure Your Ladyship would well agree."

"Oh yes," Maggie said gravely. "Do go on."

"Saffie vehemently denied the accusation and, indeed, burst into tears, telling me over and over again that she was a good girl." Trumbull paused with a look of grandfatherly concern. "'Twas quite affecting. Perhaps I erred on the side of compassion. But Saffie is…different, you see."

"Different how, Trumbull?"

"A bit feeble-minded. For any other maid in the household, I assure you, the accusation alone would have been enough for me to send her off without a reference. I will not tolerate such nonsense in His Grace's house. But with Saffie being simple as she is, I…felt she deserved another chance. After all, it's only the scullery."

"Simple?" Maggie asked.

"Yes," Trumbull said regretfully. "She's quite a pretty girl, but she's not…all there. Has the mind of a child."

"I see."

"She means well; she is sincere enough. But if I had shown her the door, only the good Lord above knows how the poor creature would have fared out in the world. Unfortunately, His Grace dismissed her anyway, along with the rest of us. I don't suppose the master realized he was throwing an innocent to the wolves."

Connor's heart sank possibly through the floor, hearing this. Trumbull would not even look at him.

"Do you know what ever became of her?" Maggie asked gently.

The aged butler shook his head. "I should hope her family took her in."

Maggie looked relieved. "At least she does have family, then?"

Trumbull could not hide his disdain. "Yes. They live not far from here, in fact. I know of an elder brother, works in the mill next to Sadler's Wells. I must say, I got the impression that Saffie was rather afraid of him. From what I understand, Mr. Diggs is a low, rough sort, given to drink and brawling."

"I see," Maggie said faintly.

Trumbull paused and gave them both a measured glance. "Normally, I would never consider a girl with such unsavory connections for employment in the ducal mansion, but given Miss Diggs' especially dismal prospects in life, Christian charity compelled me to offer her a chance—with Cook's approval, of course.

"In the end," Trumbull continued, "we were quite pleased with how Saffie turned out. She was always a hard worker, and obedient. Whatever her limitations, she is perfectly capable of strenuous physical labor."

Maggie sent Connor a worried glance; he was busy wallowing in guilt.

"It was good of you to give her a place in life," she said, turning back to the butler.

Trumbull tilted his head. "Be that as it may, it was not always easy for her at Amberley House."

"What do you mean?" she asked.

"That day I came upon the chambermaids tearing her down behind her back, well... The truth is, this was not an infrequent occurrence." Trumbull shook his head, lowering his gaze. "I regret to say that Saffie was often the target of teasing by some of the other servants. I suppose she made easy prey, simple as she is. It's not the girl's fault she was born slightly lacking in wits," he said indignantly. "At least the Lord gave her a pretty face—to make up for it, I should think—but that only brought her more hostility from some of the other maids."

The old man sighed. "Poor Saffie. She is quite innocent, and altogether well-meaning. She cannot help what she is. Nor can we all. The point is, if she lied to me when I confronted her about this ugly rumor, which I seriously doubt—I can *tell* when they are lying—if she was indeed letting some ruffian take advantage of her in the coach house, then I would venture to say there is...a *remote* possibility that *he* might've gained access to the mansion somehow, through her. But the whole thing is absurd."

"Why?" Maggie asked. "How are you so sure?"

"Because the chambermaids were saying that this lover of hers was an officer of the dragoons, no less! Honestly." Trumbull shook his head, while Connor and she exchanged a grim look of shock, having found a highly incriminating button. "The dragoons are among the elite troops of England, ma'am, our modern-day knights, gentlemen of birth and breeding, sworn to chivalry—the heroes of Waterloo! For one of *them* to use a girl like Saffie in such an unspeakable fashion would be, why, 'twould be the very nadir of dishonor. Who could believe such a thing?"

Connor could not believe the old man's naiveté.

There were, of course, those patriotic souls who tended to worship the flag and the military, especially in wartime. But they were usually not "wise old men" who understood the carnage, but impressionable young girls who thought the lads looked dashing in their uniforms.

Like a young scullery maid would have done.

God, if some cocksure dragoon had come stalking this servant girl to get to Connor, she wouldn't have had a chance. Connor's jaw was clenched and his stomach turned with the sickening realizations spinning through his mind.

Unwanted by her family, ill-equipped to face life, bullied by the other maids, she'd have been desperately vulnerable to a man's smooth lies. Especially a dragoon, those arrogant bastards. Toy soldiers on their shiny horses, all glory, no brains, infantrymen liked to say of them.

Connor supposed he should be happy that at least it hadn't been Cousin Richard romping in the carriage house with one of them, but he could not muster the sentiment, awash in self-recrimination for having tossed the girl right into this scoundrel's arms.

To be sure, he felt the sting of Trumbull's veiled reproach aimed at him—an infantry officer—by pointedly heaping praise upon those swaggering cavalry dunderheads, but Connor didn't care.

The old man had more cause to be angry at him than Connor had previously realized.

It seemed he had allowed his Irish temper to run away with him where the servants were concerned. He knew *why* he had done it, of course. He had been out of his element as a newly minted duke, taken off guard, and outraged to be offered such a welcome to his new London home: a plate of poisoned food.

His first thought, his knee-jerk reaction, had been to assume that the English staff were slyly taking a go at him because he was Irish-born and they thought him unworthy. Well, he'd been fighting that battle all his life. And before he had realized the seriousness of the situation, some part of him must have also equated the poisoning with the same sort of unpleasant initiation rituals that new recruits faced when they arrived at their regiments.

The veterans enjoyed subjecting the cherries to all manner of pranks and pummeling to test them, a rough way of preparing them to face their first battle.

Moreover, Connor's deep sense of loyalty had added fire to his outrage, to think that it should have been his best mate Rory to bear the brunt of what had been intended for *him*.

But this visit to Mr. Trumbull's cottage clearly showed Connor the error of his ways. He had acted out of anger, and prejudice, with undue haste.

Maggie was right. The staff had not deserved to be sacked. And, apparently, for some of them, his lashing out like that may have led to disaster.

He had to repair this. Now. And so, in the silence that hung on the air after Trumbull's revelations, he swallowed his pride, cleared his throat, and lifted his chin.

He tried in that moment to look as much the part of a proper duke as a bloodstained barbarian could manage. Somehow it was easier to play the role with Maggie by his side, for it was plain that she, at least, had been born to maneuver her way smoothly around the polite world.

"I say, Mr. Trumbull." He moved away from the mantel, his posture stiffening. "It is not often that I find myself in the position of having to ask for another man's forgiveness. But I fear I acted in haste in the matter of your dismissal."

The old butler's eyes became as round as the saucers on which he had served the tea.

If hearing Lady Margaret address him a few times with the honorific "mister" had startled him, a personal apology from the fourth Duke of Amberley rendered him speechless.

Connor hoped he did not stop the old man's heart with his next words.

"I, er, I should be personally grateful if you would consider returning to my employ — with a raise in pay for your trouble, of course." Connor cleared his throat awkwardly and awaited Trumbull's reply.

Maggie turned, however, and sent him a tender glance, erasing any doubt that he'd done the right thing.

Trumbull was still trying to gather his wits. Connor really did not know how the ex-butler would answer. Old as he was, perhaps he was enjoying the leisure of his retirement.

Then his future duchess chimed in with her usual delicacy. "I second that offer, Trumbull, although, of course, I wouldn't want you to feel compelled, if you do not wish to return. But it would be a great relief to me as a new bride to know that a man of such experience as yourself—and expertise—was at the helm of my new household. It is, after all, a great responsibility."

Finally, Trumbull found his tongue. He rose to his feet. "Your Grace and Lady Margaret are both entirely generous," he declared, slightly abashed. Perhaps no one of such high birth had ever spoken to him in such respectful terms before. "I hardly know what to say…"

"Will you at least think on it?" Maggie asked sweetly.

He nodded. "Yes, my lady. And Your Grace need not apologize." Trumbull hesitated, though it was clear he had felt differently about this when they'd arrived. "That is to say, I cannot blame you for being angry, sir. It was a most distressing experience for us all. I only wish I knew how the blasted thing happened in the first place."

Trumbull sighed, lowering his gaze. Stiff-spined as he was, his shoulders slumped, and Connor realized that though the old fellow still didn't believe it was attempted murder, he truly did blame himself for the inexplicable lapse.

"Whoever has done this, we will find them," Connor assured him. "This will not stand. I can promise you that."

"You see, Trumbull," Maggie said, "you may not be aware that His Grace now believes it was not just he, himself, who was targeted, but that there is some nefarious plot afoot against the entire House of Amberley."

Trumbull's white eyebrows shot upward as he turned to Connor. "Do you mean to say you believe the other deaths in the family are suspicious, Your Grace?"

"'Tis possible." Connor nodded.

"Nothing is certain yet," said Maggie.

"Good heavens…" Trumbull looked stricken. "Your Grace, I served under all three past dukes. It seems ages ago that I was a young footman serving under the First Duke, even in his bachelor days, when he was still marquess. I remember when he used to go out riding 'round the countryside with King George himself…

"And dear Reverend Lord Rupert. That's what we all called him for so many years before he became the second duke…" Trumbull's eyes turned steely. "Sir! If someone harmed either brother or young Richard, I hardly know what to say. Do you suspect that even Duke Richard was murdered?"

Connor nodded.

Trumbull sat back down slowly. "If this is true, and they were killed under my very nose, then I am thrice shamed, and in no wise deserve the post."

"Nonsense," Maggie said gently. Leaning forward, she laid a hand on his arm, which startled him. Her gaze teemed with kind reassurance. "Even Bow Street has failed to find the answers, and you had no reason to suspect. Nothing is confirmed yet, Trumbull, so, please, do not trouble yourself so. It may prove that the first and second dukes' deaths were indeed the accidents they seemed. We simply aren't sure yet."

"Maybe even Richard's crash, too," Connor added. "If the truth proves otherwise"—he shrugged—"there is no way you could have known."

"But it would put both our minds at ease if you were there at Amberley House once more, only now, alerted to whatever mischief is afoot."

"However, it could be dangerous," Connor warned. "That is why I dare not marry Lady Margaret until this threat is removed. Given your advanced years, sir, if you do not wish to get involved, I would thoroughly understand—"

"Oh, to be sure, Your Grace, I will be there." Trumbull lifted his chin and stood tall once more, rising creakily from his cozy couch, ready for duty. His dejection faded as he straightened his shoulders and looked at them with flinty determination. "When would you like me to begin?"

"I'm very proud of you," Maggie told her handsome fiancé as they walked back out into the sunshine a short while later. "You quite impressed me in there."

"Me?" Connor glanced at her in surprise, then opened the little garden gate for her at the end of the flagstone path. "You're the one who charmed him."

"Come, it is a rare man, let alone a duke, who would have the humility—and the integrity—to apologize to a servant."

"Trumbull deserved it." He followed her out and pulled the gate shut behind him. "I'm glad you got him back for me."

"Me too." Maggie smiled at him as they headed toward their two parked carriages. "We'll need an expert to get that house of yours back in order after you turned it into an army camp."

"At least my aunts will be happy now," he said, but his brief grin faded. "We've got to track this poor Saffie girl down as soon as possible and find out the name of her dragoon. If she's still alive."

Maggie froze. "You think he might've killed her?"

His glance was grim but matter-of-fact, and the dark realization promptly sank into her mind.

"Of course," she murmured to herself. "If the scullery maid knows what really happened, then she could lay information against our dragoon and send him to the gallows."

Connor gave a taut nod. "Exactly. We need her address."

"I'll fetch the servant records." Maggie strode ahead to Connor's town coach, parked alongside the sleepy dirt road ahead of the carriage that Edward had lent her for her "errands" today.

Nestor and Will leaned against the glossy black side of Connor's town coach, chatting with Penelope, while Hubert, Delia's usual coachman, sat atop the driver's box of the second carriage, waiting for Maggie.

All the Birdwell servants were still in mutiny toward Delia after what she'd done to Maggie in Hyde Park, so Hubert had been more than happy to drive her around today, and had promised her his discretion.

After much consideration, Maggie had told Edward but not Delia about Connor's proposal. She'd told her trusted brother-in-law to expect a visit from the duke in due time so he could make his formal request for her hand.

Until that day came, Maggie had implored Edward to keep her big news quiet for now, so that Delia could not spoil it for her again.

Good old Edward, he'd agreed, and had even poured them both a glass of champagne so he could toast to her triumph. "Are you sure about this man?" had been his only question. Maggie had given a heartfelt yes and joyfully admitted that she was in love with their new neighbor.

Hearing that, Edward had gladly put his extra coach at her disposal for the day, assuming that her errands had to do with preliminary wedding planning.

In a sense, this was absolutely true. She should not have liked to lie to him.

But she saw no reason to tell him about the attempts on Connor's life and this mystery they were determined to resolve, for protectiveness might have caused him to forbid her from involving herself in this.

With that, Maggie flipped the bound folio of household records open and whisked through the pages listing the employment details on each staff member.

"Here she is. Saphronia Diggs. She lives in Muggeridge Lane." Maggie looked around at the others. "Does anyone know where that is?"

No one had heard of it, so Connor went back to ask Trumbull for directions, since he had said Saffie's kin lived nearby. The butler came to the door, leaving the front window where he had been discreetly peeking out at them.

He soon pointed them in the right direction, but warned that Muggeridge Lane was a ramshackle place, peopled by the rugged bruisers who made their living doing backbreaking labor at the mill and nearby brickyard.

"Maybe we should part ways here," Connor said as he ran his hand quickly over his hair to smooth it down, then pulled his top hat on.

"Nonsense. I shall be perfectly safe with *you* there, Major. Besides, Trumbull said it's right by Sadler's Wells theater; how dangerous can it really be? And once more, you'll most likely need me," Maggie reminded him.

"She's right, sir," Will spoke up. "Saffie was afraid of you even before you fired her."

"You know her?" Maggie asked the skinny lad.

Will nodded. "She was a sweet girl. I felt sorry for her, the way the others picked on her. Half the time she didn't even know they were making fun of her. I wanted to punch them," Will mumbled, "but I didn't."

"See?" Connor said in amusement. "Will can help me get her to talk."

Maggie cocked a fist on her hip. "Your Grace, if you were a frightened girl, would you sooner trust a scowling, oversized duke and two ex-soldiers, or a lady and her maid?"

One corner of his handsome mouth quirked upward. "Point taken."

"Good, for after everything she's probably been through with this blackguard..."

"If she's even alive," Connor said, and Will blanched.

"You think he might've killed her?" the lad cried.

"What if he's there?" Nestor interjected, silencing them all for a moment.

Maggie and Penelope glanced at each other; the maid looked a trifle worried at being included in this bad business.

"Then I'll shoot him," Connor said blandly. "You ladies can look away. If you still insist on coming, that is."

"You're armed?" Maggie asked.

"Always," Connor said, and behind him, Will nodded emphatically, glancing at the major.

"Shall we?" Nestor asked, opening the coach door.

Maggie nodded, then she and Penelope hurried back to their own carriage.

With Trumbull watching from out his cottage window and Society still ignorant of their as-yet informal betrothal, Maggie had insisted on them observing propriety by traveling in two separate carriages.

Hubert and the liveried footman posted on the standing bar at the back of her coach were the only two residents of the Birdwell household other than Edward and Penelope who knew of her pending engagement.

All four had been sworn to secrecy.

"Follow the duke's coach again, Hubert," Maggie instructed the driver. "We have an unexpected stop."

"Yes, milady." Beneath the brim of his tricorn hat, however, the coachman looked a bit puzzled as he got the door for them, so she explained to avoid any risk of gossip in the servant hall.

"We just found out that one of Amberley's former servant girls may have fallen into most perilous circumstances. We need to make sure she is safe at home with her family."

He bowed his head, looking relieved at the explanation. "Of course, ma'am."

Maggie climbed in and took her seat, and Penelope followed. In short order, their little two-coach caravan wove through the rural peace and quiet of Islington, heading back southward toward Town.

Sadler's Wells was on the way—home of the famous aquatic spectacles.

Genteel folk went there all the time to enjoy a night's lively entertainment, but Maggie had never even realized there was a mill of some sort tucked away behind it.

She desperately hoped that when they found the brother's residence, Saffie would be there, safe and sound.

What they would do with the former scullery maid once they found her, Maggie did not know, but she supposed they had to remove her somehow, given the threat to her life that her dragoon still might pose, if he was indeed the ruthless soul responsible for the three dukes' murders.

Whoever he was, he sounded like a most unpleasant fellow.

She thought again of that stranger, the dragoon, who had offered her the ride home during the rainstorm. Could that be the man? The notion that she might have stood there talking to a killer that day sent an arrow of pure ice down her spine. *He knew my name. And now he knows where I live...*

A shudder ran through her, but she was glad that, at least, she had told Connor about the incident. She hadn't thought much about it until they had found that button off a dragoon's uniform in the coach house.

Trysts taking place there between Saffie and this man would explain how it got there.

With gooseflesh marching down her arms, Maggie pushed aside her anxiety over it all to focus on the next task at hand. The sooner they found Saffie alive and well, the sooner they would learn her lover's name.

Then Connor could track the blackguard down and put an end to this, and they could start their new lives together without having to constantly look over their shoulders.

Trotting on through the bright spring day, they passed a pond, open fields, and a herd of grazing cows.

In the hazy distance, they could just make out the London skyline and the gleaming dome of St. Paul's.

Then, about a mile farther down the road, they veered off to the right into the Sadler's Wells complex, with its music hall and aquatic theater, tea gardens, and the old Sir Hugh Middleton Tavern, named after the founder of the waterworks there.

Indeed, they had passed several peaceful reservoirs, owned and operated by the powerful New River Company. This august firm had built the artificial New River, channeling the region's many underground streams into a proper system that supplied half of London with its drinking water.

The ingenuity of the man-made river was most impressive, Maggie thought, considering it had been built two hundred years ago.

Weaving past another of the spas established in this area, so rich in mineral springs, they admired the New River, with its locks and genteel brick promenade. Youngsters stood fishing atop its thick cement wall.

Deeper into the winding, tree-lined lanes around Sadler's Wells, they came upon the New River Head, the largest of the reservoirs. It had an oblong shape with a walled pond at its center.

With the carriage windows open and the breeze blowing through, Penelope and Maggie enjoyed the view of shimmering waters under blue May skies, with the bright green fields rolling out behind it.

Just a little taste of the countryside…

It made Maggie think of Kent and Halford Manor, and just for a moment, she was homesick.

Hubert followed the duke's carriage onward, however, and there, tucked away at the back corner of the reservoir, stood the mill.

It was a large, plain redbrick building with great chimneys billowing white clouds of smoke, as if some great furnace burned within, and when Maggie spotted a yard full of cast-iron pipes, it dawned on her that *that* was what they manufactured here.

Come to think of it, she had heard that sections of London were in the process of having their ancient, leaky wooden water pipes replaced with new cast-iron ones. Since the mill sat upon New River Company property, it made sense that the waterworks would also be supplying the replacement pipes throughout the city.

The mill yard bustled with activity, but they hurried on by; many of the men hard at work turned to scrutinize the two fine coaches rolling past.

Just beyond the mill, they found the rows of terrace dwellings set up for the millworkers.

Sure enough, per Mr. Trumbull's directions, the last street there proved to be Muggeridge Lane.

But apparently, the butler was more of a snob about such things than Maggie was, for the place looked respectable enough to her—a neighborhood of hardworking people, poor but decent.

The redbrick terrace houses were identical and small, with walled gardens in the back, laundry flapping in the breeze of many of them.

When they spotted Number 62, Saffie's home address listed in the servant records, they glided to a halt and got out. Jittery anticipation building as to whether the girl was here or alive or dead, Maggie and Penelope exchanged a worried glance as Connor walked over to them with Will in tow.

"Ready?" Connor asked.

Maggie smoothed the tassel on the end of her reticule as her heart began to pound. Then all four of them proceeded to the door of Saffie's brother's house.

Will stepped forward and knocked, then retreated to stand behind

Connor.

Nothing happened.

They looked around at each other.

"Maybe he's at work," Penelope said.

Maggie shrugged. "Yes, but if he's got a wife, *she* should be at home—with Saffie. Don't you think?"

"Did the butler tell you if Mr. Diggs is married?" Will asked with a frown.

"He didn't say." Connor knocked this time, louder. "Anybody home? Mr. Diggs?"

The door suddenly jerked open and a rumpled man appeared.

With his fist raised mid-knock, Connor nearly rapped the fellow in the forehead.

"Wot?" he barked. "You woke me up! What do ye want?"

Maggie blinked at this greeting.

Connor lowered his hand to his side. "We're looking for Miss Diggs."

The bearded man stared blearily at them, red-eyed, surrounded by a cloud of fumes from last night's ale. He appeared to have fallen asleep in his clothes; his plain, wrinkled shirt hung open down his hairy chest, and his feet were bare.

Maggie supposed she should be grateful that at least he had on breeches.

Well, Trumbull had warned them this man liked his drink.

"Your sister?" Connor prompted impatiently.

"Why?" Diggs glanced skeptically from him to Maggie, eyeing their upper-class garb. "Wot's she done now?"

"She hasn't done anything," Maggie said in a gentler tone. "We are concerned that she might be in danger—"

"Oh, she'll be in danger, all right, next time she shows her face around 'ere, the little slut."

Maggie jolted. And she thought *her* sibling was bad! At least Delia had never called her such a name.

"Why do you say that?" Connor demanded.

"Never mind it." As he warily scrutinized them, Diggs's glance flicked to the two fine carriages with gleaming horses and liveried footmen standing at the ready. "Who are you lot?"

Finally recovering her tongue, Maggie nodded politely toward Connor. "This gentleman used to be your sister's employer."

"Ohhh, I see." The stinky fellow looked Connor up and down. "So it's your fault, then."

"Pardon?" Maggie asked in surprise.

Diggs pointed at Connor, who was scowling. "He sacked her, and now she's ended up a whore."

"Mind your tongue in front of the lady," Connor ordered.

"Beggin' your pardon, ma'am," the man corrected sarcastically. "A soiled dove." Then he gave Connor a cold look. "I hope you're pleased with yourself, sir. Not that I'm surprised. In the end, it's probably all she's good for, anyway. Chit's barely got a brain in her head."

Maggie was nonplussed.

"Do you know where she's working?" Connor growled.

"Are you joking?" Diggs retorted. "I'm her brother! If I did, I'd have dragged her out by her hair months ago, wouldn't I? But she's hiding from me, see. Knows I'll tan her hide. Little numbskull. Useless, she is. Only way to manage that girl, beat some sense into her."

Maggie's jaw dropped, and Connor's fist clenched, but Diggs noticed neither, dismissing the whole matter with a weary wave of his hand.

"Eh, let her make her living on her back for all I care. Just another mouth to feed. But that little simpleton had better not show up here with some faceless fool's brat in her belly, that I can tell you. Because I'll send 'em both on to the workhouse."

"If you see her"—Connor's voice sounded slightly strained with the effort to hold his anger in check—"will you have her call on me at Amberley House?"

"Aye, I suppose," Diggs grumbled. "But if *you* see her first, you tell Saffie that our mum's rollin' over in her grave with what she's gone and done. Now, if you *fine* people will excuse me. The mill closes late and opens early, and some of us have to work nights."

Slam!

Maggie blinked as the door banged shut in their faces.

Connor and she both stared at it for a moment, then glanced at each other, speechless. "Well!" he finally said. "What a charming fellow."

Maggie shook off her astonishment, still marveling at the man's casual brutality. "I daresay Mr. Trumbull was not exaggerating after all."

"Criminy," Will muttered from behind them. He shook his head, looking stunned and saddened at what his little friend had had to endure. Penelope shook her head.

Then they all turned away and headed back slowly toward the carriages.

"Saffie's not simple," Will muttered. "She just daydreams all the time."

Connor looked askance at him.

"Well, what do we do now?" Maggie asked once she'd found her voice again.

"I hardly know," Connor growled. "There are hundreds and hundreds of brothels in London… The city's infamous for it, even on the Continent. Girl's a needle in a haystack at this point. For that matter, we don't even know if she's still *in* London. He might've taken her elsewhere."

"Or got rid of her altogether," Maggie murmured grimly.

"God, I hope I'm not responsible for this," Connor said.

"Of course not. The dragoon who targeted her is, not you." Maggie could see by the brooding look that he begged to differ.

He looked away, glowering. "I suppose I'll have one of my useless Bow Street fellows check to see if anyone matching Saffie's description has turned up dead in London over the past few months. Will, you'll have to come along to tell them what she looks like. I don't remember her at all."

"She was pretty," Will said in a somber tone.

Connor sighed. "Unfortunately, it seems that, at least for now, our search has reached an impasse."

Maggie nodded, her heart sinking, then glanced toward the road. The sun was bright overhead, climbing toward noon.

"I suppose this is where we must say goodbye." She looked up at Connor. "I have to get back in time for morning calls."

Penelope and Will drifted away, giving the two of them some privacy as they stood near the carriages.

Connor took Maggie's hand and squeezed it gently. "Thanks for all your help today."

"Of course."

"I'll see you Friday evening, yes?"

"Aunt Lucinda's soirée." Though her heart was troubled over Saffie, Maggie smiled and squeezed his gloved fingers in her own. "I'll be there."

"Thank God," he muttered. "I'm counting on you to help preserve my sanity that night." Then he lifted her hand to his lips and pressed a kiss to her knuckles. "Enjoy your morning calls, my dear. Though I still don't understand why they call them that when it's clearly afternoon."

She chuckled and pulled away with reluctance, sliding her fingers across his palm as they parted. "I will. You enjoy your day, too. And let's both say a prayer for Saffie, wherever she is."

He nodded and sketched a bow as Maggie withdrew.

"You know, if we do find her," she said to Penelope when they got back into their coach, "there's no way we can bring her back here to that dreadful brother of hers."

"Not if he's going to beat her," Penelope agreed with a huff. "Brute."

They lapsed into thoughtful silence as Hubert drove them home, following Connor's town coach the whole way back.

When they finally rolled into Moonlight Square, Penelope was the first to spot the dark-haired man sitting on the front steps of Amberley House, idly whittling wood with a penknife.

"Who's that?" she asked, pointing toward the open window on her side of the carriage.

Instantly, Maggie leaned over to look, fearing the worst. Was it the killer? Had the dragoon returned?

But when the brawny, apple-cheeked fellow jumped up, hailing Connor's coach with a broad smile, Maggie breathed a sigh of relief.

Whoever he was, he got quite a reaction from the duke—and Will and Nestor, too.

The surgeon-turned-coachman stopped Connor's town coach in the middle of the street, blocking the way for Maggie and Penelope, to their surprise. Even more startling, Connor immediately leapt out of his carriage with Will right behind him.

"Rory!" they both cried.

The newcomer grinned, flipped his penknife closed, twirled it nimbly in his hand, and put it away just in time to return Connor's brief bear hug. "Major. Willy."

"Good God, man, where's the rest of you?" Connor cried with a grin from ear to ear as he clapped the fellow on both shoulders.

"Ha! Poisoning was good for me," the newcomer declared, slapping his own flat stomach.

"I barely recognize you!" Connor exclaimed.

The newcomer lifted his arms out to his sides. "Gorgeous, ain't I?"

Connor smirked. "I wouldn't go that far."

Penelope made a low sound of possible agreement, studying the fellow, while, out on the pavement, a laughing Will leaned close to shake his hand.

"Welcome back, sarge! You're almost as skinny as me now."

"God, I hope not," the man said, whacking Will on the back with a chuckle.

The boy went flying, but he seemed to have expected that.

The cheerful man turned last to Nestor and waved. "Better move your arse, doc—you're blocking the street. I think these pretty ladies want to get through."

"Oh my," Penelope murmured when the roguish fellow beamed a smile at her through the carriage window.

Maggie arched a brow, glancing at her fashionable maid.

Connor, standing behind his friend, looked equally surprised.

But Nestor duly laid hold of the lead horse's bridle and moved the coach aside so they could pass.

"Well, that answers *that* question," Maggie said with amusement. "At least now we know who he is."

Penelope nodded and sent her a twinkling glance, blushing just a bit after having caught his eye. "That's Rory."

CHAPTER 23

On the Hunt

"*M*an, it's good to see you! How are you feeling?" Connor stood amazed at his friend's transformation. "Never better," Rory said absently, still watching Maggie's carriage pass, and peering, in particular, at the elegant blond lady's maid in the window.

"I'll bet!" Connor said. "All trim and healthy. Look at your clothes hanging off you. How much did you lose?"

Rory snorted. "Three stone."

Will sighed. "Could've given it to me."

"Ha." Rory shrugged. "I was so ill for a few weeks there, my glorious girth melted down to nothing." He clapped both hands to his abdomen and grinned. "Once I started getting better, I just decided to keep it going. Although…now that you mention it, I am a bit peckish."

Nestor chortled, still holding on to the lead horse's bridle along the edge of the street, where he'd moved the carriage to so that Maggie could pass. "Some things never change."

"Want to eat?" Connor asked all three.

"Not here!" Rory retorted.

Will laughed.

Connor winced. "Understandable. No matter. I found us a good pub." He'd liked the one by the shopping arcade that day with Maggie. "I'll take you lads there for a meal—my treat."

"Say, Major?" Rory rapped him on the chest, then nodded down the street after the Birdwell coach. "You know those lasses? 'Cause I might want an introduction to the little blonde, and maybe her friend, too. Couldn't see her very well, but you never know."

Connor started laughing.

"Did you see her lookin' at me?" Rory hooked a thumb over his shoulder. "Women look at me now! It's the damnedest thing."

"Oh, I can introduce you to the blonde, mate. But you can't have her friend," Connor said mildly.

"And why not?" Rory tossed him a glance full of humor.

Connor folded his arms across his chest. "Because I'm marrying her, actually."

"What?" Rory hollered.

Connor laughed heartily, as did the others, and clapped him on the back. "Oh, my friend, much has happened in your absence. I have a lot to tell you."

"Is he serious?" Rory asked Nestor and Will. "He's getting leg-shackled?"

They all nodded.

"Mm-hmm," Connor said.

Rory glanced around. "Am I at the right bloody house?"

Connor chuckled and clasped his shoulder. "Come on, you lot. Let's go eat, and I'll tell you all about it. Well, not *all* about it, if ye take my meanin'."

Rory managed to shake off his shock at Connor's news, but held up a hand. "Wait. Before we go get drunk to celebrate this…impossible news, I need to tell you what I learned while I was out rambling around. It's big."

"Oh?" Connor lowered his voice, all humor fading instantly. "Go on."

"Well, I did some sleuthing like you asked me to once I was on m' feet again. You're not going to believe this. Better brace yourself, maje."

"What is it?" Connor asked.

Rory smirked. "Turns out your ancestor, the first duke? Married a courtesan. His mistress."

Connor's face fell. "Oh. We already know that."

Rory frowned, looking crestfallen for a second, then shrugged it off. "Well, I found out the name of her old pimp."

"That's new! Yes?"

"Not sure if the man's still alive, but he's called Elias Flynn. Owns half a dozen brothels and gambling hells around London. The Lucky

Stud, Paradise Inn, Aphrodite's Cove. Those are the ones I found the names of, anyway. And *I think*," Rory added with a devilish glint in his eyes, "that we had better go and have ourselves a look inside each and every one of 'em."

Connor snorted. Will cringed. Nestor shrugged.

"Might not be a bad idea," said the surgeon. "What else have you got?"

"Right," Rory continued. "Though this Flynn made his fortune as a whoremonger, he's got dreams of turning his family respectable one day. Married a lady whose family had ancient bloodlines but not a penny left to their names. Didn't manage to find out her name. She's dead now, I think, but they had two sons. The younger one was sent to study at Oxford. The firstborn became a dragoon."

Connor narrowed his eyes. "A dragoon? You don't say." He stared intensely at Rory, weighing every word.

"Aye, but then the younger one died about two years ago. I'm not sure how. Some kind of squabble in the streets led to violence. It happened here in Town."

"How did you learn all this?" Nestor asked.

Rory shrugged. "Following my nose. Just like always. Eventually led me to an old barmaid, who poured me pints of ale and told me all about how she used to entertain the sailors at Aphrodite's Cove." He winked. "You know me—I'm a good listener."

"Good work, McFeatheridge." Connor's mind was whirling. He pulled the dragoon's button out of his pocket and gave it to his friend. "Look what we found right here in my coach house."

Nestor's one-eyed gaze darted from Rory to Connor. "Maybe Flynn's been blackmailing the duchess all this time."

"Believe me," Connor muttered, "I will get to the bottom of this when I question Aunt Lucinda after the soirée. This time, I won't allow her to brush me off again. In the meantime, I daresay our first priority is tracking down a dragoon by the name of Flynn."

"Wellll, not exactly," Rory said. "Flynn's sons took the surname connected to the mother's upper-class family, but I wasn't able to find out what it was. It seems Flynn made some attempt to hide his sons' connection to his own ill-gotten gains. The whoremonger's goal seems to have been to give his boys the benefits of his dirty money, sanitized by the mother's high rank."

"I see," Connor said. "Well, sounds like visiting Flynn's brothels is our only firm lead at the moment, so let's see what we can find. But business only. Remember, boys, we're on a mission."

Rory rubbed his hands together. "I like this mission."

"Sounds sleazy," Will muttered.

"Here's hoping." Rory slung his arm around the lad's shoulder. "Hey, Major, let's get Willy a girl while we're there so he can finally lose his cherry."

"What?" Will cried, turning red and shoving him away. "What makes you think I'm still a virgin?"

The rest of them just started laughing.

"Damn," Nestor said heavily as they entered Aphrodite's Cove early that evening. "I really miss my other eye."

Will kept his head down, embarrassed at all the half-naked women everywhere. "I don't think Lady Margaret would approve of this, Major."

"I don't disagree," Connor said, but in truth, he was so smitten with Maggie that no other woman alive presented the slightest temptation. Especially not the hard-eyed, paint-crusted harlots trawling this dim, low-ceilinged hellhole.

Connor shook his head. It was inconceivable to him that queenly Aunt Lucinda could have got her start in such a place. Then again, Lord Sefton had spoken of first glimpsing "Lucky Lucy Bly" in her theater box, which was how the high-priced harlots generally advertised themselves.

Apparently, Elias Flynn had all kinds of mares in his stables, from the most exclusive courtesans selling pleasure to the aristocracy, to these poor, common trollops servicing sailors on shore leave.

The sight of them depressed Connor.

Earlier, they had visited Elias Flynn's Lucky Stud gambling hell and found it nearly empty, but that was because it had only been midafternoon.

To pass the time until these nocturnal establishments began waking up, they'd taken a meal at that good pub near the shopping arcade, and Connor had told Rory all about his little Lady Maggie Winthrop.

Rory, in turn, had regaled them with talk of his travels. They'd played darts, watched the clock. Finally, they had gone for a look around inside Flynn's brothel called the Paradise Inn.

By then, it had been about five in the afternoon, and the women had been at their freshest, frisky and loading up on liquor to help them face the night ahead.

They had hung on Rory, petted Nestor and praised his cleverness, and squeezed Will's cheeks, calling him a baby face.

They had made themselves abundantly available to Connor, as well, but he had remained coolly aloof, watching everything.

He remained so now, noting that the second house of ill repute, Aphrodite's Cove, a sailor's haven, was just a stone's throw from the docks where he had been attacked by the "cutpurse" that first night, moments after stepping off the boat from Ireland.

Rory elbowed him, breaking into his musings. "Let's get a drink and I'll chat up some of the ladies. They might know Flynn's son."

"Be careful," Connor warned him, giving his friend a look that reminded him that the man in question could be the killer.

Rory started toward the bar, but Will put up his arm abruptly, blocking the way. "Hold on!"

Nestor looked at him. "What is it?"

"Look!" Will pointed. "It's Saffie!"

"Where?" Connor asked.

"Right there, sir! In the red gown. Criminy," the boy added in awe.

Every muscle tensed, Connor followed the direction of Will's pointing finger, past a cluster of women sashaying by.

Amid the swirls of smoke, a pert young blonde in a red dress leaned against one of the tavern's wooden posts with her hands flat behind her. She was pretty enough but looked entirely bored, staring upward into space as though she was counting the ceiling rafters.

"Are you sure that's her?" Connor asked.

"I'm certain of it, sir."

"Doesn't look like a scullery maid to me," Nestor mumbled.

"I'll say," Rory said.

But it was Saffie, all right. For, at that moment, her wandering gaze fell upon Will.

She jolted, jumped forward from the post like a startled cat, and then waved eagerly to him, a look of joy breaking across her face.

"Will? Will? Private Duffy! Is it you?" She started forward—but then spotted Nestor, and when her vapid gaze swung to Connor, she froze, gasped with obvious recognition, then whirled around and fled.

Will looked wryly at Connor. "Told you."

"See if you can catch up to her," Nestor ordered the lad, gesturing after the girl. "Get her to come and talk to us."

"Tell her not to worry, that I'm not angry at her," Connor said. "Say we've only come to see if she's all right. Hurry, don't lose her."

"Do my best," Will replied, then rushed off after Saffie, trying not to look at the bosoms that were thrust at him along the way.

The others went and ordered pints of ale for the sake of blending in while they waited for Will to coax Saffie back out.

It took ten minutes, but he finally led her over by the hand. The girl half hid behind Will's slight frame, eyeing the others from over his shoulder with fear and resentment.

But she must've trusted the lad, for she followed, wide-eyed, as Will led her down to the far corner of the bar, where the three of them had sat down on long-legged stools.

"Fellows," Will announced as the two joined them, "Saffie has something she'd like to say to sarge."

Rory raised his eyebrows. "Yes, dear heart?"

The girl wrestled visibly with the notion of admitting to anything concerning the poison; guilt and angst were written all over her guileless face.

"Go on, Saffie," Will said gently. "It's all right."

"But he'll send me to Newgate!" she whispered.

"No, no, he won't. I promise."

Saffie gazed at Will with eyes full of innocence and trust, then gulped and looked again at Rory. "I'm sorry you got sick, sir. It was never meant for you."

"Ah, no matter," Rory said with a cheerful wave of his hand, putting her at ease in that particular way of his. "As you can see, I'm right as rain now. All's well that ends well."

She stared at him with uncertainty, then glanced warily at Connor.

For whom the poison *had* been intended.

He wanted to know why, but kept his mouth shut for fear of scaring her away, especially now that he knew she was slightly soft in the head.

"If you don't mind my asking," Nestor spoke up, "it would interest me as an apothecary to hear what the potion was."

Saffie shrugged. "I don't know, sir. He just gave it to me."

"Who did, dear heart?" Rory asked with his most mesmerizing smile.

Saffie flinched and backed away a bit. "I'm not tellin'. Never."

"Why not?" Will asked.

"Because I promised I wouldn't! Besides, if I do, you'll try to hurt him, and I can't have that, seein' as how he's goin' to be my husband."

Connor stared at her, shocked.

"Is that right?" Rory asked, his jovial smile pasted in place.

Saffie nodded eagerly. "Just as soon as he finishes up some errands for his father, he's taking me to Gretna Green. I'm to wait here until he's ready. Earn my keep."

Even Rory's smile thinned upon his hearing that. "Riiight."

Connor couldn't even speak upon hearing such colossal lies. Rage boomed through his veins.

Will looked flabbergasted.

Nestor took a long drink of ale, then glanced darkly at Connor with a look that said, *This chap needs killin'.*

Aye. Connor gave him the barest of nods.

"Well now," Rory finally said. "Congratulations on your impending nuptials. That is happy news indeed, Miss Saffie. But it won't be miss for long, now, will it? Tell me, when you marry this lucky fellow, what will your name become then?"

She beamed at the question. "Mrs. John Smith," she said proudly.

Connor shot up from his barstool and turned his back on them, clenching his fists.

"What's wrong with him?" Saffie asked.

"Oh—nothing." Will sounded slightly strangled.

Perfect. A fake name, to boot. Half the men who ever went to brothels were called John Smith, as everyone knew.

Everyone but Saffie, unfortunately.

Rory cleared his throat. "My dear, doesn't it bother your fiancé that you're here diddlin' other men before the wedding?"

"They don't make me do that," Saffie retorted. "My Johnny says it's fine, and he's the one that got me this job. It's a sight better than scrubbin' pots and pans, I can tell you."

Connor turned back around in astonishment.

"I get to wear pretty gowns like this one and just sit around, talk to folk, listen to music. I mean…it's not *so* much fun sometimes. You see things. And sometimes, people grab you." A dark shadow passed behind her empty eyes. "But Johnny said he's leavin' me here so he'll always know where to find me when he needs me. Ain't that sweet? People say I'm not very clever, but he knows there's one thing I'm good at. So what do you say to that?" She cocked a hand on her hip and smirked at them, pleased with herself.

"I want to kill this piece of filth," Nestor murmured.

Thankfully, Saffie didn't hear the comment, for just then, one of the other women tapped her on the shoulder and asked her whether she had finished straightening the rooms on the third floor for the night.

While Saffie paused to answer her, Will marched over to Connor with an air of desperation. "We can't leave her here, sir."

"Aye," Connor said. "Not the least because she'll tell this son of a bitch that I was here. We need to keep the element of surprise."

"Are you sure?" Rory glanced at him as the four of them formed a huddle. "We could use her as bait," he suggested. "Set a trap for him here. Next time he comes to see her, we take him down."

"No, we're on his turf. This is his father's establishment." Connor shook his head, then indicated the room with a discreet nod. "Look at all the security on duty, as well. If they work for his father, they'll be under his command. Too risky, especially with so many women and customers around. We don't want anyone getting hurt. I'm with Will. Let's just get the girl out of here somehow."

"Thank you, Major," the boy said. "I couldn't live with myself if we abandoned her in this hellhole."

Nestor frowned. "But what are *we* going to do with her?"

"We can't take her back to her brother," Will said. "That ogre. He beats her."

"Plus, that's the first place her 'Johnny' will likely look for her, once he comes back and finds her missing," Connor said. "He'll kill her for certain if he realizes we're onto him. I'm surprised he left her alive this long—but thank God he did."

"Ugh, I could throw up to think how he's used her," Will said, clutching his stomach and glancing at her again.

"Don't worry, lad. We'll keep her safe," Connor said. "Actually, I think our only solution right now is take her to Trumbull."

"The butler?" Nestor asked, taken aback.

Connor nodded. "He seemed to have a soft spot for the poor creature. She knows him. Besides, she's already been taught to obey his authority. He'll keep her in line while we finish off her dragoon."

Nestor arched a brow. "Good thing you hired him back, then. And not a moment too soon."

"Thanks to Maggie," Connor said wryly.

"All well and good," Nestor said with a nod. "Just one problem. The girl doesn't seem inclined to be rescued. She thinks this blackguard's prince charming."

Connor looked grimly at them. "Leave this to me."

When they turned back to the bar, Saffie was nodding in answer to some household task the older harlot was giving her for later. Then the haggard woman swished away to go and greet more men coming in, and Connor looked at Saffie.

So young and fresh. She did not belong here. Therefore, lying to her to save her did not trouble his conscience in the least. He should hope he had the brains to outsmart her, and besides, getting her to leave of her own free will would avoid them drawing the wrath of the guards by hauling her out kicking and screaming.

"Saffie," he said as gently as possibly, leaning on the bar. "There's actually a particular reason we came."

She gazed at him with round, somber eyes. "To take me to Newgate?"

"No—"

"I didn't want to do it! He made me."

"I know that. Don't be afraid." Connor smiled tenderly. "Will's right. You needn't worry about any of that. I shouldn't want you to do it again, of course—"

"I won't!" She looked relieved.

"Good. The main reason we're here... Well, I'm afraid it's rather bad news."

"Oh?"

"Yes. It's about poor old Mr. Trumbull, the butler. You remember him?"

This got her full attention. "Ol' Trumby? Well, of course. He was always kind to me," she said. "What about him?"

"I'm afraid he's fallen ill."

She gasped, popping her hand up over her lips for a second. "Oh no! He's not going to die, is he?" she asked. "He was like a grandfather to me! He and Cook. Like the grandparents that I never had."

Will took her hand and squeezed it, giving her a heartfelt gaze.

"Please, tell me he's not going to die!"

"His physician isn't sure," Nestor said gravely, catching on to the ruse.

"Fond of you as Mr. Trumbull is, Saffie, he was asking for you,"

Connor said.

"He was? Why?" she asked.

"He has no children of his own, remember? He's just been a butler all his life." Connor shrugged. "He's all alone now in his hour of need."

"Oh, no!" Her eyes welled up with tears.

"So, we were wondering, would you go and sit with him for a couple of hours? It would be a great comfort to him, and we could take you there right away."

"Oh, of course," Saffie said. "Let me just get my wrap… Oh, but wait." Her shoulders slumped. "Johnny said I'm not allowed to leave. Not unless I have permission."

"It is an emergency, though," Will pointed out.

"Besides, if he loves you, Mr. Smith will understand," Connor said.

"Yes… Right." Saffie mulled this. "That is true."

Will patted her hand. "We can take you there."

"Will you be going, too, William?"

He nodded. "If you wish me to."

"I do!" She had only one more question—a surprisingly sensible one, at that. "Is it catching? Whatever Mr. Trumbull has?"

"No, dear, just old age," Nestor said, startled.

"But he could die at any moment," Connor added. "Best hurry."

"Very well," Saffie said. "I'll tell the guards I'm leaving and go fetch my wrap. Be right back!"

When she rushed off, Will turned to them with fury which he could apparently no longer contain.

"That poor girl!" he burst out as loudly as he dared. "He's ruined her! Cast her off in this vile place. And she doesn't even realize how she's been used… What a devil!"

Connor had never seen the mild-mannered private in such an agitated state. Nestor stared at him, then sent Connor a puzzled sideways glance.

"What's the plan, then?" asked Rory.

"Right," said Connor while Will kept watch for Saffie's return. "You three take her out to Trumbull's cottage. Nestor, you remember the way?"

"Of course."

"You'll drive. When you get there, apprize Trumbull first of our ruse so he plays along."

"This should be interesting," the surgeon mumbled.

"Rory, you guard the cottage until you hear from me in the off chance this bastard figures out where she is," Connor continued. "He'd have no reason to look for her at the butler's house, but stay sharp, just in case. After all, now that we know he'd do this to her with so little regard, there's no doubt in my mind that he'd kill her to shut her up."

"But she's barely told us anything," Will said.

"Yes, but she still might. In fact, maybe Trumbull can coax more information out of her once she's away from this place," Connor added.

"What should I do, Major?" Will asked.

"You're in charge of keeping Saffie entertained. Clearly, she trusts you. Don't let her wander off. Keep her busy. Whatever it takes."

Will eyed him skeptically, then Rory slung an arm around his shoulder. "Hear that, Willy? You might get lucky yet. I think she fancies you."

Will huffed, blushed, and shoved Rory away.

Nestor shrugged. "The lad would be a damned sight better for her than whatever soulless blackguard brought her here."

Ignoring them both, Will stared fiercely at Connor. "You kill him if you find him, sir."

"Oh, believe me, I will," Connor said.

"What'll you be doing in the meanwhile, maje?" Rory asked discreetly as Saffie came hurrying out of the back again, clutching her wrap.

"I'm going to pay a visit to the Guards' Club and have a chat with some of the dragoons there," Connor murmured as Saffie made her way toward them through the gathering crowd. "Someone there might have information about our John Smith."

"Watch yourself. You have no idea which one of them he is," Rory warned.

Connor shrugged. "He means to kill me anyway. Maybe I can get him to tip his hand. Besides, I'll be in a room full of armed men who think I'm a bloody hero."

Rory quirked a knowing smile. "Where did they ever get a fool notion like that? Still, be careful, mate."

"You too. You lot take my coach. I'll flag down a hackney."

They wished each other luck and, when Saffie rejoined them, parted ways.

Connor paid their tab and watched the others drive off, making sure they got away safely. Then he stepped to the pavement and hailed a hackney, hungry for blood.

I'll find you yet, you son of a bitch.

If there was one place where Seth was able to muster a genuine sense of belonging, and a feeling of contentment—other than between Saffie's legs—it was at the Guards' Club on King Street, established expressly for military men.

Founded some years ago by Wellington himself as a place for veterans to congregate, the Guards' Club was known for surprisingly good suppers, restraint in gambling, and, above all, the easy sport of making fun of the dandies who displayed themselves in White's bow window across the street.

Seth was there now, enjoying the familiar sights, sounds, and smells of this haven of men. The light of sunset slanting in through the high windows cast a mellow glow over the patina on the long wooden tables, where countless former soldiers—some in uniform, some not—were digging into a hearty beef supper.

Steam curled upward from roasted chickens, shepherd's pie, and vegetables. Men eagerly helped themselves to the food, while the aproned waiters brought around wine and ale.

All the while, the high-ceilinged hall reverberated with the lulling chatter of males laughing and arguing good-naturedly, while the sound of plates and silverware clanked as the meal was served.

Seth soaked it all in as he sat on a long bench, eating in the company of his regimental mates, just watching, listening. The atmosphere of camaraderie warmed his normally cold heart—until the moment Amberley walked in.

Seth froze as his gaze clamped on the man he wanted to kill. The shepherd's pie promptly turned to ashes in his mouth.

Shock, fear, and stomach-churning dread curdled the half-eaten meal in his belly as he sat there, unmoving.

Why he should be surprised to see Amberley here, though, he did not know.

Amberley belonged here, in truth, even more than he did, but this was the first time that Seth was aware of that the man had walked through the door.

There was no mistaking him, though. The big, fierce-eyed warrior paused in the doorway, tall and formidable, dressed down in decidedly informal clothes. Brown coat, nankeen breeches, black boots.

No, to be sure, Seth thought cynically, the legendary major did not need to rely on the uniform for swagger. A third-generation soldier, the blackguard had military prowess rising from his bone marrow.

Across the club's vast hall, Seth watched his enemy speak to a few men, one of whom soon pointed him in the dragoons' direction.

Then any hope that Seth might've harbored that he was in the clear dissolved as Amberley marched toward them, his square face grim, murder in his blazing blue eyes.

Seth's heart began to pound. In that moment, he had no idea how to handle this. He was about to be exposed, he was quite sure. But how?

That he could not answer, too panicked to think. Here in the critical moment, he sat paralyzed with dread. The hairs on the back of his neck stood on end; his hands went ice-cold.

At least he managed not to let them shake when he reached for his ale and took a swig to wash down the suddenly nauseating mouthful of food.

He feigned ignorance, mild-mannered uninterest when his friends reacted eagerly to the hero's arrival. Several of them stood to greet the man.

"Major!"

"Welcome, Your Grace! It's good to see you here at last!"

"We've been wondering when you'd turn up."

The duke swept their company with a glance like a saber stroke. "I am not here on a social call, gentlemen." He planted his hands on the edge of the table and leaned down a bit, scrutinizing each and every one of them.

Seth held perfectly motionless, heartbeat booming.

His friends were puzzled.

"Is something wrong, sir?" Daniels asked.

"Yes, actually. I'm looking for one of your men."

"Who, Your Grace?" Thurnow asked cheerfully.

"The son of Elias Flynn."

Seth managed not to choke at his father's name.

Amberley took a brass button out of his waistcoat pocket and tossed it down on the table in their midst like he was rolling the dice. "Tell him he left this in my coach house."

Seth's comrades were confused.

It was then that Amberley's gaze wandered around the table and found *him*. His stare lingered on Seth for a moment, until Phillips spoke up, drawing the duke's steely stare.

"But, sir, we don't have anyone called Flynn in the regiment."

"Not openly, you don't. But he knows who he is and what he's done." The duke looked around at them with hellfire in his glance. "Just spread the word that I'm looking for him, would you? Tell him I'm ready to settle the matter between us any time he's ready to quit hidin' like a coward and show his goddam face."

Seth did not move a muscle, as if stillness could render him invisible.

His friends seemed dumbfounded at the savagery in the duke's tone.

With that, Amberley straightened up and walked away, leaving Seth's missing uniform button spinning on the table.

For his part, Seth uttered not a word, but kept his stare pinned on his enemy's back as Amberley strode out, shoulders squared, head high.

Meanwhile, all around the table, his friends began discussing what had just occurred, confused and alarmed.

Coming from any other source, such claims would be found ludicrous, but the major was so well respected...

Seth listened but could not quite absorb the men's heated exchange. Angry questions about who the imposter might be, protests, oaths, and bewildered denials flew back and forth across the table.

Right before his eyes, he saw how his secret actions had fractured his tight-knit squad into chaos. Seth had no answers to give them, however, wrapped up in his guilt.

His mind was spinning, a whirlwind whipping around and around inside his brain—terror that Amberley was on his trail, relief that he hadn't been found out entirely yet. Seth looked down at his plate, unable even to think about finishing the meal. Thank God, he was still in the clear—at least for the moment. His heart slammed inside his ribcage.

It was not Amberley he was afraid of, exactly. It was exposure. Complete ruination before his friends. And, most of all, dread of his underworld father.

Oh God, Amberley had now connected Father to this thing...

Plunged into his own private hell, Seth felt in that moment as though he was being torn in half, all for trying to stand with one foot in two different worlds. Father's fortune; Mother's name. Had he really expected this to work?

But a more important question loomed in the foreground: how had this happened? He had a sickening feeling he knew.

Saffie.

God damn it, he should have got rid of her weeks ago. This had to be her fault. She was the only loose thread he'd left untied.

Grimly, he picked up his fork again and forced himself to continue eating, shoveling down a few nauseating bites to avoid rousing his friends' suspicion. He had to seem normal.

He shrugged when they asked him his opinion of the duke's outrageous claims against someone in the regiment.

"Probably bullshit," he said.

Of course he knew nothing about it. He shook his head, denying all, as usual. This had nothing to do with him. He was Captain Seth Darrow. One of them. He had the uniform to prove it.

He had long since replaced the missing button, sewing it on himself. His mates were none the wiser. Above all, he refused to let any sign of his other life, his dark side, or his underworld origins show on his face. He knew that his well-born friends would not understand.

His stomach rebelled as he forced the rest of the food down, but it was remarkable what a man could force himself to do after going to war.

At last, when he deemed it safe, Seth wiped his mouth on his napkin, then tossed it down and stood; ignoring the queasy feeling, he bade his fellows good night and left the club.

He slung up onto his horse and rode immediately to the brothel. Darkness was falling as he stalked into Aphrodite's Cove.

He searched the tavern, shoving women out of his way, then checked the second-floor rooms, interrupting trysts in progress.

But he soon saw that it was as he had feared.

Saffie had vanished.

Oh my God, Father is going to kill me. Panic rose in him as he stood at the top of the dim, creaky stairs. *I need to end this before the old man finds out.*

He jogged down the steps on shaky legs to go speak to the guards, cursing himself along the way for not strangling her when he'd had the chance. Instead, he'd let himself become addicted to her mindless worship of him.

As if that nitwit's opinion should matter.

"Where's Saffie?" he demanded when he found the head guard.

"She left with some men, sir—not customers. Friends of the family or something. Want me to send up another girl for you tonight?"

"No, damn you!" Seth pushed the man against the wall. "What men? Didn't I make it clear she's my possession? Where is she?"

"I-I don't know, sir!" the guard blurted out. "She said it was an emergency."

"What kind of an emergency?" Seth growled through gritted teeth, gripping the man's lapels.

The large, beefy man shook his head. "She told us some old man she knows is dyin'. It was hours before we start getting busy, sir. I didn't see the harm."

"Oh, didn't you?" Seth released him in disgust. "Who were these men she left with?"

Another guard with a facial scar came over warily. "Is everything all right?"

"He wants Saffie." The head of security righted his coat, looking uneasy.

Seth turned to the newcomer. "Did you see her leave?"

The hireling nodded. "Aye, 'twas around six o'clock."

"What did these people look like?"

"Er, I'm not sure... There were three of them. Or was it four?"

"Seemed like soldiers, I thought," the head guard said. "I thought they might have been friends o' yours, sir, so I didn't worry. Surely...you didn't mean for us to keep the girl here against her will?"

"Oh!" the scarred man said all of a sudden, holding up a finger. "One of them had an eye patch."

Bloody hell. Amberley's men for certain. Seth knew of the old, one-eyed surgeon, having watched the house carefully for weeks.

"Do you know where they took her?"

"No, sir. They said they'd have her back in a couple hours."

"They were lying. You idiots. They're not bringing her back here. They've taken her." He turned away, shaking his head as he strove to clear his mind of the clawing dread.

"Is Saffie in danger, sir?" the head of security asked.

Seth couldn't help but laugh cynically. "No, she's safe. That's the problem," he added under his breath, then marched out.

Outside on the pavement, he stood for a moment under the stars, pulling deep gulps of air into his lungs, trying to steady himself.

Well, what now?

The girl who could get him convicted of murder was out there somewhere in the care of his enemies, all because he hadn't been able to get enough of her sweet, virginal pussy. *What do I do?* The question kept thundering through his mind, over and over again.

The answer seemed clear. He had to flee while he still had the chance. He resolved to rush home, throw his most vital belongings into his haversack and a couple of valises, and take the dawn packet to Calais. He was getting the hell out of England before he wound up arrested and hanged.

If Father wanted the last Amberley dead, he could do it himself. God knew he was mean enough, and besides, Seth had already done three of them.

With that, Seth untied his horse once again and rode home, already feeling the hot breath of the hangman on his neck.

But when he tiptoed into the house to collect his things, he was unable to pass by Father's study unnoticed. He tried to quiet his footsteps as he crossed the entrance hall toward the stairs, but, sure enough, heard a rough, gravelly voice.

"Seth! Get in here."

His stomach clenched. He swallowed hard. "Coming, Father."

He braced himself, then trod dutifully toward his father's study.

Elias Flynn sat in his Moroccan leather chair, his bald head gleaming by the light of the candle burning on his desk. He drew off his spectacles and studied Seth with a piercing glare when he ventured into the doorway.

"Yes, sir?"

The self-made millionaire whoremonger eyed Seth suspiciously. "How's the assignment coming along?"

Seth hid his gulp and shrugged. "It's fine."

"Really?" Flynn countered, unblinking. "Seems to be taking an awfully long time. This has been going on for nearly five months now." Father raised his eyebrows and gave Seth a look that seemed to peer down into his very soul.

Amberley's words of a while ago echoed through Seth's mind as he did his best to hold his father's gaze.

"Tell him to quit hidin' like a coward..."

Was that all he really was at the end of the day? A coward? He *was* on the verge of running away, after all. Wasn't he?

Seth dropped his chin nearly to his chest and thought of Francis dying in his arms. Little brother, the gentleman, with his lion-cub courage and his big mouth.

A heaviness moved over him, then, as he realized there was no point in trying to flee. Why bother? What did it matter? His life was a misery, anyway, and wherever he went, the guilt that hounded him day and night was sure to follow.

He had to stay and finish this. He owed Father that. For robbing him of his younger son. The one who made him happy. The son he had loved.

"Well?" Flynn prompted.

"It'll be over Friday night," Seth said wearily. "I know where he'll be, and I'm going to blow his bloody head off."

"Good." Father nodded. "See that you do."

CHAPTER 24

Aunt Lucinda's Soiree

When Friday evening finally arrived, Maggie and the Birdwells piled into Edward's finest coach, invitation in hand, and set off for Upper Brooke Street in Mayfair, and the home of the Dowager Duchess of Amberley.

Edward complimented both sisters, and Maggie complimented her brother-in-law in turn. The marquess's black-and-white formal garb of this evening was pristine; indeed, he looked as handsome as she had ever seen him.

Even Delia grumbled begrudging agreement.

His black tailcoat seemed to trim down his portly figure by a stone, and the jeweled cravat pin that adorned his throat twinkled with a sapphire that brought out the blue in his eyes.

Lady Birdwell was dressed as resplendently as ever in a gown of bluish-purple satin with silver lace trim. Her hair was adorned with an iris bloom, and the effect was striking.

Though her sister had still not apologized, Maggie went out on a limb to offer the observation that the flower's jewel tone flattered her auburn hair. Delia thanked her but still refused eye contact, and certainly did not return the praise.

No matter. Maggie sat undaunted. Not even Delia's unpleasantness could dampen her excitement over seeing Connor tonight. She dropped her gaze to her lap, where she clasped her fingers, and smiled privately, complimenting herself.

She knew she looked her best this evening—for her future husband, of course. With Penelope's assistance, she had chosen a flowing, high-waisted, watered silk gown of pearl white with a hint of pink and a crimson sash to match the rosettes that encircled the skirts at the knee. A white ruffle of lace edged the small puff sleeves and daring décolletage, which sat low around her shoulders.

He'd like that, she thought, biting her lip as it curved into a smile.

She wished she could have found a way to end the bristling silence inside the coach, though, as the horses went clip-clopping through the streets.

When they rounded the corner at Hyde Park, Maggie glanced out the window and felt a twinge of anger to recall being stranded there in the rain. But she flicked the memory away. Tonight, she'd be with Connor, and that was all that mattered.

It had been three days since they'd visited Mr. Trumbull. She wasn't sure what her darling neighbor had been up to in the meanwhile, but for her part, she'd been busy with various things, not the least of which had been a bit of preliminary daydreaming about their wedding. Each night, of course, she'd kept an eye out her bedroom window for the lantern signal, just in case.

It didn't come.

She didn't mind. She would never be the sort of woman who constantly demanded to be the center of his life. They needn't suffocate each other.

As the Birdwell carriage rolled on, she mused with pleasure on various aspects of the affection she and her wild Irishman had discovered, and the beautiful love she knew would continue to unfold…

At length, traveling north on Park Lane, with the wrought-iron gate that surrounded Hyde Park on their left, and some of the most fashionable streets in London to their right, they turned in at Upper Brooke Street.

Hubert slowed the vehicle just around the corner, where a queue of elegant carriages waited to deliver their guests to a magnificent terrace house on the right.

"Are you going to be in a mood all night?" Edward murmured to his wife as his coach crept forward the last few feet to halt before their destination.

Delia let out a small, aloof huff and looked out the window at the other homes. "I'm only here because she is a *duchess*, Ed. You can't say no."

"Charming," he mumbled.

Then the footman was opening the door for them, letting down the step. Excitement whooshed through Maggie. Edward got out first, handed down Delia, and then assisted Maggie, the lower-ranking female, as she alighted.

Delia took her husband's arm and Maggie followed, her heart pounding as they walked toward the porticoed entrance of the dragon lady's lair.

Smoothing her skirts, Maggie wondered if Connor had been introduced yet to the young ladies his great-aunt deemed worthy to be his bride—and what he thought of each one.

Not that she was jealous. She just wanted the First Duchess to approve of her, too. Then they walked into the entrance hall and her nervous thoughts were blotted out by the buzz of conversation and the distant music of a stringed ensemble playing somewhere upstairs.

Maggie estimated there were about a hundred guests present so far, a fine-sized gathering for this home, though it could have easily fit twice that number.

The duchess's house seemed about the same size as Edward's, with four stories and three banks of windows across. Ahead, a magnificent William Kent staircase waited between creamy white Ionic columns to take them upstairs.

With lacy wrought-iron rails beneath the shining oaken banister, the frothy staircase fountained up to two galleried stories, both visible from the entrance hall. The corbelled ceiling soared far above, and from the peachy painted walls adorned with white plaster garlands, a pair of marble busts peered down from round niches.

Liveried footman posted here and there assisted the glittering crowd. Throughout the entrance hall, the candlelight burnished the touches of gilt everywhere, even though the rosy glow of sunset still streamed through the large fanlights over the front door.

Maggie took it all in with wonder, joining the orderly queue of guests ascending the staircase. She carefully lifted the hem of her gown and followed Delia and Edward up the white marble steps.

As they progressed slowly to the main floor, where the soirée proper was taking place, she noticed an opulent sedan chair that had been pushed up against the wall in the ground floor corridor leading from the entrance hall toward the back of the house. For some reason, it amused her.

She had never met the First Duchess of Amberley, but the woman sounded like one of those grand old souls who enjoyed being carried around by footmen like a queen. Delia should probably buy one, she thought with a twitch of her lips.

When they reached the first floor, the splendor continued in the drawing room, where wallpaper with garden vines and delicate flowers adorned the walls above a rose-colored carpet. Small landscape paintings hung here and there, and atop the mantel of the green marble fireplace sat a large mechanical clock under a glass dome.

Ornate lamps of brilliant blue glass dangled from the ceiling, and pocket doors opened up to a music room beyond. On the right lay a small ballroom the same length as the combined chambers on the other side. It had beautiful parquetry floors, handsome pilasters, and three crystal chandeliers.

At the far end of the entire house along this floor, Maggie noticed French doors letting out onto a shallow balcony that overlooked the garden.

She did not see Connor, but realized that the large woman seated beside the empty fireplace was their hostess.

Grandaunt Lucinda wore a voluminous gown of black lace with an ebony toque to match; a cluster of rubies sparkled on the brooch at the center of her hat. Frowning, the heavyset old woman waved a tasseled fan as she presided over the trio of young debs who sat with her.

Maggie's stare homed in on them. *Ah, the approved choices.* The first was a rail-thin brunette with a large nose. The second was a tepid-looking flaxen blonde with a weak chin and a wan complexion. The third had curly red hair and a freckled face, and Maggie decided in a glance that none of them would do for him.

All the same, she did not envy them their place of honor at the moment.

None of the girls dared to move as the dowager duchess commanded their attention, holding forth on God knew what subject.

Maybe telling them how to run a home. Or raise a child.

Maggie wouldn't dream of interrupting. Instead, she gravitated toward the ballroom, where she spotted her friends. While Delia and Edward went to greet some of their acquaintances, Maggie was joyfully reunited with Trinny, Viscountess Roland.

The new mother was wearing a glorious emerald gown in one of those sophisticated jewel tones reserved for married women.

"Lady Roland!" Maggie teased. "You look splendid."

"Maggie!" Trinny greeted her with a light kiss on the cheek. "So do you."

"Truly, I'm not just saying that," Maggie said. "I love this on you."

"Do you?" The redhead beamed, smoothing her skirts. "I always wanted to wear this color before, but Mother would never allow me."

Maggie chuckled. "I'm glad to see you here. How goes the soirée so far?"

"Oh, it's lovely. Her Grace has a beautiful home." Trinny's eyes danced as she beckoned Maggie closer. "You'll never believe what she said when Gable and I were presented to her."

"What did she say?" Maggie whispered.

Visibly fighting a grin, Trinny lowered her voice as she imitated the dragon: "'Only peasants elope, young lady.' And she hoped I haven't damaged my younger sisters' hopes of making good matches with my 'wild behavior.'"

Maggie gasped. "She really is a dragon lady, then?"

"I'll say. Proceed with caution, my friend." Trinny waved the comment off. "I don't mind. I knew what I was getting into."

"God love you. How did Gable react?"

"Oh, he laughed, of course, as he always does, the cynic. Then he went to find Amberley. I'm sure the poor duke needed some moral support by that time."

"Have the Rivenwoods arrived yet?"

"Came and left, I'm sorry to report," Trinny said, shaking her head.

"What? Why?"

"Well… Serena was not as forgiving as you or I might be about the rude remark the duchess made to Azrael."

"Oh no. What did she say to him?" Maggie asked, appalled.

"Something about his bloodlines being vile."

Maggie's jaw dropped. "Vile? She actually said that?"

Trinny nodded, wide-eyed. "In front of a room full of people. Poor Azrael. He just smirked—I guess he'd rather have people say it to his face than behind his back—but for a moment there, I thought Serena might actually slap her."

"Good heavens! This woman really is a termagant, then. Oh God," Maggie added in a low tone, "now I'm terrified to meet her." She was only half joking.

Trinny shook her head, then glanced toward the drawing room.

"How those poor girls must feel, trapped beside her! I would not want to be one of them right now. Why is she holding them prisoner like that?"

Maggie gave her an arch look. "Why do you think?"

Trinny tilted her head. "No…! She's matchmaking for him?"

"She's trying, from what I understand."

"No wonder the poor man's hiding!" Trinny said with a chuckle.

Maggie grinned. "Have you seen him?"

"Yes." Trinny smiled, nodding toward the far end of the ballroom. "He's down that way somewhere with my husband. Those two seem to get on famously, don't they? Between you and me, Gable is in awe of the man."

That makes two of us. Maggie followed Trinny's gaze across the ballroom just as Connor stepped in through the open French doors.

Her mouth fell open when she saw him, for he was in full dress uniform tonight, resplendent in his scarlet coat with black-and-gold facings. His mighty shoulders looked cliff-like, gleaming with gold epaulets. The black sash 'round his lean waist accented his V-shaped physique, and his white dress breeches shone bright as snow.

Maggie stood tongue-tied, ogling him from across the room, while Trinny glanced at her with amusement.

Thankfully, Edward emerged just then from down at the music room, greeting the duke. Delia followed, and Maggie regained her wits when she witnessed the frosty nod that Connor gave her sister—but as he shook Edward's hand, he obviously realized that Maggie must have arrived, too.

His glance swept the ballroom and landed on her in a trice. At once, a grin lit up his handsome face, and Maggie smiled in return, blushing.

"My, my," Trinny murmured. "You two *are* getting on well, aren't you?"

Maggie was dying to tell her that they would be married, but somehow she swallowed the glorious news for now—though she could not quite dim her beaming smile.

"His Grace is…surprisingly amiable," she coyly admitted.

"More so than Bryce, my dear?"

"*Much* more," she said, then Connor marched across the ballroom to join them.

"Welcome, Lady Margaret," he said warmly.

"Good evening, Your Grace—or should I say Major? I hardly know whether to curtsy or salute," she teased.

"Ah, if it were up to me, I'd rather greet you with a kiss. But we wouldn't want to start a scandal now, would we?" Instead, he lifted her hand to his lips and pressed a brief kiss to her knuckles, holding her gaze as roguery twinkled in his cobalt eyes.

Maggie felt heat flooding into her face and rather feared she had just turned as red as his coat.

"You look radiant," he said. "You both do," he added, smiling at Trinny.

"Such flattery, Your Grace," Trinny said with an airy wave of her hand.

"Have I told you how much I love the Rolands, Lady Margaret?"

Maggie smiled. "As do I. How's the baby, anyway?"

"Oh, don't ask her that," Connor teased with a groan. "We'll be here all night."

Trinny smacked him on the arm, and he laughed. "He is all that's plump and happy and adorable," she informed Maggie. "But I'm sure you can bear to hear all the latest details until later in the evening. Humph!" she said playfully to the duke.

"Ah, never mind me, Lady Roland," Connor said with a grin. "Truth is, I'm just jealous, y'see. I've always thought 'twould be a fine thing to have lots of children at home. Babies everywhere, loads of 'em—the louder and stinkier, the better. What say you, Lady Margaret?"

Maggie stared at him, speechless.

Trinny laughed heartily and clapped the duke on the arm. "That's the spirit, Your Grace! You'll need help with that, though, to the best of my understanding of how it all works. Won't he, Maggie?" Trinny's eyes danced with mischief. "Know anyone who'd like to volunteer?"

Maggie's eyes widened as she stared at her friend. *You redheaded rascal!* Trinny laughed gaily while Maggie did nothing but stammer incoherently.

"Hmm, do they mean to start the dancing soon?" Trinny asked, glancing toward the musicians.

Connor shrugged.

"Think I'll go ask," the viscountess said, then sailed off to leave them alone, the little matchmaker.

"You are altogether *naughty*!" Maggie finally said, still blushing, when she finally regained her tongue.

"I was only being honest," Connor teased. "You do want children, don't you?"

"Well, of course. Not stinky ones, in particular…"

"They're all stinky, Maggie. It's part of their charm."

Laughing softly, she wanted so much to embrace him and give him a proper greeting. But that was impossible, since, for now, in the eyes of the ton, they were no more than friends. The memory of his mouth at her breast and other places on her body filled her with desire, though, as his fond gaze caressed her.

"I'm so glad you're here," he said, though she thought she detected a troubled flicker in the depths of his eyes. "Can I get you something to drink? There are refreshments in the music room."

"No, thank you, stay. How are you enjoying your party so far, my dear guest of honor?"

Connor snorted. "Surviving it. I missed you," he added in a low tone.

"I missed you, too. But, um, shouldn't you be on a receiving line somewhere?"

"Aunt Lucinda promised me we would not be so formal as that. Frankly," he murmured, glancing around, "I have no idea who most of these people are."

"But you have met the three young ladies, I trust?"

"Oh yes," he said dryly.

"Well?" As he hesitated, her sense of the nervous energy about him tonight grew stronger. "What's wrong, darling?" she murmured, briefly touching his arm. "You seem on edge."

"It's all just a little unseemly, I guess," he said gruffly. "Can you believe two of those three girls were aimed at Cousin Richard last Season? Aunt Florence told me so. Now they're being shoved at me, as though all titled men are interchangeable. It's disturbing. I feel like some sort of harlot being peddled to the highest bidder—not that it matters. My affections lie elsewhere, obviously. I should have told my aunt so before tonight, but she had her plan, and things happened so quickly between us. So I'm merely being polite until I can tell her this was all wasted effort."

Maggie smiled sympathetically. "Well, don't worry. It'll be over soon."

Indeed, the structure of the evening had been laid out in orderly fashion in the invitations. The soirée was to last for precisely four hours. From seven until nine, there would be biscuits and hors d'oeuvres, a little dancing, and cards. From nine to eleven, the guests would enjoy a light supper and cake.

And then Her Grace wanted everybody out.

To be sure, the Dowager Duchess of Amberley was a woman who knew her own mind.

"As long as you're not cross at me for this," Connor said, scanning her face.

"Not at all. I understand you must tread delicately here."

He nodded.

"Besides, what woman could be cross at so magnificent a specimen as you tonight, Major?"

He gave her a wry look. "Ah well. You're here now, and that's all I wanted. As for the ladies themselves, suffice to say I can see why Aunt Lucinda favors them."

"Oh?" Maggie lifted her head with a twinge of jealousy. "Are they very pleasant?"

"No, they're exactly like her." He paused, sending Maggie a brief scowl. "The brunette had scarcely known me two minutes before she asked if I'd ever killed anyone in the war. Can you imagine? No, I was only there to learn how to play cribbage."

Maggie pursed her lips. "It does seem an impertinent question. What did you tell her?"

"I said of course. Hundreds. Just to see how she'd react."

"You are naughty."

"Perhaps a slight exaggeration," he said with a gleam in his eyes.

"*What?* Hundreds, really?" Maggie felt the blood drain from her face.

"Well, I didn't keep count, exactly. But I was in for fifteen years, Maggie. You figure if it averaged out over time to one a month between battles and skirmishes and scouting missions, well, it comes out to…more than the number of guests here, at least." He shrugged, gauging her reaction while she stood there dazed.

He stared at her. "Why? Does that bother you?"

Actually, Maggie was reeling with the news. She appreciated his honesty and did not want to seem as unnerved by his answer as those three girls in the other room. But, in truth, she could barely wrap her mind around this revelation.

"Maggie?"

"That is…surprising," she managed at last.

He narrowed his eyes, assessing her. "You're horrified."

"N-no."

"Yes, you are."

"A little. It's all right." She felt a bit faint, but held up a hand, determined to steady herself. She just needed a moment. "I'm glad you told me. I just...never thought about it too much before. But you're right. It was a war. And without men like you, we'd all be speaking French."

"Speaking French would be the least of your worries," he said grimly. "I'd be more concerned about guillotines."

"Oh. Yes..." She finally looked up at him again, having gathered herself.

She found him watching her guardedly.

"You did what you had to do," Maggie said, determined to show her support. "And after all, as you said, you weren't there to play cribbage."

He said nothing for a moment, then looked away. "This is why I hate it when people ask me that question, and they always do. There is no good answer."

She laid her hand on his arm. "Fortunately, Connor, that life is far behind you now."

He gazed wistfully at her. "Wish I could believe that."

"Margaret!" Delia suddenly appeared with her nose in the air. "Come. We must go and pay our respects to our hostess. We mustn't be *rude*." She pivoted on her heel and stalked away again, expecting Maggie to follow.

"Far be it from your sister ever to be rude," Connor said under his breath, hiding that brief glimpse of melancholy behind another roguish remark.

Maggie sent him a smile, glad for his quip breaking the uneasy tension that had rippled between them with his disturbing admission.

Now he changed the subject. "Has she apologized yet?"

"Don't be silly, Your Grace."

"She's a hard one."

"*Aye*," Maggie said heartily, borrowing his favorite word.

Connor smiled. "Come, I'll introduce you and your sister to both of my aunts. Brace yourself," he added, then the two of them followed Delia into the drawing room, where Edward already waited.

They walked through the wide doorway and joined the queue of guests waiting to pay their respects to the hostess. The duchess's house was becoming ever more crowded, but Maggie felt all upside down to think that Connor had single-handedly killed more people than were now crowded into the house.

Now, now, who are you to judge? she scolded herself. *This man's a hero.* She wasn't judging him, though. She was just…a bit shocked.

Newly in love, she had been floating around in a bubble of happiness ever since he had proposed. Darker possibilities embedded within their alliance had not yet had time to emerge. But as she walked into the drawing room, feeling oddly numb and disjointed from reality after his revelation, she could not help wondering how well she really knew her future husband.

After all, she had known very little about Bryce, as it turned out.

What Connor had said just a few minutes ago was true—things *had* happened quickly between them. It was the first thing she had said to him when he'd offered marriage. *"We've only known each other for ten days."* To be sure, they got on beautifully together, but standing back a bit from her swirling emotions, Maggie saw that perhaps she had allowed herself to be swept away by the first blush of passion. Even so, she knew what she felt for him was real.

Delia kept her back to Maggie as they waited in the queue to greet their hostesses, chatting with various people.

Connor was also socializing along the way. As the guest of honor, he was busy and could hardly attend to Maggie alone all evening, nor did she require him to. While he spoke with various guests, Maggie gazed about, taking in her surroundings, admiring the little landscape paintings on the walls.

As they neared the spot where the First Duchess was holding court, Maggie noticed a second elderly lady standing near the fireplace. While the larger woman sat enthroned with the three would-be brides arrayed beside her, the second lady stood, smiling anxiously at people here and there.

She was a frail, nervous-looking thing with an air of hapless vulnerability. Like the dowager duchess, she was clad in widow's weeds. Her gray hair was gathered up into a chignon, and the only hint of color that she wore was an emerald brooch at her throat.

She noticed Maggie gazing at it, and her fingers rose to it self-consciously.

Maggie smiled at her. "What a beautiful brooch, if I may say so."

"Oh, you like it, dear? It's green, you see, in honor of His Grace. A-and the Emerald Isle."

"How thoughtful." Surprised but pleased by this small show of support for Connor's Irish birth, Maggie gazed warmly at her. *I wish I'd thought of that.* "It's lovely."

"Aunt Florence is very kind," Connor said from nearby, returning his attention to her. "Dear aunt, you must allow me to present Lady Margaret Winthrop, a daughter of the late Lord Halford."

"Ah. It's nice to meet you, dear."

"Lady Margaret," he continued, "this is Aunt Florence, Baroness Walstead."

Maggie curtsied, though there wasn't much room to move in the crush around the unlit fireplace. "How do you do."

"Aunt Florence lives here with Aunt Lucinda," he explained.

"Thank you for allowing me to come," Maggie said.

"Oh, we're glad to have you, dear. It's so nice to have guests again." Florence fretted, as though remembering the three recent deaths in the family.

Maggie did not wish to distress her. "You have a very beautiful home."

"Oh yes," Lady Walstead said with a vague look around. "It's quite pleasant, being close to Hyde Park."

"Aunt Florence, Lady Margaret is a neighbor of mine in Moonlight Square," Connor said. "She lives with her kin there, Lord and Lady Birdwell."

"Oh, that's nice," she said sweetly, looking relieved to find that she wasn't the only one cast upon the hospitality of relatives.

Delia, meanwhile, was immersed in conversation with some woman, so Connor did not bother making that introduction quite yet.

"Florence!" the dowager duchess suddenly snapped, making the timid little baroness nearly jump out of her skin. "What was the name of that play I told you I wanted to see? At Drury Lane."

"Oh, er, it was… I'm sorry. I-I cannot remember," Florence said, shaking her head.

"Ugh, of course not. Her brain's made of cheesecloth, I swan," the First Duchess declared to her listener.

Maggie's eyes widened, and her glance flew back to the unassuming Aunt Florence. The baroness lowered her head with a wounded air at the sting, but the dowager duchess did not take the least notice, continuing on with her conversation.

Maggie looked uneasily at Connor. He gave her a look that said, *I warned you.* Then he put his arm around his little aunt's shoulder, gave her a kiss on the temple, and playfully asked her if the punch was strong enough to get them drunk.

Aunt Florence pooh-poohed his question, but lifted her head and gave him a grateful smile as her charming nephew teased away the hurt.

Maggie fell just a little more deeply in love with him, seeing his kindness. He might be a beast on the battlefield, but his heart was pure gold.

In any case, with her own introduction to the dragon lady looming, Maggie's main concern was getting through the next few minutes unscathed.

If anyone could tolerate a few minutes in the presence of a bully like the duchess, surely it was she. After all, she'd dealt with Delia since birth.

The line to greet the dowager duchess moved slowly, in part, because Her Grace gave no thought to inconveniencing everybody present. It was her house, seemed to be her attitude, and everybody there could either dance to her tune or leave.

Just then, the butler came sidling along the wall, making his way to Connor, and trying to get his attention.

Maggie pointed him out, and Connor turned.

The butler bowed his head. "Pardon, Your Grace. The duchess earlier instructed me to inform you when the Duke of Wellington arrived: His Grace is below."

"What? Wellington? Here?" Connor blurted out, his eyes widening.

"Yes, Your Grace. The duke has only a few moments to spare, I'm afraid, but he wishes to make your acquaintance, welcome you to London, and express his appreciation for your service."

"Me?" Connor seemed tongue-tied. "I-I'll be right there!" He turned to Maggie. "Ol' Nosey's here—to see *me*!"

"Well, what are you waiting for? Go on," she said, nodding toward the doorway.

"I don't...want to abandon you."

"Nonsense. I'll be fine. Lady Walstead can do the introductions, I'm sure. Would you mind?"

"I'd be delighted, my dear," Florence said. "Run along, Amberley. Go see your field marshal."

Connor actually gulped. "Wish me luck," he said, smoothing his uniform coat.

"Good luck," Maggie said with amusement.

Lady Florence and she exchanged a glance at his boyish awe, then he excused his way through the throng and hurried off to meet his idol in person.

When he'd gone, Maggie noticed that the three approved brides had spotted their quarry standing next to her for those few moments.

Now they looked daggers at her. She turned away self-consciously, gritting her teeth.

Perfect. Delia still wasn't speaking to her. Those three were glaring at her like they wanted to snatch her up and toss her out the window. And she was about to be chained to a rock before the Kraken.

Nevertheless, she did a cursory introduction between Lady Florence and her sister before they arrived at the dragon's seat. While Delia started preening in expectation of meeting the duchess, Maggie's gaze wandered off through the wide-open pocket doors, where the crowd had parted to allow the Duke of Wellington to march up to the landing at the top of the stairs.

There, Connor met the great Irish-born general, who had masterminded the Monster's demise. As some other uniformed fellow introduced the two, Maggie stifled a grin to see Connor looking stiff, intensely serious, and a bit self-conscious upon being presented to the Iron Duke.

At ease, Major. She shook her head as the queue shuffled forward, little by little. *He is adorable.*

Suddenly, Maggie felt Delia's elbow drive discreetly into her side. Snapping to attention, she looked forward again, only to find the dragon lady's stare locked on her. "And who have we here?"

Delia took a step, putting herself forward, as she was wont to do.

Fluttering closer, Florence humbly did the introductions. "Lucinda, allow me to present the Marchioness of Birdwell and her sister, Lady Margaret Winthrop—daughters of the late Earl of Halford."

"I see," said the dragon, narrowing her eyes at Maggie and her sister in turn.

Delia dropped a deep curtsy. She'd come to curry favor, after all. "It is an honor to make your acquaintance, Your Grace. Thank you for the invitation."

"As if I had a choice," their hostess muttered. "My nephew insisted that all his friends from Moonlight Square attend, and I don't mind telling you, I do not approve of that place, on the whole."

"Why ever not?" Delia blurted out.

"I know what goes on," the duchess said. "That place has earned a reputation for scandal of late. In my view, no one of taste ought to live there. It's a haven for scoundrels." The duchess dissected her sister with a relishing stare, sizing her up, daring her to protest.

But the Marchioness of Birdwell was in no wise accustomed to being addressed in such a fashion.

Maggie was. So she saw in a glance exactly what was going on here. The dragon lady was testing her unsuspecting sister.

Unfortunately, before Maggie could restrain her, the proud, hotheaded Lady Birdwell dared to naysay the duchess—politely, of course.

Delia swallowed her startlement and forced out a superior laugh. "Allow me to assure Your Grace that most in our neighborhood are entirely respectable."

"Oh? That may be your opinion, young lady. But mark my words. It only takes a few bad apples to spoil the lot! What say you to that?"

"Certainly not, ma'am," said Delia.

Maggie kept her mouth shut, but her heart sank. *Oh, Delia, you don't bother arguing with such a woman. Trust me on this.*

"Oh, I see!" said the dragon. "You would contradict me in my own home, then?"

Delia spluttered while Maggie glanced around discreetly. *Where is Edward?* she wondered with increasing distress, but the serene marquess was nowhere to be found.

Sensible as he was, perhaps he had simply refused to go near the duchess.

Delia must have finally realized that even she was outmatched by this fearsome enemy, and it was time to beat a hasty retreat.

"Not at all, Your Grace." She cleared her throat and forced a smile. "Well! We are very glad to be here, in any case. And may I say, Your Grace has a lovely home."

"So glad you approve, Lady Birdwell," the termagant drawled. "No doubt, in your infinite wisdom, you know much more about what's in fashion than I, hmm?"

Delia floundered at this renewed attack. Maggie looked on in alarm. The dragon's eyes gleamed with cruel glee as she homed in on Delia for sport.

"Th-that's not what I meant, ma'am." Delia lowered her head, flustered. "I would never presume such a thing."

That does it! thought Maggie. She was getting her sister out of here.

"Come, Delia." She laid hold of her sister's arm. "We don't wish to take up any more of Her Grace's precious time."

The dragon's belligerent stare swung to Maggie. "Something wrong, Lady— What was your name again? Madeline? Miranda? Milquetoast?"

"Margaret. Lady Margaret Winthrop, Your Grace." Maggie's heart leapt into her throat, but she held her head high. "And yes. Something *is* wrong, actually, as it happens."

"Do tell."

Maggie knew it was unwise but could not hold her tongue. Blast it, as much as she sometimes despised her maddening sister, she would not stand by and see her abused by this bully.

"Frankly, Your Grace, I am shocked, shocked, I say, to hear such barbaric remarks directed at guests in one's home!"

The ongoing chatter around them stopped at the sound of her loud, angry declaration.

"Aha." The dowager duchess beamed as though she had just found a worthy opponent. "This one has spirit. Your sister presumes to judge my tastes, Lady Margaret."

"She gave you a compliment!" Maggie exclaimed.

"It isn't her place. Do I require praise from a self-important little marchioness that everybody hates?"

Delia gasped, her eyes widening at this unprovoked attack, then her cheeks turned scarlet. She turned around, gathered up her peacock-colored skirts, and bolted out of the drawing room in tears.

"Delia!" Maggie cried, left standing there alone.

"Somebody better fetch Birdy," one of the other guests murmured, while the duchess laughed gaily, basking in her victory.

"Yes, run, run away, little marchioness!"

Maggie turned to her, infuriated. "How dare you speak to my sister that way?"

"Oh, you object, do you?"

"Most heartily, madam!"

The duchess leaned forward. "And what are you going to do about it, then, you impertinent little baggage?"

Maggie leaned toward her, narrowing her eyes. "Why don't you ask your nephew?" she answered quietly.

The dowager's laughter stopped, and her gloating smile turned to a glare. "Ah, have designs on him, do you? Well, too bad! Don't get your hopes up. Little nobody. I know of your family. Your father foolishly died without male issue. You are therefore of no possible significance in the world, and thus have no chance of joining this family. What say you to that, Lady Milquetoast?"

Maggie saw red. "What a rare beast you are, madam! Inviting people here to your home so that you might attack them!"

The duchess merely shrugged, waving her fan. "The whole ton knows I have an acerbic wit. Those who cannot withstand it should stay at home. That is all."

"No, madam, that is not *all*." Maggie was now quivering with wrath. "*Nobody* speaks to my sister that way. You bring dishonor to my family and your own, showing such incivility to a guest."

"Dear me! Such censure from a little milk-and-water miss."

Maggie clenched her fists at this particular accusation. For, in truth, it was her worst fear about herself. "I am not a milk-and-water miss, for your information," she said through gritted teeth.

"Oh? What are you, then?"

"The daughter of the Earl of Halford, ma'am." *And the future Duchess of Amberley,* she almost said, but somehow managed to keep their secret.

"As for you, Your Grace…" Maggie leaned closer. "People warned me you were a dragon, but I see now they were wrong." She pointed her finger in the old woman's face. "*You,* madam, are an ogress!"

A loud, rude "Ha!" suddenly sounded from the back of the drawing room, which Maggie now realized, in the throes of her trembling outburst, had gone absolutely silent.

Her pulse pounding, she had forgotten all about the other people in the room.

The three approved debs were staring at her, open-mouthed, and, peeking from the corner of her eye, Maggie beheld the crowd of guests gaping at her with expressions both shocked and appalled.

At the back of the room stood Connor, however, wearing a devilish grin that stretched from ear to ear.

Maggie suddenly felt the room spinning. With a gulp, she looked over at little Lady Walstead.

Who was gazing at her in wonder.

Maggie was filled in that instant with an overwhelming need to get out of there. How she kept herself from running as swiftly as the god Hermes in his winged shoes, she knew not.

But somehow, she straightened up, lowered her hand to her side, and lifted her chin, pivoting to face the stunned crowd with all the dignity she could muster.

People cleared out of her path as she walked slowly, head high, out of the silent room.

Upon gaining the galleried staircase landing, she noted—with considerable relief—that Wellington had gone. One did not wish to make a fool of oneself in front of a national hero, after all.

But the staircase was clear, so she went right past Connor and fled down the steps as fast as her slippered feet would carry her.

"Maggie?"

She didn't look back.

The entrance hall was still thick with guests; she'd never make it out the front door. Instead, she flung around the newel post and hurried down the ground-floor hallway, forging deeper into the house, in frantic search of an exit.

Heart pounding, she tried all the while to fathom what on earth had come over her. It seemed inexplicable. But hearing that dreadful woman abuse everyone around her—even sweet Lady Walstead—was more than she could bear.

No one had ever sent Delia running away in shamefaced tears before. Seeing *that* had cracked something open inside her that Maggie had never felt before: an instinctive need to fight back, protect her own, no matter how flawed they might be.

At last, she found an exit at the back of the house and strode out into the night-clad garden on legs that had turned to jelly beneath her.

Gulping in deep breaths of cool night air, she walked off across the terrace in a daze, pressing both hands to her forehead. *Oh Lord, what have I done?*

But she knew. She was fairly sure she had just destroyed her own reputation.

CHAPTER 25

The Major

$\mathcal{C}$onnor was seriously impressed by what he had just witnessed. Upon his return from walking Wellington out, he had caught only the tail end of the row in the drawing room, but, by Jove, he hadn't thought the girl had it in her.

First she had stood up to Delia in Hyde Park; now she had defied the dragon lady herself. *I fear I've created a monster.* He could not suppress his grin while the rest of the drawing room looked confounded—except for Aunt Lucinda, whose lined, doughy face was puckered up in rage.

This defiant outburst from a social inferior had not just shocked the duchess; it had veritably roused the dragon from her cave and brought her forth ready to breathe fire.

It seemed Aunt Lucinda had just met her match in the unlikeliest of places.

She even made the effort of rising from her chair in grand indignation, but as the murmur of astonishment began to spread throughout the drawing room, Connor sent the matriarch a hard look of reproach for starting this.

She would answer for it when the party was over.

How would she react, he wondered, when he also told her he had found out about her past as Lucky Lucy Bly? Maybe the 'ton had forgotten who she'd been fifty years ago, but Connor had realized that most of Her Grace's bluster was but a façade.

She might fool others, but she wasn't fooling him. Her outrageous rudeness was meant to help cover up her own sense of inferiority, after having clawed her way up from the gutter to join the aristocracy.

How she must hate these highborn maidens of the ton, whose quality was never questioned. That would explain why she made it her business to put them all in their place.

Well, he thought, it had not worked on Maggie.

Already in motion, Connor went after her, pardoning his way past his guests. He rushed out onto the upstairs landing and looked over the banister just in time to see her flitting off down the hallway.

He ran down the steps, ignoring the guests just arriving, except for his trusty new friend, Major Peter Carvel, who had just walked into the crowded entrance hall with the Duke and Duchess of Netherford.

"Amberley!" Carvel looked amazed, hooking a thumb over his shoulder. "We just saw Wellington leaving!"

"Aye." Connor flashed a taut smile at his fellow veteran, who was likewise in uniform. "He stopped for a quick visit, can you believe it? Sorry—can't talk at the moment. Minor emergency. I'll be right back."

"Need any help?"

"Ah, not at all, thanks. Glad you all came," he added distractedly, then hurried after Maggie. He could not imagine what she was feeling at the moment.

But it was no mystery to him why she had exploded like that, never mind that Delia was no prize for a sibling. Nobody needed to explain clan loyalty to a three-quarters Irishman.

Still, he was startled and rather tickled by it all. After seeing how Society cowered from his aunt, little Maggie Winthrop was the last person in the world he would've predicted to stand up to her.

Amazing, how this woman continued to surprise him.

He strode down the hallway that led off the entrance hall, glancing around for her in every room he passed. When he saw the French doors in the morning room at the back of the house left slightly ajar, he realized she must've gone that way.

He crossed the room in a few swift strides and went outside. After pulling the door shut behind him, he spotted her wandering aimlessly a few yards down the central garden path with her hands pressed to her head.

"Lady Margaret!" he called, aware of a few guests standing on the balcony above.

Maggie looked back at him, her eyes as round as those of a spooked horse. She sent him only the briefest of glances over her shoulder, as though too ashamed to look at him.

"Are you all right?"

She didn't answer, and kept her back to him, walking faster down the graveled path. Connor followed.

His aunt's garden spanned the luxurious width of the terrace house and was bound by an eight-foot stone wall. Wrought-iron furniture was arrayed around a square flagstone terrace that overlooked the greensward, emerald and flat.

Here and there throughout the garden stood decorative pillars topped by stone busts or urns burgeoning with flowers. Connor passed sculpted topiaries, blooming flowerbeds, and a few small, ornamental fruit trees in blossom as he strode after her.

"Maggie, it's all right. Come back."

"Leave me alone!" she said in a shaky voice, sounding forlorn. "I've caused enough trouble for one night. I...I just need to collect my composure for a moment. Then I'm going home."

She walked under the trellised archway, at the end of which sat a small, gurgling fountain with a curved stone garden seat across from it.

Connor briefly deliberated on what tack to take with her. With all his heart, he did not wish to see her cry. He was bursting with pride in the girl.

Cheer her up, he decided.

"There, there, Lady Maggie," he said as he, too, passed under the trellis, approaching the fountain and the stone bench, where she had sat, looking routed.

"You cannot join me out here, obviously," she said with a sniffle. "It's not proper!"

"Why start now?" he murmured as he reached the fountain.

She looked up at him with an air of desperation as he stood there, and the moonlight caught the panic glittering in her wide, stricken eyes.

"What have I done?" she whispered.

"Darling." Everything in him wished to comfort her.

"I can't believe I just did that."

"Neither can I," he said with a chuckle, sitting down beside her. "Who are you, fearsome young spitfire, and what have you done with my meek, mild-mannered Maggie Winthrop?"

"Oh, please, don't tease me!" she begged him, tears in her eyes.

"Sorry," he said. "Just trying to put a smile back on those lovely lips."

She covered her face with both hands and shook her head. "I've made an utter fool of myself."

"On the contrary, darling, you were magnificent."

"Oh, hang your Irish charm," she whispered, turning her whole body away from him, trembling.

Connor gazed at her creamy shoulder with tender concern. "My aunt is the one who acted badly, not you."

Maggie trembled. "I should not have risen to the bait. Why on earth would I throw away my reputation for my stupid sister's sake? Delia hates me!"

"No, she doesn't. She's your sister. That's just her way." He pulled his clean, pressed handkerchief out of his breast pocket and tapped her gently on the shoulder.

She glanced back and accepted it with a grateful nod.

As she dabbed at her eyes, still half turned away from him, Connor leaned closer and kissed that pearly shoulder. "Don't cry, love," he whispered. "All will be well. I promise."

Maggie sniffled, wiping her nose. "You should go back inside. You really should."

"I can't," he said. "Not until you feel better."

"I'll be all right," she said woefully.

Connor stayed planted, resting his arm along the back of the bench and stretching his legs out before him.

Idly, he crossed his ankles, with no intention of leaving until she had fully regained her composure. It was pleasant out, starry. The spring night wrapped around them in dark, silky serenity.

The fountain bubbled and arced, its waters silvered by moonlight. The frogs sang, tucked away in their green hiding places. The cool night air smelled of lilacs.

"Your aunt's garden is beautiful," Maggie said in a weary tone after a moment.

"Almost as lovely as her temperament," he drawled.

She let out a low snort of laughter, then turned around and finally gazed at him. "Should I apologize?"

"God, no," he said. "She'd lose all respect for you now if you did."

"Respect?" Maggie echoed.

"Aye. That's how you earn it with her kind. They shove you; you shove back harder. Believe me, I've seen this sort of thing a million times. Besides, she had it coming, I daresay. So I repeat: you were magnificent."

He caressed her shoulder with one knuckle. "You made me proud."

"You would say that." She smiled uncertainly, then glanced toward the house. "They can probably see us from the balcony, you know, so you'd better behave."

He shook his head. "Not from this angle. Blocked by the trellis. We're safe." As a rifleman, after all, he understood the geometry of a clear shot.

"Humph, it's probably worse if they *can't* see us," she mumbled, sounding resentful. "Then they'll just make up whatever they want instead of reporting what they think they saw. Not that it matters anymore. I'm sure I've just become an outcast, anyway."

"Don't be silly. I wager you've just become a heroine in the eyes of countless people in the ton. But who the hell cares what they all think, anyway? You'll soon be my duchess, remember? Then you, too, shall have the luxury of behaving however you please."

"Which would never include treating people like that." She looked askance at him, a sulk on her plump, tempting lips. "Are you sure you wouldn't be better off with one of those other young ladies after that?"

"Absolutely not! I want my future sons to be fighters. And my daughters, too. You're clearly the lass for the job." He grinned.

"Hmm." She gave him an arch look. "All those babies you mentioned, eh?"

"Aye. Lots of 'em. Screaming, wild, happy, bald babies." He nudged her. "What do you say?"

She shrugged, feigning nonchalance. "I already told you I would."

"Good." He leaned over and kissed her gently on the lips. "Don't worry, sweeting. It'll be all right."

She gazed wistfully at him, mere inches away. "How are you so sure?"

"Because I love you." Connor stared at her, his heart pounding. He hadn't expected to tell her that tonight, but the words just came out, and besides, it was true.

Her eyes widened with tender amazement. She breathed his name.

"I love you," he whispered again, more forcefully.

"I love you too." Laying a hand on his cheek, she studied him.

Connor nestled his face against her palm, craving her touch more than she knew.

He leaned in to kiss her—when she suddenly gasped. "Oh my God!"

"What?"

Without warning, she threw her arms around him and pulled him down violently on top of her. Connor was quite amenable to her sudden burst of passion—except that the sound of a gunshot cracked through the night, and a bullet slammed into the stone wall behind the garden bench, making a hole and a little puff of dust.

Right where his head had been seconds ago.

Maggie shoved him aside, jumping up to point frantically. "He's there! There! I see him!"

"Stay down!" Connor roared as he rolled down off the bench and spun into a crouch. A curse escaped him when he saw her on her feet; he went to retrieve her.

"He had a long gun—a musket or rifle!" she cried, still pointing toward the high garden wall. "He was right up there! On the wall!"

"Damn it, stay down, Maggie, there could be more of them!" He shoved her down behind the low stone wall of the fountain.

She tumbled onto all fours.

"Where?" he demanded.

"By the cherry tree! I only saw one figure—dressed all in black. He was p-perched on the wall! I saw the flash of his gun!"

"Thanks for saving my life. Now stay the hell down."

"Connor!"

"Stay back!" he ordered, already on his feet, tugging loose the black stock around his neck and striding toward the garden gate.

"What are you doing?" she yelled.

"Securing our future, my love," he said wryly under his breath, nostrils flaring as air flooded into his lungs and fury pounded, red-hot, in his veins. *Let's finish this, shall we, John Smith?*

He must not give him time to reload. He flung open the gate, glanced up and down the narrow cobbled mews, and caught sight of a black-clad figure racing off through the darkness with a rifle slung across his back.

"Get back here, you son of a bitch!" Connor bellowed, then ran.

As the seconds ticked by, Maggie was still in shock, her heart pounding, as she debated what to do. She remained where Connor had put her, crouched on all fours behind the low fountain wall, dazed with the aftermath of pure panic.

Every time she blinked, she kept seeing the dark silhouette of the

Gaelen Foley

sniper perched atop the garden wall, the shape of his gun emerging from the cherry blossoms—and then the muzzle's flash.

Thank God I saw it. What if I hadn't seen it? Oh God, she could not let herself think about that or she might throw up.

That had been much too close a call. A true brush with death.

And now Connor had gone chasing after it.

Was he mad? He must be, she thought, her chest heaving. Just a little.

Her mind was spinning, and she wasn't sure how many seconds passed. Time had lost all meaning. Only vaguely did she feel how hard she'd bumped her knee when she had fallen to the ground—or, rather, been pushed by her fiancé.

She could not believe he had run off alone into the night.

With utter irrelevance, she then noticed absently that she had torn her ball gown a bit. A rosette by the knee of her skirts hung limp. As she lifted her hand, having landed hard on her palms, she saw she'd got moss and gravel on her white satin gloves from the cracks in between the flagstones.

All the while, the fountain lilted, as though nothing was wrong.

Somebody, help! she wanted to scream. But she dared not make a sound. She did not know where the killer was at the moment.

Surely, though, the guests up in the duchess's house heard the shot. Rather wild-eyed, she glanced up toward the balcony.

Somehow the music played on, spilling out from the ballroom. They must have started the dancing, never mind the absence of the guest of honor. It would have been a way, she supposed, to smooth over the awkwardness after her public fracas with the Duchess of Amberley.

Well, what the devil do I do now? Just wait here? Staring toward the alley from her undignified position, she listened for all she was worth to any sound from the mews that might indicate what was happening with Connor.

She had heard his footsteps pounding off into the darkness, but then he did not return.

Maggie gulped, trying to steady herself. *Shouldn't I go get help?* She risked a quick peek over the edge of the fountain.

The garden was empty. The gunman had fled. Chest heaving, she glanced again toward the balcony, but her view was blocked by the trellis. Any minute now, she expected some of the men from inside to come running.

Surely they would. They were probably standing around inside even now, asking each other, *"Did you hear something?"*

But in that nerve-racking pause of indeterminate length, Maggie swept the garden with a fearful glance, her eyes wide.

Worry for Connor consumed her. How could anyone help him if nobody knew where he'd gone? She realized that in order for her to bring him assistance, she had to get at least a general sense of which way he'd run.

He had told her to keep her head down, true. But Maggie simply *had* to do something to help him. The man she loved was out there alone with a murderer—and what if he was right? What if this viper had brought henchmen with him, waiting somewhere nearby?

Connor might be outnumbered. Led into a trap or an ambush.

With that, Maggie rose with caution from her hiding place, inching up onto her feet.

Glancing constantly toward the house, she was rather sure she heard voices of male guests who'd come out onto the balcony, but not knowing where the killer now was, she dared not yell to them for help.

Now that it was truly sinking into her bones that she—she!—could have also been shot moments ago, she had no desire to offer herself again as a target.

As for Connor, she did not even know if he was armed. Will had said he always was, and maybe that explained why he'd gone racing off alone like a lunatic. She hoped so.

Fighting back sickening fear, Maggie peeled off her gloves and trailed her hand through the fountain as she passed, lifting her hand to bring a bit of chilly water to her face.

It helped clear her head. Then she crept on toward the garden gate, and, ever so cautiously, peered out into the mews.

The darkness was empty, but she could hear Connor's footsteps pounding in the distance, as well as his voice.

"Get back here, you son of a bitch!"

Slipping through the waist-high gate, she stole silently down the cobbled passageway until she reached the corner. She poked her head out past the plane of the alley, risking a glance north toward Hyde Park.

No, they hadn't gone that way. Then, peering southward down the street—she did not know the name of it—she saw her love running at top speed after the still-fleeing shooter.

The gunman clearly wanted to avoid the glowing street lanterns, so he darted around the next corner to his right, into a side street. Connor raced after him.

What are you doing? she thought frantically. *Come back! I don't want to lose you!*

She was afraid to call out to him, though—and afraid to call attention to herself. She glanced over her shoulder once more, torn between going back to fetch help or following them.

He could die. I can't leave him.

Instinct took over, deciding the question on her behalf. The man she had already set in her heart as her mate was in danger. She had to be there in case he was hurt. Ignoring all protests of reason and logic along with her terror, Maggie turned the corner and began running down the street.

She resolved that if she saw anyone along the way, she would plead for their help. Perhaps some kind stranger might come driving by. Or a night watchman, though they were known to be useless. Usually drunken old men.

For now, Connor had no one but her to come to his aid. Not in a million years would she abandon him.

A dog barked in the distance. She strove to listen past its angry clamor for the sound of her quarry. Every step of her sprint jarred her hurt knees. To be sure, her little dancing slippers were not made for running down hard, paved streets.

Her breath rasped through her teeth as her stays clamped tight around her ribcage, restricting her lungs. At least the hem of her ball gown skimmed her ankles, the right length for dancing. Otherwise, she might have gone tripping down the street.

The pins in her hair began coming loose, but no matter. Maggie pressed on. Mere moments later, she reached the corner around which both men had gone. She slowed, panting as she approached it.

I hope he's armed. Please, let him be armed.

She had this terrible feeling deep in the pit of her stomach that the happiness they had just found together was about to be snatched right out of her hands.

Please, God, be with him. Don't let this man take Connor from me. I need him. Her heart thumping like it would burst out of her chest, Maggie pressed her back against the corner where the street met the alleyway. She could feel her fine, watered silk skirts catching on the rough bricks behind her.

Tamping down dread, she ventured a glance around the corner.

The dark, narrow alley led away from the streetlamps and into the blackness. But now she could hear things. Curses and shouts.

There was no motion at all in the alleyway, so she realized the two men had merely passed through it. Pressing her lips together, Maggie forced herself to follow.

Shaking, she went closer, setting one foot after the other, nigh tiptoeing down the black alley.

With each step, the ugly noises grew louder. It sounded as though Connor had caught up with his quarry on the next broad, illuminated street that the alley connected to.

Her stomach churned at what she might find when she reached the far end of the passage. A cold sweat formed on her brow, and the hairs on her nape stood on end.

Curses bounced off the pavement. A scuffle of boot heels.

"Don't you dare!"

A cry and a clatter of metal—and then a dull thud.

"Son of a bitch," Connor said.

"Let me go!" someone thundered.

Maggie hesitated, not sure if she really wanted to see this.

"Let's have a look at you, shall we?"

"Damn you, Amberley!"

She swallowed hard. Upon reaching the corner, she leaned out ever so carefully, barely beyond the length of her nose.

Oh…it's Park Lane. For across the wide, elegant avenue stood the tall fence that girded Hyde Park. She spotted a horse hitched to its wrought-iron rails in the shadows of a massive oak at the park's edge.

Perhaps the would-be assassin had left the horse there as his means of escape. But he hadn't made it that far.

For the major had captured him.

"Mr. John Smith, I presume?"

"Oh, go to hell."

She winced, closing her eyes at the sickening thud as Connor dealt him a sledgehammer punch; she heard a low cry of pain.

"I know who you are," Connor informed him.

"No, you don't." The voice sounded vaguely familiar: low-toned and sly, still mocking, even in pain.

But whomever he'd captured, she could not see the man very well when she dared look again. It was dark in between the streetlamps, and both men were in profile to her, less than ten yards away.

"You're the whoremonger's son. Why are you after my family?" Connor demanded. He slammed the lean, black-clad figure once more against the Portland stone wall of some opulent town house overlooking the park. "Did your father send you or was this your idea?"

As Maggie looked on, not daring to interrupt, her relief to find Connor unharmed was quickly infused with another emotion.

He was brutal, her lover. By the glow of the streetlamps, she could see how he'd trapped the man there and was beating him senseless.

With ease. Nay, with relish.

He was vicious, quite in his element. The thought of his revelation earlier this evening sliced through her mind.

Over a hundred kills, by his estimate. Tonight it seemed likely that he might add one to that number.

Maggie looked on with a sort of confusion, uncomprehending. For it was one thing to fall in love with a warrior, and quite another to see his talents in action.

Blood crimsoned his fist. She winced as if feeling the blows, lowering her head a bit, hunching her shoulders.

Unable to look anymore as he used his forearm like a bar, pinning his enemy by the throat against the wall, Maggie lowered her gaze, chilled to the marrow.

Weapons littered the pavement. She realized he must've torn them away from the man. A pistol lay a few feet away on the ground.

Its mate had been thrown out into the street. There was a nasty knife near Connor's boot.

As for the rifle, the would-be assassin had been stripped of that, too, somehow. It had fallen longwise against the wall where they were brawling.

Maggie gripped the bricks on the corner, steadying herself against the realization that the man had probably tried wielding each weapon against Connor while trying in vain to escape him.

Another fierce blow to the gut, and the man started coughing.

The final object she saw on the ground near their feet was a length of black cloth. She stared at it until she realized it was a mask that Connor must've ripped off his enemy's face.

"Did you kill my kinsmen? Why? What the hell have you got against my family?"

Silence.

"Why are you trying to kill me, damn you? At least have the courage to tell me!"

Let him breathe, Maggie thought. *And don't break his jaw if you want him to talk.*

Connor picked up the knife. "If you won't answer my questions, I have no reason to spare you. Now, I'm not goin' to ask you again. Why are you persecuting my family?"

"Ask your aunt!" the man shouted bitterly. "Ask your aunt, you stupid sod."

"Why? What about her?"

"She killed my brother." The man's voice was garbled with rage — and pain, considering the blood pouring down his face.

"Don't be ridiculous. She's an old lady."

"She sent hirelings, idiot."

"And why would she do that? Answer me or you die. I don't need you, you know." Connor menaced him with the blade, still holding him fast. "I can kill you and still get truth from your father. I'll find him, and I'll rip his throat out. What say you to that?"

Maggie covered her mouth with her hand.

"Let him be. This doesn't concern him," the man fairly whispered.

"Oh really?" Connor seemed to think he'd found a weakness. He tapped the flat of his blade against the man's cheek. "What if I don't believe you? Perhaps I should kill your father. Aye, maybe I will. You want to wipe out my line? What if I do the same to yours first?"

"He knows nothing about this. But suit yourself!" the man said boldly. "It won't go well for you, duke. The old man's survived worse enemies than you."

"You think so?" Connor seemed to be having increasing difficulty reining in his temper. Maggie could hear the rage building in his voice. "All right, then. Let's talk about Richard. Did you kill him, too? Tamper with his curricle? Maybe one of those times you hid in the coach house, waiting to use my servant girl like she's your whore?"

The man laughed coldly, as if he was past caring what happened to him. "She *is* my whore."

Connor punched him for that with a massive right hook; the man spun toward Maggie with the force of the blow and fell onto all fours on the pavement.

When he lifted his head, she drew in her breath, recognizing him now that she saw him straight on by the lamp's glow.

It was the dragoon who had offered her a ride that day in the rain.

328   *Gaelen Foley*

He shook his head to clear it, and when his dazed eyes focused after the blow, he looked up and saw her standing there, four or five yards away.

Maggie stared back at him, her heart in her throat.

Connor had not yet noticed her. "I'm warning you," he snarled, closing in once more, looming over the man, "I don't give a damn for your life."

A low, almost drunken laugh escaped the dragoon as Connor took hold of him again. "But, Your Grace, surely you wouldn't kill me in front of your lady?"

CHAPTER 26

Killer Unmasked

onnor glanced over from the depths of savage fury and saw Maggie standing there, her hair disheveled, her gown torn at the knee. By the light of the moon, her face was pale, her eyes wide as she stared at him holding his enemy's knife to the man's throat, knuckles dripping with blood.

The thought swept in as though from a great distance as he stood there, his chest heaving: *What the hell is she doing here?*

Then the look on her face snared his attention.

The horror. The shock. The fear.

Fear of *him*. That was what jarred him. Aye, the woman he loved was gazing at him as though she had just realized that the real killer here wasn't the man on the ground.

And no wonder, that. Connor had completely dominated his foe, just as he had been trained to do. The sharp, bitter taste of the threats he had uttered moments ago lingered on his tongue. Threats he may or may not have carried out; it just depended.

But Maggie must've heard them, and now she saw him standing astride his sprawled enemy, blade in hand, in position, if need be, to cut his throat.

He had made it his business to ensure that Flynn's son believed that he'd better start talking if he wanted to live. Whether the dragoon had been convinced of Connor's willingness to murder him there in the street, that remained to be seen.

But Maggie believed it.

So said the terrified look on her face.

Seeing himself through her eyes like that took Connor completely off guard, and in his fleeting hesitation, the dragoon grabbed the nearby rifle off the ground, lurched to one knee, and swung it like a club, smashing Connor in the side, where his wound from the duel was still healing.

Connor bellowed and staggered a step to the left, knocked off balance by the force of the unblocked blow, and the momentarily blinding burst of pain to feel his side split open again.

He heard Maggie cry out in alarm while the dragoon scrambled to his feet, already stumbling to a run.

"Get back here!" Connor tried to yell, but could not quite catch his breath as the man spun past him—not toward Maggie, thank God, but across the street.

Beaten half to a pulp, the blackguard ran for his life, and Connor took a few winded steps after him. Unfortunately, the fresh reinjury slowed him down.

Chasing the pain out of his mind by willpower, he snatched the rifle's ramrod off the ground by his feet. He had removed it immediately upon capturing his enemy and tossed it aside so the man could not reload. Connor gripped the ramrod now and started after him. By God, he would skewer the bastard with it.

But then Maggie cried, "Connor, don't!"

Again, she made him waver. He whipped a glance over his shoulder, fearing she might be in danger, that another enemy might've appeared, but she was just standing there as before, and by the time he looked forward again with the iron rod in his grasp and his side throbbing, Flynn's son had reached his horse.

Damn it! Why had she interrupted?

The dragoon jumped into the saddle.

"You won't escape me!" Connor thundered, running toward him. "I know where to find you, you son of a bitch!"

"And I know where to find *her*!" Flynn's son yelled back from beneath the great tree overhanging the park fence. In the next instant, a dark horse charged out of the shadows across the street, and Connor's would-be assassin galloped off into the night.

Connor remained standing in the middle of Park Lane, staring after his enemy until the man had disappeared.

With a curse under his breath, he tossed the ramrod down in disgust.

It clattered onto the cobblestones, then he threw his head back and let out a garbled shout of frustration at the sky.

"You there! What is going on down there?" a prim female suddenly called down from some window above. "I'm warning you, I've sent my footman for the constable!"

"Perfect," Connor muttered. He turned around, still panting with rage and extreme irritation. Holding his side, already hot and sticky with seeping blood, he glanced up at the opulent townhouse and saw a worried head peering out from between the curtains of an upper window. "Go back to bed! The show's over!"

The woman's head disappeared.

As he trudged back toward the pavement, Maggie rushed out onto the street toward him.

"Are you all right?" She reached for him, trying to see his side and gauge how badly he was hurt, but he pushed her helping hand away.

"What are you doing here?" he demanded.

Her head jerked upward at his curt tone. "What?"

"I told you to stay back. Did you not hear me?" Connor asked crisply.

Her lips parted, but no words came out.

He shook his head, exasperated. But, doing his best to let the matter go, he stepped past her. "Come on. We need to get out of here. The last thing we need right now is a chat with the constable."

He winced as he bent down to pick up the weapons that he had removed from Flynn's son. Perhaps they would bear some telltale sign of evidence. For now, they'd serve if any more threats should appear.

Then he picked up the dragoon's knife and gave it by its handle to Maggie.

"Here. You carry this," he said without meeting her gaze. She grimaced and held the thing like a dead rat. "Let's go."

She followed a few paces after him as he stalked back down Park Lane, toward the mouth of the alley, through which they had passed earlier.

"Connor?"

He remained coldly quiet.

"Say something."

He stopped short and pivoted to face her. "Very well. When we are married, madam, if I give you an order, I expect you to obey it—without question. Particularly in matters of life and death. Damn it, Maggie, have you no concept of the chain of command?" he barked at her.

She jumped, then her mouth fell open.

He pivoted on his heel and continued marching forward. "Come. Let us hasten back to the party," he said with a biting undertone of sarcasm.

She spluttered a little behind him, then hurried after him in her dancing slippers, skipping to keep up. "Chain of command? Well, pardon me, Major! I was not aware that becoming engaged to you meant I'd enlisted in the Army."

He harrumphed.

"I was worried about you!" she exclaimed. "That's the only reason I followed. I thought you might need me to send you reinforcements."

"Did it look like I needed help?" He stopped and turned to her, intensely annoyed. "I told you, I neither want nor need a mother hen. Obviously, I had everything under control."

"Oh really? And did you have *yourself* under control?"

He narrowed his eyes. "Do not make excuses. You were clearly in the wrong."

She huffed with indignation, but he didn't care. There was a time for kisses and a time for laying down the law, and by God, he'd dealt with enough neophytes in his day to realize that the chit's safety required that he nip this defiance in the bud.

That bastard had just threatened her. Given that the dragoon had already murdered up to three members of his family, Connor wasn't taking any chances with his future wife.

Her survival until he finished this business might well depend on her following his orders to the letter. Why was that so difficult for her to understand?

She gave him a wounded pout, but he did not soften his expression. Letting her off the hook here could get her killed. On the contrary, this was essential training.

"I was only trying to help," she said with a sulk.

"Oh really? And what were you going to do? Give him a frosty set-down? This isn't a ballroom, Margaret. It isn't even a duel governed by some pretty code of honor. Do you understand me? Good. End of conversation. Do not disobey me again.

"Now, hurry up. He might decide to come back, and I promise you, if the bastard does, you won't like what you see. Your presence won't stay my hand a second time."

He pivoted around the corner, making sure she was right behind him.

Her silence as they walked through the dark alley onto the wider, illuminated street beyond told him that she was mulling his words.

Clearly, he had given her much to think about.

Alas, his declaration that the topic was now closed had been overly optimistic.

She kept glancing up at him as they walked up the elegant street, side by side. For his part, Connor was just glad to have passed through that tight, claustrophobic alley, for a place like that was a fine spot for an ambush.

"What?" he finally grumbled.

She was shaking her head. "I don't believe it... You're blaming *me* for this?"

"I had him! You distracted me. He got away. Ergo?"

Admittedly, some of his anger came from hurt male pride that she had seen him fail at such a vital task—even though *she* was the one who had caused him to blunder.

Still, the only person in all of London whose opinion he really cared about had just seen him at his most ferocious.

Gentle soul that she was, he did not expect the girl to take it well. Old, hardened defenses in him had already braced for some sort of rejection or another.

"So, I get no credit for courage or...or loyalty?" she demanded.

Connor just looked at her.

"Here's a thought, Major. Why don't *you* learn to follow *my* orders once in a while?"

He snorted.

"Well, look at you!" She gestured angrily at him. "Your hand's bleeding, your eye's swollen, your side's ripped open again—all because you had to go charging off alone into the night like a lunatic! Why did you not just stay with me in the garden like I asked you?"

"What, cower behind a female?" he retorted with a scoff as they stopped to squabble in the street like an old married couple. "Hide behind your skirts? You've obviously mistaken me for Bryce, darling!"

"You could have been killed!" she shouted.

"I know my craft!" Connor roared back.

Maggie's posture stiffened. She folded her arms across her chest, and her chin came up a notch.

"Do not bellow at me, sir." She looked away, nose in the air. "*Humph.* If I wanted to spend the rest of my life with a bully, I might as well stay at Delia's."

Connor froze, scrutinizing her by the light of a nearby streetlamp. *Did she just threaten to call off the match?*

But he refused to let his horror at this possibility show on his face, keeping his expression cool. "What's that supposed to mean?"

She lifted a dainty finger and poked him in the chest. "*Never* do that to me again! *That* is what it means, Major."

He swallowed with relief as he held her imperious stare.

"I want your word that you won't go running off on me again like some...some sort of Celtic berserker on the loose, w-with his face painted blue!"

Connor clenched his jaw, relieved that she was not ending it here and now after what she had just witnessed. He was not sure he would have blamed her.

He really wished she had not seen that side of him.

Nevertheless, even though he knew he was pushing his luck, he refused to lie to her. "Sorry. I can't promise that. Berserkers only quit once the battle's won."

"Or when they are dead," Maggie replied crisply.

He gave her a stern look, then walked on.

"Bullheaded man," she said, following him up the street, around the corner, and back into the mews behind Aunt Lucinda's house. "So, that's it, then? You're completely unwilling to compromise? Because that is not how marriage works—you give the orders and I obey?"

"Frankly, when it comes to situations like this, yes, darling. That's exactly how it works."

"Oh, indeed?" She sounded nigh strangled with indignation now, but the lady maintained her prim façade. "Well then, Your Grace. Perhaps I need more time to consider your offer more carefully!"

With that, she whooshed ahead of him back in through the garden gate, while he grimaced behind her in the darkness.

Unfortunately for Maggie, her grand ultimatum lost much of its punch when they returned to the garden only to find that over a dozen guests had poured out to see what was the matter.

The panicked looks the moonlight revealed on their faces confirmed they'd heard the gunshot.

Connor tamped down a smug flicker of satisfaction over all these witnesses who'd come rushing out only to find the two of them alone in the dark out here together.

How scandalous.

"Sorry, love," he murmured, sending her a wicked half-smile as he pulled the garden gate shut behind him. "Looks like there won't be any backing out now. Just *think* of your reputation."

She shot him a withering glare just as Major Carvel came striding out through the trellised walkway.

"What happened? We heard gunfire!" he said.

"Aye, you did," Connor said as Maggie and he reached the fountain. "Bit of unpleasantness out here, I'm afraid."

"Were you hit?" Carvel asked.

"No, no. I'm fine."

His fellow soldier looked at her. "And Lady Margaret?"

"I'm all right," she answered with a nod.

Connor held up his hands in a calming gesture to the arriving throng of shocked guests, both men and a few women. "Don't worry, ladies and gentlemen, we are both unharmed. It was just a footpad of some sort."

"He shot at you?" Netherford asked, hurrying after Carvel, his brother-in-law.

"Aye. I gave chase—old instincts, don't you know," Connor said. "We traded a few punches, then he ran off. I let him go. After all, no harm done. Don't worry, he's gone. Everything's fine now."

"Good God!" someone murmured.

There was no point in mentioning the blood seeping from his wound. He would simply rebandage it, and perhaps a servant could run home and fetch him a fresh shirt and coat.

Only for a split second did he consider canceling the rest of the soirée, but given the battered condition in which he'd left his enemy, he felt reasonably sure the danger had passed. There was no need to make a fuss.

People trying to kill him was nothing new, after all. Aunt Lucinda had gone to a lot of trouble for his sake; everyone seemed to be having a good time—until just now, anyway—and the soirée was only scheduled to last another couple of hours.

Plenty of time for him to mentally hammer out a plan of action for dealing with Flynn and his son for once and for all.

Connor knew that, first and foremost, he wanted his womenfolk out of harm's way. And then, the moment that Maggie and his aunts were removed from the equation, stowed someplace safe, by God, he would return and rain down bloody fire and brimstone on his enemies.

They'd soon regret the day they'd ever heard the name of Amberley.

His first order of business, however, as soon as the guests were gone, would be to question Aunt Lucinda—*finally*—and make her tell him exactly what the hell all this was about.

Because, clearly, there was something even worse going on here than he'd previously guessed. He did not appreciate her leaving him to muddle his way through such treachery blind. She wasn't going to like it, but it was time for the dragon lady to cough up the truth.

Maggie sent him an uneasy look while the men who'd crowded around scanned the shadows, as though half expecting another attack.

The ladies' reaction was different, however. Their eyebrows had shot up and they began exchanging *"hmm"* looks as they realized the "footpad" had interrupted some sort of tryst between Maggie and him.

"So…the two of you were out here…together?" one gossip asked.

Maggie blanched, and Connor knew it was time to speak up, though he did not answer the question directly.

"Ahem. We have wonderful news, ladies and gentleman," he declared without warning. "She said yes!"

Maggie gasped as he captured her right hand in his unbloodied left one, raised it to his lips, then smiled at everyone with his most dazzling show of self-assurance.

Then he made his bold announcement—whether she liked it or not.

"Lady Margaret Winthrop will soon become the Fourth Duchess of Amberley!"

Gasps abounded. Huzzahs and stunned congratulations followed, though the latter were a little more tentative, given how they'd startled everyone.

No one, he gathered, was more shocked than Maggie.

Her smile looked pasted in place, and in that swift heartbeat before the guests encircled them, she whispered, "You devil."

Connor gave her a hard glance. *No getting rid of me now, love.*

He'd just saved her reputation, obviously.

Besides, she was daft if she thought he'd ever let her get away. He knew he had infuriated her with his abrupt announcement, but at least he'd made sure she no longer had the option of backing out of their match.

She was staring at him as though finally understanding just how ruthless he could be.

Connor looked away, unrepentant. An old proverb came to mind, *All's fair in love and war,* along with *He who hesitates is lost.* What was there to dither about?

He wanted her, he needed her, and indeed, his survival instincts warned that the peaceful future he craved would be meaningless without her.

So he'd done what he had to do.

Shortly thereafter, they and all the guests who had come outside returned en masse to the party to break the news to Grandaunt Lucinda.

And her list of would-be brides.

Seth barely remembered the wild gallop through the dark streets that brought him back to his father's house. It was fortunate that his horse knew the way, for, with his head reeling from Amberley's thunderous punches, it was all he could do to stay on the animal's back.

Blood coursed down his face from the cut above his eye. Several teeth had been knocked loose. Everything hurt, especially his pride.

He couldn't even think straight. It took all his concentration simply to keep his feet braced in the stirrups and hold on to his gelding's mane long enough to reach his father's doorstep.

Since it was Friday night, he knew Father would not be at home. The old cutthroat would be making the rounds at his establishments, ensuring that everything was operating smoothly.

Knowing this was the only thing that gave Seth the courage to go inside. He could not have faced him otherwise.

As he ducked his head against his shoulder to wipe the blood out of his right eye, not letting go of his horse's mane, it was hard to say which he was more frightened of: Amberley tracking him here and killing him, his father's reaction to his failure tonight, or the law catching up to him and sending him to the gallows.

Seth did not intend to let any of these disasters befall him. He had not survived the goddamned war just to come home and swing from a noose in a futile effort to satisfy his father.

No, thank you. He was giving up. Amberley had won, and Seth just didn't care anymore. He was getting the hell out of England.

As his horse clattered up to the house, he slithered off the side of the animal and landed with a wince, whispering his thanks to the beast for getting him home. He had no time to cool the horse, though, for he wasn't staying long.

On legs that shook beneath him, he tied the blowing animal up as best he could with his latest broken finger. Moving slowly, indeed, weaving on his feet, he noticed he was seeing double when he turned to face the few stairs that led up to the back door.

In and out fast. He would quickly clean himself up, get his things, and flee. He made a mental note to take more money out of his father's desk.

Seth knew where Father kept the ready blunt, and was not above stealing it. Alas, he could kiss his huge inheritance goodbye, but he could still set himself up somewhere on the Continent, where officers on half pay could live in relative ease.

His hands were shaking as he reached for the door. When he opened it and went inside, he grimaced at the light from the sconces. It was too bright; black blotches appeared across his field of vision.

He shut the door quietly behind him, and almost didn't have the nerve to glance into the mirror as he passed it in the foyer. He did not want to see the mangled mess that Amberley had made of his face this time.

Nevertheless, he caught a glimpse of himself out of the corner of his eye on his way to the staircase.

What he saw chilled him. He had been pounded into some sort of misshapen, blood-covered monster.

As self-hatred for his latest failure spurted through his veins, mingling with dread in a hellish concoction of inner turmoil and pain, Seth gripped the banister and steadied himself on it, then began to climb the stairs.

He had only gone three steps, however, when a terrifying sound reached him from above.

"Back so soon?"

He froze. Father's voice.

When Seth looked up to the top of the staircase and saw his old man standing there, feet planted wide, bald head gleaming by the lamplight, he felt his stomach drop all the way down to his feet.

He gripped harder to the railing to keep from tumbling back down the stairs under the force of his sire's withering gaze.

"You failed. Didn't you?" Father's tone was accusing, yet he did not sound surprised.

Before Seth could answer, two females came skipping out of the upstairs hallway, both scantily clad, one toying with a riding crop.

They were gorgeous creatures, the kind of girls his father reserved for the richest ton clients. They pranced over to hang on the rugged seventy-year-old, one on each still-strong shoulder.

Elias Flynn ignored them. They were merely merchandise, after all, but apparently, he hadn't felt like waiting for Seth's return by himself.

He shook his head at Seth. "You disgust me," he finally said. "Go clean yourself up. I'll handle matters henceforward."

Flynn took the riding crop from the long-legged blonde on his right. He tapped the girls on their lovely hips with it, shepherding them back toward one of the rooms. "Go put your clothes on. I have an assignment for you."

They obeyed instantly, of course. He was king around here.

"And as for you"—Flynn pointed at Seth with the riding crop—"I'm taking over. God, I should've known. If you want something done right, ye do it yourself."

"Father," Seth pleaded, "what did you want me to do? I took the shot. Someone was with him—she saw me! She pulled him out of the way."

Flynn's face turned incredulous. "A *woman* bested you?"

Seth lowered his head, hating that girl, that lady. God, he wanted to hurt her.

"That hardly speaks in your favor. Well, it's obvious the duke caught up to you." Disgusted, his father scoffed at the bloody pulp Amberley had made of Seth's face. "I thought the Army taught you how to fight."

Seth stood shaking on the stairs. He wasn't sure how many more minutes he had in him to remain upright. But he could not bring himself to admit the worst of it yet to his father—that Amberley knew about *him*, as well.

The girls returned, elegant and tall, a pair of leggy sylphs. As they quickly buttoned up their tailored pelisses and perched expensive hats atop lovely heads adorned with shiny, coiffed hair, one could not distinguish them from proper ladies.

Seth thought wistfully of Saffie. Who was nothing like them, of course. Those two could probably converse with their clients in French.

Father was as rough with them as with any others, but the girls knew he was the god deciding their futures. Under his management, they, too, might marry lords, just like ol' Lucky Lucy Bly, devil take her.

340   *Gaelen Foley*

"You two get your arses over to Moonlight Square and watch the Duke of Amberley's house for me. Now. You know the place?"

"Oh yes, yes, sir." The pair exchanged sly smiles.

"You see anything, one of you report back to me, while the other stays in place and keeps watch. I want to know if anyone comes or goes. Find out whatever you can."

"Yes, Mr. Flynn." They sketched curtsies to him and flitted off down the side corridor to slip out the front door into the night.

"As for you." Father turned and studied Seth with cold disgust. "Clean yourself up, for God's sake. You do not have my permission to black out until you tell me exactly what happened." He started to turn away, but could not seem to help himself. "You are a disgrace, you know that?"

"Oh yes, Father." Seth lowered his head. "You've made that very clear."

"Good. And as for this Amberley, watch carefully and learn, son. You want to destroy someone? Let your old man show you how it's done."

Later that night, once he'd finally got rid of the guests, Connor closed himself up in the drawing room with Aunt Lucinda and told her what he'd learned about her past and what she needn't bother hiding anymore.

Now he stared at her, waiting for her to fill in the blanks.

She had already tried a few verbal dodges, but this time, he refused to relent, and when she read it in his face that he was not letting her go without answers, she gave up the game, though she was still entirely defensive.

"Is it my fault I was born in poverty and did what I had to do to survive?" she exclaimed, her fleshy face trembling as she gripped the head of her cane. "What was I to do? I had no way of knowing Elias Flynn was so vicious until he had already trapped me in his web."

"Extortion is a crime. As a victim, you could've gone to Bow Street."

"Oh, don't be naïve!" she retorted with a scowl. "Flynn has incriminating information about half of London, including Bow Street. How do you think he gets away with so much? Besides, I'd agreed to it, and Charles could afford it."

"Did your husband know about Flynn's monthly fees?"

"Of course not. There was no need to tell him. Why make a fuss? I simply took it from the pin money he gave me every month. He was very generous with his gold to me. But fifty years was long enough to pay any blackmailer, I daresay."

"And to keep a secret from your husband?" Connor said, raising an eyebrow.

"For God's sake, man, don't delude yourself! Your granduncle was a devil. You think he married me for love? Don't make me laugh. He did it to impress his friends and horrify his parents. And he succeeded in that. But don't worry; he regretted it in due time. Just like his father said he would. Especially when we discovered I could not have children."

Connor shook off his astonishment at her blunt response, trying to stick to the topic at hand. "So, after Uncle Charles died, you told Flynn you would no longer pay?"

"Yes. It seemed reasonable to me, but that's Flynn for you. He's quite mad. How was I to know he'd send his stupid son to go push Rupert off a cliff? Rupert," she added with a snort, shaking her head as she gazed at the fireplace. "Self-righteous prig. Though not as bad as that dreadful wife of his. Caroline. Ugh, pair of Pharisees. You'd think that precious God of his would've protected him from Seth if he was as holy as he pretended to be."

Connor looked at her in amazement. She seemed to have no remorse whatsoever that her own decision had got her brother-in-law killed. "What about Cousin Richard? Did he deserve to die, too?"

She rolled her eyes. "That ponce."

"My God, I've never seen anyone so hardhearted."

She cackled. "Wait until you meet Elias."

Connor frowned at her, then pushed away from the mantel where he had been leaning and paced. "What can you tell me about him?"

"Other than he doesn't have a soul?" She sneaked a quick swig from a little silver flask, wiped her lips, and continued. "Elias Flynn is one of the most well-established criminal chiefs in London—and the most ruthless. He has dozens of men at his disposal. Spies everywhere. And all the dirt he has on the fellows in the Home Office makes him quite immune to prosecution."

"Does he have any weaknesses I can exploit?"

She lowered her head, as though searching her thoughts, then finally said, "No. Not anymore."

"What do you mean?"

She glanced about impatiently. "From what I understand, he had a certain soft spot for his younger son. That died."

"Do you know anything about this lad's death?"

"No. Nothing," she said.

"What of the elder one, then?"

"Seth. Captain Seth Darrow. The sons took their mother's surname."

"Is that even legal?"

She heaved a sigh. "How many times must I tell you? Flynn can get away with anything. He is a…a force of nature!"

"I see. So, this Seth fellow. Tell me more about him."

She shook her head, lowering her gaze. "Flynn forced me to use my influence to get him into the dragoons. 'Twas easy. Considering I used to bed the young officers who are now the old generals."

"Oh God," Connor said under his breath, wincing at this revelation. For a moment, he wondered if that could be why he'd been given such great leeway in the Army and selected for just the sorts of assignments he liked.

All this time, he thought sardonically, could it have been not so much due to his own prowess or his fine military heritage, but because the old goats knew who his grandaunt was?

Was it possible the brass still got giddy over Lucky Lucy Bly, the way Gable's father had? Connor rather wanted to bang his head against the wall at that thought.

"Please tell me you never knew Wellington."

She chortled. "Oh, please, he's half my age."

Thank God.

Putting Her Grace's scandalous past aside, Connor weighed what she'd told him with a chill down his spine. He was glad to have some answers, at last, but this information merely steeled his resolve to remove the ladies from Town as quickly as possible—both of his aunts as well as Maggie. Only males in his family had been harmed so far, but if it came down to it, he would not put it past Flynn and his son to hurt the ladies.

Especially after the way they'd made their fortune.

Connor studied his aunt with lingering suspicion. Because, for the life of him, something here still didn't seem to add up. "So, Elias Flynn has done all this to our family—sent his soldier son to kill Uncle Rupert and Cousin Richard—simply because you stopped paying his extortion fees after your husband died? Because that certainly seems excessive."

She shrugged. "That's how he is," she replied, then pursed her lips. "He had to make an example of me. He blackmails all the girls he marries off to rich men. He can't have them all refusing to pay like I did. He had to crucify me."

Connor considered this for a long moment in silence, still unsatisfied.

"Aunt Lucinda?" he prompted gently as he sauntered closer. "What are you not telling me?"

"I've told you everything!" She looked offended, but it was hard to tell if she was being genuine.

"But to kill two innocent men over a bit of money—"

"Killing means little to him, while money means a great deal."

"Then why didn't you warn Rupert and his son of the danger they were in?"

She faltered. "I really didn't think he'd go that far. But, apparently, arrangements like mine are too lucrative a source of income for him to let his married girls begin balking about the payments after he'd set them up in life. That is why, as I said, he had to make an example of me, since they all know I'm the strongest. He had to show the others what would happen if they tried it." Then he saw her bulldog jowls tremble. "He thinks he can break me, but he can't. I won't let him."

Just for a moment, Connor thought he caught a glimpse of the fiery beauty she'd once been. But the strangest thought occurred to him; he got the feeling that maybe it wasn't Lucy Bly's looks that had made her stand out, but her indomitable spirit.

The very trait that made her so damned impossible now.

"I see," he said at last. "So all this is just business, then? Begging your pardon, aunt, but I'm still having trouble believin' that."

"Oh, very well!" she said with a huff. "If you must know, Elias and I were...involved."

Connor's eyebrows shot up.

Aunt Lucinda nearly smiled, staring into the fireplace. "He said I was the only one who ever got under his skin."

To go to such lengths for a bit of money did not quite ring true to Connor's ears, but if Flynn's love had turned to hate for Lucinda somewhere along the way, at least that made sense.

"Ah well," she said, staring into the unlit fireplace. "Whatever it was that Elias thought he felt for me, all I know is that he did not object when I got the offer from the young marquess, who soon became the First Duke

344   *Gaelen Foley*

of Amberley."

She looked cynically at Connor. "He sold me to the highest bidder: your granduncle. And from that moment on, Elias Flynn was dead to me. Oh, I paid his fees faithfully, of course. I did the favors he insisted on, regarding his sons' places in Society. But I sure as blazes never let the blackguard touch me again."

Connor gazed at her.

"The fool actually thought I would keep him for a lover once I became a duchess." A bitter laugh escaped her. "Instead, I told him after the wedding that I wanted nothing more to do with him. Oh, he didn't like that much, I assure you. He had the nerve to claim that I had used him. But what," she whispered, "does that *devil* know about being used?"

"I am sorry, Aunt Lucinda. Truly. For everything you've been through."

She looked up at him with a sea of unshed tears in her eyes. "Kill him if you can, Amberley Number Four. Put a bullet in his black heart, and Lucy Bly will dance a jig on his grave."

CHAPTER 27

Leaving Town

The delicate, rosy light of early morning illumined Maggie's bedchamber as she finished folding up her favorite dressing gown, which she had taken off less than half an hour ago. Hectic with the knowledge that Connor's traveling chariot was already waiting outside to whisk them away to some remote country house, she squashed the bulky garment down as small as it would go into her brown leather traveling trunk.

Meanwhile, Penelope, mid-task, lingered at the window in distraction near Maggie's dressing table, gazing down onto the street where Sergeant McFeatheridge lounged atop the driver's box.

"If you can drag yourself away from the view, my dear, I think I need you to sit on this thing if we're ever going to close it," Maggie said. "I'll do the latches."

Penelope turned with a startled glance, then hurried over to help. "You sit, my lady, I'll latch. Just admiring the scenery, even though our journey hasn't even started yet."

Maggie chuckled and sat atop her traveling trunk. "You like him, do you?"

"He has a nice smile. And a very jolly laugh."

Snap went the first latch.

"Although," her maid added, "Major Carvel is certainly handsome, too. Not much of a smiler that one, of course."

"No," Maggie said. "Fortunately for us, he does seem very capable, though. It's good of him to help us."

Penelope snapped the second brass latch shut and nodded.

Last night, after the other guests had left the soirée, Connor had put Major Carvel in charge of the small group of handpicked men tasked with transferring Maggie from the dragon lady's house back to Moonlight Square, while he had remained there to interrogate his aunt in private.

Instead of being taken back to Edward and Delia's, however, Maggie had been escorted to Rivenwood House, one of the large ducal mansions on the four corners of Moonlight Square—in this case, the neo-gothic home of her friends Serena and Azrael.

Apparently, Connor deemed Azrael a fierce enough fellow to be entrusted with protecting Maggie, while he saw to the safety of his aunts, questioned the dowager duchess, and made his preparations for today's journey.

It had been awkward, to say the least, arriving on her neighbors' doorstep in the company of armed men, with no idea of how to begin to explain. She remembered what Trinny had told her about the couple leaving in a huff after Grandaunt Lucinda had been so rude to them.

Curiously enough, the Rivenwoods had taken Maggie's unannounced arrival in their stride. It didn't take long for Maggie to realize they'd had their own violent encounters with unpleasant people in the past.

Apparently, Connor had found out—most likely at the Grand Albion's gentlemen's club—that the pale-haired duke had a deadlier side than Maggie had ever suspected.

At least she'd be safer there than at Edward's—and she certainly couldn't stay all night at Amberley House. Not until they were married.

Which, it seemed, was going to happen whether she liked it or not.

In any case, along with Major Carvel, Azrael and Serena could not have been better about the whole debacle. And now that Connor had mentioned it, Maggie could see what he meant about the silver-eyed duke.

Cool and quiet, Azrael was a mysterious man with the deadly elegance of a fine sword forged by a master smith. While he and Carvel gave low-toned instructions to the men, the unflappable Serena had taken charge of Maggie, who was still bewildered by it all, gaily welcoming her into the house, and adopting a blithe attitude to cheer her up, as if it were all a lark.

"Come!" Serena had said. Carrying Azrael's ridiculous little white dog under her arm, she had beckoned Maggie into the library on the first floor and shown her that, in fact, Rivenwood House was full of secret passageways.

"This way, if danger should come," Serena had said in a reasonable tone, as though attacks on one's life were de rigeur, "there are always escape routes."

All of which made Azrael himself even more intriguing as a neighbor, Maggie thought, but one did not dare ask questions about all this, or the master of the house. She had heard the occult rumors about his ancestors, after all, the ones that had apparently bothered Aunt Lucinda. Who hadn't?

While Serena had entertained Maggie, and various men discreetly guarded the house, Edward had been ordered to take Delia home from the soirée.

By Connor, of course.

Once the crisis had struck, he had not shown the slightest hesitation about giving orders to everyone in sight, just like he'd done to Maggie. Indeed, it was fortunate that the Duke of Wellington had not stayed, or Amberley probably would've been giving him orders, too.

At least the mighty major seemed to know what he was doing.

Still, Maggie's head was spinning from all that had happened last night.

"Do you think all this fuss is really necessary?" she asked her maid out of the blue as Penelope finished packing Maggie's smaller bag of toiletries and hair ornaments. "I don't see the point."

Penelope gave her a bolstering look and shrugged. "I'm just doing as I'm told."

"Hmm," Maggie said archly. "I think *you're* looking forward to getting to know Sergeant McFeatheridge better on the way to Dorset. I'm on to you, miss."

"Pshaw!" Penelope said coyly. "I've never been that far west, is all."

"Neither have I."

Connor had told Maggie last night that today's journey of nearly a hundred miles would entail ten to fifteen hours of nonstop travel, depending on the weather. It sounded utterly grueling.

Frankly, she couldn't believe he was making them do the trip in one day—especially the two old ladies—but apparently, he was unimpressed by the distance, being used to forced marches this way and that across the Continent.

For the rest of them, it was going to be a long, arduous day until their convoy rolled into the gates of Dartfield Manor around sunset, but he considered time of the essence, so they'd have to make the best of it.

And change carriage horses often along the way.

Maggie checked her wardrobe one last time to make sure she hadn't forgotten anything important. She felt ready, more or less, yet she couldn't help but sigh.

After all her disappointments on the marriage mart, it irked her immensely that just when the world found out she had snared herself a duke—which would have been a moment of triumph for any young lady—now that it was safe to bask in the ton's amazement at her brilliant match, here she was, being whisked away to the dull, dreary countryside.

So much for gloating, she thought with amusement.

To say nothing of the fact that, at the moment, she still wanted to wring her duke's neck. The autocrat.

"I'm sure it'll be very pretty in Dorset. The moors in that country are said to be very dramatic, and the sky," Penelope said, breaking into Maggie's thoughts. "It's not far from the sea, I understand. I wonder if the house is on the coast?"

Maggie shrugged. For her part, she was absolutely dreading the long, dragging journey closed up in the coach with the dragon lady.

Especially after her outburst at the woman last night.

Ah well. She had no intention of apologizing, as much as it went against the grain with her to let the matter lie. As Connor had said, Grandaunt Lucinda would lose all respect for Maggie if she yielded ground now.

And besides, the truth was, she wasn't really sorry. Nobody talked to her sister that way. The dragon lady ought to be the one apologizing.

No doubt, however, Her Grace would be unpleasant to her the whole way there.

Thank God that Aunt Florence would also be in the carriage. And Penelope. Both of them were pleasant-tempered enough to smooth away at least *some* of the tension that was sure to make the drive all the more nerve-racking—even without the threat of a murderer after them.

"Well, I believe that's everything, my lady. Are you ready to go?" Penelope turned to her.

Maggie glanced around her bedchamber. "I think so... Did you bring my velvet bonnet?"

Penelope nodded and pointed at the hatbox. "It's in there."

"Good. And you have all your own things?"

She nodded. "My bag is packed. I just need to fetch it from my room."

"You may go, then."

Penelope bobbed a curtsy, then bustled to the door. "I'll send a footman to carry these out for you on my way."

Maggie smiled with gratitude. Penelope was more loyal to her than she had to be, and she truly appreciated that.

She had given her trusty maid the chance to decline making the trip, but Penelope had refused to send her off alone.

Admittedly, Maggie suspected that her maid's enthusiasm for the journey might have a slight something to do with the brawny, roguish soldier sitting on the driver's box of Connor's traveling chariot. But Penelope was right. Rory McFeatheridge did have a warm, ready smile — and better still, he seemed equally admiring of her.

I guess it's time to go. Maggie took one last glance at herself in the mirror. She had donned a dark blue traveling costume for their all-day trek. It was well-tailored, of sturdy, practical material, with a pelisse she could remove if the coach grew stuffy. Her comfy kid half-boots were warm and suitable for taking short walks to stretch her limbs when it was time to change horses along the road.

She'd heard Connor tell Delia and Edward to pass along the story to the ton that, out of respect, he was taking her to meet Grandaunt Caroline, the Second Duchess, in the country before the wedding.

Caroline was Duke Rupert's widow, and the mother of dead Cousin Richard.

Now that the public knew about their heretofore secret betrothal, it was finally sinking into Maggie's own mind as a reality that she, Maggie Winthrop, would become the Fourth Duchess of Amberley.

Such a grand title for such an unimposing person! She supposed she hadn't quite let herself believe it till now. Gazing at her subdued reflection, she wondered if she looked the part of a future duchess. She didn't feel any different.

Of course, now that their match was out in the open, Society had already begun to view *her* differently, to be sure. She shook her head, still embarrassed about how the other guests had discovered her outside alone with Connor last night, with only a crazed gunman for a chaperone.

That alone should have caused a scandal, but far worse was her outburst in the drawing room. She still cringed to think of how she'd called the First Duchess an ogress to her face.

Ah well, it was pointless to worry about strangers' opinions of her, or other such tempests in teapots, when their lives were at stake.

Honestly, though, Maggie had no doubt that once they left London, they'd be quite safe at this country house.

She really wasn't too worried about this dragoon, despite his escape. Not after what she'd seen last night, the way Connor had thrashed him so handily.

This sneaky jackal did not stand a chance against her lion of a fiancé. No, what preoccupied her most right now was Connor himself.

He was a problem.

And she really did not know what she was going to do about it.

She was glad he was safe—that was the main thing, of course.

But their argument and his complete lack of remorse for either the savagery he'd unleashed or the hard way he'd spoken to her afterward left her at a loss. She was still a bit in shock at what she'd witnessed.

To be sure, it was better that Connor should be the one doling out the violence rather than receiving it, but she struggled to make peace with the knowledge of what the man she loved was capable of. On top of that, he could be so blasted domineering!

She never would've dreamed he'd bark orders at her like she was some new recruit in his regiment who needed whipping into shape. An uncomfortable thought went through her mind: *I honestly did not know what I was getting into here.*

True, it had been an emergency situation. She'd give him that. If he had to go into blue war-paint Celtic-berserker mode when it came to matters of life and death, then fine. She could accept that.

As a temporary state of things.

But could he ever truly turn it off? He'd been one of the lucky ones who'd come home alive with all his arms and legs, but what in God's name had that war done to him...on the inside?

Uncertainty entwined with worry for him sent a chill down her spine.

Maggie knew she had to try to address it with him somehow, but she had no idea what to say—or if she even dared, especially now. Who would want to make *him* angry? She knew he'd never hurt her, but still.

Standing up to Delia was one thing, defying the dragon was another, but trying to rein in that wild warrior? Success seemed extremely unlikely.

Yet if she failed, then she faced a lifetime ahead of being ordered around, having her wishes trampled underfoot by a will far stronger than her sister's.

A flash of anger sparked through her at the thought, and Maggie knitted her brow. Blast it, she was not backing down!

Not to him. Maybe not to anyone ever again.

And if the major didn't like it, then he only had himself to blame, for he was the one who had encouraged her—how many times?—to start standing up for herself.

Well, by Jove, that was exactly what she meant to do now. She was a lady of gentle birth, and no one was entitled to speak to her that way.

Not even a war-hero duke.

With that, unsure but still determined, she squared her shoulders and marched out of her chamber, ready as she'd ever be for their duel of wills, if it came to that.

She passed a footman on his way to fetch her bags when she stepped out into the upstairs hallway. Already she could hear Connor's deep voice floating up to her from the drawing room, where he was speaking with Edward.

Her heart beat faster, but she kept her chin high, her face impassive as she started marching down the stairs, sliding a gloved hand along the banister.

To her surprise, though, before she reached the bottom, her sister stepped out of the music room below and held up a hand to halt her.

Startled, Maggie paused halfway down the steps, gazing down at her sibling. Her haughty sister wore an almost chastened look on her face. Nevertheless, out of mere habit, Maggie braced herself as Delia lifted the hem of her skirts and climbed a few of the stairs to meet her halfway.

"Mags, I wanted to talk to you before you go," Delia said in a low tone.

"Yes?" Maggie held her breath, desperately hoping that her sister was finally ready to make peace. Their fight had been going on for days now, and she did not want to leave Town still at war with her sister, when the truth was, there was a slim chance she might never come back alive.

Not if the murderer managed to follow them.

"I..." Delia began, instantly faltering.

Maggie waited, on her guard.

"I heard you stood up for me last night," Delia said, toying with the banister, "and I...I just wanted to say thank you. I sort of know I didn't really deserve it."

No, you didn't.

"Look—I realize we haven't been getting along for the past couple of weeks. But I don't want to part on bad terms."

"Neither do I," Maggie said cautiously.

Delia studied her with a strange look in her emerald eyes, as though she were seeing her for the very first time. "I can't believe you defended me against that dreadful old hag."

"Don't be silly. You are my sister. Papa told us to look out for each other, did he not? You've done your part, letting me live here." Maggie shrugged. "I had to do mine."

Moisture sprang into Delia's eyes as she held Maggie's gaze. "You're very good."

Usually, she said that sort of thing as an insult, but this time, she sounded sincere. Delia looked away with a quick sniffle. "I fear I haven't been easy to live with of late."

Maggie's lips quirked. "Never were, as I recall."

Delia shrugged haphazardly, still avoiding her gaze. "I don't know why I get so moody. I...I haven't been myself, quite, lately. But I acknowledge, selfishness is, um, a fault."

Intrigued by this rare offer of the olive branch, Maggie opted to be gracious. "We all have our faults." She paused. "At least I'll be out from underfoot here, once I marry Amberley."

Delia bit her lip. "I think I'll actually miss you." She quickly looked away, trying to wipe off a tear that had gathered on the outer edge of her eye. "The truth is, I'd be lost if anything happened to you, Mags, so you'd better stay safe."

"Oh, don't worry—with Amberley, I'm in no danger, I assure you." She pursed her lips in an attempt at a smile. "I'll be back before you know it."

"Well, when you return, I'll help plan your wedding." Delia swallowed, taking a businesslike tone. "We'll make it even finer than whatever that tedious Portia Tennesley is concocting."

Maggie gave her a dubious half-smile, recalling how Portia had stood up to Delia in Hyde Park. "Only if you promise you won't try to take over the whole thing."

"I will try," Delia said solemnly, and they both started laughing in spite of themselves.

To Maggie's astonishment, Delia suddenly reached out and hugged her.

Balanced on the stairs, Maggie hugged her back, closing her eyes. A lump rose in her throat.

"Take good care of yourself, sis," Delia whispered.

"I will. Try not to worry. You and Edward do the same—and take care of each other." Maggie pulled back slightly, still holding on to Delia's arms. "Go easy on him, would you? He's such a good man and he truly loves you."

"God knows why," Delia said softly, lowering her gaze. "I can't imagine what he sees in me. What's wrong with him? Can't he see I'm just some 'haughty little marchioness that everybody hates'?"

"Now, now," Maggie chided gently, taking her sister's hand as she recognized the dragon lady's words from last night. "That is not true. Your friends are very loyal to you, as am I. But our affection for you pales in comparison to Edward's. He doesn't just love you, he is *in love* with you, you know."

Delia bit her lip and stared at Maggie.

"What?" Maggie murmured, hating to ask. "Is there someone else?"

"No, no. Nothing like that. It's just—I hate all those drippy, tedious emotions! It's embarrassing. It's not the done thing!"

"Oh, I don't know about that," Maggie said with a laugh. "All sorts of passions seem to be entirely in fashion around here. Haven't you noticed our neighbors?"

"Easy for you to say," Delia retorted. "You don't seem to care in the slightest what anyone thinks. You called the Duchess of Amberley an ogress in front of a packed drawing room."

"Yes, I did," Maggie declared. Then she stepped down with a grin and slung an arm around Delia's shoulders. "And, oh, sister," she added, "you should've seen the look on her face."

They were still laughing—and trying to stifle the sound of it—when Edward appeared in the doorway of the drawing room below.

"Ah, Maggie, my dear, there you are."

"Good morning," she replied with a smile.

Edward's curious glance darted from her to Delia and back again as the two of them walked the rest of the way down the steps. "The duke is here," he informed her. "Amberley would like to speak to you. Alone."

Delia sent Maggie a sidelong look and raised her eyebrows.

Edward stepped aside, gesturing Maggie into the drawing room with a taut smile. The puffiness around his eyes hinted that the marquess had not slept well last night after seeing danger strike so close to home.

As Maggie went toward him, she was a little surprised that her brother-in-law did not mind her going unchaperoned into the drawing room with Connor, but she supposed he must have his reasons. Then Edward withdrew and pulled the door shut quietly behind him.

Suddenly feeling uncertain, Maggie looked across the elegant, pale blue room at her fiancé. Connor gave her a tense bow.

My, that's a formal greeting. If that was the tone he wished to set this morning, very well. She sketched a stilted curtsy in return.

He cleared his throat.

Once more, he had donned his uniform, though it was a less formal one. The ivory breeches and black boots were identical, but the scarlet coat looked more worn, less ornamented, for every day. Probably the clothes he usually wore when people were trying to kill him...

The thought sent a tingle of fear down her nerve endings, but she lifted her chin and waited, schooling her face into an expectant expression to hear what he had to say.

He started simply. "Good morning."

"Good morning to you."

"Are you ready to leave?"

"Yes. I just need to fetch my reticule and a book for the journey. Why? Was there something you wanted, Your Grace?"

A moment to grovel, perhaps?

"Er, ahem, yes." He stepped closer. "I brought you this."

He was clutching something in his fist, and as he approached, he seemed to hesitate ever so slightly. She wasn't sure why, but when he stood before her, she could sense an extraordinary nervousness coursing through his broad-shouldered frame.

"Are you well?" she asked, puzzled.

"Yes. Yes, of course," he said, nodding awkwardly and avoiding her gaze. He cleared his throat.

"Well, what's the matter, then?"

He sighed, as though casting off whatever thought had been in his mind, and held out his hand, opening his fist. "Here."

She looked down at his white-gloved palm and saw a ring with a diamond of astonishing size, surrounded by glistening emeralds.

"This is for you. It may not fit you perfectly yet, but it can be fixed, and I-I think it best if you put it on now for propriety's sake." Though his head was down, his black hair still damp from his morning ablutions, his glance flicked up to meet hers.

His cobalt eyes were sincere, and by the morning's light, Maggie could just make out a faint bruise on his cheekbone. His left eye was slightly blackened.

She blinked in astonishment, then stared again at the ring, and pointed at it. "That's for me?"

"Aye." He lifted the jewel up between his fingers, presenting it to her when she made no move to take it herself. "It certainly isn't for anyone else."

"Oh…" she said faintly.

"You did agree to marry me," he reminded her.

"Of course. Yes, yes." She gulped. "It's not as though I have forgotten."

"Well, that's a relief," he muttered.

Maggie's heart, admittedly, had begun pounding from the moment she had laid eyes on him this morning. All the restless energy in him seemed to be seething with pointed intensity.

But his touch was gentle as he took hold of her left hand and slid the ring onto her third finger over her glove. "There."

She looked at it on her hand, amazed. "It seems to fit rather well over my glove." She tilted her head back to meet his gaze as he loomed over her. "I don't think I'll lose it."

"Please don't." The worried look in his blue eyes seemed to say, *That thing cost me a bloody fortune.*

She pressed her lips together to hide her smile. "Don't worry, I'll keep it safe."

She paused as he frowned, looking a bit confused.

"It's nice," she added just a bit begrudgingly, because if this stubborn man thought that he could bribe his way back into her good graces with a large and expensive engagement ring, he was mistaken.

Of course, the jewelry didn't hurt. But it could not take the place of him admitting that he had been beastly to her.

"You're sure you like it?" he asked.

"I do."

"Well, er, good." He gave a crisp nod and prowled off away from her. "You keep the ring safe, and I'll keep you safe. Which is why I

356   *Gaelen Foley*

wanted to speak to you alone before we set out. I just wanted to go over the details of our plan today."

"Oh, yes, right." She nodded, bemused at his all-business attitude, but could not resist letting her gaze travel rather hungrily over his muscular physique as he paced across the drawing room in commander mode.

"To review: our destination is Dartfield Manor in Dorset. It is a journey of about a hundred miles, but if we press on all day, we'll get there by nightfall. I chose it because it is easily defensible out there on the moors, with broad, empty approaches, and it is my primary duty to keep all of you…womenfolk safe."

Let's hope your aunts' old bones survive it, she thought.

"I, ah, hope I can count on you to be civil to Aunt Lucinda during the journey."

"Always," she said crisply, matching his no-nonsense tone.

"Thank you," he said. "I cannot promise the same from her, but I did speak to her about behaving herself."

Hmm, Maggie thought.

"Continuing: Dartfield Manor is also the home of Aunt Caroline, Second Duchess of Amberley, and her two young daughters. They've stayed away from Town due to their mourning."

"Understandably so," Maggie murmured. "The poor woman. Both her husband and her son murdered…"

"Which she does not yet realize," he pointed out. "Aunt Caroline is still under the impression that both their deaths were accidents."

Maggie studied him. "Are you going to tell her?"

"Not immediately, but once we're settled, yes. I'm afraid I have to. I am not looking forward to it, to be sure." He pivoted and marched slowly past the empty fireplace, but as he passed the window, the sunlight gleamed on his gold epaulets. "Dartfield Manor is also the place where Uncle Rupert fell from the cliff. While we're there, I mean to hunt around for any clues I might find. Things I might've overlooked on my one— brief—prior visit there, since I did not yet know the truth then. That it was foul play."

Maggie furrowed her brow. "But if that's where Rupert was killed, doesn't that mean that the dragoon may be familiar with the property?"

Connor nodded. "Yes, that likely is true. He most likely was stalking my uncle for a while before he made his move. Just as I'm sure he's been stalking me ever since I stepped off the bloody boat."

He shrugged. "That is the one part of this plan that I do not much care for, but I have no choice. Without knowing the full scope of the threat, I dare not leave Aunt Caroline and the girls out there unprotected. Our friend has now failed three times to kill me. He cannot be happy about that."

"Maybe he'll give up."

"Have you ever met a dragoon?" he asked wryly.

One corner of her mouth lifted, then she leaned against the cushioned arm of the sofa and folded her arms across her chest, listening attentively.

"No, he'll redouble his efforts now. Which is why I want all you ladies out of the way before I go to war with him properly. My men will protect you once I've seen you settled in at Dartfield Manor. I've summoned ten of the best fighters from my regiment. It may take them a couple of days to get there, but they'll come. When they arrive, I'll return to Town and put an end to this for good."

Maggie lowered her head, disturbed. Again, all he spoke of was killing...

But it seemed that Connor mistook her silence for fear about the situation.

"I wish I'd never dragged you into this," he said in a heartfelt tone, taking a step toward her.

She looked up in surprise. "I don't regret it."

He stared at her. "Even after last night?"

She nearly answered the question with a ready *"Of course not,"* but she suddenly caught herself being too quick to smooth away the trouble, as usual.

Just in the nick of time, she remembered her newfound resolve. He had not apologized for barking at her yet. So she merely lifted her chin and, instead of giving him the soothing answer he expected, waited for *him* to continue.

He narrowed his eyes, scanning her face. Then he quirked an ebony brow, surprised at her cool manner, turned away, and, rather stiffly, continued his report. "Ahem. Well, then. Moving on."

She clenched her jaw in frustration at his recalcitrance. *Surely he knows how rude he was to me.*

"About our 'footpad' of last evening," he said. "Saffie's dragoon."

Irked as she was at him, Maggie remembered something important. "Connor, in all the excitement last night after we returned to the party, I never got the chance to tell you that was the same man who offered me a ride home in the rain."

His square jaw tightened. "I assumed so."

"Do you know who he is?"

He looked relieved to have another topic to discuss other than the tension between them. "Yes, now I do. He goes by the name of Seth Darrow—Captain Seth Darrow—though he is the son of a man called Elias Flynn."

"And who's that?"

Connor hesitated. "I probably should've told you this earlier, but I was afraid it might change your view of my family sufficiently to make you refuse our alliance."

"Good God, what is it?"

A taut expression crept across his hard, sun-bronzed face. "It seems that Grandaunt Lucinda originated as the First Duke's mistress. She was, er"—he winced—"a notorious woman of the demimonde, I'm afraid."

"What?" Maggie's jaw fell open. "Are you jesting?"

"No. And Elias Flynn was the man in charge of, shall we say, hiring out her services to his titled, wealthy clients."

Maggie stared at him in astonishment, then lowered her voice to ask, "The dragon lady was a *harlot?*"

"Hard to believe, I know, but yes." He grimaced. "I spoke to her last night about all of it. Indeed, I grilled her after the guests left. She finally admitted that her former, er, pimp—forgive the word—has been blackmailing her ever since she married Granduncle Charles."

"Good Lord," Maggie murmured, wide-eyed.

"There was a monthly allotment that had to be paid as Flynn's recompense for setting her up as a top courtesan and helping her to land a wealthy husband."

Maggie shook her head in disbelief.

"For fifty years, Aunt Lucinda dropped off the money every month, as ordered. But after Uncle Charles died, she no longer wished to pay. And it is there that our current difficulty started."

Shocked, Maggie slumped her shoulders where she leaned on the scrolled arm of the sofa.

"I had no idea about all this," Connor informed her. "My grandfather in Ireland never discussed all the old family secrets he had left behind, and Aunt Lucinda was certainly not inclined to tell me when I arrived here. She was exceedingly unhappy that I had learned of her past, the mule-headed woman. Must've taken her decades to live it down, and then finally Society let it go or forgot about it. The last thing she wanted was having it brought to light again."

"How *did* you find out?"

"Lord Sefton told me. Gable's father."

"You've known that long, and you didn't tell me?" she asked indignantly, irked anew. "I was supposed to be helping you!"

"And I had determined to keep you away from the danger, remember? I wish I'd kept you out of it entirely, because look what it's led to." He gestured angrily toward the waiting carriage outside. "Now the bastard knows where you live."

"Oh, I'm not afraid of him," she said with a dismissive wave of her hand.

Her words made him smile curiously, but she was not about to compliment him outright on his fighting prowess when that very skill was part of what had come between them. She didn't dare give him the impression that she was in favor of him going around thrashing whomever he pleased.

"Well," he continued, "according to Lord Sefton, fifty years ago, our dear dragon lady was quite the scarlet woman, stealing hearts all over town. Believe it or not."

Maggie pressed her lips together, holding back a smile. "It is…difficult to imagine."

Connor's blue eyes danced with mirth, but he attempted a stern look. "Do not laugh in her face—that is all I ask of you."

"You know I never would. She has long since changed her ways, obviously."

"Just so. And let he who is without sin cast the first stone. Which certainly isn't me," he mumbled.

Maggie's ears perked up. Was this the beginning of an apology?

But no. Apparently, mulishness ran in the family, for he stuck to the topic at hand. "I am not making excuses for the way the woman treats people, mind you," he said. "But I thought if you knew a little about her past life, it might help to explain her behavior last night, and perhaps make your time in the carriage with her today more bearable. We can hire a hack horse for you at one of the livery stables along the way if you wish to escape the coach for a leg of the journey. Or," he added, eyeing her, "you could share a horse with me."

Riding double with him across the moors sounded terribly romantic, she had to admit. But the rogue was not getting off the hook that easily. "We'll see."

He furrowed his brow and looked away with a silent oath on his lips. He probably hoped she had not seen it. Had he forgotten how stubborn she could be? He need only ask Delia.

"Thank you for explaining about your aunt," Maggie told him in a lofty tone. "It does add context. Which will help me in finding patience with her. In fact, she sounds much like my sister. Relying on her rank to put others in their place before they can do the same to her."

A brooding look had come over Connor's face as he studied the carpet. "I suppose it's just her manner of establishing her dominance in a situation. Maintaining control."

Maggie arched a brow, unsure if they were still talking about his aunt, or if, perhaps, they'd drifted on to the major's talent for establishing his dominance, but she let the question go.

If he wanted her forgiveness, he was going to have to do better than dropping subtle hints. *By God, I will civilize him yet.*

With that, she left her perch on the sofa's arm and glanced again at the giant ring he'd given her: proof of her full right to his respect.

"Well," she said in a cool tone, "whatever Lucinda's excuses, I am not sorry that I stood up to the bully. Those who shove others should expect to be shoved back at some point. Don't you agree, Your Grace?"

His gaze flicked up to meet hers, and he frowned warily. His Grace deigned not to answer, however, battened down in his male pride.

Let him suffer, then, Maggie concluded. He'd get the message eventually.

He would get nowhere with her until he said he was sorry.

"Shall we get underway?" she inquired, already drifting toward the drawing room door. "Or was there something else you wished to say?"

She glanced over her shoulder, and when she saw him grit his teeth again, was slightly amused at his obstinacy. The intensity was back in his blazing blue eyes, but it mingled now with real puzzlement at Maggie's continued refusal to play her former role of appeaser.

Indeed, he did not seem to know what to make of the new Maggie, whom he himself had helped to shape.

"That is all," he answered uncertainly.

She forced a bland smile past her irritation with him. "Very well."

Without waiting for him to dismiss her—she was no servant, no soldier under his command—she let herself out of the drawing room and went nonchalantly down the stairs to the entrance hall, glad about her small victory.

He hadn't apologized yet, but she was quite sure now that he got the message.

They made their last-minute preparations, and Connor walked out as well, still eyeing her curiously as he crossed the entrance hall and went back outside.

This day-long journey in the coach had just become a good deal more interesting, Maggie thought. What he had told her about his aunt had been most enlightening, and of course Maggie would never use the information against the old woman.

She could only imagine what torments the haughty ladies of the ton must have put the First Duchess through in her day. Maggie wouldn't dream of repeating that behavior. No doubt they'd been judgmental and cruel.

Still, as she looked around at their three-vehicle convoy of traveling chariot, servant coach, and baggage wagon, surrounded by several outriders, including Major Carvel, Maggie's heart sank.

It was going to be a *long* ride to Dorset.

Soon, she said her goodbyes to Edward and Delia.

"Stay safe, my dear," Edward said, hugging her. "We love you."

"I love you too." She gave his portly waist a squeeze, then accepted Delia's embrace.

"Try not to go mad," her sister murmured, glancing toward the carriage. "You want my advice? Tie the old harpy to the carriage roof with all the luggage if she gets nasty again."

Maggie laughed. "At least I'll have proper chaperonage, eh?"

Delia chuckled, then the two sisters parted.

As Maggie turned toward the carriage, where Connor waited by the open door to hand her up, she noticed Penelope's look of wonder at Delia's change of attitude.

Indeed, Maggie *was* feeling a bit like a miracle worker today. But as Penelope handed Maggie her reticule and novel for the journey, she just hoped that her newfound powers would work on the fire-breathing duchess and her iron-willed nephew as well as they'd worked on her domineering sister.

As she headed toward the luxurious traveling chariot, the birdlike Aunt Florence poked her head out the door with an eager smile and waved.

"Yoo-hoo! Good morning, everyone! Good day, Lord and Lady Birdwell! Don't worry, we shall take good care of her!"

"Thank you, Lady Walstead!" Edward replied, waving back as he put his arm around Delia.

Maggie was quite pleased to see her sister slip her arm around Edward's waist. She noticed Sergeant McFeatheridge tip his hat to Penelope, then Connor handed Maggie up into the coach.

There was no help for it; his brief touch still made her blood zing.

Then she had to slide across the seat to make room for Penelope—which put Maggie directly across from the duchess.

"I suppose you think you're very clever," Aunt Lucinda said with a glare when she saw the ring on Maggie's finger.

She just smiled. "Shiny, isn't it?"

Penelope whipped her face to the side, pretending to look out the window as she stifled laughter, while Aunt Florence ducked behind her lady's magazine, doing the same.

"Humph," said Aunt Lucinda, but Maggie thought that she detected a slight undertone of begrudging respect in that one gruff syllable.

Then Connor, astride his silver stallion, gave the order, and their well-armed convoy rolled into motion...

Leaving Moonlight Square.

CHAPTER 28

On the Road

"Nice! Nice, she says." Connor huffed as he sat on the driver's box beside Rory. "That thing cost more than most people's houses, and she calls it nice."

"What did you want her to say?"

"Very nice, at least!" he exclaimed.

Rory chortled and shook his head as they rolled along atop the traveling chariot at the head of their convoy.

"I don't know what the hell that girl wants from me," Connor grumbled to no one in particular. He kept his voice down, but he could hear the women playing some sort of traveling game to while away the time a few hours into their journey.

Everyone had relaxed a bit as soon as they had cleared the sprawling perimeter of Town. With every mile they put between themselves and the city, Connor felt the dark underworld shadow of Elias Flynn fading behind them.

As the sense of danger receded, he could finally allow his thoughts to return to his vexing little fiancée.

He rested his elbows on his bent knees as he stared down the westward road in discontent. Knowing he wasn't very good company today, he wondered if he should keep to himself. Maybe rent a hack horse at the next coaching inn, since he had sent Hurricane back with the head groom once they had reached the edge of London.

That weathered fellow was among the handful of servants old Trumbull had already tracked down for Connor and sent back to work at Amberley House. The butler himself would soon resume control of the household, but for now, he was still tasked with keeping Saffie hidden away for her own safety.

Someone had to do it, God knew. The little henwit was a danger to herself, but then, thought Connor, weren't they all?

Women.

At length, he blew out a sigh and shook his head. "I don't think she liked it."

Rory glanced at him in surprise. "What, the ring? Are you still on about that?"

Connor scowled, and Rory quickly hid his amusement.

"Of course she did, mate. What woman doesn't like a diamond ring?" Rory sighed. "Wish I could afford one."

"Maybe I should've asked her first what kind of ring she wanted. There wasn't time!" he insisted.

"Not with somebody trying to blow your head off, there wasn't." Rory nudged him, a merry glint in his eyes that made Connor suspect his friend was only humoring him. "She's lucky she got a ring at all, eh?"

"Exactly," he huffed.

But deep down, Connor feared the situation was far worse than that: that Maggie was not so much disappointed in the ring, but disappointed in *him* and already regretted their match.

It was the only explanation for her cold, distant attitude toward him this morning.

"God's truth, I've never seen her like this before, quite so stubborn. I can't tell if she's happy or cross or if she even wants to marry me anymore. For all I know, she's only doing it now because there'd be a scandal after last night if she didn't."

"Ah, settle down, mate. This isn't like you. You're blowing things out of proportion, I'm sure."

"Am I?" He gave his friend a worried glance.

"She just needs a little time, most likely. And to punish you for a while." Rory grinned.

"Punish me," Connor muttered. "What did I do? Try to stop a murderer?"

"You yelled at her. Remember? You told me so yourself. You don't yell at a lady, ye great oaf."

"Well, I'm sorry if I am not Edward Birdwell! I didn't get out of the Peninsula alive by being a sweetheart of a gentleman."

"Me neither!" Rory agreed, a bit too cheerfully.

Connor narrowed his eyes. "I am beginning to think you are enjoying this."

"Does it show?"

Connor cursed at him in Gaelic, and Rory laughed heartily.

"Enough of your grumbling. Tell me about Miss Penelope." Rory waggled his eyebrows. "What a beauty, eh? O' course," he added, "a woman wouldn't touch the likes o' me with a punting pole."

"Why ever not?" Connor asked as Rory took a loud, crunching bite into his apple.

"Lard ass. Got no manners," he said through a mouthful. "And I'm broke."

Connor laughed. "Then why does she keep lookin' at you?"

"Nah, she doesn't, ye bastard."

"Aye, she does. Go and talk to her when we stop to change horses. We're all due for a break soon."

"I couldn't."

"What, you, tongue-tied?"

"She's so elegant! She'll think I'm an ape."

"Some women like apes. Too bad Maggie isn't one of them." Heaving a sigh, Connor leaned back on the seat and stretched his legs out before him as much as the seat would allow. "What the hell am I going to do?"

"Take your own advice. Talk to her."

"Easy for you to say, you and your silver tongue. She wants nothing to do with me today—unless I go to her groveling. And we both know I have a policy against that."

Groveling was for the weak and the cowardly, and Connor was neither.

"I don't know, at least you've got to try, mate."

Connor eyed Rory darkly. "I have nothing to apologize for. She's the one who's got to learn how to obey," he said, though he kept his voice down for fear of enraging her all over again if she should hear him. "Anyway, it's not as though I'm making unreasonable demands on the girl. All I wanted was to keep her safe. Stay back, I told her. But could she do that? Of course not."

He shifted restlessly on his seat, brooding and annoyed. Lost in the lulling rhythm of the team's six horses clip-clopping along, he failed to wave back at a friendly carriage driver going by the other way.

Rory, however, called a cheery greeting.

"I thought all females were taught from the cradle that, one day, they'd have to follow their husband's commands," Connor finally said, refusing to let it go.

"Welllll," Rory said, "they're *taught* that, I hear. It's just..."

Connor looked at him. "What?"

"Some of 'em don't like it very much," Rory said, then shuddered. "Some of 'em don't like it much *at all*."

"Well, too bad!" Connor harrumphed. "Next she'll be tryin' to change me."

Rory coughed.

"What?" Connor said.

His friend merely gave him one of his charming grins.

Connor narrowed his eyes in dawning realization. "You think she already has? Changed me?"

Rory's grin widened. "Oh, just a wee bit."

"How? I don't see it."

"We would never have been having this conversation in the past. Because you wouldn't give a shit."

"Well," Connor said with a shrug of concession.

"By the way," Rory said, "I think Will's in love with Saffie."

"What?"

"Yes, and—you'll love this—she offered to bed him as a thank-you for being so sweet to her." Rory laughed while Connor's jaw dropped. "Lad nearly fainted. She said it right in front of me and Nestor. Told the boy she wanted to be his first."

"Jaysus," Connor muttered.

Rory snickered. "Guess she learned a thing or two at that brothel."

"How did he react?"

"You should've seen him. His face turned redder than your coat. He denied being a virgin, but she just laughed."

Connor cringed.

"Our little boy's growin' up," Rory said with a wicked chuckle.

"Tell me he hasn't slept with her."

"No, not our wee Galahad. He was appalled. At least, at first he was."

"But then he started thinking about it?" Connor asked in amusement.

"Of course. Nestor headed off that trouble, though. He told Will the girl needs a thorough check from a physician first to make sure she hasn't got diseases." Rory tossed his apple core into the stone-fenced meadow beside the road. "And just when the boy had nearly worked up his nerve to ask the old Cyclops if he'd do the honors, Nestor saw that comin', too, and said there's no way in hell he's gettin' involved with all that. Reminded the boy he's not a lady doctor; only treats animals and men."

Connor rolled his eyes and shook his head.

"Besides, young Saffie's still in love with this dragoon. I think she's starting to wake up to reality, though, poor thing."

"Hmm. Sad."

Rory stared down the road, as though weighing his next words. "Want to know something worse?" he asked quietly.

Connor looked askance at him, instantly worried by his friend's grim tone. "Do I?"

Rory gave a cynical flick of his eyebrows, but his lips had drawn into a somber line. "I think she's pregnant."

Connor stared at him. "Saffie?"

"Aye," he said. "She's got that look."

"What look?"

"I can't explain it." Rory shrugged. "But I know it when I see it."

"And you'd know this how?" Connor stared at him, hoping desperately that the sergeant was wrong.

"I got four older sisters, don't I? Each of who's got half a dozen children. Uncle Rory knows what he's talkin' about."

"Shit," Connor said, with a twist of remorse in his gut. "So I'm going to orphan this infant before it's even born." He looked away. "Perfect."

"You have no choice, man. He's the one that's been comin' after you. It's you or him. At least now she'll have Will, though, maybe. He'd be a good father to the babe, kindhearted as he is."

"Yes, but he deserves better," Connor muttered with a frown.

"Don't tell the boy that. He's smitten. I think the way the other maids treated Saffie tugged at his heartstrings back when she still worked for you. And all the time we were at Trumbull's, he treated her like she was a princess."

"She's the first girl who ever paid attention to him, that's all."

"Yes, but she trusts him, and that's sayin' something after all she's been through."

"Who wouldn't trust Will?" Connor replied.

"Exactly," Rory said, and they both fell silent, pondering the riches of the heart that their skinny, homely, innocent friend possessed in such abundance, and, mysteriously, had somehow retained throughout the war, while the two of them had lost much of their own somewhere along the way.

It was half an hour before the next coaching inn with a livery stable came into sight ahead, and when Connor saw it, he made up his mind.

Inspired, perhaps, by thoughts of the softhearted Private Duffy, who sat atop the heavily laden supply wagon beside Nestor, Connor decided to lay hold of his courage and take Rory's advice.

It was time to try again to reach out and go talk to Maggie.

He'd been all business with her this morning in the Birdwells' drawing room, unsure what sort of reception he would meet. Well aware that he was on shaky ground with her after all that had happened last night, he had stayed on his guard with her, merely surveying the lay of the land.

But Rory was right. He'd have to try harder. With a little more effort, he was confident that they could put this unpleasantness behind them — their first real quarrel since they'd met — and return to their usual state of happiness together. This was no blasted way to begin their official engagement.

And so, when their convoy reached the white galleried coaching inn tucked into a tree-lined bend in the road, Connor jumped down from the driver's box, determined to take his friend's advice.

He was not without skills when it came to charming his way back into a lady's good graces. All he had to do, he reasoned, was get her to smile at him once or twice. Maybe offer up a glib jest. She'd always liked his sense of humor.

He was damned sure not groveling, though. Not him. Not ever.

Instead, he merely wanted to explain his view of all this, once he'd broken through the ice that had formed between them. In truth, he wanted her to understand and accept him for who and what he was. He had thought she did, up until last night. But now, he was not sure where he stood with her, and it upset him more deeply than he cared to show.

Unfortunately, his plan to try to charm her first crumbled when she climbed out of the coach and he saw the annoyance on her face.

Ah hell. Not in a good mood. It was no mystery why, after she'd just spent the first leg of their journey closed up with Grandaunt Lucinda. *Riiight.* The direct approach, then, since she was clearly not in a joking frame of mind.

He gave her a few minutes to stretch her back and wander off across the inn yard while he strode over to the other vehicles in their party to ensure that everything was going smoothly.

Pete had been bringing up the rear. The major swung down from his horse, told Connor he had not noticed anybody following them, and made his way into the tavern, no doubt tempted by the delicious smell of pub food floating across the cobbled inn yard. Grilled sausages, fresh-baked bread, fish and chips, flaky mincemeat pies right out of the oven…

Everyone milled about, using the facilities as needed, and buying themselves beverages or light refreshments while the livery's grooms swapped out their horses, just as they'd been doing about once an hour, every ten miles.

Connor had not allowed a proper break till this one, however. It was now about noon, and they'd just crossed out of Surrey into Hampshire.

He checked his fob watch and decided they could take twenty or thirty minutes to stretch their legs, get some food, and make themselves more comfortable for the next long push through the wide county of Hampshire.

He wandered into the pub himself to do the same. A little while later, he stepped back outside into the bright, sunny day.

Across the busy inn yard, he spotted Maggie, alone, leaning under a large, shady oak tree. She had seen him, as well, and was eyeing him warily.

Penelope stood over by the carriages drinking a glass of lemonade that Rory had just brought her, Connor surmised.

The sergeant, who also had a glass of lemonade, was now smiling from ear to ear as he worked to chat her up. Connor mentally wished both himself and his friend luck with their chosen ladies. Then he marched across the inn yard, slowing his pace as he stepped onto the grass, approaching with caution.

Maggie pinned him with her gaze, never taking her eyes off him. Not that she looked entirely pleased to see him, but at least she acknowledged him. "Your Grace."

"Maggie, we need to talk," he said as he sauntered over to her in the shade. There was no point beating around the bush, after all.

She lifted her chin, still wearing that cool expression on her face that made it nearly impossible to guess what she was thinking. "Agreed."

Connor searched her face. "I can tell you are upset with me, but I'm not sure I understand why." He was being cagey, admittedly, but he was trying to draw her out, get her to show her cards first. "What did I do wrong? I'd like to hear it from you. Was it the violence? Because I was attacked, Maggie. Was I to supposed to let him kill me?"

"Of course not." She already looked riled up by his opening statement. "But there is such a thing as the *law* to deal with such people, you know."

"The law," Connor echoed, registering a twinge of offense. A thousand brutal memories swept through him of vicious death matches on the battlefield. Blood, smoke, sweat, mud, screams. But she knew nothing of all that had been his normal world until lately. So he checked his impatience with her suggestion, and decided it would be rude to point out that Bow Street had already failed him.

"I don't think Darrow plays by those rules," he said coolly. "Therefore, neither can I."

"So you're just…going to kill him," she said slowly.

He stared at her. "First chance I get."

"I see." She looked away, paling.

It occurred to him that the night they'd met, she'd come to him begging him to spare a man's life, and then last night, another man who deserved even less to be spared had escaped him because of her meddling.

He had cause to be cross at her, for his part. "You do realize that I could've ended all this last night if you wouldn't have interfered."

"So this is my fault now?"

"A little. But mostly, it's mine. I'm the one who hesitated because you were there." He paused. "In all actuality, though, it's Seth Darrow's fault, and he deserves exactly what he's going to get. I'm sorry if you disapprove, but there it is."

She looked at him.

"When somebody hits me, I hit back twice as hard," he informed her with a shrug. "It's the only reason I'm alive now. I'm sorry if you do not like it, but this is who I am. Take it or leave it."

"Take it or leave it?" she echoed, raising her eyebrows. "I'm in no position to leave it now even if I wanted to, am I?"

Connor flinched but just stared stubbornly at her, masking his horror at her words.

"You saw to that," she continued, "announcing our engagement to the world without so much as a by-your-leave!"

"What difference does it make?" he said. "You had already agreed to marry me—quite enthusiastically, as I recall. I was the one who asked you to keep it a secret, merely to protect you from this madman. That's all I care about—can't you see that? Damn it, I saved your reputation by announcing our betrothal when I did. Doesn't that count for anything?"

"Well"—she dropped her gaze primly—"considering you're the one who compromised it in the first place, don't expect me to fall down and kiss your feet with gratitude, Your Grace."

Connor had no answer to that. He was now quite sure she was only marrying him because she had to. And probably because he was a duke.

"In any case," she continued, her cheeks rosy with anger now, "while it's true that seeing you almost kill that man with your bare hands was upsetting enough, it was how you yelled at me afterward that was quite beyond the pale. You were utterly disrespectful. Even worse than Delia."

Connor's voice vanished. So that was at it, then. And deep down, he had known it. He'd just been hoping he was wrong.

Because he knew how serious this was.

He had to fix it somehow. Now. Without looking weak. But he was rattled at the thought that he'd already lost her. "I was not trying to be disrespectful to you, Maggie—"

"Well, you were."

"Forgive my lack of manners in the midst of somebody trying to kill me!"

"Is that an order?" she inquired.

Bloody hell. His heart pounded, because it seemed the more he tried to make this better on his own terms, the worse it all became. God, he wanted this to be over. He strove for logic and clarity, wishing that for just one moment, she would look at this like a man.

"Don't you think you're being a little unreasonable?" he asked.

"Unreasonable? I only followed to help you, and you nearly bit my head off!"

"*After* you disobeyed a direct order from me, you mean? When you left cover and safety and followed me into the darkness, and could've got yourself killed?"

"I couldn't help it!" she all but yelled, her gray eyes blazing. "I was worried about you!"

"And I appreciate that," he said in frustration. "But as you saw for yourself, I don't need some sheltered young lady to protect me, for God's sake."

She turned her head, looking stung, then regarded him from the corner of her eye. Instead of looking soothed, she only looked more annoyed. "I *thought* you came over here to make up with me, not insult me."

"It's not an insult; it's true! You are sheltered. I *like* that you're sheltered." *It reminds me of everything I'm fighting for.*

"Well, stop browbeating me."

He checked his temper. "I'm not. We're just...having a conversation."

"It seems like browbeating."

"Maybe you're just too sensitive," he muttered, and immediately regretted it, for Maggie narrowed her eyes at him.

"Maybe *you* are just a barbarian," she replied, enunciating every word clearly. "If Your Grace will excuse me." With that, she pushed away from the tree and headed for the carriage.

Connor turned. "Maggie, you cannot just run away from me. We need to settle this. I don't want to fight with you, especially not with so much at stake. It's a distraction!"

"Fine. I'm listening." She stopped, pivoted, and lifted her chin with a grand air. "Apologize for being a barbarian, and then perhaps I'll forgive you."

"I'm sorry!" he said much too hotly, throwing his hands up.

She just looked at him, arching a brow.

Connor cleared his throat and shrugged nonchalantly, trying to play it off, but even he knew that, as apologies went, that was a disaster.

Lack of practice, no doubt.

But, cheeks flushing with embarrassment and half the inn yard looking on, he tried to brazen it out. "There. I said it. Happy now?"

She shook her head at him, then turned around and walked away.

He dropped his chin to his chest, praying for patience.

"Do you at least like the ring?" he asked, casting about for any source of encouragement.

"More than I like you right now," she drawled, not bothering to look back, merely giving him an idle wave.

Connor's eyes widened at her saucy retort. *When in the world did she turn so cheeky?* He stared at her retreating figure, lovely and slim in that striking blue gown, then shook his head, mystified.

"Glad I did at least *one* thing right," he called after her indignantly.

"Must've been your Irish luck."

Connor gasped, then laughed with shock at her sarcastic reply.

Then he could not decide if he was outraged or amused. *What on earth has happened to my sweet, mild-mannered, little Maggie?*

This new version of the girl practically swaggered back toward the carriage.

He noted Aunt Florence bustling over to her, but he paid the old woman no mind, for only one thing was certain.

Lady Margaret Winthrop had never acted so cheeky till she'd fallen in with him.

I am a bad influence on that girl, he thought, not for the first time. And, in spite of his defeat just now, Connor walked away smiling.

"Lady Walstead, you look distressed," Maggie said. Putting that maddening Irishman out of her mind, she took hold of the old lady's forearm and drew her gently out of the way as another stagecoach came thundering into the inn yard, loaded with passengers, its six horses' hooves clattering.

The little baroness glanced over her shoulder, startled by its arrival, then chuckled at her own state of distraction for having missed it bearing down on her. "Thank you, dear. And please, call me Aunt Florence. We will soon be family, after all."

"Aunt Florence," Maggie echoed, and smiled, glad of the sweet old lady's unassuming company after Connor's latest outburst, but then she noticed her worried expression. "Is something wrong?"

Florence glanced around uncertainly, her brow puckered. "Well, it's just, I wondered if I-I might ask a favor of you."

"Of course. Anything. What is it?" Maggie guided Florence safely into the shade of a budding pear tree planted next to the cobblestone courtyard.

"There is something I need to tell my nephew, but I-I don't think he wants to be bothered right now, what with all the hubbub and him being responsible for leading our journey today."

"Nonsense. Shall I fetch him for you?"

"Oh, no, please. Do not bother him, dear." Wringing her bony hands, Florence glanced around nervously. "He's so very large. And I fear what I have to tell him might make him angry, a little. I confess, I find him a little...intimidating sometimes. Especially when he's cross."

Understanding dawned.

"You want me to give him the message for you?" Maggie asked gently.

"Oh, would you, dear?" Florence said. "I should be ever so grateful, if it's not too much trouble."

"It's no trouble at all," Maggie assured her, giving Florence's spindly arm a soothing caress. "As you said, we are soon to be family. What would you like me to tell him?"

"Oh, I knew I could count on you." Florence beamed. "But, of course, you're not afraid of him. You're not afraid of anyone, are you?"

"I don't know about that," Maggie said in surprise.

Florence leaned closer, lowering her voice. "You were magnificent last night, standing up to Lucinda that way." She lifted her gloved fingers over her lips, stifling a giggle. "I've never seen anything like it!"

"Oh, I was very rude—"

"*She* was rude. Just like always. You had every right to dish it back to her. No one ever dares, because of her rank. But for my part," Florence said with a guilty glance around, as though the dragon lady might be listening, "I was cheering for you, o-on the inside."

Maggie lifted her eyebrows. "You were?"

"Oh, you have no idea how I've been wanting to do that for years myself!"

"I'll bet," Maggie said, holding her gaze in twinkling amusement. "To be honest, it felt rather good. Perhaps you should try it sometime."

"Oh, I couldn't. It's easier—for me, at least—just to put up with her nonsense. But you, why, you have such courage. Which is why I thought perhaps my nephew might, er, better receive my information if it came from you."

Maggie nodded. "I am at your disposal."

"Thank you, my dear." Once again, Florence glanced around, looking as nervous as the little birds that alighted in the tree above them, hopped from branch to branch, then flitted off again. "Well, to begin, it's a wee bit embarrassing. I know it was wrong of me, but, last night, while my nephew questioned Lucinda"—she hesitated—"I eavesdropped."

Maggie swallowed a laugh. "You did?"

Florence closed her eyes and nodded. "It is a dreadful habit of mine, I do not deny it. But…living with Lucinda, sometimes, well, as the Poor Relation in a family, no one ever tells me what is going on. My life must seem rather empty, to do such a thing. But I was afraid! A gunshot, right in our garden! I may be nosy, but I am no fool. I realized our very lives might be at stake. So I felt compelled."

"Understandably so. It's all right. And, believe me, I can sympathize more than you know." Maggie patted Florence's forearm. "What did you hear, then?"

Florence gave her a grateful look. "Has His Grace told you anything about Lucinda? Her past?"

"He did, just this morning."

Aunt Florence wrinkled her nose. "So, you know, then. What she used to be."

"I do. It was Amberley's way of explaining to me why we had to flee."

"It's so good he tells you things, dear. So many men don't." Florence scanned Maggie's face. "How much did he say?"

"Well, he told me he'd just found out that for many years now, the poor duchess has been the victim of a blackmailer connected to her past."

"Yes," Florence said, wide-eyed. "It's about time someone other than me knew about it."

Maggie was startled. "So, you were aware of this, then?"

"Oh yes." Florence glanced around again. "I kept my mouth shut, of course. I'm very discreet. Far be it from me to criticize *her*. It's not my place, I'm sure, and if there was someone Lucinda had to pay, what business was that of mine?" She shrugged her frail shoulders. "Charles was never stinting with his money toward her. Indeed, he always bought her everything she wanted."

"Did he?"

"He liked flaunting her in Society's face. His parents were very strict with him when he was a boy, you see, and he went through…a rebellious time in his youth. His choice of Lucinda, I daresay, was a product of that time in his life."

"I see." Maggie noticed some of their party drifting out of the pub and back toward the carriages.

Soon it would be time to go.

Florence seemed to realize it, too, and hurried her story along, while the breeze made the dappled shadows of the leaves dance around them. "Anyway, last night when I overheard Amberley questioning her, I noticed that, well, let's just say Her Grace *erred* on some dates."

"How's that?" Maggie tilted her head.

"Well! *She* told my nephew that she decided to stop paying the blackmailer *after* Charles's death. But this was not accurate." Florence closed her eyes briefly and shook her head. "I'm very good with such details, and I am certain that Charles was still alive when Lucinda hired those two brigands to go tell the extortionist that she had paid for fifty years, and wasn't giving him another farthing."

"She hired *brigands*?" Maggie said, astonished. "Connor did not mention that."

"Because she didn't tell him," Florence whispered. "I was listening; I know. Perhaps it slipped her mind. But I doubt it."

"So she lied to him, gave the wrong order of events, *and* left out vital information?"

"It would seem so." Florence gulped. "I was shocked that she did not mention them to him, for, in my view, her hiring these two outlaws was where all the trouble started."

"What happened?"

"I'm not sure, exactly. But something must've gone wrong that night. For when her two hired ruffians came back to collect their pay for their errand, they were all out of temper and demanded far more money than Lucinda had previously agreed to pay." Florence leaned closer. "I think they might've killed someone."

Maggie's eyes widened. "What makes you say that?"

"They told Lucinda they had to flee the country. They wanted her to pay for their passage across the Channel that very night. I overheard them threatening that if she did not help them flee and they were arrested, they'd tell the magistrate that *she* was the one who had hired them.

"In the law's eyes, they said, that would make *her* an accomplice to whatever dreadful thing had occurred when they went to confront the blackmailer. Then she might be arrested herself, and the whole lurid story would come out in the papers. And all the scandals around her that she worked for so long to expunge would explode into life again. That, Lucinda could never abide.

"It's the one thing she fears—not that I blame her. She suffered such cruelty at the hands of the ton. Treatment I wouldn't wish upon my worst enemy. She is a hard woman, but at least I know why."

Maggie nodded, and the baroness continued in a hushed tone.

"Anyway, realizing all this, of course Her Grace paid whatever it took to make those dreadful mercenaries go away. But that was not the end of the problems they'd caused in the course of their errand.

"Indeed, it was only the beginning. For that was when the family's awful run of bad luck started. First, Charles died in his sleep. Then poor Rupert stumbled off the cliff. He was such a lovely man! And then young Richard broke his neck in that dreadful carriage accident. I always told him he drove too fast, poor thing. And then when I heard about Connor nearly getting poisoned..."

Florence shuddered. "Until that happened, the others' deaths all seemed reasonably explainable. We could lie to ourselves. Even after the poison, since Connor survived it, we hoped for the best. We ignored our suspicions. We're just two old ladies, after all. We live quietly. Who'd want to hurt us? To think that there should have been deliberate and purposeful malice behind these events, why, it just seemed unthinkable!

"But last night in the garden, that was the last straw. When some killer tried to shoot my poor nephew—at his own welcome party!—even I could no longer hide from the horrible truth: that what I'd always feared deep down was, indeed, happening."

"And what's that?" Maggie whispered.

"That Lucinda's past would get us all killed." Florence's sweet face was grim.

"Dear Aunt Florence, why did you never say anything about all this before?" Maggie asked when she finally recovered her voice.

Florence shrugged. "Whom would I tell? Before Connor came to London, there *was* no one to tell. Besides, she terrifies me—Lucinda, I mean. I did not know what she might do to me if she found out I'd told on her, such a woman as that. Considering where she came from. She would know it was me who had blabbered the truth, after all. Who else could it be?"

"Ladies, we shall be leaving as soon as you're ready!" Nestor called from across the inn yard.

Maggie waved to acknowledge him. Then she looked again at Aunt Florence, who was staring at her.

"Please, will you explain all this to His Grace on my behalf when you have the chance?" the old woman asked anxiously. "I don't want him to shout at me for not telling him sooner."

Maggie nodded. "I don't think he would yell at you, dear Aunt Florence, but of course I'll take care of this for you. I know how intimidating he can be. I'll relay everything to him that you've shared with me, just as soon as I can."

"I thought it might help," Florence replied.

"I should think so."

"Could you ask him to try to be discreet, please?" she added timidly. "That is, I pray he would not tell Lucinda I've spilled her secrets. They're not mine to share. But when I heard her lie to him, I knew I had no other choice."

"You did the right thing, and I'll make sure he keeps your name out of it. But Aunt Florence, you needn't be so afraid of her. You have me now. I am your friend and I will defend you."

Florence clutched Maggie's hand. "Such a sweet child. He's lucky to have you, dear Maggie. We all are. You are going to be a wonderful duchess."

"I shall do my best," Maggie replied, touched by the old lady's faith in her.

"Oh—one more thing," Florence said, almost turning away. She returned, still clutching Maggie's hand. "My nephew probably doesn't realize this, but the first and second duchesses positively *hate* each other—Lucinda and Caroline."

"I'll bet," Maggie murmured. The ex-harlot and the vicar's wife?

"Do warn him. I should hate for him to accidentally, you know, step into the crossfire."

"Yes, indeed. Thank you for the warning."

"Absolutely, my dear. We all need allies in this world." With a conspiratorial wink, Florence signaled for silence with a finger to her lips, then bustled off toward the carriages, where Lucinda now stood, already bellowing for her.

"Florence! Where is Florence?"

"I'm here, Lucinda! Yoo-hoo! Coming!"

Maggie could see the party reassembling to continue their journey, but for her part, her head was still reeling from the little lady's revelations.

She strove to absorb it all as she walked back slowly toward the traveling chariot. At least her mission was clear.

As irked as she was with Connor right now, she was going to have to speak to him at the first opportunity…

Alone.

CHAPTER 29

Dartfield Manor

*O*f the several country houses Connor had inherited, Dartfield Manor was his least favorite. The house was an ugly mishmash of two clashing styles.

The brown brick Jacobean façade with three rounded Dutch gables might've been well enough if it had been left alone to brood in its ancient ornateness. But, at some point over the centuries, some ancestor—perhaps poor of sight—had hired an equally blind architect to add on a whole new block in an entirely different style.

A white, gleaming, neoclassical addition thrust out inexplicably from the south wall, all self-important pillars and huge, arched windows reflecting the sky.

There had been no attempt he could see to make the two styles, centuries apart, match. It would've made more sense simply to build two separate houses. But there they were, joined for all eternity. One dark and twisty, one bright and airy, symmetrical and pure.

Connor shook his head, beginning to wonder if the match between him and Maggie was as ill-conceived as that massive eyesore.

After being trounced by his lady at noon, he had not spoken to her again. Not from pouting or sulking—he was a man, for God's sake—but merely from the necessity of focusing on the task at hand. The girl exasperated him and he needed a clear head as the leader of this journey. Besides, he didn't want to make it any worse.

Later, he supposed, he would try a third time to reach some sort of peace treaty with her. For now, he did not need the headache. In truth, he was still kicking himself for botching it, and was rather sure that Maggie would have liked to kick him, too.

But he sighed and put her out of his mind, preferring to focus, as he had been doing for the last several hours, on staying ahead of the weather that had begun blowing in from the southward sea.

By midday, they had passed through Surrey, with its sculpted gardens and prosperous estates. The temperature had climbed to its average in the low sixties for this time of year, and the skies then had been bright blue, full of big, puffy clouds overhead. He had heard some of their travelers entertaining themselves by saying what shapes they could find in them.

Moving ever southwestward, they'd spent the long afternoon pressing on through the fertile chalk lands of Hampshire, where sheep grazed on the downs and the farm fields burgeoned with the spring wheat and watercress.

But the cloud cover had gradually thickened, so that, as the day passed, the once-cheery sunshine could only squeeze through now in piercing silver shafts, and the golden light turned to a hard gray glare that forced them to squint and gave them all a headache.

The temperature had receded accordingly into the high fifties, and the wind had picked up, gusting up from the south, and the hint of sea salt it brought with it on the air reminded Connor of home.

Meadows eventually gave way to heaths, and in the waning light of day, they knew they had crossed the county line from Hampshire into Dorset when they spotted wild ponies grazing on the moors.

By then, even the silver glare of the overcast afternoon had faded to a warning pewter gray, and the temperature had dropped further. Rain was definitely on the way, and Connor feared what would become of these remote country roads if they did not reach their destination before it started.

Their pace was already slow enough without slogging through mud, and he was worried in particular about his old ladies.

Aunt Lucinda walked with a cane and did not move well on a good day due to her arthritis. Connor had realized that when the dragon stopped complaining altogether, her physical discomfort must have turned to agony.

He'd moved his horse alongside the coach and looked in on the Amberley womenfolk frequently throughout the eleven hours they'd been on the road so far, but without another coaching inn in sight in this remote stretch of Dorset, there was nothing he could do other than hurry their party along as best he could.

With every mile, he was feeling more and more like a hardhearted bastard for doing this to all of them. But it was for their own safety, and just one day of discomfort...

By the time Dartfield Manor came into view in the distance, standing out on its lonely moors, huge thunderheads had begun forming overhead, and the wind was now steady.

Connor put his own weariness aside and smiled over his shoulder as a cheer went up from all their travelers to spy their destination in the distance.

The only road left for them to travel now was the manor's long, winding drive. He checked his annoyance when he saw the tall iron gates standing open, for the family of mother and daughters living here were not aware of the threat.

The old mansion had a gatehouse, too, but it was presently unmanned.

"That'll be your post tonight," he said to Rory, pointing at it.

His friend nodded.

"Pete, would you close the gates behind us?" Connor called.

His fellow veteran nodded and urged his horse to the side of the drive, letting everyone else pass.

As they all filed in through the gates, Connor checked his fob watch—at dusk, there was still enough light out to read its face.

Seven p.m. *Not bad.* They'd made it in just under twelve hours.

Now it was time to deal with Aunt Caroline. He hadn't even warned her he was coming, bringing all these people. He wondered how she would react. He barely knew her, but he could guess that the Second Duchess would be about as thrilled as any woman who'd just had twenty unexpected houseguests show up on her doorstep.

Ah well. At least they'd brought their own supplies.

And, technically, the house *did* belong to Connor. He had let Uncle Rupert's family continue living here because it was home to them, they'd already lost enough, and he certainly didn't plan on living there. They were welcome to it, as far as he was concerned.

Urging his hired horse from the last livery stop into an easy canter, he rode ahead of the convoy to give the lady of the house at least a few minutes' advance warning that they were here.

His excuse, at least in front of her two children, was that he had come to visit out of eagerness to introduce them all to the girl he had chosen for his bride.

Later tonight, he would take Aunt Caroline aside and tell her what was really going on. How she'd take the news that he suspected her son and husband had been murdered, he shuddered to think. He could only hope that, as a vicar's wife, her faith would see her through.

For now, though, as he reined in before the front door, Connor's lips quirked. *Let's just hope she remembers who the blazes I am.*

When Maggie climbed out of the carriage, her bones aching after bumping along over the roads from London to Wessex all day, she could only imagine how much pain Aunt Lucinda was in by comparison.

It took three servants to help Her Grace lumber down from the traveling chariot. By the gray of twilight, Maggie saw the First Duchess stubbornly pressing her lips together as if to hold back a groan.

Maggie and Penelope got out of the way as Her Grace's two footmen helped their mistress toward the house.

Aunt Florence also required some assistance. Maggie had been helping her, but the little baroness's own maid scrambled out of the servant coach back by Nestor's supply wagon and hurried over to her side, then helped her go limping toward the house.

Maggie stood with her hands planted in the small of her back, stretching her body a bit. She was just glad to have escaped the coach. After nearly twelve aggravating hours confined with the others, she was ready to part ways even from Penelope's company.

Now she faced the prospect of trying to seem charming when she was introduced shortly to her soon-to-be relatives. Never mind that she was cringing at the rudeness of this imposition, the lot of them descending on the Second Duchess without warning.

The worst part was knowing that Maggie herself was being portrayed as the cause of why they were here—so that Connor could introduce his aunt and cousins to his future bride without delay, the sooner that they could be married.

As a result, the Second Duchess was probably going to despise Maggie for this as much as the first one did. She sighed and scrounged up a smile, though, as the front door opened and an army of the manor's servants came pouring out into the graveled courtyard to assist.

In moments, the whole front entrance of the house bustled with activity as everyone—servants, soldiers, and passengers alike—fled the vehicles in which they'd been imprisoned all day.

Lanterns were brought out, instructions were shouted to and fro about where the luggage should be brought, where their servants would be quartered, and how quickly the stable could be made ready for a herd of uninvited horses. Half a dozen people had to use the loo. In short, the whole place was in an uproar.

The butler had rushed out and put himself at Aunt Lucinda's disposal. For her part, Her Grace was already making detailed, specific requests about what sort of accommodations she required. Aunt Florence was insisting she did not wish to be a bother as the two old ladies hobbled toward the house.

Maggie stayed behind, trying to prepare herself to meet the people they were imposing on so dreadfully. She could not deny that she was nervous. Meanwhile, her maddening fiancé had disappeared, leaving her standing there feeling like an interloper.

His horse was there; a dazed-looking footman who apparently worked here stood holding the reins. But the Fourth Duke himself was nowhere in sight. Maybe Aunt Caroline had murdered him inside for this inexcusable bout of rudeness.

Maggie and Penelope exchanged a dire glance, merely trying to stay out of the way amid all the hubbub. Her maid still looked a bit green around the gills, for while Maggie was merely sore, Penelope had grown a bit motion sick, especially after the last leg of their journey.

It seemed today that the farther they went from London, the rougher grew the roads. But at least the weather had held. The wind flapped through Maggie's wrinkled blue skirts and tugged at her pelisse. Its brisk caress, however, helped to wake her up after the lull of endless travel.

Judging by her maid's improving color, Maggie gathered that the fresh breeze with a faint hint of ocean in it was making Penelope feel better, too—although her newfound friendship forged on the road today with a certain sergeant might have something to do with that.

Rory was doing a fine job of directing the men and the servants who'd made up their party, and Penelope watched him admiringly.

Still waiting for Connor to reappear, Maggie stretched her neck and glanced down at her hand again to make sure she still had the ring. She knew full well she was walking around with a fortune in jewelry on her person, and it gave her a strange feeling.

But all of this did.

The one thing clearest in her mind was that she still needed to find an opportunity alone with Connor to relate Aunt Florence's vital information, never mind the tension between the two of them. She doubted she would get the chance tonight, though, for she fully expected to spend the entire evening under intense scrutiny from the Second Duchess and her children.

Maybe by tomorrow the novelty of her as the soon-to-be bride would begin to wear off, and then she could take a turn with him in the garden or a discreet stroll upon these intriguing moors.

They had a haunting beauty, she thought, gazing at the lonely landscape under the lowering clouds. In this remote place, London and all the dangers they had left behind there seemed a world away.

Maggie caught sight of Connor just then through the front door.

He stepped into view within the open doorway, the light from the foyer casting a halo over his black hair and shining down on his broad shoulders.

She caught her breath at the sight of him, oblivious for a moment to the servants scurrying about in all directions. It was no easy feat staying angry at such a beautiful man.

Her heart beat faster as she saw him gesture to a plump, blondish woman in perhaps her early fifties, inviting her to go ahead of him. Maggie gathered that this was Aunt Caroline, and concluded in a glance that the woman looked far more like a vicar's wife than any sort of duchess she had ever seen.

Her clothes were unpretentious, her manner that of an ordinary country gentlewoman. Trailing after her came two bounding girls, not yet out of the schoolroom. Maggie was surprised to notice they were twins; they looked to be about fourteen.

The two chubby youngsters seemed fascinated by all the chaos, but hung back shyly together, while the vicar-duke's widow proceeded with caution toward Maggie.

For a moment, the woman glanced from Maggie to Penelope, as though uncertain which one was the bride.

Maggie was instantly mortified, and Penelope seemed appalled to have been mistaken for her mistress. She bowed her head and quickly backed away.

Do I look that *rumpled?* Maggie pressed her lips together in what she hoped passed for a smile and lifted her chin as the woman approached.

"Aunt Caroline," Connor said with a warm, mellow timbre in his brogue-tinged voice, "allow me to present Lady Margaret Winthrop, the daughter of Lord and Lady Halford, my future wife."

"Lady Margaret," Caroline echoed, flicking a tentative glance over her, while the gawky girls stared.

"My dear"—Connor turned to Maggie—"it is my honor to introduce you to Grandaunt Caroline, the Second Duchess of Amberley."

Maggie ignored her body's stiffness to offer a curtsy of the utmost respect, bowing her head. "Your Grace."

When she lifted her gaze to meet that of their reluctant hostess, the woman's brown eyes blinked, as though she were still a little in shock about all of this. But then she seemed to click back into the expected reaction. "Lady Margaret, I congratulate you on your betrothal and wish you both every happiness."

"Thank you, Your Grace. I am so sorry for this imposition," Maggie said.

"Not at all." The Second Duchess gestured toward the house. "Do come in. You all are most welcome."

The words sounded rather forced—not that Maggie could blame her.

"Lucinda," their hostess said coolly, glancing at her scowling sister-in-law.

"Caroline," the dragon lady answered.

"Florence," Caroline said with far more warmth, turning next to the frail baroness.

"Oh, Caroline, it's so good to see you again!" Florence said.

Lucinda rolled her eyes as her companion gingerly embraced the lady of the house.

While the twins curtsied to the dragon lady with trepidation and were largely ignored, then sprang over to Florence and hugged her till she winced, Maggie and their hostess exchanged another glance, sizing each other up.

Maggie offered a tentative smile, and Caroline blinked. "Oh! My daughters. Allow me to present them," she said, turning to the pair. "Girls?"

The chubby twins went over to their mother, one sidling up shyly to her, the other galumphing over with a wide, self-certain grin. They both glanced at Connor in awe along the way, then peered eagerly at Maggie.

She instantly found them very dear, these callow country girls, raised in seclusion. Oh, they were at that age when everything a person did was awkward, no matter how hard one tried, she thought with an affectionate tug at her heart. She remembered those days well. She liked the children right away, at least. The mother she still wasn't sure about.

"Lady Margaret, these are my daughters, Hope and Faith."

"Twins," Maggie said with a smile.

"Oh yes, and quite inseparable. Girls, this is Lady Margaret Winthrop, who will become the Fourth Duchess of Amberley when she marries Cousin Connor. Isn't that happy news?"

While the twins managed breathless curtsies without falling over, which was something for creatures their age, Maggie noted a faint gulp from the Second Duchess, as though she had a lump in her throat.

The briefest shine of tears appeared in her dark eyes by the light of the lanterns, and in an instant, Maggie realized why. She must have been thinking of her late son, who ought to have been the duke now if he hadn't been murdered. His mother must have surely expected it would be Richard bringing home a bride to meet his family one day.

Of course, Cousin Richard would have rather brought home Bryce, by the sound of it. But Maggie doubted the duchess had known anything about her son's proclivities in Town.

"Well!" Caroline said. "Do please come in and let us make you welcome. No doubt it has been a long, trying day for you all."

"If you ladies will excuse me," Connor said, after standing there in silence all this while, "I must decline, but I'll be in to join you shortly. First, I must see to matters out here and get my staff settled in before the storm brewing over there hits." He pointed to the south, where the thunderclouds had been amassing.

Maggie sent him a discreet, imploring stare, begging him not to leave her alone so soon with people she barely knew and a hostess whom she feared was entirely annoyed. It was *his* idea coming here, after all.

But while the older women all headed inside, the furrowed-brow look he gave her made Maggie realize he had no choice. There were too many things he had to make sure were sorted out by what light still remained of the day.

Inspiration struck, however.

"You know," Maggie said suddenly, addressing their hostess, "I wonder if Your Grace would mind if I took a brief walk around the grounds with my maid for a bit before we come in—so we might stretch our limbs after that very long ride."

Certain that Caroline must be craving a little time to organize her household to receive this invasion, Maggie gestured at Penelope. "We're both a little motion sick, as well, I'm afraid," she lied with a self-deprecating laugh. "This cool breeze is so refreshing. If it wouldn't be too much trouble, of course."

"Oh, no, by all means," Caroline said with relief, looking ready to go rushing off in ten directions at once. This way, she could at least see that the battered old ladies were made comfortable first. "Girls," she said to her daughters, "why don't you show Lady Margaret your father's old walking path? That's a pleasant stroll—but not too far!" she warned. "If you feel a raindrop, come in at once. I don't want you catching colds."

"Yes, Mama," the twins said, then whipped around to face Maggie.

Caroline seemed to be warming to her task. Obviously, hospitality would have been a chief virtue required of her in her role as vicar's wife.

Whatever dark cloud of lonely grieving had hung over her life since the deaths of her husband and son, she suddenly seemed to gather herself, for she launched into action with admirable skill.

Amid the influx of strangers arriving, Maggie heard Caroline give orders to one of her servants to take the wagon and hurry into town to buy more bread from the bakery, hampers of prepared foods from either the inn or the coffeehouse—a baked ham and roasted turkey, if he could come by them—a barrel of ale from the brewer at the pub for the men, and anything else they might need in the larder to feed their guests tonight and over the next few days.

"Aunt Caroline, that is not necessary," Connor said. "We brought our own supplies. We don't wish to be a burden to your household."

"Nonsense, Your Grace," she said with a smile. "You are the Duke of Amberley and deserve a proper welcome, you and your future duchess. Besides, all of your people must be starving by now, and cooking you all a proper supper could take hours. The village isn't far, and, after all, whatever we don't eat tonight, we'll have for tomorrow."

With that, she bustled off. Maggie saw Connor bite his lip, as though tempted to argue. But perhaps he, too, realized that their arrival seemed to have given the bereaved woman a much-needed new topic to occupy her mind.

"This is most generous of you, Aunt Caroline. Thank you!" he called after her, but Maggie wasn't sure the duchess heard him.

She was already marching back over the threshold of her domain, directing the porters in the entrance hall toward the rooms for the two old ladies, and ordering hot water for baths with mineral salts to ease the travelers' aches and pains.

Connor called to Peter and Rory to come with him, while Nestor and Will took over the process of moving horses and servants into their respective quarters.

As the major strode off with his cohorts, Maggie turned to smile at the twins in the waning half-light. She surmised that their mother was glad to shoo them away for the time being, for the pair were standing around getting underfoot, and watching everything, agog.

For her part, Maggie mainly planned on following Connor, observing what he was up to—she loved watching him in commander mode—but the girls were welcome to come along. "Shall we, ladies?"

"Sarge, you forgot this!" Will shouted after the men, holding up the knapsack that Rory had carried over his shoulder for most of the day. He must've left it on the driver's box of the traveling chariot, since that had been his main post throughout their journey.

But the men had already gone out through the garden beside the house, heading for the fields, so Penelope dashed over to fetch it for him.

"I'll take it to him, Will!" She quickly retrieved Rory's knapsack from the skinny lad before the traveling chariot was whisked off to the stables.

They had to wait briefly for her return, as the servant carriage leaving Dartfield Manor rolled past in between them, heading off to bring supplies from the village, as ordered.

Off it went down the drive, but the gates had been closed, thanks to Major Carvel—a fact that probably annoyed the driver.

If she were in his shoes, Maggie thought, she'd be cursing her bad luck for being chosen for the task, heading out onto the roads with foul weather bearing down on them.

Hunkered down on the seat, the man clapped the reins over the team's backs to hurry them along, no doubt nervous about making it there and back before the storm hit.

This seemed unlikely, however. The wind was gaining speed while the skies continued to darken.

Maggie turned her gaze from the roiling clouds overhead to the two young girls. "I do love storms, don't you? So exciting."

One friendly question was all it took to open the floodgates of their enthusiasm.

"Once I saw lightning strike a tree and it nearly exploded!" said the slightly taller twin.

"Really?" Maggie said, but dashed if she could tell the two apart.

Once they had moved from their original positions, she had no idea which was which, but they both were delightful.

From that moment, the youngsters did not stop talking, chattering away on a dozen random topics as they strolled along. Maggie and Penelope exchanged an amused glance as the girls led them first through the garden on one side of the house, and then out onto the windy moors.

The pair seemed thrilled to have new people to talk to—Londoners, no less—out here in the middle of nowhere.

As they took their refreshing post-travel constitutional, hawks wheeled high overhead, riding the unsettled currents of air.

The wind shook the clumps of thorny yellow gorse, making their nettles rattle like old dried bones. It whispered in the rugged Scots pines that grew here and there, and rippled through the mounds of pink and purple heathers that stretched on seemingly for miles, covering hill and dale.

When the walking path climbed to the crest of a gentle rise, Maggie spotted the men in the distance once more. They seemed to be taking the lay of the land. Connor was pointing toward the deep, narrow chine that nature had cut through the chalk hills on the edge of the property.

A swift stream ran along the bottom of its steep, pale sides; they could hear its babbling current rushing along on its way to the sea.

While the talkative twin told them all about their local village and their studies and how *boring* it was there, the quieter one gave up trying to get a word in edgewise. Instead, she took it upon herself to act as their guide, running farther up the footpath, then pausing to beckon to them.

"Here, come this way!"

"Hope, I don't want to take them that way! It's depressing!" said the talker—apparently this was Faith.

Maggie looked at her in question.

"It's where our father died. He tripped. It's very high up," Faith said. "Overlooking the stream."

"It's a nice view!" Hope said. "I'll bet they want to see it."

"Is it dangerous footing there?" Penelope asked.

"Not really. It was just muddy that day, and I'm sure he wasn't watching where he was going. That's just how he was," Faith said with a sigh. "He was probably holed up in his Thinkery for hours with his books, and walked out with his head still in the clouds."

"What's a Thinkery?" Penelope asked with a blink.

"That." Faith pointed. "See? That little castle sort of building on the rise? It was Father's favorite place."

They followed the direction of her pointing finger, and there, tucked in a fold in the heather-clad landscape near a copse of trees, they could just make out a gothic folly in the distance: a miniature castle, complete with two dainty spires.

"It's filled with boring stuff. Books." Faith shrugged. "He had his study there and his prayer closet."

"It was his one luxury," Hope chimed in, rejoining them. "You should see it. It's cozy."

"I don't want to go there," Faith mumbled, turning away. "But I'll walk to the cliff with you, if you really want to see it."

"There's no need to go there for our sakes," Maggie said gently. Orphaned herself, but by illness, not by foul play, her heart went out to the twins. "I'm so sorry, girls. Please know, both of you, that Connor would much rather *not* be the duke, if only your father or brother could still be here with you."

"We know," the twins mumbled, lowering their heads.

Penelope sent Maggie a pensive frown.

"Thank you, Lady Margaret," Faith added.

"Please, call me Maggie. And this is my maid, Penelope, by the way. She is a genius at hair."

"Are you?" the girls asked eagerly, cheering up again.

And while Penelope answered their questions about braids and topknots and the newest styles in London, Maggie scanned the gloomy landscape up by the whimsical Thinkery.

Walking up over the rise, she now saw the men in the distance not far from the sturdy little folly.

As she watched them, Connor sent Peter riding north, probably to scout out the grounds, keeping an eye out for danger.

He pointed Rory back toward the gates, which the exiting carriage driver had left open behind him again.

As for himself, Connor went to stand on the rocky promontory where his uncle had fallen.

With the wind riffling his hair, making his long coat billow around him, he faced the coming storm as though he welcomed it, as though it called to his very nature…

Just as he called to hers.

Riveted, Maggie found him magnificent—proud, brooding,

temperamental as he was. She could not tear her gaze away from him, and when he turned, sweeping a glance over the moors, he found her watching him, and from the distance, he captured her stare.

What passed between them in that moment in the twilight was like nothing she had ever felt before. A certainty. A knowing, deep in her belly.

And a hunger that she could no longer deny.

CHAPTER 30

Vendetta

"Father, we need to take shelter," Seth said, while beside him, Elias Flynn peered through the folding telescope that had been glued to his eye all day.

Flynn said nothing in reply, but slowly lowered the telescope and folded it. He seemed impervious to the increasingly temperamental weather.

Seth masked his impatience. This was hardly the father-son holiday he'd always dreamed of, but beggars couldn't be choosers. "The man at the last inn said there's a town not far south of here."

"Use your eyes." Father nodded toward the drive of the estate where Amberley's party had gone. "Have a look." He handed him the folding telescope, and Seth lifted it to his eye.

From their perch atop a windy ridge about a half-mile away, they had a clear view of the misshapen estate and the drive leading to it.

Seth went very still. "A carriage is leaving. He's opening the gates."

"One day you'll learn to trust me."

Seth could not help but marvel. His father seemed undaunted by the grueling hours of travel.

While Seth felt wrung out, achy and exhausted, the seventy-year-old man beside him had seemed only to grow stronger throughout the day, driven by a maniacal intensity, perhaps, to see his vendetta against Lucinda through once and for all.

For his part, Seth was still recovering from the thrashing he had taken at Amberley's hands last night.

Pain had further slowed his pace today, not to mention his annoyance at everyone on the way here staring at him on the roads and the inns. You'd think they'd never seen black eyes before, plum-colored bruises, swollen jaws, men who limped with cracked ribs.

Of course, Father had taken scarce pity on him during the day, driving on endlessly, powered by rage. Now he seemed prepared to weather the storm out here on this naked hillside with nothing but a few mounds of gorse for their cover.

Seth was tempted to leave the mad old bastard there to finish his quest alone, but, naturally, he did not dare. It was his fault that all this had happened, anyway. So they watched and they waited, but at least they need travel no farther in chasing their quarry.

A few minutes passed, and Seth thrilled to see that the driver left the gates open behind him.

They both ducked down like lion stalking prey when the carriage rumbled closer, heading toward them down the road.

"Should we make a run for it? There's a folly on the grounds where we could—"

"Wait." Father stared, assessing the situation.

Three minutes passed. Four. The storm fired a few warning shots in their faces. Cold, angry bullets of rain.

"What are we waiting for, Father? Full darkness? I'm sure they won't see us—"

"Hold!" Father snapped, staring again through the telescope. "You must've failed to observe there's no cover once we get through the gates. It's all open ground. We'll never get near the duke."

A moment later, Seth saw once again that he should have trusted the old cutthroat's instincts.

It was damned lucky they hadn't gone charging in when *he* had wanted to, or they'd have been caught. The tall, brawny soldier they had seen driving the ladies' coach all day galloped up to the gatehouse just then, swung down from his horse, and instantly clanged the gates shut.

The sound of it carried to them on the gale.

Seth frowned and turned to his father. "Do you think they know we're here?"

"No. They just know they're in trouble, that's all."

Locked out again, Seth wasn't sure what his father wanted to do next, but he could feel the old man brooding, thinking it over.

When the plain black coach passed them on the road right beneath the hill where they sat, Father scrutinized the driver through the telescope.

"Servant," he reported. "No one inside." As the coach hurried off down the road, Father turned to Seth. "Tell me, son, what would Mother do if twenty people showed up at our country house without any warning?"

Seth considered. "She'd want to feed them, of course."

"But what if she wasn't expecting so many mouths to feed, eh?"

"She'd send a man out for supplies. Ah…"

"He'll be back." Father nodded toward the road.

"Until then?"

"Be patient."

Seth heaved a sigh and leaned back against the boulder, taking a swig from his flask to dull the pain all over his aching body. Thunder rumbled. His misery climbed as the temperature dropped.

Lightning stabbed at them from the dark sky but missed.

At last, an hour later, the carriage came trundling back, laden with supplies. They saw its front lanterns gleaming feebly in the now-inky gloom as it neared, and heard the horses' nervous whinnies. The clip-clopping of their approaching hoofbeats picked up speed as they scented home.

Father climbed to his feet and slapped Seth on the shoulder. "Come on now. It's time."

Before he quite grasped what his father was about, Elias was already striding down the hill.

"Father, what are you doing?" Seth whispered loudly.

"What do you think? We're taking the carriage. We'll use it to get inside."

"But the staff will know that we don't belong there!"

"Nonsense. If anyone from the manor asks who we are, we'll say we came in with the duke's entourage. And if any of the duke's men should see us, we'll say we're part of the staff here. That's why I told you to dress plain. Need to be ready for all eventualities. Now, come on, dullard, we mustn't miss him."

Seth thought it was madness, but knew all too well by now that there was no point in arguing. Instead, he just shook his head, then trudged down the rough slope after his sire.

"How do you mean to kill him?"

His father looked askance at him. "Silently," he said with a smirk.

Then he took a length of garrote wire out of his pocket and wrapped it around his two hands.

"It's been a while," Flynn remarked as the carriage rumbled closer down the road. "Let's hope I haven't lost my touch. Otherwise, it might be up to you. And we both know how that's likely to turn out."

Seth gave him a hard look. But Father needn't have worried. Unfortunately for the wagon's driver, the old rookery rat hadn't lost his touch at all.

While Seth stepped out of the darkness in front of the horses, lifted his arms, and said, "Whoa," Father sprang up onto the driver's box like a goblin and attacked Her Grace's astonished employee.

It only took moments.

The horses had halted, though they tossed their heads and pawed the gravel in protest.

Seth ran to assist his fierce sire.

As the driver slumped out of his seat, a dead weight, the corpse fell heavily onto Seth. He caught it with a wince, then dragged the dead man off into a drainage ditch by the roadside and hastily covered the body with vegetation.

By the time he turned around, Father was already sitting on the driver's box with the reins in his hands. He nodded behind him with a glint of wild satisfaction in his eyes.

"Get in the back, boy!" Then he put on the dead man's hat and pulled the brim lower over his eyes.

Seth swung up into the carriage and ducked out of sight, his heart still pounding.

Father drove on.

Seth took a deep breath and looked around to gain his bearings. The most delicious smells filled his nostrils, and as his eyes adjusted to the deeper darkness inside the carriage, he found it filled with baskets and hampers with warm, scrumptious food of all kinds. Seth's mouth watered.

Killing did not dull his appetite. Not after all those years at war.

While Father drove the carriage up to the gates, Seth reached into one of the hampers stacked up on the coach floor and helped himself to a wedge of cheese, a hunk of ham, and a few rolls.

Ahh, the rolls were still warm. They were heavenly on a cold, wet night like this. Just getting out of the constant wind was a boon. He ate one of the rolls on the way to the gates and put a few more in his knapsack for later.

Then the coach slowed and he lay down sideways on the squabs to keep out of sight, listening.

Holding his breath, he waited to see if the soldier Amberley had posted at the gatehouse would realize that a different man had driven the carriage back from the one who had driven it out.

Apparently not.

For, in the next moment, Seth heard the lock being undone and could not resist a cautious peek over the edge of the carriage window to see if the guard posted there seemed at all suspicious.

The man barely looked at Father.

A cynical smile curved Seth's lips when he spotted some pretty blond woman who had apparently come out to bring the soldier some comforts for his long night watch—a lantern, an oilskin to keep him dry, and a serving of rations.

The two were so absorbed in their flirting that the smiling soldier barely took his eyes off the blonde long enough to unlock the gates and haul them open.

He waved the expected carriage back onto the property with nary a glance at old Mister Garrote. Seth shook his head in amazement that his father's plan had worked. But why was he not used to it by now? Elias Flynn had not become a king of the London underworld by lacking nerve, resourcefulness, or wit.

It all went exactly as the old bastard predicted. They parked the carriage outside the kitchen entrance around the back in an area that looked about right for receiving deliveries, then they abandoned it, slipping into the workaday regions of the manor without anybody questioning them.

They just acted like they knew what the hell they were doing. Seth found it fun. Father's glance told him he thought so, too.

Oddly enough, it was the closest Seth had ever felt to his father.

Perhaps they had bonded over killing that poor bastard together. To be sure, Father never could've done *that* with his darling Francis.

Then the rain hit, and an army of servants scrambled outside to start carrying in the food they had just delivered.

"Where's Jackson?" the cook asked, looking puzzled and frumpy in her apron.

"The coach is back, so I'm sure he's here somewhere, ma'am," said a hurried footman. "Does anyone have an umbrella?"

Seth and his father politely stepped out of the way.

"Do you boys need anything?" the footman called to them, mid-scurry.

"Er, no, thanks," Father said quickly. "We serve the duke."

"He wanted to know how long until dinner," Seth chimed in.

The man blanched. "Please give His Grace our apologies. It'll be ready in no time. Everyone, hurry!" The footman dashed off to help the effort underway to carry the food into the kitchens and get it served before it got any colder for the great Duke of Amberley.

Seth slid his father a sly glance. Father chuckled.

Then they walked slowly and deliberately, oh so casually, through the maze of workrooms. Passing the scullery with its big sinks and draining holes in the cold flagstone floor made Seth think of Saffie.

But he pushed her out of his mind. Just another reminder of his previous failures to impress his father. Tonight, surely, was the last chance he'd ever get. He had to make the best of it.

Father beckoned him down another hallway and into an ancient-looking stairwell with a low, arched ceiling. The next thing he knew, they were holed up in the dim, dank wine cellar, where they retreated to the darkest corner available.

Finally, they could relax, still dripping rain and shaking with the thrill of what they'd done.

"See? Easy. I told you." Father took off his spectacles and polished away a few flecks of road dust and rain.

"You did," Seth said. Reaching into his knapsack, he offered his father a bread roll.

Flynn took it and tore off a bite.

"So, what do we do now?" Seth asked.

"Now we wait," Father replied through a mouthful.

"For what?"

"Till they all go to sleep."

"And then what?"

"Killin' time, lad."

Seth paused, bracing himself. "It won't work."

He hated to say it, and his father clearly didn't like hearing it.

"What do you know?" the old cutthroat retorted, scowling at him.

"With all due respect, sir, you're not killin' this man. He's too good."

"Eh, you've let him get inside your head," Father said with a dismissive wave. "Leave it to me. Everyone's got to sleep sometime."

"Fine. So you use your wire on him, then? He wakes up and kills you. He's unbelievably strong. How do you think I ended up looking like this?" Seth pointed at his mangled face. "He'll snap your neck like a rabbit's, sir."

Father shrugged. "So you say."

"Very well. Let's say you find his room, shoot him the moment he closes his eyes. The sound wakes the whole household. They catch us; we hang. I'm not liking these plans, sir."

"Well, what do *you* suggest, then?"

As his answer, Seth broke off a small piece of cheese from the wedge he had stolen. He placed it on the mousetrap set up nearby, then gave his father a meaningful look. "All we need is the bait, sir. Then we can kill him with ease. Trust me, he won't even fight."

CHAPTER 31

Landfall

*L*ater that night, Connor caught an hour of much-needed sleep, but was awakened by a rumble of thunder. He lay in his bed for a few minutes longer, listening to the rain gusting against the window panes.

The long-promised storm had finally hit.

At length, he sat up, wincing at the pull to his wounded side with the motion. Leaning against the ornate headboard for a moment, trying to wake up, he had an unfettered view of the tempest raging beyond the huge windows across from his bed.

The guest chamber he'd been assigned sat in the Georgian addition to Dartfield Manor. Maggie and his aunts were far away in the original Tudor section.

His room was spacious, high-ceilinged, and dark. Shadows clustered in the distant corners, fingered the neoclassical cherry furniture, and tucked up into the coffered ceiling. But lower, the feeble illumination from the small fire crackling in the white marble fireplace licked over the impressive four-poster where he rested. It was the show of nature's fury outside his window that held his attention, however.

The violence of it reminded him vaguely of battle. Silver slashes of rain beat against the windows. Flashes of fiery lightning streaked through the night's deep indigo. Thunder reverberated like cannon fire; its waves shook the glass.

God, he was not looking forward to going out there.

Not when the massive bed beneath him was comfortable as a cloud.

It was an impressive bit of business, the kingly four-poster. Rich blue bed hangings to match the drapes that he'd left parted over the windows. A mound of pillows, most of which he had thrown onto the floor.

Crisp white sheets swaddled his half-naked body. A blue and gold satin duvet kept him warm. He felt downright lordly lying in this thing. And lazy as hell.

As another lightning bolt tore across the sky, he would have much preferred to lounge here contentedly savoring the memory of royal pudding, tender Portland lamb, and the other excellent local dishes that Aunt Caroline's trusty staff had managed to procure from the village.

But it was Connor's duty to check on his men, who were out there keeping watch, poor bastards. He wanted to ride out to Pete and make sure he was doing all right in this mess. Connor wasn't overly worried about him, though. If the man had tasted the monsoon season in India on his adventures, then an English springtime storm would hardly prove too much for him.

Besides, Connor had pointed out the peat-roofed stone shooting hut on the moor where Pete could take shelter for the night while keeping watch—an old refuge for shepherds and grouse hunters alike.

Rory was in the gatehouse, meanwhile, probably shivering his arse off. The thought of these two loyal companions finally pulled Connor out of bed. Not in a thousand years would he put his men out on sentry duty in weather like this without also joining the effort.

They all knew that until reinforcements arrived, vigilance was key. And so, with a sigh, he dragged his weary bones up and out of bed, and went over to the washstand to splash himself fully awake.

At least he'd got the horrid conversation with Aunt Caroline out of the way, he thought as he poured water from the pitcher into the washbasin. He'd had to, to explain why he needed to post his own men and some of her footman around the property to keep an eye on things.

Not that he expected any real trouble tonight, as he had assured her.

The Second Duchess had been stoic at the news of his suspicions, and finally admitted that she'd had doubts herself about the official story of the deaths in the family. He'd seen her mentally cursing Lucinda—and Charles—for bringing this on their family, but she had been nearly silent, taking it in without a tear.

Their talk, in fact, had been startlingly brief. Her spine ramrod straight, she had thanked him for journeying to Dartfield Manor to make sure that she and her daughters were also safe. They had agreed it was up to her to determine when and how to tell the twins the awful news, but, clearly, their mother needed at least a few days to absorb the awful news herself before sharing it.

When their talk was over, Caroline had ordered her staff to do whatever Connor said. Then she had retired to her chamber, for the hour was late, no doubt to cry her eyes out in private.

As Connor splashed his face over the washbasin, he was just glad to have that burden lifted off him now.

Ducking his head before the mirror, he ran his fingers over the stubble that darkened his jaw. "You need a shave, mate," he mumbled.

That could wait till tomorrow. Then he dried his face and went to get dressed, pulling a pair of gray woolen trousers on over his drawers.

Shirtless, he peered down at his side, which was bandaged again after last night's debacle. The reopened wound hurt, and now a big purple bruise was added to where that blackguard had bashed him with the rifle butt.

Not that he was complaining. God knew it could've been worse.

All the while, the violent gales outside shook the manor, yet inside, the house seemed eerily quiet.

Connor wished he could say the same for his own thoughts. But in truth, he felt weary and sad. His heart ached a bit with the question of whether the peaceful life he'd always dreamed of would ever come to fruition.

He'd clung to hope for so long, but now he was beginning to doubt it. He knew he'd feel better if only he could make up with Maggie.

This discord with her still had him all out of sorts. When had she grown so essential to his basic functioning? And he ached to think that he had made her feel like he didn't respect her, even for a moment, for it was so untrue.

He *had* barked at her, though—she was right—but it was only out of his state of intensity in the moment last night, not from a lack of care for the girl herself. Equally true was the fact that she *was* sensitive, as he'd stated earlier today, but that was no flaw. On the contrary, it was exactly why he felt so drawn to her. He vowed to himself that he'd be gentler with her in future, no excuses.

Adding to his general disgust with himself was the gnawing sense that he was missing something vital here.

None of this rubbish with Seth Darrow made any sense.

Why in the world would Elias Flynn send his son to keep killing off

Dukes of Amberley—all because the harlot he'd once been attached to quit paying his blackmailing fees?

That was fifty years ago.

Unanswered questions continued whirling in his mind like the leaves circling in the wild eddies of wind outside. They set his teeth on edge. Ah well, maybe lightning would strike him out there and send down divine inspiration.

If it didn't kill him.

Just then, he heard a timid knock at the door of his bedchamber. He assumed it was the servant who'd promised to wake him for sentry duty.

Still shirtless, he walked over to tell the man that he was up, but when he opened the door, he was astonished to find Maggie standing there holding a punched-tin lantern. His gaze trailed over her, wrapped up all cozy in a comfy velvet dressing gown, thick woolen socks on her feet.

Her skin was still pink and warm and rosy from a recent hot bath, he presumed. The telltale evidence was the little curling tendrils of her still-damp hair. It hung in long, flowing waves past her shoulders, and that, he had never seen before.

It entranced him to behold her like this, with her crowning glory unbound, a rich reddish brown in the candlelight.

How on earth was he not to ravish her when she kept showing up on his doorstep like this late at night?

Maybe that is her intention, his starved libido suggested.

Ha, said his better sense, considering the lady had barely spoken to him all day. Small hope flamed in him when he saw her glance admiringly down his bare chest, then she looked away, blushing.

"May I come in?" When she sent a nervous, almost guilty glance down the dim hallway outside his chamber, Connor remembered his wits, beckoning her in.

He closed the door quickly behind her.

"What are you doing here?" he asked, striving for nonchalance when, in fact, his heart had started pounding.

If she'd come here to scold him again, he really ought not to feel such joy at her arrival. But a scolding was better than being ignored.

"I hope I didn't wake you up," she said in a conspiratorial hush, tiptoeing deeper into his chamber.

"No. I was just getting ready to get back outside."

Her eyes widened, and she glanced toward the window. "You're going out there?"

God, he wanted nothing more than to pull her into that big, luxurious bed and ride out the storm with her under the covers.

Instead, he gave her a taut smile. "Figured I'd ride the perimeter. Make sure everything's quiet."

A frown puckered her brow. "Is that really necessary?"

"Probably not, but it will make me feel better." Connor stole a glance at her hand and was relieved to see she was still wearing his ring.

After the way things had gone between them since last night, he barely knew what to expect. "So, ah, was there something you wanted?"

"Yes." She gave him a businesslike nod and set her lantern down on the chest of drawers. "I've been waiting all day for a chance to talk to you in private. There's something I need to tell you. But be warned: you're not going to like it."

His stomach lurched, and he froze. *Oh God, she's going to break off our engagement.*

She can't. I need her. His heart took up a sickening, breakneck pace, but Connor rested his hands on his hips with a small nod, listening intently.

It was her decision—and he would have to respect that even if it killed him. He forced himself to be stoic, but braced for the onslaught like the stalwart infantryman that he was.

"Yes?" Belatedly, he recalled his manners and cast an awkward gesture to the chair by the wall. "Er, would you like to sit down?"

She shook her head. "No, thank you. I-I mustn't stay long."

"Very well." He took a deep breath, but really, would have rather been skewered with that damned dragoon's bayonet than stand here and hear the woman he loved reject him for being a bloodthirsty killer and a hardheaded Irishman.

He suddenly felt very naked, half dressed as he was, but he was too proud to cover himself. Folding his arms across his chest, he lifted his chin.

"What is it?" he asked coolly.

"I spoke to Aunt Florence today," she said, much to his surprise. Connor furrowed his brow. "Oh?"

She folded her arms. "We had a rather disturbing conversation…"

Utter relief poured through him as she embarked on her unexpected topic—so much so that he almost couldn't concentrate at first on the shocking details of what she'd been told.

She carefully recounted Aunt Florence's secrets as the minutes passed, and soon left Connor flabbergasted.

He stared at her, incredulous. "I don't believe it... Aunt Lucinda lied to me? She lied to my face?"

Maggie nodded. "According to Aunt Florence, she did. She claims she heard the whole thing, and that Lucinda botched the timing of when this all happened—that it was *before* her husband's death, not after—as I told you. And then she left out the entire part about the brigands."

"Brigands... No, she didn't mention that little detail at all." Leaning one shoulder against the nearest bedpost, Connor stared unseeingly across the shadowed room, his thoughts swirling. "So this has nothing to do with the blackmail itself, then."

"It would seem so," Maggie said grimly. "Lucinda hired those ruffians to tell the blackmailers their scheme was over, and someone got killed. *That's* what all this is about. But who?" She shrugged. "Aunt Florence did not know, and I have no idea."

Connor stared at Maggie as the pieces finally started fitting together. "Rory had heard Flynn had a younger son. He died a couple of years ago."

"That timing sounds about right. Didn't Granduncle Charles die about two years ago?"

"Aye," he said. "Of natural causes," he added sarcastically, shaking his head as he pushed away from the bedpost. "So that's why he's killing us. It's all revenge."

"It would seem so," Maggie said softly. "I've been waiting all day to tell you this. I hope the delay did not cause a problem."

"No, not at all." He raked his fingers through his hair, head down in thought. "Damn, though, this changes everything."

"How so?" Maggie finally sat, perching on the slender wooden chair by the wall.

"At least it explains his persistence. This Seth fellow. He's avenging his brother. Flynn's avenging his son. But why come after me instead of Lucinda? Not that I want him to, of course, but she is the one responsible. I sure as hell had nothing to do with it."

"Maybe he's saving her for last," Maggie said in a dark tone.

Connor stifled a curse. "Maybe so. Aye, I'll bet you're right. God, what a debacle. I had a feeling she still wasn't being completely honest with me."

"Well, you were right. But, Connor, if you do decide to confront her, please try to keep Aunt Florence's name out of it, will you? The poor thing's terrified of Lucinda."

"Aren't we all?" he muttered, then sighed. "I'm not sure there's any point in confronting the woman if all she's going to do is lie. Maybe it's just as well to spare Aunt Florence the headache."

They both fell silent.

Then Connor spoke, now that his astonishment was fading. "By the way, how did you get on with the dragon in the carriage today?"

Maggie smiled ruefully. "Better than expected. Still, I shall sleep well tonight. With all due respect, that woman wore me out."

They chuckled, sharing a warm gaze for a moment.

Then another thunderclap banged at the manor's ancient rooftop, and Maggie jumped like a child.

She frowned at him and rose, crossing to peer anxiously out the large window. "I really don't want you going out there."

"I'll be fine." Connor followed, staring at her silhouette framed against the flashes of blue lightning.

"It's dangerous," she said as he came up behind her. "Maybe you could just wait a little while until it dies down."

"Ah, don't worry about me, love." He touched her shoulder to soothe her. The velvet texture of her dressing gown cradled his fingers. In spite of himself, he wondered what she had on beneath it.

Maybe nothing. His mouth watered at the thought, though he knew that his good little Maggie was no doubt draped in something warm, clean, and sensible under there.

God, he loved her.

She turned around and caught him adoring her. Her cheeks brightened as she read his thoughts in his stare. At once, she lowered her lashes demurely, but the pink tip of her tongue darted out between her lips, enticing him all the more.

He could think of one reason to delay going out there...

"Ahem. Well," she mumbled, "I probably shouldn't stay. I'm sure all three of your aunts would be scandalized if they knew I was here, especially the vicar-duke's wife. So I shall bid you a good evening, Your Grace. Do please be safe out there."

"Maggie, wait." Connor gently barred her exit with a forearm across her waist. "Please. There's something I need to say to you."

"Yes?" She lifted her gaze to his, the firelight limning her delicate profile and glistening in her gray eyes, wide with hope and vulnerability.

He lowered his arm to capture her fingers, moving closer. "I…I owe you an apology."

She lifted her eyebrows, looking amazed.

"I'm so sorry I hurt your feelings, Maggie. And I *do* respect you. I want so much for you to know that." He lifted his shoulders in an expressive shrug. "How could I not? You saved my life."

Connor faltered while she gazed at him. "The truth is, I hate that you saw me fight Darrow last night. That's the real reason I got so angry. I…" He looked away, speaking with difficulty, but offering her the raw honesty she deserved. "I never wanted you to see that side of me. You, of all people. It was bad enough that you witnessed that, but then I made it worse by how I treated you. And I truly am sorry."

Dry-mouthed, he glanced at her again. To his relief, she hadn't fled the room yet. "I, er, I lost my cool because I was scared of what you would think of me. When I saw the look on your face…" His words trailed off, for he didn't have the heart to finish them.

That was the moment I knew I'd lost you.

Connor lowered his head, his soul heavy as a stone. "I just wanted you to know that it wasn't so much that I was angry at you for following me. I was angry at myself, seeing through your eyes for that split second, what I've become. What I *had* to become. At the war."

She nodded, listening. A sheen of moisture had sprung into her eyes.

"I didn't mean to scare you," he whispered. "You're such a gentle soul. A true lady. You should never be exposed to such brutality. But I'm afraid that's just a part of who I am. So if you don't want to marry me anymore, I'll understand." He swallowed hard. "Or, if you feel we ought to marry for propriety's sake, I'll do whatever you want. Everything that's happened is my fault, after all. I just want you to be safe. And happy."

"Oh, Connor." She took a step toward him and then captured his hand in her own. "I don't think you understand at all how I see you."

He nodded, bracing himself for whatever hard truths she might hit him with. "Tell me."

She searched his eyes tenderly. "First, I know how you *think* I see you. As an 'Irish savage,' or some brutal killing machine. But that is not the case. When *I* look at you, I see my friend." She lifted her soft, warm hands and cupped his face gently between them. "My lover. My darling. The man who taught me courage, and how to stand up for myself. You want me to be happy? Then you must not speak another word of canceling our marriage, for I can never be happy unless you are mine to love."

He stared at her, amazed at her clemency as her words slowly sank in.

"Well?" Maggie whispered. She lowered her hands from his face to her sides again, waiting.

Overwhelmed, Connor barely knew how to answer.

"You are so generous to me," he finally whispered. "You always have been. You gave me a chance when nobody else would. You stuck by my side when I didn't deserve it."

"You believed in me," she countered. "Nobody ever really believed in me before like that, and I certainly didn't believe in myself."

His heart clenched and he reached for her hand.

They stared at each other in wonder.

"Besides," she ventured after a moment with tears in her eyes, "you've been generous to me, too. Have you seen my ring?" She lifted her hand with a teasing sparkle in her eyes.

Her little jest took him off guard, but, touched by her transparent effort to cheer him up with humor, he answered softly, "Plenty more where that came from, love."

She smiled. "But you know that's not the main thing that I want from you."

He nodded. "You want me to be a good husband and behave myself, and I shall try."

"No." Shaking her head, she rested her hands on his chest. "I merely want to know that you love and respect me as much as I do you. That's all."

"I do, Maggie. God, you are on the highest of pedestals to me." He captured both of her hands and held them. But as he gazed at her, his voice failed him as he realized how desperately he needed her in his life.

The future he'd dreamed of was useless without her at the heart of it. "I just don't want to lose you. Especially not now, before we've even begun, with all this still hanging over our heads."

"You'll never lose me now that I've finally found you, my beloved." She stepped into his embrace and laid her head against his chest.

Connor wrapped his arms around her slim body and thanked heaven for this woman—and her patience with him. Closing his eyes, he lowered his face against her head, inhaling the perfume of her hair.

He stared into the fire as he held her, his thoughts drifting faraway.

"I'm such an animal sometimes. I've had to be. There's no use denying it. If you're still with me, then perhaps it's best you know that."

"Connor, you survived that long, bloody, horrible war." She looked up at him earnestly, resting her palms on his chest. "You're here now, and you love me. That's all I need to know. Everything else, it's all in the past. The war's over now. Napoleon's defeated. And it's time for you to start a *new* chapter of your life, yes? With me."

"Will you help me do that?" he breathed.

"Of course."

He nodded wistfully, clinging to that promised hope. Yet, oddly enough, the welling misery tucked away in the back of his heart came on stronger at her tender vow. For she touched something in him; her gentleness woke the sadness he always avoided over the things that he'd seen and done.

It wasn't easy to live with sometimes. And, deep down, he knew damned well that more than just his wounded side needed healing. But there was never time to ponder such things with bullets flying around one's head. So he had merely pressed on day after day, year after year, and he'd learned young to cover up sadness with laughter. 'Twas the Irish way.

She must've noticed the pensive cast of his face, for she drew him back to the present with a soft caress on his jaw.

"I love you," she said.

Her sweetness, her artless sincerity, and above all, her innocence brought a lump to his throat. He'd have done it all over again to protect the likes of this precious girl.

Then he mentally shoved the past away, refusing to let it swallow him like Jonah's mighty fish and carry him down into the abyss.

Maggie was the present, here in his arms. She was his future.

"I love you too, my darling." A low burst of breathy laughter escaped him in his embarrassment at how well she saw through him. "But, God's truth, I'd rather fight a battle with the Grand Armee than ever argue with you again."

She grinned, resting her chin against his sternum. "I'm not so scary."

"No. But I have a feeling you're usually right. Which means I'll usually lose."

"Ah, don't worry, Major," she said, "you shall find me magnanimous in victory. I confess, however, I might enjoy claiming the spoils of war…" She ran a naughty fingertip down the center of his chest to his navel, and tilted her head with a coquettish smile.

"I surrender," Connor whispered heartily.

Then Maggie bit her lip and gave him a rough little shove toward the bed.

CHAPTER 32

At Last

A rare boldness filled Maggie as she thrust him playfully onto the nearby four-poster. With a husky laugh, Connor dropped to a seated position on the edge of the bed. Handsome as sin in the firelight, he leaned back slightly, his hands propped behind him. The way the fire's flickering illumination played over his magnificent body had been driving her mad from the moment she'd arrived at his chamber.

Delicious man, he was more temptation than she could resist.

His apology had touched her heart, and now Maggie felt closer to him than ever. Hope glowed within her at seeing they'd had their first real scuffle but made amends.

Besides, she had no intention of letting her darling fiancé go outside in the middle of this storm. That was even more dangerous than what *she'd* done, sneaking here to his chamber at this hour.

Of course, having come this far, Maggie figured, why quit now?

Her belly quivered with want as she watched the shadows dance across his massive shoulders, the muscular curves of his chest, and down his sculpted abdomen.

She dragged her gaze up from perusing his physique. All it took was one look into his cobalt eyes, and she threw caution to the wind. Her need for more of him tonight was urgent, elemental.

"I see. Queen Maggie the Magnanimous, is it?" he taunted as he trailed a smoldering gaze over her.

"That's right." Maggie untied the cloth belt of her dressing gown.

"You can conquer me anytime, love."

"Good. Because you're not going anywhere right now." After sliding the velvet belt free from around her waist, she tossed it, looped, over his broad shoulders, capturing him. "Now I've got you," she whispered with a smile, leaning closer. "And I'm never letting you go."

"Ah well." He smiled, watching her with hawklike intensity.

Then she closed her eyes and kissed him for a moment. Beneath his playful banter, she could sense his throbbing awareness of her. It thrilled her, as ever—and told her all she needed to know.

Ending the kiss, she straightened up then shrugged off her dressing gown and let it fall to the floor. His lips curved when he saw her white cotton night rail, but the tingling heat racing through her at his nearness made her loath to continue wearing much of anything.

"Whatever are you doing, my dear?" Connor murmured, and licked his lips.

She climbed onto his lap in answer, kneeling astride him. She slid her arms around his neck. "Don't you think we ought to make up properly now?"

"Mmm, I do. What did you have in mind?"

"I'll show you." She claimed his mouth in a deep, hungry kiss, gathering him closer.

His hands curled around her waist. She ran her fingers through his hair, trembling with a surge of feverish yearning. His tongue stroked hers in swirling seduction.

When she ended the kiss, Connor swallowed breathlessly. "I suppose the boys can manage on their own for a while longer."

"Ah. A man of sense," she panted. Then she pushed him down onto his back on the bed and braced herself above him on her arms.

"My, you are an insistent lady," he not-quite-protested.

Deliberately caressing his body with her own, she meant to rout any more foolish talk of his leaving. "You should know by know how stubborn I can be," she purred.

"Almost as stubborn as me," he said, then let out a low groan as she gently brushed her thigh back and forth between his legs.

"Perhaps, then, we really are perfect for each other," Maggie whispered as she set out to entice him.

His eyes swept open and he gazed at her. "On that, my darling, we are in perfect accord."

She went very still, holding his stare for a heartbeat. *I want you.*

412   *Gaelen Foley*

"I love you," he whispered.

Taken aback by his tender declaration, Maggie felt her heart clench. "Oh, my darling man, I love you too." She kissed him, moved. Then, filled with decision, Maggie pressed up onto her knees.

Still straddling him, she took hold of her loose night rail and lifted it off over her head with a smooth motion, offering herself to her chosen mate without another word.

Connor's lips parted as his gaze drifted over her naked body. Maggie let him look, her pulse pounding. Her nipples peaked in the chill, but she wasn't cold, merely yearning for his touch.

He laid a warm hand on her thigh planted next to his hip. The other he raised to the center of her chest, trailing his fingers slowly down the middle of her torso.

His reverent gaze followed his caress. "You are an angel," he said hoarsely.

Her lips twisted. "Usually, Your Grace. But not tonight." Then she leaned down and claimed his mouth in a series of deep, drowning kisses.

As his arms wrapped around her waist, the feel of his bare chest to hers for the first time was blissful. Her hair swung down to veil the intoxicating kisses they exchanged, and, in moments, she abandoned herself to the pleasure of Connor's hands gliding all over her body.

His sensuous caresses molded the curves of her back. He gripped the cheeks of her backside in both hands with a low growl of lust.

Without warning, he flipped her onto her back on the bed and rolled onto his side next to her. Maggie tilted her head back, eager to yield control to his expertise.

Connor nuzzled her cheek for a moment. She moaned as his warm, sure hand cupped her breast. But the restless pleasure of his thumb chafing back and forth across her swollen nipples wasn't enough. She needed his mouth.

She asked for it wordlessly, urging his head down, arching her back. He swung lower in a swift, eager descent and then feasted on her breasts. Maggie smiled with erotic relief at his lusty moans while his hot, wet mouth devoured her, tugging roughly at each nipple in turn. The roughness of his day's beard against the delicate skin of her breasts heightened her arousal.

Her groans of climbing ecstasy joined his when he slipped two fingers inside of her. Passion exploded in her veins with a wave of even sharper need.

Suddenly, panting and wild, she reached down to unfasten his breeches, impatient to touch and stroke the erection she could already feel waiting for her there, straining at the placket. She had visited this region before, after all. She'd even had her mouth on him, had drunk his salty juices. She was eager to do that to him again, but not tonight.

Now only the hard, glorious length of him buried to the hilt inside her body would do.

He seemed pleased to oblige her. Unfortunately, her fingers were clumsy with haste and inexperience—not to mention shaking with unbearable desire. The buttons of his placket seemed all backward from her angle, frustrating her in seconds, but with an indulgent half-smile against her lips, Connor assisted.

When he had freed his member, he returned to kissing her madly. But Maggie only stroked him for a moment or two before the silken feel of his throbbing shaft in her grip drove her to a state of utter craving for the man.

She drew him atop her and parted her legs to receive him. Connor groaned as she guided the head of his manhood to the threshold of her dripping passage, letting him taste her body's wettest kiss.

He breathed an intoxicated oath and shuddered, barely holding himself back. Having made her wishes explicitly clear, Maggie slid her hands up his arms and held on tightly to his broad shoulders, weak with hunger, waiting for him to take her.

His eyes swept open, and they stared at each other in the firelight.

His chiseled face was stark with the torment of raw desire, and his blue eyes burned into her very soul.

"Are you sure?" he panted, hesitating.

"God, yes. Connor, please."

"I want you so much," he said, his voice guttural.

A needy groan escaped her at his words.

"But, sweeting, we aren't married yet," he forced out. "If this bastard should manage to ki—"

"No! Don't even say it," she ordered, laying a finger across his lips. "I won't allow it." She looked deep into his eyes. "I'll kill him myself before I'll let him take you from me."

His expression changed as he absorbed her fierce vow. Something deeper than lust filled his eyes. He seemed to realize in that moment that perhaps the two of them were more alike than he had previously grasped.

414   *Gaelen Foley*

Maggie also understood that now. She lifted her hand and cupped his beloved face. "I'd give my life for you," she whispered.

He shook his head, looking speechless for a moment. "I'd never want that. But aye, I'd do the same for you. In a heartbeat."

"I know you would, my warrior." She licked her lips, shifting beneath him. "Please, Connor, make love to me."

His effort to withstand temptation crumbled before her eyes. A surge of thrill swept through her as he bent his head and kissed her with devastating tenderness.

The scruff on his jaw chafed her chin, but his mouth claiming hers was satiny smooth. She parted her lips eagerly for each mesmerizing stroke of his tongue and slid her splayed fingers up through his hair, caressing his head. Her pulse pounded with anticipation as he lowered his body onto hers, his elbows planted on both sides of her head.

While his tongue swirled in her mouth, she was breathless with wonder, shaking with need, and acutely aware of his delicious incursion as he entered her, inch by inch. No words were spoken, but he paused for a heartbeat when he came to the maiden barrier within her; then he thrust into her, and Maggie cried out.

The sensation was raw for a moment, but he held himself in check with a hard swallow, letting her absorb the sweet pain of this blood oath, joining them forever.

She dragged her eyes open and looked at him. Connor was staring down at her with stormy devotion, his eyes glittering like sapphires. "You are so beautiful."

"I'm yours." The simple words escaped her without forethought.

Tenderness sobered his expression, then he kissed her brow. As a few moments passed in his patient embrace, her fleeting discomfort receded. She explored the curve of his lower back, his lean hips, and muscled derriere, gradually getting accustomed to the size of him within her.

After a bit, she lifted her head and nibbled a sensuous kiss along his shoulder that let him know she was feeling quite splendid now, and ready for more. He glanced down at her with that irresistible, roguish half-smile, and, slowly at first, they carried on right from where they'd left off.

He was gentle with her; his light kisses skimming along her jaw line filled her with delight. Meanwhile, each coaxing motion of his hips cautiously lured her back into realms of dreamy enjoyment.

"Mmm." Maggie felt the tension of a moment ago dissolving. Indeed, any lingering fears flowed out of her entirely at his efforts. By God, she'd begged him—shamelessly—to make love to her, and now that was precisely what he did, with luxurious skill.

Soon, even the memory of shyness or the initial pain of her deflowering drifted far behind her. He kissed it all away, lipping her wrists, her arms, her shoulders, her neck, as his hard length glided in and out of her. Maggie felt her senses catch fire anew.

She wrapped her legs around him, moving with him now, as need, lust, hunger returned, while the storm crashed outside. His jaw tautened as he struggled to restrain himself, but he was losing the battle, and watching that, feeling it, thrilled her.

He rose on his arms above her, thrusting, claiming, taking her.

"Yes," she told him breathlessly.

She gave herself over to wanton pleasure, knowing she was safe with him, so safe with this dangerous man. His every move intoxicated her, his every touch as he clutched her body and rocked her in his arms. He grew rough with her, but Maggie relished it, raking her nails down his back. She wanted nothing but to fulfill his every need, even as he shattered hers.

Soon she was writhing beneath him while the tempest buffeted the house. The rain lapping at the window panes was like his wet, warm kisses devouring her neck. His rhythm hammered at her breasts. She bit back a wild cry of ecstasy as he lunged between her thighs; the low grunt of savage pleasure that escaped him thrilled her to the core.

Wrenching cries of desire tore from her as he brought her to a white-hot climax, raining sensuous kisses all over her brow, her cheeks, then he joined her in frantic surrender. They clung to each other, both covered in sweat, as his big, hard body pulsed with release.

It was fortunate the night was filled with thunder, for its roaring crescendo drowned out Connor's riotous groans of ecstasy.

Maggie's pulse continued slamming away as he collapsed on top of her, all sixteen stone of him, pure muscle.

She laughed weakly. "Can't...breathe."

"Oh. Right. Sorry." Panting, he withdrew from her body with a wince, then lifted off her and collapsed onto his back beside her. "Good God."

"Aye," she agreed in amusement, then looked over at him, dazzled, and glowing with joy. She felt as though he'd turned all her bones to honey and replaced the beating heart within her with a bright, pulsating star.

He turned and held her stare, still catching his breath, his chest heaving. "When will ye marry me, woman?"

The blunt question startled but pleased her. But, truly, it was the best thing he could have said after what they had just shared.

Though she barely wanted to move, she could not resist rolling over to snuggle into his arms. "The sooner the better after that, I should think. You know, just in case."

"Just in case, eh? You mean a child?"

"That's what I mean," she replied.

He kissed her brow. "That would make me very happy," he whispered, wrapping his arms around her. He glanced down and met her gaze, his heart, so brave and true, glowing in his eyes.

Maggie cupped his cheek in her hand and gazed at him: such a beautiful man. He looked dreamy-eyed with satisfaction, and she couldn't help wondering how an ordinary girl like her had ever been so lucky.

He pressed another doting kiss to her head, then held her for a while in blissful silence while the rain drummed against the window panes and the fire crackled cozily across from the bed.

Though Maggie longed to stay with him all night, she did not wish to horrify the aunts, let alone offer a scandalous example to the two young girls.

"I should go," she finally said with a sigh of regret.

As she sat up and started to move away from him, he clasped her wrist and pulled her back. "Pay the toll, lady."

She smiled and dutifully kissed him, lingering with a low chuckle as his hands went wandering, then she barely managed not to get herself seduced a second time.

It was tempting, but she extricated herself somehow from his light, playful hold. He heaved a sigh of contentment but didn't fight her, letting her escape. He watched her with a lazy smile as she climbed out of his bed and shuffled off toward the trifold wooden screen in the corner of his chamber to clean herself up in privacy.

"Cute bottom," he observed.

She shot him a coy smile over her shoulder, "Why, thank you very much, Your Grace," she replied, and shook it at him.

He whistled, and Maggie laughed as she ducked behind the tall wooden screen, rather shocked at herself. The rogue had turned a proper English lady into some sort of a wild woman, it seemed.

After a moment's inspection, however, noting the blood on the inside of her thighs, she peeked back out around the side of screen. "Um, could you possibly bring me a basin of fresh water, some soap, and a washcloth?"

"Oh—of course." He heaved himself up from the bed at once. That was when he glanced down at himself and must've noticed traces of her maiden blood on him, as well. "Er, does it...hurt?" he asked anxiously as he brought her what she'd asked for. "Now I feel terrible—"

"No, no, it's all right. It's natural," she told him. "Besides, it was worth it." She flashed a cheeky grin to reassure him, protective as he was, and then disappeared behind the screen again.

Nevertheless, unseen by him, Maggie winced as she wiped away the blood. He was a big man—everywhere—and her womanly parts were already sore.

At least she did not have to worry about incriminating evidence being left behind. Under normal circumstances, a bloodied washcloth and water would seem exceedingly strange to the servants who collected them in the morning. Indeed, it would provide the telltale evidence of what had taken place in this room tonight.

But since Connor was already wounded, that, at least, would help to hide the truth. Maggie did not like lying, but soon, she told herself, they wouldn't have to sneak around anymore. She couldn't wait until they could always be together. It wouldn't be long now...

Maggie reemerged from behind the screen, clean and tidy, then it was Connor's turn. While he went behind it, she glanced around, spotted her clothes on the floor, and went to put them back on.

She was dressed when he returned two minutes later, but to her surprise, he was scowling and looking unsettled, maybe even angry at himself.

At once, she knew why: because he'd made her bleed.

Beaming with affection, she went over to him and laid her hands on his still-bare chest. "I'm *all right.*"

"Are you sure?" he asked glumly.

"I've never felt better in my entire life!"

He smiled ruefully, then gathered her into his arms. "If you say so." After a moment, he kissed her head. "I hate to let you go. But you need to rest, and I suppose I'd better get outside."

She pulled back and gazed up at him with a frown, then glanced toward the window. "Humph." She supposed she could live with him joining his men on sentry duty, since it sounded like the storm was moving a bit farther off now.

Still.

"Promise me you'll be safe out there," she said, resting her palms on his chest.

He wrapped his arms loosely around her waist. "I will. As for you, don't get caught going back. My aunts will die of apoplectic fits."

"Two of them will, maybe. But one of them can hardly talk, from what I hear."

Connor laughed.

"For my part, I'm mainly wondering what the devil to say to Penelope. They set up a servant cot for her in the corner of my room. Maybe she fell asleep and I won't have to explain where I've been."

"Oh, I think she's going to know."

Maggie looked at him, and they both laughed softly, neither with the least trace of remorse.

He chucked her gently under the chin and smiled. "Good luck, sweeting."

"Till tomorrow, Your Grace."

He slung his arm around her waist, pulling her up onto her tiptoes to give her one last, lingering kiss goodbye. "Sorry. Couldn't resist," he whispered, then begrudgingly released her. "Sleep tight."

He'd left her in such a state of perfect contentment that Maggie knew she would drift into dreamland the moment her head hit the pillow. "I love you. Good night."

"I love you too."

Reluctantly, she pulled away from him with a sigh and headed for the door. She tugged the cloth belt of her dressing gown tighter around her waist, then peeked out the door to make sure no one would see her on her way.

"Psst!" Connor said from behind her. She closed the door again without a sound and glanced over her shoulder at him in question. He pointed to her lantern, which she'd almost forgotten. "Better take that with you or you might get lost."

"Oh! Yes, I probably would. Thank you. I've got a long way to go, and this place is a maze." She whisked back to retrieve the lamp from the chest of drawers where she'd left it.

"If you meet any nosy servants on the way, tell them His Grace will reward them well for their silence."

"You naughty boy."

Connor grinned, then peeked out the door on her behalf. Finding the way clear, he beckoned her through, opening the door wider for her. He stole a kiss on her cheek as she slipped past him. Maggie giggled, turning left out of his room; she blew him a quick kiss over her shoulder, then stole off down the dark corridor.

Aunt Caroline had done her best to keep them apart by giving Connor the grandest chamber in the center of the Georgian wing's second floor, while Maggie had been tucked away in the far corner of the Tudor wing.

His room was flanked on both sides by those of his trusty men. These were empty now, however, as all four were presently on guard somewhere around the grounds, along with most of Aunt Caroline's footmen.

Maggie, meanwhile, had had to sneak past the guestrooms given to Aunt Florence and the dragon lady.

Over creaking, ancient floorboards.

Fortunately, both old ladies were so exhausted from the day's journey that they were no doubt sound asleep—Maggie hoped.

For now, she padded down the hallway with stars still in her eyes from her first experience of lovemaking. Indeed, she could barely wipe the smile off her face. *Ah, that man.*

He gave her such joy. Now she could hardly *wait* to get married. She had not let herself think much about the actual wedding yet. But suddenly, she was buoyant with enthusiasm to start planning the big day.

Delia would probably make fun of her, but at least Portia would understand.

After passing Will and Nestor's empty room, Maggie came to the stairwell and turned right. She steadied herself on the banister as she hurried down the airy classical staircase to a sort of atrium, where an attempt had been made to join the two distinct regions of the manor with well-placed columns.

She wasn't sure if the atrium quite succeeded, but overall, she found the house with its two disparate parts thrown together like this charming and original. And out on the moors, the vicar-duke's Thinkery in a third style entirely—the neo-gothic—seemed like a whimsical act of defiance.

Of course, Delia would've hated it all.

Reaching the bottom of the white marble steps, holding her lantern behind her for a moment in case anyone was out there, Maggie swept the atrium with a wary glance, and determined with relief that no servants were nearby to catch her at her mischief.

She quickly darted to the left-hand corner of the atrium, where another staircase — of heavily carved wood, old, dark, and dramatic — led up into the Renaissance side of the manor.

The three-hundred-year-old steps squeaked accusingly under her footsteps, refusing to be muffled even by her woolen socks. She might as well have worn metal patens.

With a wince, Maggie hitched up the long hem of her dressing gown and hurried up to the second floor as quickly as possible just to get it over with, squeaking all the way.

The carved angel on the newel post seemed to smirk at her as she exited the staircase, making a right into the dark, narrow, slightly wavy-walled corridor, at the end of which lay the rich Elizabethan chamber she'd been given.

Almost there.

Her heart pounded as she tiptoed past Aunt Lucinda's chamber.

Meanwhile, her lantern's tiny flame flickered over the faces of esteemed ancestors whose portraits hung along the walnut-paneled corridor. Garbed in antique styles of various eras, they all seemed to scrutinize her as she crept past.

So, you think yourself fit to be the Fourth Duchess of Amberley, do you? Carry on our bloodlines? Eager to get started on that part, though, aren't you?

Lusty wench.

She frowned at their disapproving stares. *Humph.* This place was like all old houses in England: *Definitely haunted.*

Right on cue, a floorboard creaked, and Maggie mouthed an oath she'd learned from Connor.

After clearing Aunt Lucinda's room, Maggie glided past dear Lady Walstead's like a ghost, and finally reached the third door on the left: her own guest chamber.

As she reached for the door latch, she heard thunder rumble overhead again and wondered if Connor had gone outside yet. The thought of him warmed her anew.

But even as she lifted the latch, she floundered, trying to think of what to say to Penelope.

Her maid was not the judgmental sort. Still, even Maggie knew that her actions over the past hour had been scandalous in the extreme.

She herself could scarcely believe she had just lost her virginity.

A half-smile quirked her lips. Sans regret, she opened the door to her chamber, but immediately frowned to find the room pitch-black.

That's odd, she thought. Penelope must have nodded off, for she had let the hearth fire burn down to embers.

Maggie stepped into the chilly chamber, shut the door behind her, and held up her lantern. "Pen?"

Pausing where she stood, she let the dim illumination of her lantern lick over the various quarters of the room as she lifted it higher and moved it about, looking for her maid.

Its feeble glow revealed the dark, spiral-carved posts of the canopy bed, draped in heavy green velvet bed hangings. It reflected off the colorful diamond panes of the mullioned windows.

Maggie frowned. *I thought I closed those drapes.*

They were bunched up on both sides of the window now.

As her gaze traveled on, a fading unicorn stared back at her from the ancient tapestry on the wall.

An uneasy feeling filled her as she took a few steps deeper into the chamber, reaching the edge of the jewel-toned rug. She looked at the servant cot stationed in the corner, and the chair beside the massive Tudor wardrobe.

But Penelope was nowhere to be seen.

Maggie furrowed her brow as she walked slowly into the center of the room. *Surely she's not out there with Sergeant McFeatheridge.*

Penelope *had* mentioned taking her new friend some food. Had she never come back from her errand to the gatehouse?

My goodness. Maybe Penelope was the one who had some explaining to do! Maggie thought. Could her normally well-behaved companion have proven as wayward tonight as she had?

There's just something about a soldier, I guess, she thought with a grin.

Still, this seemed very unlike Penelope.

With deepening curiosity over her trusty maid's whereabouts, Maggie began crossing toward the fireplace to see if she could nurse some flames back to life. But then, as she rounded the bed, she stopped cold, and a horrified gasp escaped her.

Penelope was lying unconscious on the floor.

At once, Maggie flew to her side, dropping to her knees. "Penelope?"

she exclaimed. "Are you all right? Penelope?" Heart pounding, she laid a hand on her maid's shoulder and gave her a gentle shake. "Penelope? Can you hear me?"

Then Maggie drew in her breath, spotting some blood on her maid's blond hair, as though she had fainted or fallen somehow and struck her head near her temple.

"Oh God," she breathed. *What on earth happened?*

Nestor, she thought at once. The surgeon would know what to do. She had to find him.

Half panicking, Maggie left her lantern on the floor and shot to her feet, but even as she drew breath to shout for help, a hand clapped over her mouth, roughly silencing her as she was captured in a viselike grip.

"Good evening, Lady Margaret."

Her eyes flew open wide with terror and the blood in her veins turned to ice.

She had heard that voice before.

"Would you be so good as to come along with me and my father?"

CHAPTER 33

Two Lanterns

*O*utside, the fullest violence of the tempest had passed. The slashes of lightning had dwindled to distant flickers of blue light, and the rumbles of thunder had moved off to the north. What remained of the storm now was a strong, steady rain that poured from the dark skies and soaked deep into the thirsty earth.

The rain felt good to Connor, the smell of it drenching the turf, the feel of it on his face, the roaring music of the swollen brook rushing through the boulder-strewn chine nearby.

Draped in a loose black oilskin cloak, rain pouring off the brim of his old shako, Connor rode one of the manor's hack horses at a plodding walk down the drive to the gatehouse, checking first on Rory.

"Anything to report?" he asked, throwing back the loose hood of his dripping cloak as he joined his friend inside the little stone tower.

Rory shook his head. "All's quiet. You want a smoke?"

Connor accepted a cigar but only took a few puffs from it, savoring his experience of this night as he stood beside his friend, gazing out at the dark landscape. Yet he saw only Maggie in his mind's eye.

God, but he still felt absolutely glorious after their joining. He hadn't a care in the world. He knew he was a smitten fool, but he couldn't stop smiling to himself about how shy she'd been that first night in his sitting room at Amberley House, back in Moonlight Square.

It had taken all his charm merely to dare the prim little miss into showing him her ankles, and then, tonight—*whoosh!*—off came her clothes.

He laughed to himself and shuddered with admiration of that sweet body even now. Ah, 'twas a memory he'd savor until he was old and gray. She never ceased to surprise him, that girl…

"What's with you, mate?"

Connor looked over to find Rory eyeing him with a skeptical frown.

"Who, me?"

"You seem…funny," his friend said suspiciously.

Connor gave him a secretive smile. "I have no idea what you're talking about."

"Oho, you made up with Lady Maggie."

"Aye," Connor said.

Rory chuckled. "Good for you. I'm glad your mood is improved, at least."

"More than you know."

Rory laughed, then looked askance at him. "Miss Penelope came to see me."

"Oh, did she, now?"

"We're taking a stroll in the garden tomorrow, two o'clock."

"Well, how about that. Well done, man. And you said she wouldn't look at you twice."

Rory snorted. "No accountin' for taste, eh?" Then he shrugged, his expression turning more serious. "She's a fine woman."

"They're out there," Connor agreed. "You just have to look."

At length, he put out the cigar to finish for later, since there was no point in taking it out in the rain with him. Then he clapped Rory on the shoulder, asked if he needed anything more, and when his friend said no, that he was set till the end of his watch, Connor left the gatehouse and went back out into the downpour.

The horse snuffled with indignation at being put through this, but Connor patted the animal's neck. "It's for a good cause, mate. I wouldn't do this to you if it weren't necessary."

Then he rode back up the drive, clipping along at a more hurried walk to go check in with Pete. Passing the garden, he reined out across the fields and moors, where he and the men had looked around earlier.

Well aware that the heathlands were filled with treacherous footing for horses, he kept his mount to a walk and followed an eastward trail that branched off from Uncle Rupert's main footpath to the Thinkery.

He eventually found Pete sitting stoically under the shelter of the old shooter's hut out on the moors. The grouse hunters' refuge had a small stone hearth, where he'd built a fire to warm him.

"How are you faring out here?" Connor called as he approached.

"Feels like old times," Pete answered wryly, rising to his feet. "What time is it, anyway?"

"Quarter past midnight," Connor said. "Have you seen anything?"

Huddled under his oilskin, Pete shook his head. "Quiet as the grave. Except for the thunder."

"Good," Connor replied.

"Am I missing anything exciting back at the manor?"

If you only knew, Connor thought. But he just shrugged and shook his head. "Everyone's asleep."

"Have you got someone ready to take the next watch?" Pete said. "Because if not, I can stay out here till dawn. I don't mind."

"No, one of Aunt Caroline's footmen will replace you." Connor looked at him, both of them splashed with firelight. "I truly appreciate this, Major. It's a lot to go through for someone you barely know."

Pete smiled sardonically. "Eh, bloody peacetime. What else have I got to do?"

"Well, I owe you," Connor replied.

"Nonsense." Pete waved him off. "I'm sure you'd do the same for me."

"Count on it. If I ever can repay you, I shall do so gladly." Connor paused, glancing out at the landscape. "Although I must say, I certainly hope you never face the prospect of someone trying to kill off your family."

Pete gave a snort. "Can't even imagine it. Anyway, there's only Felicity and me. And Jason, if you count my brother-in-law. And his two children." His weathered face softened a bit. "Fond of them."

"Aye? How old?"

"Simon's five, and Annabelle's three, and has the lot of us wrapped around her little finger…"

For a few minutes, Connor listened as his fellow warrior revealed this unexpected soft spot for his wee niece and nephew. He thought of Gable, rhapsodizing over his three-month-old son.

It would be good to start a family of his own with Maggie, he thought. Such things were on his mind tonight after deflowering his soon-to-be wife. But as he stood there by the fire, on a night watch like the many hundreds of them he'd been on in his life, he made a private vow that he'd never force any son into the military for the sake of family tradition, the way his father had signed him up as a mere child.

God willing, there'd be no need. He prayed there would not be another war in his lifetime—or theirs.

"Well," he finally said, clapping his fellow veteran on the back, "time to move on, then. You need anything?"

Pete covered a yawn and shook his head. "No, I'm fine. Just make sure I have a room with a dry bed to sleep in when three o'clock rolls around, would you?"

"You already do. Second floor of the new wing. I believe yours is the third door on the right. You're bunking with McFeatheridge, by the way. Hope you don't mind."

Pete shrugged. "Doesn't bother me."

"Good hunting."

Pete held up a hand in farewell, and Connor went on his way to continue making the rounds to see if the footmen he'd stationed around the sprawling perimeter of the property's hundred acres had anything to report.

Riding through the darkness, it wasn't long before his thoughts filled up again with Maggie. The kisses they had shared, the delicious softness of her silken arms and legs wrapped around him. The enchantment of her eyes, the welcome of her virginal body. Her passion had astounded him. Made him feel so loved.

Truly, what he'd found with her had so far surpassed all his fondest hopes for the future that he was in awe. What he felt for her was deeper than anything he'd ever expected to experience. She'd drawn forth a side of him that he hadn't known existed...or had lost long ago.

Perhaps it had been wrong not to wait for their wedding night, but now the peacetime life he had envisioned for so long danced before his eyes, so close that he could almost touch it.

These were the soft, satisfying thoughts that filled Connor's mind as he rode the horse along slowly, continually scanning the sable landscape, pounded by silvery rain.

Then he rode the horse up over the next rise and spotted something strange in the distance.

He pulled the horse to a halt and stared, unsure of what he was seeing.

A burnished ball of light glowed in the middle of the blackness where no light ought to be, about a mile and a half across the moors.

Instantly, his defenses went on alert. He urged the horse forward again, brushing the rain out of his eyes, and squinting until he realized where the light was coming from.

The Thinkery.

What the hell?

He could just make out the spiky silhouette of the miniature castle standing black against the indigo sky.

Who on earth would be out there at this hour?

Maybe one of his sentries had needed a break from the weather.

But as he urged the horse a little closer, the light he had mistaken at first for one lamp or torch split, on closer inspection, into two.

And Connor stopped cold.

Two lanterns set in the upstairs window…

He stared in disbelief as time dripped to a halt.

Two lanterns.

The signal he and Maggie had devised.

Come to me, it signified.

Two lanterns meant it was an emergency.

Staring at them there, like devil's eyes burning in the night, his own blurred with rain, Connor felt a horrifying rush of deep, instant knowing.

His throat closed with dread, for there was no possible way that Maggie could be out there. Not of her own volition.

Nor did she have any possible cause to summon him now. Not after the way he had just left her, ravished, completely satisfied, and ready to tumble into bed.

No. Whether by logic or instinct, Connor instantly grasped the import of what he was seeing, and he went numb.

Numb and clear as a crystal blade.

Then came the slow drip of rage into his veins as he stared, drawing in a breath through flaring nostrils. His hands tightened on the reins.

It was a trap, of course. But he didn't care.

He had no idea how his enemy could've learned about their lantern signals. He only knew with steely certainty that they had been followed all the way to Dorset.

He has her. He's here.

"I should have let Amberley kill you when he had the chance," Maggie spat, thrashing uselessly against the ropes that bound her wrists behind her and fastened her to the hard desk chair in the Thinkery's upper room.

"Yes, you probably should have." Pacing past her to check out the other window, Seth Darrow smirked at her despite his black eye and swollen lip. "Mercy is a common fault of ladies. But then..." He paused and leaned down to whisper in her face, "You're not a *real* lady, after all. Are you, my lovely?"

Maggie turned her face away in disgust.

His breath stank of stale liquor, and his cold hazel eyes were deadened of any emotion but lust-tinged scorn.

He snickered at her and straightened up again, then continued on his way, tracking muddy boot prints across the oval carpet.

After he'd passed behind her, Maggie glanced over her shoulder, barely daring to let the murderer out of her sight.

But the battered dragoon merely went to peer out once again from between the long green curtains drawn over the window nook, looking for any sign of Connor.

Likewise, his father was keeping watch out of one of the two windows that flanked the unlit fireplace on the back wall.

A short, stocky man, rugged and compact, Elias Flynn had a bald head, wire-rimmed spectacles, and a weathered face carved with a stony expression.

Other than snapping orders at his son, he had said very little so far.

His lack of conversation made Maggie nervous. For, despite his smaller frame and greater age, Elias was clearly the more dangerous of the two. Napoleon was supposed to be a man of small stature, too, after all, but that hadn't stopped him from wreaking havoc across the Continent for over a decade by sheer force of will.

Occasionally, Elias patted his rain-dampened face with the loose-hanging end of the plaid scarf wound around his neck, tucked inside the collar of his black wool coat. Other than that, he seemed impervious, indifferent to the weather, and nonchalant about the crimes he had underway.

He'd glanced at her a few times in a calculating manner that made Maggie extremely uncomfortable. She knew he owned brothels, after all.

She had a horrible feeling he was wondering how much money he might be able to make off her. But he was impossible to read behind the candle's glint off his little round glasses.

Far easier to interpret were his son's randy leers. These made her skin crawl. Seth Darrow had a cruel, petty quality that made her think he probably enjoyed rape far more than seduction.

Ruthlessness emanated from both father and son, though. A family trait, perhaps. For neither seemed perturbed that their plan to lure her noble Connor into a trap using her as the bait was the very nadir of treacherous dishonor.

Maggie felt sick to think that they were going to use his love for her as the very weapon with which to kill him.

As soon as he saw the lantern signal, she knew he would come, just as they'd promised each other. But the moment he stepped through the door, her captors meant to open fire.

Please, God, no. Maybe he wouldn't see the signal. Or, maybe, seasoned a warrior as he was, he would realize something was wrong. They had just been together, after all.

Surely he'd sense it was a trap.

But with his very life at stake, Maggie didn't dare take that chance.

Somehow, she had to figure out a way to warn him it was an ambush before he walked in.

Unfortunately, fear and fatigue both clouded her mind. The powerlessness of her situation made her furious, as well, to say nothing of her sharp physical discomfort, her arms pinned behind her, ropes chafing her wrists.

Wet and muddy from having been dragged out of the house by way of a servant stairwell that she hadn't even known existed, and then out into the night, past the lifeless body of some poor footman who'd been guarding the morning room door that let out onto the garden, the father and son had hauled her out across the moors in her night rail and dressing gown.

They had pulled her into the Thinkery, where she presently sat shivering and soaked to the skin.

None of this mattered, though, compared to her rising desperation to find some way to save her love.

Every tick-tock of the mantel clock in the vicar-duke's study warned her that time was running out. Any minute now, Connor would walk through that door and they'd shoot him—and shoot her, if she screamed to alert him.

Tick-tock, tick-tock...

The sound frayed her nerves. *I have to think of something.*

Finally getting hold of her terror, Maggie scanned her cozy prison, searching for anything that might be of help.

The rectangular room was partly lined with tall, pointy-arched, gothic bookshelves. Matching wooden arches adorned the red-painted walls above the door, the three windows in the room, as well as the curtained window nook overlooking the chine.

Before the unlit fireplace, an oval rug marked out the area for a comfy grouping of jewel-toned furniture: a deep-cushioned sofa and two slouchy armchairs, with a small, round table between them. On it sat a double-armed candelabrum, whose two ivory candles provided the chief source of light inside the Thinkery.

Her captors had also lit a small jar candle on the mantel, but none of this was enough to quite dispel the gloom. There were also the two signal lanterns, of course, but these perched on the windowsill on the other side of the drawn curtains, their light beaming out into the ebony night.

Calling Connor to his doom.

Maggie swallowed hard, kept trying to twist her hands free of the ropes, and continued her wary search of the vicar-duke's study.

It was a very personal space, and its contents soon led her to conclude that the churchman must've made an even more unlikely duke than Connor.

The room also gave her a strong impression of the sort of simple, goodhearted family man he had been, and it saddened her to know that one of these two monsters had murdered him for no reason at all.

The sight of his orphaned daughters' framed embroidery samplers proudly hung on the wall enraged her. But, from the cross on the mantel to the religious paintings on display, showing scenes from the Acts of the Apostles, certainly, Maggie got the impression that Uncle Rupert had been sincere in his calling.

His writing desk, about a foot away from her, was positioned under the largest window in the room, where the lanterns had been set.

Though she did not enjoy being tied to the wooden desk chair, from here at least the vicar-duke must've had a very inspiring view of the moors when he'd sat here writing his sermons and spiritual essays.

His notes and writing instruments had been left untouched since his death, it appeared. On the desk sat a well-worn Bible, paper and ink, a few quills, and a beautiful bronze statue of a dove in flight, carrying an olive branch in its beak.

Maggie gazed at it. A symbol of peace and reconciliation—of which her captors wanted no part.

Tick-tock…

"What's wrong with you?" Seth asked, eyeing her suspiciously. Restless as ever, he had prowled over to the little table between the armchairs, where he picked up the candle branch and used it to light a cheroot. "You look like you got indigestion or something. Problem?"

"You," she said. "You make me sick."

"Oho! Saucy. You hear that, Father? I don't think she likes me." He set the candelabrum back down and sauntered toward her again, puffing away.

Maggie glared at him. "You must think yourselves such brave fellows, clobbering a poor young maid and terrifying old ladies."

"Shut her up," the father ordered the son.

Casually exhaling a stream of smoke, Seth glanced over at his sire. "I'm sure that won't be necessary." Then Seth looked at Maggie again with a speculative gleam in his good eye; the blackened one was nearly swollen shut. "Are you going to be quiet or do I have to gag you?"

"Don't touch me."

He seemed amused by her snarl. "Then be polite." His tone was soft, but a world of ominous meaning danced behind his simple words; Maggie knew a threat when she heard one.

She swallowed hard and tried to slow her pounding heartbeat.

Think. Maybe agitating them was not the best idea, she admitted, even if it would take their minds off Connor.

Still, it made sense to keep them talking as best she could. A bit of conversation would distract them, and she might even learn something useful.

Surely that was worth making the effort to be civil.

Unsure how to begin, she studied the dragoon, who at least seemed interested in her, while the father was entirely focused on the darkness outside the window.

Seth held her wary gaze, simply watching her as he smoked.

"How did you find out about our lantern signal, anyway?" she asked. "Have you been stalking me?"

"Him, mostly. You, some." Brushing past her chair, Seth leaned across the vicar's desk to glance out briefly at the landscape, then he let the curtains fall shut again and turned around. "Watching you's more fun, I admit." He perched on the edge of the desk right near her.

"I'm honored," she said dryly.

"Oh, I'm a very observant fellow." His leisurely gaze traveled down over her body. "I was minding my own business one night, y'see, merely taking a stroll around Moonlight Square, when, lo and behold, I noticed two lanterns burning side by side in your upstairs window. Then you came out."

He shrugged and took a pull off his cheroot. "That was quite a show the two of you put on in the gazebo. I daresay I enjoyed it almost as much as you did."

Maggie gasped. "*Pervert!* You watched us?"

He grinned, revealing a chipped tooth—most likely from Connor's fist.

A furious curse exploded from her lips, the likes of which she had never uttered aloud in her life.

"My, oh my, Lady Margaret," he taunted. "You're spending too much time with the major. You're even beginning to swear like a soldier."

Rattled, she shook her head and let out a huff of disdain, struggling to regain her composure. "What on earth does Saffie see in you?"

He idly arched a brow at the mention of his plaything. "Well, you know, she isn't very bright."

"You're a dreadful man, using that poor girl."

"Trust me, she wanted to be used. So many of them do. I wouldn't mind using you for a few hours. Would you fancy that, milady?" He blew a stream of smoke in her face, anticipating her response.

Maggie coughed, turning her face away. "Go to hell."

Seth laughed. "Ohh, I'm wounded. Do you not find me handsome?"

"Hard to say. You look like an eggplant with eyes at the moment, thanks to Amberley."

Across the room, his father chortled at her jibe.

Seth glanced at the old man, then narrowed his eyes at Maggie. "Droll."

Then he lifted off the desk and slouched away to check out the window nook again.

Pleased with herself for finally landing a hit on him, Maggie sent a cold smile of aristocratic hauteur at his back. "I think it only fair to warn you that my fiancé will do much worse if you lay a hand on me. He shall tear you limb from limb. He only spared you last time because I was there, but this time, I won't stop him. In fact," she said, "I'll cheer him on."

"Spitfire, eh, Father?" Seth let the curtain fall back over the window nook and turned around to stare icily at her. "How about this, Lady

Margaret? Whatever your precious duke does to me, I'll take it out on you after he's dead. How does that sound, hmm?"

Though she gulped privately at the threat, Maggie refused to cower before him. Instead, she turned her attention across the room. "You've raised quite a prince here, Mr. Flynn. You must be so proud."

"Not really," Elias muttered, glancing over his shoulder.

Maggie's heart pounded. She knew it was dangerous, but if she really wanted to turn their attention elsewhere, only one topic was likely to serve. "I hope your other son was more agreeable than this cretin."

It worked.

From the corner of her eye, she saw anger flood Seth's face as he took a swift step toward her.

"Don't you dare speak of him, you little slut!"

Maggie ducked as he lifted his hand to strike her.

CHAPTER 34

Conflagration

"**H**old!" Father ordered, and Seth's hand froze in midair.

Damn it! To his fury, the girl's outrageous mention of his dead brother had snared his sire's interest.

But of course it had, Seth thought cynically.

Even in death, Francis was still his old man's favorite topic.

Elias Flynn turned from the window and eyed Lady Margaret suspiciously. "How do you know about Francis?"

"So that was his name." She seized on this as though she sensed an opening. "You have my condolences, sir. How did he die, may I ask?"

Father snorted and looked back out the window. "The old bitch murdered him, of course. That's why we're here."

"Surely you don't mean the Duchess Lucinda?" the girl asked, frowning prettily.

Seth didn't trust her for a minute.

"What happened?" she asked with an innocent look.

Father and he exchanged a dark glance fraught with bitter meaning and a shared history to which she was not privy.

"Please," Lady Margaret said. "If your son is the reason you're doing all this to me and my future family, I think that, at least, I deserve to know."

Seth shot her a seething glare, but it seemed his old man did not mind passing the time with a little talk.

Elias turned around slowly, letting the drape swing shut behind him. "He was a good lad," he said, his gravelly voice taut.

The little blueblood offered a sympathetic nod. "How old was he when he died?"

"Only eighteen."

"Father, it's none of this wench's business," Seth growled.

She ignored him, all her attention homed in on his sire. "But, Mr. Flynn, I don't understand. Her Grace is an old woman. Infirm. She walks with a cane. How could an old lady kill a strapping young man of eighteen?"

Father's spectacles glinted. "Her hirelings did it."

"Perhaps it was an accident."

"You think that matters?" Father said. "The result is the same. My son is dead. There's no atoning for what she's done." With that, he turned his back on them both and stared again out the window.

Seth looked at the girl and shook his head. *You shouldn't have started that.*

Her dainty chin came up a notch, and her gray eyes took on an even more determined gleam, despite her having her hands pinned behind her.

Seth let his gaze skim over her wet, cold, shivering body. He could definitely see the appeal she must've held for the soon-to-be dead man.

Truth be told, he rather liked seeing her tied up. He'd enjoyed the way she'd struggled and squirmed as he'd held her fast. When all this was over...

"Very well, Mr. Flynn," she said in that cut-crystal, aristocratic accent. "Even if you have a valid claim against the duchess, why kill off the Amberley men? They had nothing to do with this. The man whose study we're in, for example, he was a vicar. From what I'm told, he didn't even like Lucinda!"

A sharp, cynical bark of laughter escaped Elias. "A common problem for ol' Lucy, as I recall. Men either wanted to rut with her or reform her."

"What about you?" she countered, and to Seth's disgust, Father was weak enough on this point to indulge her.

"Me?" The old cutthroat nearly smiled. "I liked her as she was, I suppose, acid tongue and all. Now *there* was a spitfire. Ah, she was something back in those days."

Here we go again, Seth thought wearily.

But now Margaret was staring at Father with a dawning look of shock. "You cared for her," she said, "but…then she married the duke. My God, is that why you hate her so much to this day?"

"Be quiet," Seth warned her.

She ignored him, staring at his father. "Did she love you too? Might you have been happy together? And yet you sold her to this man?"

Elias took his glasses off and stared at the girl. Then he wiped them and put them back on, saying nothing.

Seth glanced over at his sire. "You want me to gag her now?"

"Leave her alone."

"Father, she's playing you!"

"Oh, shut up. Seth. Women don't play Elias Flynn," he said.

But Seth knew full well that one had, once, long ago.

This goddamned dragon lady who'd ruined all their lives.

Well, tonight, he and Father would finish ruining hers by destroying the family she had joined, just as she'd destroyed theirs. And then perhaps they could finally be done with this hellish obsession.

"Go check the other window," Elias said, but, for a long moment, Seth made no move to obey, itching to tell his father off.

He did not like the way the old man was treating him in front of this upper-class woman.

As the tension stretched thin, Seth noticed her watching them with a crafty stare. She was looking to sow division, he knew.

Divide and conquer.

But it wasn't going to work. Seth decided this wasn't the time to let himself rise to the bait of Father's constant goading. He swallowed his long-nursed resentment.

With a shake of his head and another idle puff of his cheroot, he simply went and did as he was told, as always.

He would punish his little captive later for her trickery. The thought cheered him up considerably.

Now, *that* he would enjoy.

Tick-tock, tick-tock…

In the brooding silence that followed her captors' curt exchange, Maggie pondered her next move. The friction between Elias and his surviving son could not have been more obvious.

She knew she was taking incredible risks, but picking at the scab of this unhealed wound between the two seemed the only way she had left to help Connor.

So much for being a peacemaker, she thought, calculating how to drive a deeper wedge between the pair.

Maybe she could turn one against the other. It was a heartless plan, but if she could focus their anger on each other rather than on Connor, that would make it all the easier for him to dispatch both of them when he arrived.

Which should be any minute now, she thought. She'd wager he had seen the lantern signal burning in the window by now, out riding the perimeter, as he'd told her he was going to do.

He was probably on his way even now. *Tick-tock.* This could be her last chance to let him know what he was walking into.

With the sand mentally pouring through the hourglass, Maggie gathered her courage to try playing her risky game. "Ahem, well. If I may say so, I'm very sorry you lost your son, Mr. Flynn, and your brother, Captain Darrow." She faltered. "What was he like?"

"I'm warning you," Seth uttered, seeing through her deception, she feared.

But Maggie would not be cowed.

"What does it matter if I ask about Francis?" she said, deliberately using the dead boy's name, for it seemed to have a potent effect on the old man. "I had nothing to do with his death, yet here I sit, being punished for it."

"It's nothing personal against you, young lady," Elias conceded, now that she had softened him up a bit.

"Nothing personal?" Maggie exclaimed. "You're about to murder the man I love! Why, in the name of heaven? Amberley is a good man! He had nothing do with this! He grew up in Ireland. He barely even knew his English relatives until he inherited the title. Is this what your son would really want?"

Elias stood very still. Maggie almost dared to hope he was considering her plea for a moment. But when she looked from one to the other, she saw that, at least, Seth would not be swayed.

He'd come too far to quit now, she supposed, had too much blood already on his hands. And, clearly, the dragoon had no sympathy for the major.

On the contrary, that cold smirk he wore said Seth wanted to make Connor suffer for the thrashing he'd taken last night.

Elias shrugged off his moment's hesitation. "It's nothing personal against your fiancé, either. This is all about Lucinda."

"How do you mean?"

"Isn't it obvious?" Seth muttered, looking disgusted even to be having this conversation. He crushed out the remainder of his cheroot with a scowl.

"Oh, I see." Maggie held the old man's gaze for a long moment. "You're ending the Amberley line, just like Lucinda's hirelings nearly ended yours."

"Clever lass," Elias said, studying her again in his unnerving way. "You could be of use to me when this is over, if you wish to live. The choice is yours."

Maggie stiffened. "I'd rather die with Amberley than be locked up in one of your brothels somewhere, thank you very much."

"That's not what I was thinking." Elias paused. "You remind me a little of my wife. Doesn't she remind you of Mother, Seth?"

Maggie went very still as Seth squinted skeptically at her.

She wasn't sure what Elias was getting at, and by the sound of it, she wasn't at all sure she wanted to know.

"You are from a good family, are you not?" Elias asked.

Suddenly wary, she did not deign to answer.

"Of course you are." The old cutthroat seemed amused. "Too proud even to answer the question from some cheeky commoner, eh? That haughty glare tells me all I need to know. A blueblood for certain."

"She's the daughter of an earl," Seth said. "Her sister's married to a marquess."

"My, my, how very lofty." Elias's cynical gaze shifted from her to Seth and back again. Then he announced his decision: "You'll make a fine bride for my son."

"What?" they both said.

"We've got to do something with her," Elias told his heir with a shrug. "Might as well use her to our advantage. If you want to keep rising in the world, you'll need the right kind of girl with good connections as your mate. Besides, you seem to like her."

"Oh, I do. How could I not?" Seth grasped Maggie's jaw and lifted her face to inspect it. "Can I have her, Father? Really?" he asked like a child pleading for a puppy, just to taunt her.

Elias shrugged. "Once Amberley's dead, I don't see why not."

Seth smiled and released his rough hold on her face. "You hear that, sweet? We have my father's blessing."

Maggie's stomach twisted. She fought not to panic. But, behind her back, she began pulling frantically at the ropes chafing at her wrists.

"I wouldn't be so sure you have the wherewithal to kill my fiancé," she said in a brittle tone, determined to keep a dismissive look on her face. "He *is* a war hero, after all. A real one," she added pointedly to Seth. "In my view, it is far more likely that when he comes—*if* he comes— you're both going to die."

"Oh, he'll come," Seth replied. "But from there, you have it backwards, my dear. Because the moment he steps through that door, I pull this trigger." He lifted his pistol to show her. "And your war hero dies."

"Amberley's not a fool," she said. "He's going to know something's wrong."

"Really? How?" the father asked.

When she floundered, suddenly fearing she'd put her foot in her mouth, Seth stared at her like a disapproving husband. "Aha, she's already been with him tonight." He grasped her face again. "You little slut, is that where you were while we were waiting for you in your room? Were you off fucking him?" he demanded as if he owned her already.

"Of course not! I was having a late-night cup of hot chocolate with my future kinswomen! Th-the Duchess Caroline and her two girls."

Seth leaned closer and stared hard into her eyes. "I'll know if you're not a virgin," he said softly.

He was a terrifying man. Holding his gaze, Maggie saw in his eyes that this particular ex-soldier truly was just a bit demented.

Tick-tock…

Suddenly, instead of dreading Connor's arrival, she couldn't wait for him to get here and save her. Who else could possibly protect her from these two?

Shivering uncontrollably with dread now, she strove to gather her wits, then steered the conversation back to the only topic that, so far, had been of any use. "So, you're blaming Lucinda. Her hirelings. The entire Amberley clan," she said in taut anger. "But with all due respect, Mr. Flynn, your son was practically a grown man, so isn't it possible that your Francis might've been at least partly responsible for his own death?"

"Mind your tongue!" Elias said. He paused, scowling at her, but then could not seem to hold back. "I will say this, though. *Someone* was responsible. Only it wasn't Francis. Was it, Seth?"

His glance wandered back to his firstborn.

Maggie saw that Seth's face had gone ashen; even his bruises had paled.

The battle-hardened dragoon flinched as though his sire had just punched him in the stomach.

"Not now, Father, please," he said quietly.

"Oh, was it *your* fault?" Maggie asked.

Seth cast her a tormented look.

"Go on, tell her, son. Tell her how you sent your little brother to his doom, all for your own laziness."

Seth whirled to face his father, fists clenched. "It wasn't laziness! My God, how many times must I explain it to you? I was trying to *teach* him the family business instead of always sheltering him like you did! Is it my fault he got cocky with those two thugs? I didn't tell him to start a fight with a pair of men twice his size!"

"He should've never even been there!" Elias bellowed.

"Why not?" his firstborn roared. "If I was expected to do those things, then why not your precious Francis?"

"Oh, quit whining," Elias said.

Seth strode toward him. "Damn it, you will listen to me this time! If you really want to know who's to blame for all this, Father, I suggest you look in the mirror!"

Elias's face turned white. "What's that supposed to mean?"

"You and your blackmail schemes. You and your obsession with that insufferable duchess. The girl's right." Seth gestured angrily at Maggie. "If your thrice-damned Lucy Bly meant so much to you, then why the hell did you sell her to the duke? Oh, but I already know the answer," Seth said. "Profit's all that ever mattered to you. Profit and position!"

"*Francis mattered!*" the old man howled. "And you got him killed!"

Maggie watched, wide-eyed, as Seth stepped toward Elias.

"No, Father. *You* did."

"How dare you?" Elias took a step toward his son.

"It's true." Seth shook his head. "You spoiled him. Praised everything he did to the rafters till the little peacock came to think himself invincible. I know full well you wish it was me who had died, but at least I know better than to go slapping a man twice my size across the face."

"Which is why I sent *you* to do the task, not your brother, you fool. Francis had nothing to do with the family business. He was a *gentleman!*"

"*No, he wasn't!*" Seth erupted, red-faced. "Stop fooling yourself! He was nothing but a whoremonger's son! Just like me."

Good God, Maggie thought, heart pounding. She had wanted to get them squabbling with each other, but she wasn't quite sure what she had started here.

The way Seth had exploded at his father reminded her of herself that day in Hyde Park, when her patience with Delia had finally snapped.

It sounded like this fight had been a long time coming.

But Seth's father was having none of it.

"Don't you dare speak against Francis." Elias gripped Seth by the lapels, though his son towered over him. "You're the reason he's dead, you useless piece of shit. Your incompetence. I charged *you* with the task of collectin' the money. It was *your* job, and like always, you had to shirk your duty. You made him do it, so quit tryin' to shift the blame!"

Seth thrust his father away from him, loosing his hold on him by force.

"Shift the blame?" he echoed incredulously. "First of all, no one could *make* Francis do anything. He was far too spoiled for that, your little gentleman! He did as he pleased, as you may recall. I'm the only one you could ever count on, you ungrateful son of a bitch."

"Oh, why don't you just admit it?" Elias wrenched out with murder in his eyes. "We both know you purposely set him up."

"*What?*"

"You wanted Francis dead."

"Don't be absurd!"

"You hated that boy."

"Why, because you loved him more?" Seth scoffed. "I don't give a shit, Father. I just want your money."

While they continued battling over the sins of the past, Maggie looked around discreetly.

The two were so engrossed in their hatred of each other that they seemed to have forgotten temporarily about her.

Flooded with newfound hope at this sliver of a chance to warn Connor somehow while they were distracted, she swept her gaze over the vicar's writing table, a slender Chippendale piece on long, spindly legs. There had to be something here that she could use to her advantage.

It was then that she looked at the bronze dove statue and suddenly received what could only be divine inspiration.

She drew in her breath and quickly lowered her head so they would not notice the sudden excitement flaring in her eyes.

She sneaked another glance at the desktop statue and felt her pulse quicken.

This might actually work. If she gave the desk a good kick in just the right spot, the hefty bronze dove would slide off and crash right into the window.

The glass *should* break, then she could scream out to Connor that he was walking into a trap.

She eyed her captors briefly, making sure they were still distracted; their quarrel raged on.

With that, Maggie began inching her chair carefully into position.

She didn't have far to go—she merely had to turn herself around a bit to get lined up with the desk.

Her captors did not notice her movement, and the rug beneath her muffled the sound of any bumping and scraping of her chair legs as she shifted herself around.

Halfway there, she glanced over again at the criminal duo, making sure they were still engrossed in their argument.

Heavens, it looked like it soon might come to blows.

Elias had whipped off his spectacles, and a vein popped out on his forehead as he gave his son a vicious tongue-lashing. The red hue of his face had crept all the way up toward his bald head.

Seth, for his part, looked like he'd had all the humiliation for one night that he intended to take.

Still, the seconds felt like hours and brought a cold sweat to Maggie's brow as she finally lined herself up in a good spot across from the vicar's desk.

She stared at the slim drawer right in the middle where she wished to strike it with her feet. Her wet, muddy, woolen socks would be slippery.

Just give it a good shove.

The two men were paying no attention to her as she slowly lifted her legs and planted both feet against the edge of the writing table. Her heart pounded as she said a brief mental prayer, then gave a sharp, sudden thrust against the side of the desk with both feet.

Her eyes widened as everything on the desk tilted toward the window.

The dove rocked off balance and began sliding toward freedom like it wanted to fly away out the window, escape these horrible men.

Everything else on the desk went sliding in that direction, as well: books, papers, inkpot.

Her chair legs thumped back down to the floor as the bronze dove went crashing into the window.

Through the drapes, she heard the sound of shattering glass, then the dove itself disappeared between the curtains.

Both her captors spun to face her, but then Maggie saw what had actually occurred.

Instead of simply breaking the window, the dove had also shattered the glass surrounds of the two lanterns on the sill.

And that, in turn, had fed the drapes right into the spilled lamp oil: the curtains promptly ignited.

Both her captors let out astonished curses as the drapes burst into flames.

"You bitch!" Seth said.

"What have you done?" uttered Elias.

"Connor!" Maggie screamed through the hole in the glass.

The cold rush of oxygen into the room only teased the flames higher.

Seth backhanded her in the face on his way to put out the fire.

Maggie cried out, tasting blood, but the dragoon wasn't finished with her yet.

As he swept her chair aside roughly so he'd have more room to fight the flames, his motion was so swift and violent that the chair tipped off balance.

Maggie shrieked as her chair went falling sideways onto the carpet.

She landed on her shoulder with an *"oof!"* and the side of her head banged hard against the floor. Her eyes watered at the pain. Amid her terror, black dots floated across her field of vision.

Clobbered in the head by her fall while her captors struggled to put out the fire, she felt the hot, sticky wetness of blood oozing from a gash somewhere above her ear.

Amid the wooziness, she wanted to scream for Connor again, but the fall had also knocked the wind out of her. She could not seem to draw a proper breath for a moment.

Meanwhile, gray and black smoke had begun billowing from the curtains, roaring out the Thinkery window and curling up all around the ceiling.

Elias and his son worked frantically to stop it from spreading.

"Use your coat!" Elias bellowed. He had taken off his own rain-sodden jacket and begun beating at the flames on one side.

Seth set his pistol down to follow suit, perhaps fearing the gunpowder might catch a spark and explode in the holster.

Unfortunately, their efforts did them little good, for the curtains were ablaze, and when the flames leapt to the fine oak framing around the window, it burst into a raging inferno, as though the wood had been treated with some highly flammable varnish.

The smoke took on a different smell, sharp and acrid.

Maggie's eyes watered as she glanced up from the floor as best she could to gauge how far away from her the fire was. Only seven or eight feet. She could already feel the heat of it.

God, this was not what she'd intended!

Worse, she saw that, in moments, the flames would reach the vicar's bookshelves, and then there would be no stopping them.

Maggie could hear both of her captors coughing while she, too, choked at the smell. That varnish on the wood paneling seemed to be giving off some sort of noxious fumes.

Between the throbbing pain on the side of her skull and the lung-squeezing smoke filling the room, she could feel herself starting to pass out.

Stay awake! she ordered herself while the blood oozed from the gash on her head and the ropes held her fast. She'd never felt so helpless.

What if they run away and leave me here? Tied to the chair, she couldn't get up—indeed, she could barely keep herself conscious.

The room had gone wavy. The floor seemed to spin slowly while the flames writhed nearby. Maggie struggled to stay alert, but her eyelids grew heavy. She could feel herself fading…

The last thing she saw before she lost consciousness was the room door blasting open with an explosive kick from Connor, and, through the drifting smoke, his face filled with wrath.

CHAPTER 35

All or Nothing

*A*fter his horse had tripped three times on the boggy, pathless moor, Connor had abandoned the animal and finished crossing the longest mile and a half of his life on foot, running through slog and rain in the blackness, up and down the hillocks, through puddles up to his shins, wrenching his old gammy knee on a thorny clump of sedge, finally reaching the Thinkery about twenty minutes after seeing the lantern signal.

He'd heard two males arguing inside as he'd crept silently into the building on the ground floor, closing in for his attack. When one called the other "Father," he realized that not just Seth awaited him upstairs, but also Elias Flynn.

Good. That meant Connor could remove both threats at one go.

Maggie's presence in the room complicated matters, of course. With a dagger in one hand, a pistol in the other, he had climbed stealthily up the steps, calculating how best to get her out of there unscathed.

But then he'd heard glass shatter and a startled cry from her, followed by a thump.

With that, he'd sprinted the rest of the way up the stairs.

He could smell the smoke even before he'd seen wisps of it pouring out from the crack at the bottom of his uncle's study door.

Then he'd kicked the door in.

Now, stepping over the threshold into the smoke-filled room, Connor assessed the situation in a glance.

Both men were using their coats to slap frantically at the fire that

446　　*Gaelen Foley*

now engulfed the front wall of the study. Flames consumed his uncle's bookshelves.

Where is she?

His heart lurched until he spotted Maggie unconscious on the floor, tied to a chair that had toppled over sideways.

His stare homed in on her head. *Is that blood?*

But then the old man, turning in response to Connor's arrival, reached for a weapon.

Connor reacted instinctively, hurling his knife at Elias, striking him in the chest. A garbled expletive escaped the old whoremonger.

His son gasped.

Elias stumbled backward, looking shocked as he reached for the blade sticking out of his chest.

But not even Connor expected what happened next, as Elias pitched back clumsily against the wall, stumbling over his heels into the flames.

His clothes ignited.

"Father!" Seth shouted, as a horrific scream rose from the burning man's throat.

Connor went to Maggie while the dragoon stood by helplessly, watching his father in shock.

"Go outside! Run out into the rain!" the son cried.

The father thrashed from side to side, howling.

Connor was glad Maggie was not seeing this as he stepped over her inert body, ready to protect her. But it seemed his enemies were preoccupied at the moment.

The room now stank of charring flesh.

"Get the rain on you, Father!"

Elias leaned out the window as if to take his son's advice, but, writhing in pain, lost his balance and fell.

His inhuman scream was cut short.

"Oh my God," Seth said. He turned to Connor. "What have you done?"

Connor lifted his pistol, took aim, squeezed the trigger.

Nothing happened.

Seth sneered. "Got your powder wet, eh, Major?" Then he reached for his own pistol, which he'd set aside.

Connor charged him, running at the gun even as it was pointed at him. He reached Seth in a heartbeat, grasped his arm and drove the muzzle skyward in the same split second that the bastard pulled the trigger.

The bullet bit into the ceiling somewhere above the door in a burst of plaster dust. Connor wrenched the spent weapon out of his enemy's hand, but Seth abandoned the fight with a glare that promised vengeance later.

For now, he ran out of the room to go down to his father. Not that much could be done for the man at this point, if he was even still alive.

Connor let him pass at a safe distance, checking his own fury for the moment. He would deal with him later. First, he had to get Maggie out of here.

The place was burning down. He tucked the empty gun into the back of his trouser waist in case he found some dry ammunition to use later. He did not intend to let Seth get hold of it again.

"Sweeting, can you hear me?" he asked, willing his voice to be gentle as he crouched beside Maggie and quickly untied her hands.

He cursed to himself when he saw how red and raw the delicate skin at her wrists had become.

He pressed two fingers to her neck, checking her pulse. She was alive, still, but his rage turned flinty when he got a closer look at the blood trickling down the side of her face from the gash above her ear.

It erased whatever trace of pity he might've felt for the man he had just set on fire, to say nothing of his son. To be sure, the dragoon had merely postponed his death, not escaped it.

"Maggie, can you hear me?" Connor asked again. He was frightened to move her until he was sure she had not sustained worse injuries that he could not see.

To his unutterable relief, her lashes fluttered when he caressed her cheek with one knuckle. "Connor," she mumbled. "I knew you'd come."

Then she coughed in the thickening smoke. His own lungs were straining, and the smoke stung his eyes. He glanced around to find that the fire had now spread to the opposite wall.

Time was of the essence.

"I need to get you out of here, love. I'm going to pick you up now. Are you able to move?"

"I think so..." She tested it, stretching her fingers, flexing her feet in her mud-caked socks.

Thank God. More than once on the battlefield, he'd seen blows to the head kill or paralyze men instantly.

"Put your arms around me," he forced out. "Here. Try for me, love."

Maggie lifted her hands to his shoulders while Connor slid his arms under her back and the bend of her knees. Moving smoothly and carefully, he rose to his feet, carrying her toward the door.

Coughing again, Maggie laid the uninjured side of her head on his shoulder.

To his relief, they left the roaring blaze behind them.

Connor cradled her gently in his arms as he sped down the dark, narrow staircase. Slowing his pace when he reached the bottom, he scanned the darkness on the ground floor of the Thinkery.

It was possible that Seth was lying in wait there, but a wary glance around confirmed the lower room was empty. The dragoon must've run out to his father, as Connor had initially assumed.

Still, not knowing what sort of trouble might await him at the front of the building, he had to keep Maggie out of the line of fire. Put her somewhere close enough where he could still protect her, but as far as possible from the burning front section of the neo-gothic folly.

With that, Connor carried her out the back door of the Thinkery, into the wet, chilly night.

The steady rain poured off the deep, medieval-style eaves overhanging the back wall of the Thinkery, but at least these provided the two of them with a narrow strip of shelter.

Connor set her down there, on the stone foundation at the corner of the building farthest away from the fire.

Miserable as it was outside, the wind-driven mist of the shower blowing just past their noses felt like heaven after the ovenlike heat and smoke of that blasted inferno.

Maggie leaned back wearily against the exterior wall, looking somewhat revived by the cold sprinkle they both were getting in the face, while Connor kept scanning the blackness around them for movement.

To his relief, there was no sign of Seth.

As he'd anticipated, the dragoon must have remained with his dying father at the front of the burning building, facing the distant manor house.

By now, for that matter, Connor trusted that his men had seen the flames towering out of the Thinkery window.

They would not understand what the hell was happening, but being well trained, they'd hesitate about leaving their posts, sensing some trick of the enemy. Aunt Caroline's staff would surely respond within a few minutes, however. They could deal with the blaze.

Until then, Connor's chief concern was for Maggie. The moment she was secure, he would go and hunt Seth. Finish this thing.

And this time, that bastard would not get away.

"Sorry about the fire." Maggie coughed again, wincing. "It was my fault," she confessed.

Connor arched a brow and looked at her again, leaving off scanning the darkness. "You started the fire?"

She nodded wearily. "I had to try and warn you it was a trap. I didn't mean to burn the whole place down."

"Oh, I knew you were trouble from the first moment I laid eyes on you, Lady Maggie Winthrop," he whispered tenderly, and leaned close to kiss her brow for a long, shaky moment, his heart clenching.

God, I thought I'd lost you.

The fact that his enemies had gone after her redoubled his hunger to end this. He pulled back again, then lifted her hand and gave it a quick kiss. "I must go. Time to see matters sorted. You stay here."

She clutched his arm. "There are two of them."

"Not anymore," he said.

"Oh." She grimaced. "I must've missed that part."

He nodded grimly. "Be glad."

She stared at him, still clinging to his arm. "I don't want you to leave me, Connor. I'm scared."

"I know, sweeting. I have to. Don't worry," he promised, finding a smile for her—a mask for his rage. "I'll be right back. Be brave for me just a little while longer."

She closed her eyes. "Very well."

"Hey." He squeezed her shoulder gently, and her eyes swept back open. "Stay awake," he ordered softly. "You need to keep alert after a nasty blow to the head like that, you understand? Don't drift off. We'll have Nestor take a look at that as soon as I'm done here."

She nodded. "Connor, I love you."

"I love you too, Maggie. With all my heart." He leaned down and pressed a kiss to her lips.

"Be careful."

"What fun is that? I'm jesting," he whispered at her look of alarm. "Here." She looked so damned vulnerable sitting there that he gave her the second knife he always kept in his boot, sliding it out of its hidden sheath and offering it to her by the hilt.

Not that she knew how to use it. But he could not leave her here unarmed when she still looked so small and alone and defenseless.

"Take this," he said. "If anyone comes near you, cut them and call for me."

She took it, wide-eyed, but obviously grateful. "Don't you need this?"

He shook his head meaningfully.

"Oh… Right." She dropped her gaze and gripped the weapon uncertainly.

He wished like hell that he could've trusted his pistol instead, but after its mate had failed to fire upstairs, he couldn't take that chance.

Of course, he was still cursing himself for that amateurish mistake. He'd been so panicked to reach her that he'd somehow let the rain run into his ammunition pouch. It had been hard to avoid, splashing and slogging his way across some thirty acres of boggy heathland in the dark.

But no matter. The mishap had only delayed Seth's death, not averted it.

"Righty-ho," Connor murmured with a wry smile, determined to ease some of the fear from her eyes. He rose to his feet. "See you soon, love. Carvel's out that way," he added, pointing to the north. "He may well come."

"So I shouldn't stab *him*, right?" she jested halfheartedly.

"You see?" Connor grinned. "You're catching on more every day to this whole battle business."

"Well, I'd better, if I mean to marry you."

He nodded, his smile fading at thoughts of the ruthless task ahead. "You see anything wrong, you yell for me."

"I'll be fine," she said, clutching the knife in both hands, her forearms resting on her bent knees. "Good luck."

Connor took one last, long look at her, memorizing her in that moment. Truly, she was the most beautiful thing he'd ever seen—even wet, muddy, bedraggled, her cheek bloodied, her hair a mess, her clothes dusted with ash—and he had never loved any creature more.

Her eyes were so solemn and brave. How could any man leave her there to fend for herself, even for a moment?

But he had to, so they could be free.

And by now, God's truth, he knew this woman's quiet strength.

"Go on, Major," she urged him with a grim nod toward the corner. "Go do what you do."

As her words sank in, his face hardened with resolve. To be sure, she understood him now. He felt it deep down into his very core, and it lit him with power from within like he'd swallowed the lightning.

"Be right back," he whispered with a wink, then he kissed his fingers to her in farewell and left.

Maggie watched him go, her heart in her throat.

Sitting there shivering and wet against the cold stone, her head hurt, her shoulder ached where she'd landed on it, and her lungs burned, though the fresh air helped. She was still concerned about Penelope back at the manor and what would become of them all. But, mainly, her full awareness trailed after Connor.

Tall and broad-shouldered, he slid through the shadows under the eaves, angling his body as he kept to the side of the building.

Maggie gripped his knife, hoping with all her heart that she wouldn't have to use it.

As she watched him in the darkness, her heart in her throat, Connor paused at the corner, assessing whatever there was to see at the front of the burning building.

Yet, holding her breath, Maggie could not help cursing herself. All of this tonight was her fault. Why oh why hadn't she let Connor neutralize Seth when he'd had the chance? Some naïve sense of justice? But she had not known then what sort of monsters they were dealing with in Elias Flynn and his son.

Who did she think she was to second-guess the warrior in his area of greatest expertise? This all could have been avoided if only she had trusted him.

Anxiously flicking her fingers tighter around the hilt, Maggie swallowed down a wave of cold regret, dread churning in her belly.

Well…it was too late now to go back and do that awful night over.

But she swore that if anything happened to him out there, she would never, ever forgive herself.

Connor stole a guarded glance around the edge of the building, half expecting to be shot at. But when he poked his head out just far enough to see what he might find, he spotted the dragoon crouched by the smoking body of his father, rain dripping off his nose.

Elias Flynn lay in a twisted heap, unmoving.

Dead. Must've broken his neck when he hit the ground, Connor thought. A mercy, that. At least it would have been quick, putting him out of his misery.

Better than burning to death. Though he was probably burning now, where he'd gone.

Steeling himself, Connor stepped around the corner and warily walked back out across the front of the Thinkery, his stare fixed on his enemy.

"You killed him," Seth said in a low tone, looking up at last.

"Don't worry," Connor said as he stalked toward him. "You'll be together again soon."

The dragoon's face hardened. He shot to his feet. By the glow of the blaze above them, Connor saw the man's fingers flex by his sides.

Then they curled into fists, and Seth charged.

Connor stepped back with one foot to brace for the onslaught and bent his knees to lower his center of gravity, raising both hands, palms open, to block the punches he knew were coming.

The dragoon dropped his head and shoulders as he ran, clearly determined to knock Connor's legs out from under him and slam him to the ground.

Connor was ready for him, however, sidestepping the main line of attack; although Seth managed to grab hold of his upper thigh, Connor's wide stance kept him solidly planted. Connor snaked his arm around the blackguard's head, cranking Seth's neck to make him loosen his hold.

As Seth cursed, Connor brought his elbow down like a spear into his back.

Seth stumbled away, twisting about to lunge at him with a brutal right punch at his jaw. Connor blocked and struck back with a speedy jab straight to the nose. Seth's head snapped back but he absorbed the blow rather impressively.

Then they circled by the lurid glow of the inferno raging out of the upper window. By now, the roof was burning, too.

Seth launched at Connor again, his movements wild with fury. A vicious brawl ensued. They traded savage blows, slipping around in the muck and mud, until they both were bloodied and the fight ground down to a grim, brutal slog.

The only sounds were the hiss of the rain, the crackling of the fire coming out of the upper window, and their own harsh panting.

As those few long moments of full-force effort stretched on, Connor began to wish he hadn't given his knife to Maggie. A gallant gesture, aye, but he was tired, soaked to the skin, and so very sick of fighting.

Then Seth got in a hammer fist to his chest and half knocked the wind out of him—such blows could stop a man's heart if done right—but as Seth moved in for the kill, Connor summoned up a burst of strength. His fist shot out, and he left the bastard coughing with a throat strike.

Pressing the advantage, Connor swept Seth's feet out from under him and dropped astride the man, determined to choke the life out of him once and for all.

Seth reached up and jammed his palm under Connor's chin, straight-armed, trying to hold him at bay.

Losing patience, Connor punched him across the face with an angry roar. "Give up, damn you! That's enough!"

"Go to hell," Seth said, coughing. "You killed my father."

"You killed two of my uncles and my cousin, and tried to kill me at least three times!"

"So?"

Panting, Connor shook his head. "You abducted my fiancée. And for that…you die." Then he wrapped his hands around Seth's throat and began to squeeze.

Seth gripped his wrists, trying to claw Connor's hold loose as the rain pelted both of them. An old, familiar rage came over Connor as he focused all his hate on the man at his mercy.

Tonight he had none. Not after what he'd done to Maggie.

At the thought of her, however, something strange happened.

Seth was choking, thrashing, fighting, and suddenly, all Connor could think of was the horrified way she had looked at him when she'd stepped out of the alley to find him well on his way to beating this blackguard to death with his bare hands.

Now that the moment had come for him to finish the job, Connor realized he did not have it in him to end the life of a man he had already bested—never mind how much the bastard deserved killing.

He was a soldier, after all. Not a murderer.

Maggie was right. Let the law deal with him.

He released his hold on Seth's throat. "I said that's enough," he repeated wearily, chest heaving.

Seth clutched his neck, coughing and gasping for air as Connor lifted off him.

Connor planted his foot on Seth's chest, though, to hold him down and stop him from trying to get away.

"What, you're sparing me?" the dragoon wrenched out.

"Handing you over to the constable," Connor said, panting with exertion. "Let the judges decide what to do with you. I'm taking you into custody."

"The hell you are. I'll not swing by a noose!"

With that, Seth grasped Connor's bad knee above the foot pinning him to the ground and wrenched it violently, twisting Connor's leg and throwing him aside.

Connor stumbled back, slipped on the mud, and landed on his arse with a curse of pain as Seth sprang instantly to his feet.

In the blink of an eye, Seth was up and running. He bolted off around the corner of the building on the side opposite from where Connor had left Maggie.

"Get back here!" Connor climbed to his feet, limping a bit, but infuriated anew. He gave chase.

He could not risk the blackguard seeing Maggie hiding back there, for he knew full well that Seth would not hesitate to use her as a hostage if he got the chance.

He was right on Seth's heels, gritting his teeth against the pain of the old injury from when a horse had been shot out from under him once and nearly took him with it when it fell. He thrust the awful memory out of his mind and went tearing after the bastard through the darkness.

There was a span of about twenty feet between the east wall of the Thinkery and the rock ledge of the chine's little canyon. Down the center of this dark, grassy stretch, Uncle Rupert's walking path wrapped around the side of the little building and continued out onto the moors.

Around the side of the Thinkery, the exterior wall amplified the sound of the swollen river rushing violently along the bottom of the nearby chine.

Pouring on a burst of agonizing speed, Connor caught up with Seth on the walking path, grabbing hold of the back of his shirt and tackling him to the ground. Mud splashed, slippery under their feet.

It was pitch-black here, away from the blaze. Connor punched him and Seth struck back.

They brawled, rolling toward the precipice, exchanging savage blows, crushing tall grasses and tufts of heath. Connor felt a stone dig into his back. Seth found one, too, and ripped it out of the turf.

Connor ducked as Seth tried to bash him in the head with it; he blocked with his forearm, but Seth got in a glancing blow. Then mud flew up into Connor's eyes. He could barely see for a moment, but had the presence of mind to trip the son of a bitch as Seth stumbled to his feet again to flee.

How it happened, exactly, Connor wasn't sure, since his vision had not quite cleared yet from the mud flung into his eyes, but Seth must have slipped or misjudged his distance from the ledge.

Falling with a scream, Seth caught hold of Connor's good leg to try to save himself, but only succeeded in dragging Connor toward the precipice, too.

"Get off o' me!" Connor raked his hands behind him as he was pulled over the same ledge where Seth had murdered the vicar-duke.

In the final instant, Connor flipped over onto his stomach, clawing at the slippery turf and barely catching himself on the rock ledge.

It took all his strength, but he hung there somehow, defying gravity, holding up not just his own weight, but Seth's. The dragoon clung on at Connor's knees.

All the while, the swollen river thundered by some seventy feet below them. *Oh my God, we're both going to die.*

"Let go of me!" Connor bellowed.

"I—can't!" Seth sounded terrified. He flailed his feet around, trying to find any solid support on which to brace himself. But there was only empty air beneath him, white water and jagged rocks, a few scraggly trees.

Connor could feel his grip on the wet rock ledge slowly slipping.

He willed himself to hang on, fastening his hands even harder to the sharp stone outcrop, his arms and shoulders screaming with exertion, while the rain dripped off him and onto Seth below.

Seth shrieked as his grip slipped down a few inches, caught at Connor's ankle, and there, he lasted only a few seconds longer before he plunged into the gully with a scream.

The sudden shift in weight as Seth dropped made Connor lurch. He cursed, nearly losing his hold, then clung to the rockface for dear life, while a sickening thud cut short Seth's scream. It was followed by a splash from below.

Connor glanced anxiously over his shoulder.

"Darrow!" he bellowed, but there was no answer.

Heart pounding, Connor scanned the dark, frothing river below for several seconds, though he knew there was no way his enemy could have survived a fall from that height. He must've hit the rocks, then slumped into the swollen stream.

By a stray flash of lightning just then, Connor caught sight of Seth's lifeless body floating facedown in the rushing stream. The current sped the killer's corpse away, carrying him off toward the ocean.

The lightning vanished, and Connor strove to gather his thoughts in the distant rumble of thunder that followed a few seconds later.

Seth's fall had unnerved him. The dire thought snaked through his mind that he would surely follow suit any minute now. His strength was nearly spent. He did not know how much longer he could hold on.

His arms were shaking, his fingers bloodied and raw from clinging to the wet, jagged rockface—when, suddenly, Maggie appeared above him.

Her face was a pale oval peering down at him over the ledge.

"I've got you!" She flung herself down onto her belly flat on the ground above, reached down, and clasped his forearm with both hands, steadying him. "Hold on."

"Let go of me, Maggie. I'm too heavy for you."

"No."

"It's too dangerous, woman! I'll pull you down with me—"

"I told you, I don't follow orders. Now, *climb!*" she roared.

He very nearly laughed at her vehemence amid his terror. But when he looked at her delicate white hands clutching to him, refusing to let the darkness swallow him, Connor caught sight of the ring on her finger.

Her engagement ring—the very promise of their future.

Although the diamond and its crown of emeralds were smeared with mud from this night's ordeal, he could still see their sparkle by the lightning's flash, and somehow, at the sight of it, he found the strength to reach deep down inside himself and take hold of a final burst of determination.

He would not be denied a life of loving her.

She held on to him, steadying and coaxing him, until he pulled himself up over the side with a last, savage heave.

He crawled a few feet away from the ledge on his hands and knees, drawing Maggie with him toward safety.

His chest heaving with exhaustion, Connor pulled her into his arms and held her fiercely amid the blood and smoke, both of them on their knees in the mud, while the rain coursed over them.

This moment, with its terror and the nearness of death, brought him right back to every battlefield he'd ever known, only, this time, overriding the past was his love for her, and Maggie's love for him.

She was crying, hugging him desperately. "Oh, God, I thought I'd lost you."

"Shh, it's over. I'm here, darlin'. You saved me."

She lifted her lovely face to the rain. Connor cupped her cheek in his palm, staring at her with helpless adoration.

"You saved me," he whispered again.

She cupped his face between her hands, searching his eyes as though to reassure herself he was indeed alive.

"How many times is that now?" she forced out, her lips trembling as she worked up a brave smile.

The little lady quite slayed him. He shook his head as he held her gaze tenderly. "I've lost count."

She laughed, teary-eyed and slightly hysterical.

"It's all right now, love," he whispered, cradling her to him. "It's over." Then he lowered his head and kissed her for all he was worth as the rain drenched them with its cold baptism.

Meanwhile, the servants began arriving to try to put out the fire, to no avail.

The Thinkery was a total loss.

But no matter. It was a small price to pay for what he'd gained here tonight, Connor knew. The woman he cherished, so warm in his arms. Peace and hope.

Life and love and finally…freedom.

EPILOGUE

The Fourth Duchess

Three Weeks Later

The bells of St. Andrew's pealed wildly, filling Moonlight Square with their joyful noise on a brilliant Saturday morning. The wedding day—the first of June—was balmy and bright, everything sparkling with dew and as green as the emeralds surrounding the diamond Maggie wore on her finger.

Her heart pounded, her gauzy white veil wafting gently in the breeze as the garlanded open coach rolled to a halt before the church entrance. While Delia and Edward rode in the coach with Maggie, Penelope was already waiting for her there, along with Sergeant McFeatheridge, dashing in his smart red uniform. After all, he had been given the lofty honor of serving as Connor's best man.

Behind her veil, Maggie smiled to see the fond caress that Rory gave her lovely maid as the wedding carriage approached. It warmed her heart to know that Penelope had not only recovered from that bump on the head, so like the one that Maggie had suffered at the hands of the late Elias Flynn and his horrid son, but now, she, too, had someone taking care of her.

Not that she needed it, independent as she was. But Penelope was happy with her affable soldier, and that was all that mattered.

The two waited side by side as the liveried footman jumped down to get the carriage door while the vehicle rolled to a halt.

The mahogany barouche had been a wedding gift from Connor, just as he had promised. Of course, its luxurious seats had also served as the site of previous naughtiness between them that splendid day in the carriage house. But even though Maggie still felt a wee bit guilty about having the wedding night before the wedding, nevertheless, she wore her bridal white with pride.

Her gown was a glorious confection of ivory lace with a heart-shaped neckline and a small train edged with rich embroidery. The gown was high-waisted, with short puff sleeves, below which she wore elbow gloves of ivory satin.

Her simple gauze veil was held in place by a tiara that the previous Duchess of Amberley, Aunt Caroline, had passed down to her.

As the moment of her momentous walk down the aisle drew ever nearer, Maggie could not wait to see Connor's reaction to her appearance this day.

He was already inside the church, along with a throng of guests. Naturally, the groom had been kept in the dark about her bridal attire. But, playful as ever, he did not mind.

The arrival of his Irish relatives had kept him busy, as had the raucous celebration that the gents of Moonlight Square had thrown for him over at the Grand Albion.

Reinforcements for their mischief that night had arrived in the form of more soldiers from his regiment, as well as his merry Irish cousins. Rumor had it there had been a great deal of drunken singing; the cousins had informed her that Connor had a beautiful baritone voice when you got enough whiskey into him, but he denied any knowledge of this.

Meanwhile, Maggie had been honored to meet his charming mother and grandmother, both great beauties for their respective ages. It was clear where the man had come by his looks. Of course, in planning the wedding, there had arisen the delicate question of religion.

Although the maternal side of Connor's family was Catholic—rather alarming Delia—the Irishwomen had long since accepted the fact that their connection to the highborn House of Amberley came with certain political duties that required the English line of their menfolk to hold to the Protestant faith. Given the current laws, it was just easier that way, though his mother had told Maggie that her son had always had an almost Catholic devotion to certain saints.

Maggie was just relieved that his dam and granddam liked her. They could not have been kinder, bringing her gifts of fine glass and elegant linens from Ireland. So far, in fact, Maggie got along smashingly with all her soon-to-be relatives.

She had even achieved an uneasy truce with Grandaunt Lucinda.

Of course, Aunt Florence remained her favorite, though Aunt Caroline's rambunctious twins had divided her heart between the two of them. The youngsters had been thrilled to find themselves in London.

The twins were inside now…along with nearly the rest of the world, Maggie thought with a gulp.

All of Moonlight Square had said they were coming—whether she had invited them or not.

Maggie suspected this was due to Connor's joviality as he went about befriending half of London, as he was wont to do, now that he no longer had to be suspicious of everyone he met.

Ever since that night by the Thinkery, when he had rid the world of their tormentors, he had been like a different person, effusive, lighthearted. Seeing him happy gave Maggie such joy.

But she snapped back to attention and curbed her drifting thoughts when the footman opened the door and Edward rose. The marquess got out first, then turned to assist his lady.

Delia looked ravishing in a mint-green gown with a dark green sash. Edward wore a silver gray suit with a coordinating mint-green waistcoat.

Watching them together, Maggie saw the intimate little smile they exchanged, and could still only shake her head, mystified, at the wonderful change she'd witnessed between the pair.

Ever since her return from Dorset, she'd been amazed at how well Delia and Edward were getting along.

It made her all the gladder that, as of today, she would be moving in with Connor, because, clearly, Delia and Edward's time alone as a couple without *her* underfoot had done their marriage a world of good.

Maggie was happy for them, and deeply relieved. They both deserved happiness, even Delia, who had been showing a real sisterly side ever since Maggie had returned from Dorset. She had been most helpful in planning the wedding, marshaling her formidable energies to help Maggie see to all the details. Whenever she had started taking over the whole operation, a polite "ahem" had sufficed to remind Delia that it was Maggie's wedding.

Yet now that the momentous day had arrived, Maggie could not help but feel a twinge of sadness, wishing their parents could have been here. To know that, at least, she still had a sister who truly did love her helped to soothe the loss.

"There you are, my love," Edward said cheerfully, having handed his wife down safely to the pavement. Then he turned back to assist Maggie.

Penelope hurried closer to help manage the gown's train, while Delia stepped back, temporarily holding Maggie's lush bouquet of June's first red roses.

"Lady Margaret, you are truly a vision," Rory declared, standing nearby. "Well, there—I've enjoyed calling you Lady Margaret for the last time. When we leave this church, it'll be Your Grace."

"Nonsense," Maggie said with a smile as she stepped down. "Anyone who helped in the grand effort to save my neck has earned the right to call me Maggie, including both of you." She glanced at Penelope.

"Duchess Maggie, then," Rory amended with a grin.

Penelope chuckled. "Maggie and the major."

Rory gave a carefree laugh. "I'll go let him know you're here."

"Is he nervous, sergeant?" Edward asked in amusement as Rory strode toward the heavy wooden doors of the church. "I mean, *I* was on my wedding day, but then, I was never a war hero."

"Just a wee bit petrified," said Rory with a wink.

"Well, that makes two of us," Maggie muttered as she smoothed her skirts and adjusted her veil, her pulse racing.

Meanwhile, the white carriage horses swished their tails calmly, oblivious to the importance of the destination they had brought her to this day.

"Ah, you have nothing to fear, sis." Edward offered Maggie his arm, and she took it gratefully. His smooth, unflappable demeanor helped, as always, to calm her nerves.

He truly was the best of men, or at least the second best, she thought. As they walked toward the entrance, who should appear but Nestor and Will, also in uniform.

Right on cue, they opened the heavy double doors and held them open for the arriving wedding party.

"Criminy!" Will said, his eyes widening when he looked at her, while Nestor's jaw dropped.

"Now I *really* wish I had both eyes," said Nestor. "Lady Margaret, you look beautiful."

"Aye, you do!" Will chimed in.

Maggie laughed. "You both are too kind." She squeezed Nestor's hand as she passed. He'd been magnificent about looking after all three of them who'd been wounded in Dorset—Maggie, Connor, and Penelope, too.

If only Aunt Florence would stop interrogating him about her many ailments, both real and imagined…

"I wish you most happy, my dear," the old surgeon said fondly.

"Me too!" Will gazed adoringly at her, loyal as a spaniel. "Thank you for making our major happy, milady."

"The honor's mine," she said earnestly. "I'm happy for you and Saffie, too."

"Aww," Will said, blushing.

The most remarkable thing had happened.

Luckless as she'd been, Saffie Diggs' fortunes seemed about to turn in the most dramatic way.

Indelicate though the topic was, Connor had confided in Maggie that, apparently, Seth Darrow had got the girl with child. With Elias Flynn dead, and his sons dead, too, the last surviving heir who stood to inherit the millionaire's fortune was none other than Saffie's baby.

The situation was a bit complicated, since Seth had presented himself to the girl under a false name. But, with a bit of probing at the Officers' Club, Connor had managed to track down the one dragoon in Seth's regiment who had found out about his dalliance with Saffie.

This highborn cavalryman had become Seth's closest friend in the regiment, mainly because the miscreant had once saved his life. Of course, the other dragoon had noticed that Seth was not exactly honorable, and had privately warned him about his disgraceful behavior once he'd learned of Seth's game with the unfortunate girl.

This dragoon was willing to tell the Chancery court that, to the best of his knowledge, Seth was indeed the father of Saffie's child. Along with Aunt Lucinda's written testimony, as Seth's former patroness, that he was, indeed, the son of Elias Flynn, the money should go to the underworld king's unborn grandchild.

In the meanwhile, Saffie had already hinted to Will several times that she wanted him for her husband. Will was already so smitten with her, and felt such tenderhearted sympathy both for her and for the fatherless child, that their eventual union seemed inevitable. A million pounds sterling was sure to make their future bright. But Will had vowed that if he *did* marry Saffie, he was shutting down all those horrid brothels first thing.

As he and Nestor held the doors open, admitting Maggie and

Edward, Delia and Penelope into the church's dim vestibule, Maggie could not help but applaud her fiancé's taste in friends.

She'd thought them a ragtag bunch at first, but they had all become quite dear to her.

Then Will and Nestor let the exterior doors shut behind them, closing out the sunshine, and went to get the next pair of doors, leading into the sanctuary.

"Wait!" Maggie said. "I need a moment."

"You all right?" her brother-in-law murmured, turning to her.

"I-I think so." She gulped. "D-do I look all right?" She turned to Penelope, who smiled with reassurance.

"You're radiant."

"She's right." Delia handed Maggie her flowers. "You look perfect, and you know I'd never give you a false compliment."

Maggie chuckled. "To be sure."

"Good luck, sis. You'd better get to your seat," Delia told Penelope, who glanced at Maggie in question.

"You may go." Maggie nodded to her. "And thank you for everything, Pen."

"Oh, you're very welcome, my lady. Well! I think I'll go take advantage of this chance to stare at Sergeant McFeatheridge. Doesn't he look handsome in his uniform today? I should have a perfect view, since he's standing up at the altar next to His Grace."

"Enjoy it," Maggie said with a grin.

"Signal to the choir when you go in! Let them know we're ready," Delia stage-whispered, shooing Penelope away.

"Yes, Lady Birdwell." The maid disappeared, but Delia remained by the sanctuary doors, peeking through the crack.

"I hope she can find a seat," the marchioness said. "This place is filled to the rafters. Uh-oh, there's Lord and Lady Gable." She glanced wryly over her shoulder. "They brought their baby. I hope he doesn't scream." She let the door drift closed and turned around to face the others, hands on hips. "Well? Are we doing this or not?"

"I'm ready," Maggie said firmly, gathering herself.

"Good! Let's get you married off already, then. It's taken you long enough." Delia leaned past Maggie's fragrant bouquet to give her a kiss on the cheek. "Be happy, sister."

"Thank you," Maggie said dazedly. "I will. You too," she added, but Delia was already bustling off to take her place near the altar.

464   *Gaelen Foley*

The opening bars of the first wedding hymn began, and Maggie started to tremble.

"Easy!" Edward teased, patting her fingers as she curled them around his biceps. "You're going to break my arm, dear."

"Sorry," she said, loosening her grip. "I'm just not used to being the center of attention."

"Well, you'd better get used to it awfully soon, considering that in a few minutes, you're about to become the Fourth Duchess of Amberley."

At his succinct summation of the moment at hand, Maggie gave him a breathless smile. Joy infused all her jumpiness.

"Listen," Maggie whispered to him while the choir sang. "I just want to thank you for all your kindnesses to me. You are the best brother-in-law anyone could ever have."

"Ahh, you know I adore you too, Mags."

"And thank you for being so good to my sister."

"Yes…" He flashed a sudden, mysterious smile. "About that."

Something about his sly tone made her glance at him curiously.

"Should we open the doors now?" Will whispered.

"Ready?" Edward asked her.

Maggie nodded, momentarily distracted. "What were you going to say?" she said while Nestor and Will hauled the sanctuary doors open.

At once, the choir's song flooded the vestibule where they stood at the threshold of the church.

The whole congregation turned around to look.

"We're having a baby," Edward informed her.

"What?" Maggie nearly shouted while the whole church stared.

Edward grinned. "This winter, you'll become an auntie."

The entire congregation saw Maggie's jaw drop as she gaped at her brother-in-law. They then heard the bride giggle inexplicably from behind her veil.

Maggie immediately wondered if that might explain why Delia had been extra moody these past couple months, but realized she was making a wee bit of a spectacle of herself at this most important moment of her life. Her questions would have to wait for the reception waiting for them at Amberley House under Trumbull's eager supervision.

For now, she pressed her lips together, vowing to keep her sudden wave of nervous humor under control. "Er, congratulations, Edward."

"Thank you," he said mildly, looking pleased with himself.

Maggie divined then that he had only told her the big news now, of all moments, to distract her from the tension. "You are proving to be a bit of rogue, aren't you, marquess?"

"No, there's the rogue." Edward nodded toward the tall, broad-shouldered silhouette of her waiting fiancé standing by the altar in a dazzle of golden sunshine. "You want to go marry him, then?"

"Oh, I do," she answered fervently.

"Good. Right foot first?"

"Let's go. I'm ready."

And she *was*. So they went, processing down the red-carpeted aisle at a sedate pace while the music floated around them and the rosy morning light streamed in through the tall, translucent windows of the vaulted nave.

Edward held his head high while Maggie trailed her gaze with great fondness over all her friends and soon-to-be relatives as she passed them.

Gable and Trinny, holding their apple-cheeked, black-haired tot, with the stately grandparents, Lord Sefton and his wife, standing with them in the pew.

Connor's aunts, all three of them, and the beaming twins. Aunt Lucinda narrowed her eyes at Maggie, ever the dragon, but then gave her a discreet smile and a nod of respect—much to Maggie's astonishment.

She had barely recovered from the shock of that when she noticed Aunt Florence already weeping copiously. Maggie gave Florence a comforting pat on her bony shoulder as she passed.

The Irish relatives smiled at her. The soldiers bowed their heads; a few even gave her brief, playful salutes. She grinned at them from behind her veil, then passed her friends, Jason and Felicity, the Duke and Duchess of Netherford, who had brought Jason's two children along.

Beautiful little Annabelle sat contentedly in her ducal sire's arms, while the handsome five-year-old boy stood on the pew next to his godfather, Felicity's brother, Major Carvel.

Maggie smiled at them all, but gave Peter a look of gratitude after his help with the whole Dorset matter. He nodded a wordless *You're welcome*.

Lovable Lord Sidney was sitting with the Netherfords. The golden-haired flirt sighed like some disappointed swain and shook his head as she passed.

Maggie fought a smile at the charmer's usual teasing.

Azrael and Serena stood nearby, their shoulders touching. They both gave Maggie affectionate looks as she and Edward walked past. *I hope Connor and I will always be as happy as those two,* Maggie thought. *I have a feeling we will.*

The last person who caught her eye was her wedding-mad friend, Lady Portia Tennesley.

The clever blonde had supplied Maggie with plenty of useful advice in planning this day, though she did seem to treat it more like the grand production of some elaborate stage play, rather than the joining of two souls in holy matrimony.

But then, unfortunately for Portia, that was all her own wedding day would likely be, poor girl, pledged to a man in whom she had no earthly interest.

No wonder her smile seemed slightly wistful.

Maggie truly pitied her friend. Maybe Portia's parents would change their minds, or failing that, perhaps she could learn to love her future husband, if he wasn't too odious.

Of course, Maggie could not deny that some men were simply easier to fall in love with than others.

And with that, finally, as they approached the altar where the robed clergymen waited in full High Church regalia, her gaze came to rest on Connor.

Delight in him tingled through her.

Resplendent in his scarlet uniform with gold epaulets, his broad chest adorned with war medals he had apparently been too modest to wear on the night of Aunt Lucinda's soirée, his silver dress sword glittering by his side, his hands encased in snow-white gloves, his black hair slicked back neatly, he waited for her at the altar, the very embodiment of her dreams, and then some.

He was staring at her in awe, his cobalt eyes glowing, his lips slightly parted. Edward released her, and Maggie went to take her place beside him.

The major. The Fourth Duke of Amberley.

As his gaze traveled over her with sheer, doting reverence, Maggie gulped at the profundity of the everlasting vow they were about to make.

The time had come. It was a great responsibility when someone loved you so much. He had entrusted her with his heart, as she had him.

Her pulse thumped faster.

Ah, but when Connor smiled at her, so calm, strong, and sure, any lingering nervousness she might have felt scattered like a handful of bright spring petals flung to the wind.

Love had found her at last, and together, the two of them had nothing to fear. He took her hand in his and smiled at her. Then they turned to the priest.

The future waited.

Previous Moonlight Square Books

One Moonlit Night (Prequel Novella)

At the ripe old age of two-and-twenty, Lady Katrina Glendon just can't seem to snare a husband. Whether her frank tongue or slightly eccentric ways bear the blame, she faces a houseful of younger sisters clamoring for her, the eldest, to marry and move aside before they all end up as spinsters. When her latest suitor defects and proposes to another girl, Trinny throws up her hands in despair of ever finding a fiancé. But sometimes destiny waits just around the corner...and love lives right across the square!

Duke of Scandal (Book 1)

Jason Hawthorne, the Duke of Netherford, made it clear to the young, lovesick Felicity Carvel long ago that nothing could ever happen between them. He has *earned* his reputation as the Duke of Scandal—and she's his best friend's little sister. For honor's sake, he vows to stay away from the lovely innocent. But even now, all grown up, Felicity still wants Jason for her own. And after getting her heart broken once before by Naughty Netherford, does she dare attempt to play with fire again—and this time, can Jason resist?

Duke of Secrets (Book 2)

When shocking family secrets emerge, they turn Lady Serena Parker's world upside-down, sending the bold, raven-haired beauty on a quest to find answers. Her search soon points her right across the street, to the home of her most mysterious neighbor in Moonlight Square—the enigmatic and solitary Azrael, Duke of Rivenwood. He alone can give her the answers she seeks, but at what price?

Visit other story worlds by Gaelen Foley

Contemporary Romance
DREAM OF ME: Harmony Falls, Book 1

Author-sister duo *New York Times* bestseller Gaelen Foley and Jaz Kennedy present *Dream of Me*, an emotional, uplifting romance set in a small town with a heart as big as the great outdoors. Nestled in the lush green Laurel Highlands of Pennsylvania, Harmony Falls is a nature-lover's paradise...the perfect place for friends, family, and falling in love.

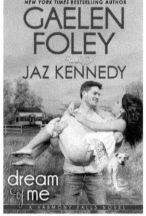

"There are some romance authors whose novels pretty much guarantee a good old-fashioned, joyful read. One such author is Gaelen Foley. Foley's storytelling is so even and consistently entertaining – and her lovers so warm and attractive – that it's easy to get lost in the romance. And that's the best gift a writer of happily-ever-after love stories can give her readers." ~Lifetime TV Books Blog

Fantasy Romance
PALADIN'S PRIZE: Age of Heroes, Book 1

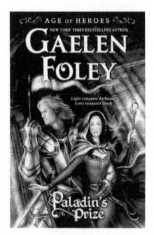

New York Times bestselling author Gaelen Foley leads readers on a magical journey to a fairytale land where good battles evil, adventure beckons the daring, and epic love awaits the true of heart.

"One of the finest adventure/romance authors does it again. Foley never sacrifices character or romance while whisking readers away on fast-paced escapades and daring missions and giving them a glorious deep-sigh read." ~Kathe Robin, RT Book Reviews

Enter a world of wonder & whimsy, adventure & peril in the Middle Grade/YA series that's as much fun for grownups as it is for kids!

Gaelen Foley writing as E.G. Foley
THE LOST HEIR: The Gryphon Chronicles, Book 1

Jake is a scrappy orphaned pickpocket living by his wits on the streets of Victorian London. Lately he's started seeing ghosts and can move solid objects with his mind! He has no idea why. Next thing he knows, a Sinister Gentleman and his minions come hunting him, and Jake is plunged headlong into a mysterious world of magic and deadly peril. A world that holds the secret of who he really is: the long-lost heir of an aristocratic family with magical powers.

But with treacherous enemies closing in, it will take all of his wily street instincts and the help of his friends—both human and magical—to solve the mystery of what happened to his parents and defeat the foes who never wanted the Lost Heir of Griffon to be found…

"A wonderful novel in the same vein as Harry Potter, full of nonstop action, magical creatures, and the reality that was Queen Victoria's England." ~The Reading Café

About the Author

Noted for her "complex, subtly shaded characters, richly sensual love scenes, and elegantly fluid prose" (*Booklist*), *New York Times*, USA Today, and *Publisher's Weekly* Bestselling author Gaelen Foley has written over twenty (and counting!) rich, bold historical romances set in Regency England and Napoleonic Europe. Since her debut in 1998, her books have been published in seventeen languages worldwide and have won numerous awards, including the National Readers' Choice Award, the Booksellers' Best, the Golden Leaf (three times), the Award of Excellence, and the HOLT Medallion.

A versatile and hardworking writer, Gaelen's passion for the craft of fiction keeps her exploring new creative ground. While continuing to entertain her Regency fans, she has branched out into contemporary small-town romance as well as fantasy romance. Since 2012, Gaelen has also been co-writing fantasy middle grade/children's novels with her husband, a former teacher, under the penname E.G. Foley. The Lost Heir, Book 1 in their Gryphon Chronicles series, was a #1 Amazon Children's Bestseller (and was optioned for a movie!).

To learn more about Gaelen and her books, visit her at GaelenFoley.com.